FLAWLESS

Adam Barrow

FLAWLESS

A DUTTON BOOK

DUTTON

Published by the Penguin Group
Penguin Books USA Inc., 375 Hudson Street, New York, New York 10014, U.S.A.
Penguin Books Ltd, 27 Wrights Lane, London W8 5TZ, England
Penguin Books Australia Ltd, Ringwood, Victoria, Australia
Penguin Books Canada Ltd, 10 Alcorn Avenue, Toronto, Ontario, Canada M4V 3B2
Penguin Books (N.Z.) Ltd, 182-190 Wairau Road, Auckland 10, New Zealand

Penguin Books Ltd, Registered Offices:
Harmondsworth, Middlesex, England

First published by Dutton, an imprint of Dutton Signet,
a division of Penguin Books USA Inc.
Distributed in Canada by McClelland & Stewart Inc.

First Printing, September, 1995
1   3   5   7   9   10   8   6   4   2

 REGISTERED TRADEMARK—MARCA REGISTRADA

LIBRARY OF CONGRESS CATALOGING-IN-PUBLICATION DATA:

Barrow, Adam.
Flawless / Adam Barrow.
p.   cm.
ISBN 0-525-94047-2
I.   Title.
PS3552.A738F53   1995

813'.54—dc20   95-6859
                                                   CIP

Printed in the United States of America
Set in Garamond Book and Gill Sans
Designed by Steven N. Stathakis

This book is printed on acid-free paper.

For Tom and Daniel

The best way to suppose what may come is to remember what is passed.

—GEORGE SAVILE

Picture this scene:

A cocktail lounge somewhere. In a hotel, say. Or attached to a fashionable eatery. Or off by itself, free-standing, bold, autonomous. Doesn't matter where. Oval-shaped bar. Booths along the walls, puddle of a dance floor. Subdued lights. Smoke vapors suspended in the air, dense as ground fog. Trendy crowd, some of them gorgeous, some plain; a few, not many, homely. Young mostly, mid-twenties, early thirties, here and there the occasional over-forty fossil still on the prowl. All of them fevered, yearning, restless at the edges. Maybe it's the music. Ax-wielding trio produces a thunderous electrified roar. Dancers twitch and jiggle, casting long, frenetic shadows. Lurid shadows frolic on the walls. Voices emerge raw and hoarse from hours of bellowing over the din. And the hour grows late. Approaching what some here, the plain ones, call ruefully the Hour of Inner Beauty, when desires, hopes, standards begin to plummet in the desperate run of time.

See it? All right, now this:

On one side of the oval sits a woman sipping a Kahlúa and cream. Sharp, angular, lacquered face, the skin deeply tanned, bordering on leathery. Hair short and expertly feathered, silvery with a pinkish tinge, the color of cotton candy, a bottled color. Gold hoops dangle from her ears. Gold chain at the neck. Abundance of rings. She wears a sheer white blouse, top two buttons undone, cleavage flaunted; black miniskirt with thigh-exposing slits in front and back, black hose, scarlet spiked heels, gold ankle bracelet. Her figure is perhaps a bit plump for the girlish outfit. A heavily scented woman, she is not unattractive but decidedly not young.

On the other side of the bar, directly opposite her, sits a man who is mid-twenties, by her estimate, thirty at most. A slender man, nicely dressed, handsome in an intense, expressionless way. Handsome enough that several women approach him, offer to dance. He shakes his head negatively. This cheers her.

For he seems to be watching her. Unless she's mistaken. She tests it with a sidelong glance and a practiced, dimply smile. He appears to return it slightly. Hard to be sure. So she picks up her drink, weaves through the crush of bodies, comes around the oval, and settles onto the barstool next to him. Chirps a *Hi.* He responds with a pronounced nod, just short of a bow. Very formal, very dignified. She is taken by that. She asks if he's having any fun. He makes the so-so gesture with a flat hand in the air, then adds shyly, *Till now.*

This is encouraging. They talk. Exchange names, pleasantries. Trade cautious snippets of their lives. He buys her a drink. Lights her cigarettes. He is attentive, polite, well spoken, at times witty. A refined wit, never crude or suggestive. She likes that too, at the outset of an adventure. Up close she discovers he's even better looking than she thought: strong jaw; planed cheekbones; flawless, creaseless skin. And the most remarkable eyes, astonishing pools of green. She is consumed with wanting. Aching want.

"I notice you don't dance," she remarks.

"Not to this."

"Slow music, then? Soft?"

"Yes."

"I got that kind. At my place."

He arches a perfect brow, indicates her wedding band. She gives a so-what shrug, says, "Not to worry. He's out of town. Anyway," she adds disdainfully, "he's a dink." He opens his hands, an acquiescent gesture. She can't believe her luck, landing this one. Must be he appreciates maturity in a woman, richness of experience. On him, she'll gladly lavish that generous experience.

A commonplace episode. Two lonely souls finding each other. But there's more:

They leave in her car. The night is clear. A cold glitter of stars reaches from one rim of the earth to the other. The setting is urban. Fast as she dares, she drives along an expressway twined like an artery through the city. Exits at a towering apartment building. She parks. Gives him a sugared smile. "Home sweet home," she says, somewhat ironically.

They take the elevator to the seventh floor. The apartment consists of a living room, kitchen, small dining space, two bedrooms, bath and a half. Predictable furnishings. A bit untidy. He asks what her husband does for a living. He is curious about the man whose phantom third presence hovers over the rooms. She makes a vinegary face. "Sales," she says, "pharmaceutical sales." She makes a brushing motion, as if to dismiss the topic.

She directs him to what she calls the liquor cabinet in the kitchen. Asks him to fix drinks while she freshens up. That's how she puts it: *freshen up.* Then she vanishes into a bedroom.

In her absence he pours brandy. Full glass for her; thimble's worth for himself, the rest water. Next he forages through a drawer, spies a wooden-handled steel cylinder. Eight inches of burnished steel tapering to a dagger-spiked point. Peculiar-looking utensil, unfamiliar to him. A meat skewer perhaps. He takes it into the living room, fits it between two sofa cushions, out of sight. Returns for the drinks, places them on the coffee table. Sits. Waits. And while he waits his eyes sweep the room, recording everything he's touched, every item, committing them all to memory. He is a punctilious man, his memory is exact.

Soon she's back. She dims the lights, puts on music. Sinatra sings. "I just adore Frank," she coos.

"Nice voice," he allows.

She snuggles beside him on the sofa. Lays a hand on his thigh. They listen raptly to the drowsy, dreamy ballads, whose poignant lyrics speak of lost love. When, after a time, he makes no moves, she grows fretful. A taut bundle of uncertainties, cravings. Maybe he's having second thoughts. Regrets. Older woman, handsome young man, he could have left with anyone. Any one of those flashy, slutty Bambis. So young, so young. *He didn't though,* she thinks, brightening some. *He's here with me. He chose me.*

Thus fortified, she invites him to dance. They come to their feet. She drapes both arms around his neck, stows her head in the hollow of his shoulder. Their movements are patternless, unrhythmic, more shuffle than dance. And slow, tantalizingly slow. Frank sings of black magic and its inexpiable spell. She clings tighter, thrusts her pelvis against him. Her breath quickens. His does not. She licks his neck. Inclines her head backward and gazes searchingly into those lovely eyes.

They kiss. Tongues lap and probe. But there's curiously little heat in it and, so far as she can tell, not a trace of stiffening down below. Now she's truly worried. Also a little irked. She wonders if there's something wrong with him. Something dysfunctional. Or aberrant. But come this far, she's not about to give up yet.

She disengages her mouth. "There are other ways to dance," she murmurs in his ear. "Let me show you. Let me please you."

She leads him back to the sofa. Instructs him to wait. Only be a minute, she pledges, disappearing for a second time into the bedroom. Affecting a husky, ruttish tone, she adds, "Oh, and you might want to lose the threads."

A seduction scene, then? Familiar salacious sketch? Well, not exactly:

He rises. Dutifully disrobes. Folds his clothes neatly, taking particular care to preserve the crease in the trousers. Sits back on the sofa, naked, chin lifted, hands clasped, knees pressed together. A somewhat prissy posture. Waits wrapped in calm, preternatural calm, unmoved by ardor or expectation. Yet something is gathering in him. An odd sensation, as though he were not quite himself, a stranger to himself. He seems to be entering an alien country, some dark region within, a transcendent zone. Destiny-driven. Sinatra croons on.

Her voice sails in from the bedroom. She's asking, "Are you ready for this?"

He replies affirmatively.

She displays herself in the doorway, clad in a most wondrous costume: underwire half-bra, satin G-string, garter belt, fishnet stockings, stiletto heels. All in black. A carnal mourner. A gold chain circles her ample hips. Gold ankle bracelet still intact. "Ta-da!" she exclaims, striking a siren pose. His face registers nothing.

She comes swaying into the room, undulating to the music. He seems to examine a point somewhere just above and to the left of her shoulder. She slinks toward him, looms over him, filling his field of vision. Leaving him no choice but to inspect her. An incongruous image, unbidden, appears to him: a shimmying, quivering, wriggling slab of meat, ambulatory meat, miraculously invested with powers of cerebration, with hopes, memories, fancies, fears, schemes, appetites.

She bends at the waist, clutches her propped powdered bosoms, big as inflated gas balloons, and jiggles them in his neutral face. The nipples, he notes, are purplish, slightly off-center, pulpy-looking. She twirls about, shakes her substantial hams. For his delectation, evidently. Even in the softened light he can detect pockets of fat, like tiny moon craters, near the apex of the loamy thighs. Assorted assaultive odors sting his nostrils. His hands remain serenely folded in his lap.

She turns, glances downward, discovers he is unaroused. Abruptly, she discontinues the vamping dance. "Don't you like me?" she asks.

"Of course I like you," he says. There is a flat, monotone quality to his voice.

"Then what is it? What's the problem?"

"It's been a while."

"Studmuffin like you? I'd think you'd be beatin' off the girlies with a stick."

"No."

"Maybe just beatin' off?" she says with a harsh laugh.

"No."

"Not that either, huh? Well, *what,* then?"

"It's been a while," he repeats. But he's thinking how coarse-grained the world is, how vulgar.

"Maybe you need a little priming is all."

"Maybe that's it."

She sinks to her knees. Pauses a moment to assimilate him with her eyes. Unlike her husband and the legion of other apish men who have occupied this same sofa, experienced this same treatment, this body is lean and symmetrical and muscle-ridged, the flesh as silky and hairless as an infant. Exquisite body. A familiar tingly candescence, emanating from her loins, flows outward through her torso and limbs. Snakes seem to coil and squirm just beneath the surface of her skin. She pries open his legs, squeezes herself between them. She grins at him roguishly. Moistens her crimson-varnished lips and fits them gently around the limp member.

Her head bobs vigorously. Watching it, he is reminded of a childhood Halloween game, bobbing for apples. Also does he recall, dimly and with a relevance murky to the moment, something his father once said, quoting some obscure bard, something about the skull beneath the skin. The confluence of memories prompts a desolate smile. He strokes her hair tenderly.

But for all her efforts, all her expertise, there is still no perceptible reaction. Not a sound out of him. Not the slightest reciprocal motion. Not a trace of swelling. Nothing. And her neck is beginning to ache. She releases the slack organ, lifts her head, and stares into the eyes that, only an hour or so ago, seemed so dazzling, so ripe with promise. "Y'know," she says, a sneery edge to her voice, "if it's a mommy you're lookin' for, you come to the wrong place."

It's the wrong thing to say, though there is of course no way for her to know this. He gazes at her steadily. He smiles, but it's a remote smile, wintry, and it goes through her like a splinter of flying glass. She experiences a flash of dread, but it's not enough to dispel her resentment, disgust. "That it?" she demands. "You lookin' for your mommy?"

He seems on the verge of a reply, hesitates, looks at his hands. A violent tic, like a nerve convulsion, comes into the muscles of his face. He grips her at the shoulders, whirls her around and pins her upper back to the sofa. He straddles her. Mistaking it for rough action, she delivers a pleasured moan. Rough she likes. And if that's what it takes to crank his engines, she's more than willing. She plants her feet on the floor. Parts her thighs. Tightens her buttocks and elevates her hips. The moan shades over into a series of agitated yips. "Fuck me!" she pleads. "Nail me! Make it hurt!"

To him it all sounds rehearsed, absurdly theatrical, not to say prophetic. As though he had orchestrated the scene himself, authored her lines. For the very next thing he does is lay the palm of one hand over her mouth, throttling the raptured squeals, and with the other he reaches down between the cushions and removes the kitchen utensil, and in a sudden grinding rotary motion gouges out her eyes, each in its turn.

Jets of blood squirt from the punctured sockets. Beneath him there is more wriggling, considerably more, but of a kind altogether different from when she was on her feet, gracelessly prancing. With the covering hand still firmly in place, to muffle the inevitable squawk rising to her lips, and with his knees lifted and wedged into her elbow joints, to anchor the wildly flailing arms, he plunges the utensil deep into her throat. The frantic wriggling dwindles to an occasional spasmodic twitch. And then she slumps back and seems just to float away.

Uncomplicated by rage or passion or spite or malice or remorse, he continues to penetrate her by now lifeless body, employing the utensil methodically, slow, sensual jabs and thrusts, almost loving, some might say. And indeed, the instrument eventually finds its way into her most intimate cavities, so perhaps this was something of a sexual encounter after all.

Fatigue overtakes him. A certain heaviness in the shoulders and arms. He eases back onto the floor and allows himself a moment's contemplation. A moment to scrutinize her blood-spattered face. A look of intense distressed bewilderment is written on it, as though she realized, too late, she had been ambushed by something terrible, something called death. A comic little rivulet of spittle leaks from a corner of the mouth that had lately sipped a liqueur, puffed a cigarette, shaped words, greedily fastened itself on his, engulfed a part of him. A mix of blood and intestinal gas bubbles up out of the numerous breaches in her flesh. Though he is himself drenched in gore, and though his own face is veiled in clinical detachment, nevertheless a flock of images, clouded and imprecise, flutters behind his eyelids. Death, he thinks, must surely be the ultimate act of purity.

A practical man, he soon enough recognizes the inutility of such airy speculation. No time to linger. He rises. Surveys the room with a calm, analytic, utterly dispassionate eye. Much to be done here. Starting with himself, his own body, sodden with blood.

He steps into the bath, showers, towels himself down. Damp towel in hand, he returns to the living room, gets into his clothes. Unreeling from a tight spool of memory the catalog of everything he's come in contact with, every object he's handled, he wipes them all clean, every one. He works rapidly but unhurriedly. *Thorough,* he reminds himself, *meticulous and thorough*. Since he'd not been near the tape deck, he leaves the music on. Sinatra has switched to a snappier tempo, inviting the listener to come fly with him.

Once he's satisfied with the living room (inapt designation for it now, he thinks), he takes the two glasses and the utensil into the kitchen. Washes and replaces them in proper cabinet and drawer. Scrubs the handles, surfaces, counter, sink, faucets, and, in afterthought needlessly, but in the interest of caution and perfection and even a certain fastidiousness, refrigerator and stove. Rinses the towel, folds it, and leaves it in the sink.

At the door he pauses for a final look around. Final summary check. Apart from the corpse sprawled in a widening swamp of blood, staining the carpet, the place is otherwise immaculate, certainly cleaner than when he first arrived. Something to be said for that. He turns the doorknob with a hankie-covered hand, peers into the hallway. Empty. He pulls the door shut behind him. And the last thing he hears, appropriately enough, is Frank warbling about strangers finding each other in the umbral depths of night.

There's no high drama to it. No swelling emotion or unbearable suspense. Nothing particularly moving. Nothing even remotely approaching catharsis. A routine episode. But then that's the way lives are often dispatched, routinely, while in nearby apartments (in instances such as this) couples bicker or make absent love or attend to the joys and quips and sorrows of images flickering across screens; and out on the roaring streets of the city, beggars beg, pimps pimp, sundry predators prey, and ordinary folk scoot resolutely from place to place; and farther still, in the tranquil fields and barnyards of the countryside, placid livestock bred for slaughter dream their bovine trustful dreams; and farthest of all, from the farthest reaches of space, a bedazzling wash of stars, winking mischievously, presides over an earth still spinning on its reliable, appointed axis.

Part

ONE

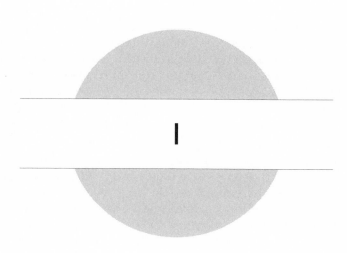

I

When you thought about it clearly, rationally, hearing voices was certainly no foolproof test of sanity. Everyone's got a voice going inside his head every waking moment of every day of his life. Voice says, *Get up now, it's time.* Voice enjoins you to shower, shave, brush and floss, dress in your dark vested suit, arctic white shirt, understated silk tie, spit-polished shoes. Same as always, invariably the same. Consume a light, sensible breakfast; assemble a public face much like the face you're showing now: attentive, thoughtful, ready with the reflex smile. Voice says to gather up briefcase and leather-bound notebook and go to work, concentrate, focus, analyze, problem solve, perform, achieve. Voice escorts you through the catalog of ordinaries that weave the tapestry of that generally amiable dreamwalk we're pleased to call living. Everyone has it, that familiar voice. Everyone.

But it was an altogether different voice, this one only dimly recognizable, buzzing away in a distant chamber of Michael Woodrow's head this morning. Nagging, prodding, insistent. Swelling sometimes, sometimes scarcely audible, like a trumpet muting and unmuting. Clashing with Max's nonstop drone and Jiffy Jack's occasional interjected grunts and Briggs's periodic throat clearing. A confusion of sounds and voices, inside and out, battering at his ears.

". . . So the system's in place," Max was saying, oiling out the words with that chameleonlike talent of his to adapt both vernacular and the mystifying argot of their trade to whatever the audience, "and all your key personnel checked out on it. Know it better'n the back of their own hand, Mike here tells me. Am I right, Mike?"

His turn to produce some words. Embroidering them with a touch of the control-management cant that came tripping effortlessly off his tongue, he averred, in roundabout fashion, Max was surely right.

"Good, good, good," Max cut in on him, signalling enough already, project's a wrap, let's spare the overkill. "Okay," he continued, ticking off the summary steps on the fingers of an elevated hand, "plan's in order, procedures manuals updated, all the reporting forms standardized, exceptions accounted for . . ."

And on it went, building toward a peroration. While the relentless voice in his head kept up a steady taunting chatter. Something dark, twisted, impenetrable. Something about last night.

It was called the Windup, what they were doing. Stroking the client, assuring him the advice and services he contracted for were indeed value-added, even as advertised. The Alexander X. (for Xavier, he'd heard, though the company joke had it standing for X, you're cancelled, eliminated, gone) Stoltz and Associates final flourish.

Folded into a cushy swivel chair behind an imposing mahogany desk, J. Willis Zulewski tugged at an underchin pensively and watched them with the blank, piglet-eyed gaze of the natural-born cheat who expects nothing less than swindle in return. Once known simply as Jack Zulewski, it was that dangling initial that gave him away now. J. Willis Zulewski, founder and sole owner of thirty-eight Jiffy Jacks scattered across metropolitan San Antonio: *Oil, Filter and Lube— While-U-Wait—$14.95—Ten Minutes or Less—Guaranteed!—Or You Don't Pay a Cent!* "Got in on the ground floor this bin-us," he liked to remind them, "before your goddam Wards and Kmarts, rest a them Johnny-come-latelys figured it out."

Jack Zulewski, high school dropout, millionaire many times over. Grease monkey with a vision. Fiftyish, sooty hair, dumpling cheeks, skin the color of boiled lobster, a mountain of baggy meat bulging his Omar-tailored suit. Cardinal tonnage of this and any other room he occupied. Watching everyone shrewdly, like a Buddha nursing a grudge. Attending to Max's monologue with the fatty's phleg-matic dispassion, waiting for it to run down. And when eventually it did, his upper lip curled back in a twist of a smile, and he said, "So you boys gonna make me even richer yet, huh? That it?"

"We forecast a seven percent increase in productivity over the next three quarters," Max declared stoutly, the barest edge of defen-siveness in his delivery, "with a corresponding dip in operating ex-penses. What're we lookin' at here? Four percent in on-site labor costs, two percent in materials, and up to six percent in office clerical."

The figures, rehearsed at tedious length and in painstaking detail yesterday afternoon and reviewed again early this morning, along with all the rest of the rhapsodic Max Stroiker assertions, were in fact accurate. Assuming, of course, the Jif and his lieutenants under-stood the system and followed it scrupulously and without deviation. Risky assumption.

Max, ever alert to risk, stabbed a finger at a ponderous manual, handsomely bound, on Zulewski's desk. Its title read: *Jiffy Jacks— Operations System—August 1992.*

"Right there's your bible," he said. "You follow it chapter and verse, and you'll realize a volume increase of—" He hesitated just a beat. "What's that number again, Mike?"

Yanked back suddenly from the persistent interior thrumming, Woodrow supplied the number. "Factor in the cost reductions, and it comes to the equivalent of approximately eleven thousand units annually."

That figure was accurate too. He ought to know; he wrote the manual. As acting installation manager, this was—always had been— his project. Max, coming off a rumored bitter divorce, was coasting lately, getting by on bluster and smoke, a share of which he was dis-pensing now. "So to answer your question, Jack, I gotta say yes. This should translate into more profit for you."

"But it's absolutely essential that the system be adhered to strictly," Woodrow heard himself cautioning. "Particularly the scheduling and weekly status reports. Otherwise we can't guarantee those results." It seemed to help some, this generating of audible words, to muffle if only for an instant the flood of them still going a mile a minute in the echo chamber of his skull. And anyway, they needed to be said.

A ghost of a frown crossed Max's face, but he recovered quickly, slid around the unsolicited caveat, and allowed to Jack, "No reason to think your people won't implement the system properly, now that they've got it mastered."

Jack tossed an imperial, finger-bejeweled hand at the man seated significantly to his immediate right. "Whadda you say, Dwight? Them numbers stand up?"

A dry, obstructed rasp, something like a grating scrape of sandpaper, rose from the stringy throat of Dwight Briggs, chief operations officer, central office manager, CPA and don't you forget it (his routine phone salutation: "Dwight Briggs, CPA, here."). In stunning contrast to his employer, he was a cadaverous splinter of a man, narrow of shoulder, hollow of chest, with a pale, pinched face, beaked nose, prim little mouth, wormy, bloodless lips, retrograde chin. His eyes, a couple of watery black beads shielded by glasses as thick as goggles, were focused on Jack. Throat properly purged, he conceded grudgingly, "That's about how it's worked since they've been here." After a pause pregnant with meaning, and with a baleful sidelong glance at the two consultants, he added, "So far, anyway."

"I ain't talkin' yesterdays," Jack growled at him. "It's them future projections I'm askin' your opinion on."

The CPA squirmed uneasily in his chair. "Yes. Well, I suppose it's possible they could be achieved. That is, if we're willing to terminate all those people. These are loyal employees, family men and women, many of them with us for years."

Max, who had only skimmed the manual, lapsed into an uncharacteristic silence. So it was left to Woodrow to meet the piously intoned objection. "I'd call your attention to the Personnel Control chart," he put in quietly. "Page 93. If you'll look at it again, you'll see that a good share of your staff reduction will come about simply by retaining the hiring freeze we've initiated. That, and predictable normal attrition, of course."

Briggs fixed them with a hostile glare. His jaw, as much as there was of it, was set in a challenging thrust. "A good share," he repeated, pitch and tone just short of mimicry. "But certainly not all of it."

"You're quite right," Woodrow said mildly. "Not all of it. There'll have to be layoffs."

The worm lips parted in a point-proven smirk. "Rather ruthless, don't you think? In these recessionary times?"

Woodrow shrugged. Nothing to say to that.

Jack's eyes, full of a sly peasant cunning, swung back and forth between them. "Fuck 'em," he said. "Somebody ain't pullin' their weight, I say fuck 'em. I ain't in the welfare bin-us." He leaned back, clasped sausage-roll fingers under his arc of belly, as if to forestall its precipitous plunge through the very seams of his trousers, spilling a puddle of polychromatic guts on the richly carpeted floor.

The jeering voice in Woodrow's head, hushed while he spoke aloud but never fully still, pronounced the words that shaped a bizarre image, like a visual memory, and set it madly prancing behind his eyes. Ghastly image. Grotesque.

"So what else burnin' your ass, Dwight?" Jack was saying. "Now's time to spit it out."

Briggs winced. Made his laryngeal bleat. With his compassion for the little guy argument, which fit him about as well as a Goodwill suit of clothes, summarily dismissed, the CPA had to think a minute, regroup. Finally he said, "Well, I have to confess it's difficult for me to understand or justify the substantial outlay for advertising in this plan's budget."

"Let me address that," said Max, resuming center stage. "What we're proposing is a one-shot media blitz, tapering off by the end of the third quarter. We're talkin' newspapers, billboards, radio, TV—the whole nine yards. Y'see, the competition, those Kmarts, Wards, they're anonymous, faceless. We get Jack on the tube, show-case him, sorta like your Dave, of Wendy's—homespun, regular guy, down-home—and people will identify with the business. It's a sensational marketing ploy. Inspired, if you ask me."

Max's failure to credit the source of that inspiration didn't escape Woodrow. Didn't matter. What he desperately wanted to do was get out of there, get to the airport, get home. The shells of his ears seemed to ache from the battery of voices assailing them, either side.

"In my judgment," Briggs said frostily, "it's extravagant. Bordering on fiscal irresponsibility, at this point in time."

Max ignored him, directed his words at Zulewski. "What's your take on it, Jack?" he asked innocently. Not for nothing was he section chief. He had all the moves.

But then so did Jack, who knew exactly where the inspired idea had come from. Nobody's fool, Jack. He looked at Woodrow narrowly, demanded, "Mike. Whadda you say?"

"Ad agency thinks you're a natural, Jack. So do I. Always have."

About half a grin rose through the porky J. Willis face. He leaned forward now, squared his hands on the desk, and in a voice as thick as blackstrap molasses, voice of a man readying himself for the television cameras and a predestined celebrity, said, "Well, I'm thinkin' maybe we'll give 'er a go. Couple of months, anyway. See what it does for them numbers." An expectant twinkle came into the mean little eyes, but when he turned to Briggs it vanished suddenly, the way a social smile will evaporate. "You got anything else, Dwight?"

The CPA, thoroughly beaten, shook his head negatively. Studied the floor. Apart from the small, relieved sigh Woodrow was certain he heard out of Max, there was an instant of silence.

It was Jack who broke it, saying, "Okay, I got one for you, Maxie. S'pose we run into some snags, this fancy system, couple months down the line. You gonna send somebody back here for a tune-up?"

"Absolutely. Follow-up check's part of the package."

"That's free for nothin', right? That follow-up?"

"Won't cost you a cent. It's part of the agreement. Written right into the original letter of engagement."

"Okay, that's good," Jack said. He paused, made the wet, lip-smacking sound of the man who's just swallowed a bonbon. But then he continued, interrogator-tough, "Now what I wanta know is *who* you're gonna send."

"Well, certainly somebody familiar with the project."

"I don't want no green peas," Jack rumbled ominously, displaying his mastery of the consulting lingo for an inexperienced man. Quick study, Jack. "What I want is this boy here," he went on, indicating Woodrow without ever once lifting his squinty eyes off Max. "He's the one done all the grunt work."

"I should, uh, think that could be arranged," Max said, the tiniest stutter in his voice.

"*Think* don't cut no shit. Word I wanta hear is *guarantee.*"

Max put a flat palm in the air, half placation, half pledge. "All right, Jack. You've got it."

Now the intense J. Willis Zulewski features opened in a huge sunburst grin. Triumphant grin, just a trace of wickedness in it. He hauled himself up out of the chair, signalling meeting's close, and the other three came to their feet automatically. Well wishes were exchanged all around, hands extended, pumped vigorously, warmly. All but Briggs's, which felt to Woodrow as limp and chilly as a death hand and which sparked yet another dreadful image in a province, no longer quite so remote, behind his eyes.

"We gotta run," Max said in parting. "Got planes to catch." And with the purposeful stride that signified the relentless pace and burden of their profession, he led the way to the door. Woodrow followed, and a moment later they were gone.

WHEN YOU'RE AN ALEXANDER STOLTZ ASSOCIATE, you don't do any high-fives or Toyota leaps on the successful completion of a project (never, never referred to as a *job*). You're much too professional for that, too coolly detached. What you do though, if time allows, is treat yourself to a celebratory loosener or two (or more, in Max's case). And that's what they were doing now, in a hole-in-the-wall airport bar as murky as a cavern, on their feet and hunched over a tiny disk of a stand-up-and-pop-'em-back table, and lucky to get that. For the abbreviated space was crammed full with end-of-the-week business travellers (preponderantly male, though lately more and more gimlet-eyed, tightly smiling women), their power-dress outfits, either gender, wilting under the scorching Texas heat. Every one of them was looking as strained, anxious, impatient, exhausted as Woodrow knew he had to look. Certainly that's how he felt.

And certainly Max, three gulped straight-up J.D.'s and working on a fourth, looked no better. Probably worse. The way large, tall, blocky men will rumple easily. Nevertheless, he had shifted into mellow gear. His speech, while a little slurred, returned to its habitual and carefully cultivated mix of the sardonic, the savvy, the profane, and whatever slangy jargon was currently in fashion (though absent altogether of the dropped *g*s and all the other cornmeal rhythms). "You catch the expression on the wuss CPA," he was chuckling, "after Zulewski squashed him on that advertising budget?"

Somewhat gravely, Woodrow nodded. "I saw it. But I doubt he's going to back off, now that we're out of there. He's about as stubborn a dragon as I've ever come up against."

Dragon was their in-house code for an executive openly hostile to consultants—a coinage out of dragging, foot-dragging, resisting every step of the way. No project was without one, and it was no small share of the installation manager's job to outflank him. With Briggs, Woodrow wasn't so confident he'd succeeded in that crucial task.

"Maybe so," Max said. "But we nailed him this time."

"For however long it may last. Make no mistake—he's got Zulewski's ear. And the dragon never dies. It was you taught me that, Max. Remember?"

Max gave an indifferent shrug. "Yeah, well, that's Warsaw Jack's problem now. He wants the system to fly, he's Polack-in-chief."

"Could be mine, another six weeks."

"You'll handle it," Max said, clearly no longer much interested in the topic. "I got faith in you, boy."

Faith. Sure. Easy for him. Woodrow made no reply. He was sipping at a Lone Star beer, taking it straight from the bottle. When in Texas . . . It was only his second, but it had an agreeable limbs-slackening effect, and along with their seamless talk and the steady hum of the many conversations rising through the room (broken occasionally by a particularly grating peal of brittle female laughter) and the obligatory racketing television tacked to a wall above the bar—all of it, in confluence, seemed to have silenced the alien heckling voice ringing in his head. For the moment anyway, and you take your relief where you find it.

"Listen," Max said, "you did a helluva job, this project. A real AS&A kick-ass-and-take-names piece of work. Couple more like that, and they'll be scrubbing the 'acting' off your IM for good. You got my vote."

Woodrow said he appreciated it, but looking at him there, fleshy shoulders slumped, pink-veined eyes beginning to glaze, droopy-dog jowls sagging, he had to wonder about the weight of a Max Stroiker vote. It was probably somewhere midway between feather and fly.

On the television screen, a smirking anchorlady, conventionally, forgettably pretty, was delivering the noonday news, mostly cheery patter about the upcoming Labor Day weekend. Which prompted Max to ask, "So what are you up to, the big three day-er?"

"No plans."

"Spend it with your old man?"

For Woodrow, this was dicey territory, slippery turf. Somehow Max had learned about his father, and now whenever he alluded to him it was in that studied, mournful tone touched by a sly, insinuating malice that carries as subtext: I know your shameful little secret, and I'll use it if I have to.

"More than likely," Woodrow said stiffly. To parry any further questions, he added, "How about you?"

Max cupped a hand along the side of his mouth and leaned

across the table, establishing a confidential zone, two confederates in intrigue. "Got this squeeze in Atlanta. Stew. She's twenty-four, ripe." His bleary eyes did a lewd roll. "For her I got plans."

Max Stroiker, aging lothario. With an Atlanta squeeze, at twenty-four exactly half the mounting tally of his own desperate years. Among pathetic and contemptible and repellant it was a tight three-way race, pathetic out front by maybe a length, no more. Small wonder he was on what they liked to call in the consulting trade the long, greased slide: booze, broads, broken marriage, crumbling career. Poor Max. Woodrow generated an indulgent smile. He never knew quite what to say to these vulgar disclosures. So he said simply, "Good luck."

"Luck's got nothing to do with this one," Max allowed around an inebriate, slow-motion wink. He propped an elbow on the table's surface, laid his chin in an open palm, and gazed at Woodrow a moment, judiciously, as though a heavy thought had just occurred to him. Finally he said, "Y'know, Mike, you got to lighten up a little yourself, grab some of that good action while you still can. A young guy like you—"

Before he could finish, his and Woodrow's attention, as well as that of most everyone else's in the room, was drawn to the image of the anchorlady up on the screen. Her smirky face had gone solemn, grim. A brutal murder, she reported, female victim, body discovered early this morning, details withheld by police pending investigation and release of woman's name, sources (not identified) on the scene (quick shot of a high-rise apartment building, cluster of squad cars at its entrance, bubble lights pulsating like accelerated heartbeats) hinting at a savage stabbing, particularly grisly . . .

A spasmed shudder, sudden as an electric jolt, charged through Woodrow's neck and torso and limbs. His jaw tightened. He lowered his eyes. And his own face, could it be seen clearly there in the dim light, was white as bleached bone. And the jeering voice in his head started up again: *Better hurry, Michael. It's time.*

Max turned back from the screen, lifted his glass, took a long swallow, and remarked, "Guess the message there is don't rile your Texas rednecks. Cowboys down here, they don't dick around."

Under his breath, scarcely a whisper, Woodrow mumbled, "Could be anywhere."

"What's that?"

"Said it's not just here. Those . . . things happen everywhere."

"I don't know. This state always struck me as the bunghole of the universe. Been a back door to the Alamo, there wouldn't even be a Texas." He chortled at his excellent wit, adding, "Which might not be all bad."

It's time, Michael. Time.

Woodrow glanced at his watch. "I've got to get to my gate," he said. "Leave in just a few minutes."

It wasn't a lie (because when you're Michael Woodrow you don't tell lies), but it wasn't precisely the truth either, since the few minutes translated into something under an hour. But there was a need for reflection now, deliberation, solitude, silence. Urgent need. Almost frantic. *Hurry.*

Max gestured languidly at the Lone Star bottle, still half full. "You could finish your brewbie."

"Can't do it," Woodrow said, conscious of the uttered words coming out clipped and toneless, like a computer simulation of a human voice.

Max squinted at him. "You okay?"

"Fine."

"Looking a little tweaked."

"I'm fine, Max. Fine." He stooped down and recovered his briefcase from the floor. "So. See you sometime."

Hurry, hurry, hurry.

"Could be early as next week," Max said.

"Any idea where?" Woodrow asked him, not really caring. But he knew he was expected to ask.

"Buzz is some Bible-thumper college, up in Michigan someplace. Puff project, strictly recommendations."

"Your assignment?"

Max scowled. A trace of doubt, not that far removed from fear, scored his used-up face. "Don't know. Nobody telling me anything lately."

Hurry!

"Max, I really do have to leave now."

Ritual handclasp. Should have been perfunctory, quick. Only Max didn't seem to want to let go. Haltingly, eyes averted, he said, "You think maybe you could, uh, get that wrap report out to the Bunker?"

Bunker was the field man's term for the Stoltz headquarters in New York. And the report he referred to was the final summary on the Jiffy Jack project, by rights the section chief's responsibility. "I'll draft it on the plane," Woodrow said. "Fax it off in the morning." He'd say whatever it took to retrieve the still-clutched hand.

Max released it. "Sensational," he said, clapping him on the shoulder in a show of warm camaraderie. "I'll owe you one." And as Woodrow threaded through the jammed bar, Max called after him, "You're on wheels, boy. I'm proud of you."

ON WHEELS OR NOT, the report didn't get written, as promised, during the flight home. Try as he might, Woodrow couldn't focus, couldn't seem to narrow his thoughts in on the tribulations and triumphs of the Jiffy Jack project. But to discourage any conversation with the traveller seated next to him (a woman whose hatchet face was buried under a layer of makeup so gooey and thick it appeared to have been applied with a cement trowel, and who, at first glance, reminded him vaguely of his aunt as she might have looked in her later middle years), he kept his notebook open on the tray table and covered its empty pages with words. A busy man, busily preparing a document of monumental import.

But what he actually scribbled there, across those blank and brilliant white sheets, was a trail of cryptic, rambling, disjointed, unpunctuated words, rather like spirit-writing. The scrawled symbols were connected to nothing other than the parade of images from the now, the near present, and the distant past, by turns innocuous and appalling, floating behind and before his bedeviled eyes. Or like those absurd word-association tests the Stoltz people required you to take as prerequisite to employment, so transparent an imbecile could fake them.

But now, since he was merely protecting his privacy, his space, there was nothing to gain or lose by fakery; and so among the accumulating pages of hyphenless combinations could be found such peculiar mates as: cloud clay, glass grief, sun run, son wail, bright soot, white dust, crimson lady, pen spike, scarlet meat, blade weed, father storm, grass worm, stone dead. And the final entry, made just before the squawky stewardess voice filled the cabin with instructions to fasten seat belts (his was) and to return seats to their upright positions (which his also already was) and to replace all tray tables to the backs of the seats ahead of them (which he obediently did) in preparation for landing at Chicago's O'Hare (where the time, they were told, was 4:15 P.M., and the temperature a not unpleasant 79 degrees under partly cloudy skies), that last entry read: nothing no thing.

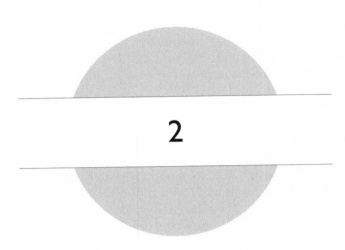

2

The voice in Norman Woodrow's head that same morning, while equally persistent, was considerably less sinister than the one tormenting his son. Stern, familiar voice, it directed him to rise automatically and without necessity of alarm exactly at 5:30 A.M.; to scrub down his lean and still-muscled sixty-year-old body in one of his two—sometimes three—showers of the day; to scrape the salt-and-pepper stubble from his bladed, fissured face; to pull on the T-shirt and baggy chinos habitually worn for work; to climb the stairs to the kitchen and prepare a pot of bitterly harsh coffee and, while it was brewing, light the first in a chain of forty-plus Marlboro reds. And then, precisely at 6:15 A.M., braced by the twin hits of nicotine and caffeine and obedient to the dictates of that interior voice, he descended the stairs and returned to his room on the condominium's lower level, seated himself at the desk located along the windowed wall opposite the bed and nightstand and bureau, and set to work.

Unlike his son's study (or office, as Michael chose to call it, for tax purposes) upstairs, Norman's cramped work space was, to all appearances, a riot of disorder. The desk was almost insanely cluttered with reference books, month-at-a-glance calendars, butts-heaped ashtrays, yellow legal pads, and assorted scraps of paper. Bolted at a right angle to its side was a small typing table upon which sat an IBM Wheelwriter, treasured gift from his son, and above which, Scotch-taped to the wall, hung a bewildering array of illegible notes and charts and communiqués to himself, and frequently amended master plans. The carpeted floor, on this end of the room, was littered with the further accoutrements and detritus of his labors: manila file fold-ers, ring binder notebooks, journals, and more loose paper scraps—some discarded, some to be saved. The fabric blind at the window, once a soft pastel peach, was now woefully discolored by the linger-ing smoke of thousands upon thousands of cigarettes. Altogether a schizophrenic room, one half, the sleeping half, neat as a squared-away-for-inspection military barrack; the other, chaos. Physical mani-festation (if you thought about it, which Norman often did) of his tangled life.

Schizoid or not, that's how he worked. What he'd discovered, quite by chance, was the terror of the blank page, for him a literal ter-ror that could be repulsed only by the conscious suppression of the perpetually buzzing voice in his head, the Norman Woodrow voice, and by the adoption of an entirely different persona. He liked to think of the process as a kind of binary fission of the brain; this sundered, albeit temporarily, half of him free to explore, through pages accu-mulating at a pace painfully slow, the terrible mystery of what hap-pened, what went wrong.

Because he had once, about a hundred years ago, been a minor scholar; and because the script that proceeded from the ballpoint gripped in his tremor-struck hand was utterly indecipherable to anyone but himself; and because, finally, no one really cared about an old joint rat's eccentric scribblings, there was not the slightest danger his son would suspect the work in progress to be anything other than what Norman had told him it was: a critical biography of the seventeenth-century English dramatist Nathaniel Lee. Mad Nat Lee. It was Norman's private joke.

And so he sat down that morning, as he did every morning, un-der the narrow band of light falling from the gooseneck lamp at the back of the desk, and produced the words that compiled the frag-ments that, once assembled, would reveal the melancholy history of his life. Or that peculiar skewed conception of his life, full of capri-cious side trips, idle reveries, and whimsical baubles of memory summoned by the stranger who occupied, these morning hours, the frontal lobes of his brain.

After the lapse of the first of those hours, the lower regions of his viscera, with clockwork regularity, began to churn, and he got up from his chair and padded into the adjacent bathroom and evacuated his bowels. Close to three years of free-worlding and yet the procedure still felt odd, bare buttocks no longer in direct contact with chilly porcelain. Good, but odd.

Two hours after that, he happened, in a reflective moment, to lift his eyes from the yellow sheet and glance out the window. Across the patch of lawn he saw a moving van pulled up at a condo on the next street over. A youngish-looking woman—short, slight, pretty (as near as he could tell from this distance)—stood in the entrance, gesturing worriedly at two burly men balancing, somewhat precariously, a large, glass-faced china cabinet. The scene registered in a pocket of the Norman Woodrow consciousness, but not in the stranger's; his eyes lowered to the scrawlings on the sheet of paper, and he resumed stalking the fugitive thought lost in the momentary distraction.

Three hours later the stranger departed, as he always did, like a figure vanishing leisurely into a swirl of fog, engulfed in shadow. No good-bye, no oath to return. No promises. Six hours, three pages, one of which was maybe salvageable. Heavy on that *maybe.*

But Norman was inescapably back again, inhabiting the clay of himself again. So he put away his writing materials and changed into sweatsuit and Nikes. He went through the door and crossed the spacious room dominated by wide-screen television, ten-piece sectional couch, magnificent dark oak book- and bric-a-brac shelves (a room designated, with only a pinch of irony, as "family"), and entered the nine-by-twelve storage area, half of which was set aside as his gym. Fitted into that tiny space were Olympic bar, three hundred pounds of plates, bench, squat racks, and treadmill—all of them gifts from his son.

Today, Friday, was exclusively weights. He shook out the stiffness with a short calisthenics drill (shoulder and knee joints creaking) and commenced his workout. Thirty years on the nails had taken their toll, but he could still bench one-fifty for reps and max out on the squat at a respectable two hundred. The withering skin of age had blurred most of his definition, but at five-ten and one hundred-eighty pounds there was still a certain solidity and volume to his muscles, and even a fair taper from shoulders to waist. Not bad, for an old fart. Yet he was not inordinately proud of, or concerned over, his body. Exercising it was just something you did, like brushing your teeth and shaving your face, minimum of expended thought. Anyway, he'd learned soon enough in the keep that, old man or not, if you're going to get by you've got to stand up, and if you're going to stand up you'd better be ready to shove.

Midway into a set of presses, the doorbell chimed, and while the intrusion *(any* intrusion in his by-the-numbers life) was vexing, he knew he had to respond. This was, after all, Michael's crib, not his, and messages arrived frequently in the overnight mail, particularly as a weekend approached. So he racked the bar and started up the stairs. As the bell dinged again, he muttered irritably, "All right, all *right."* He swung open the inner door, and there, on the other side of the screen, stood a woman clad in scruffy jeans and denim workshirt, smiling at him tentatively, timidly. Most diminutive woman, somehow vaguely familiar-seeming. "Yes," said Norman, inflecting it upward, but only barely.

"I'm awfully sorry to bother you. But I'm having a little, uh, difficulty. With my water heater. I saw your car parked out front. And there's no one else around."

It was the voice (Norman would determine, much later) that first took him. Not exactly breathless, more of a flutter in it, or maybe it was a ripple, feathery as the healing touch of a ghost of a breeze on a sun-smothered day, full of unstudied modulations and the sustaining music of promises pledged, and kept.

"Who are you?" he said with a solitary man's ragged bluntness. He tilted his head slightly, to catch more of that music.

"Lizabeth Seaver. I just moved into the unit behind you. Today, in fact."

"Say it again."

"What?"

"Your name. Say it."

"Lizabeth Seaver."

"Lizabeth," he repeated, stringing out the syllables. "Without the initial *e."*

She gazed at him curiously. "That's right. How did you know?"

"Wild guess."

"Most people think I'm just slurring when I say it. They're sure it's got to be *E*lizabeth."

"Lizabeth as in Lizabeth Scott. Minor forties actress. Played in a couple of lesser Burt Lancaster vehicles. *Desert Fury,* if memory serves, and *I Walk Alone.*"

"Now that's really weird. Your knowing that. She was my dad's favorite actress. He named me after her. I never saw those movies you said, but I can remember him talking about them."

What's going on here? Woman appears at your door. Perfect stranger. Suddenly you're chattering easily about names and orthography, and films seen and unseen. Like picking up a conversation left off years ago with an old and valued friend (assuming you had one). Very strange.

His eyes travelled over her. He listened, he stared. First the arresting voice, then the hair, great electric puff of it, Niagara of honey-colored curls spilling over the reed of a neck and brushing the thin shoulders, framing a face of such delicate loveliness it dispatched a yearning ache to the very core of his cloistered, crusted heart. Needle to the heart. But then, remembering what it was she looked at, what she saw: freeze dry in soiled sweats, thinning hair, corded throat, life-battered face complete with bent nose, worry gorge between the remote, skeptical eyes, vertical scar stitched into the forehead, slice of a mouth parenthesized by two deep creases and amnesiac of smiling—remembering all that, he was hauled back to the shell of himself. "What is the nature of your problem?" he said gruffly. That's the way he spoke, the way words came to him.

"It's the pilot light. I can't seem to get it lit. I'd call someone, but my phone's not in yet. But really, if you're busy—"

"I'm not busy. Wait here."

He went back down the stairs, got his glasses off the nightstand and fitted them over his nose and ears. State-issue wire frames, they were retained, against his son's protests, as reminder of where he had been, what he'd done, what remained to be uncovered. Like some *objet trouvé,* prized for its power of summoning the substance of his dark experience. He thought about things like that, Norman did; all the time he thought about them.

But not quite so much when he returned and found Ms. Lizabeth (without the frontal *e)* Seaver waiting patiently, as instructed, on the porch. Should have invited her to step inside. Too late now. All the commonplace amenities long since lost. She rewarded him with another smile, offered no comment on the anachronistic glasses. "Let's go have a look," he said.

Her condo was smaller than Michael's, a telescoped version, same machine-stamped layout: protuberant single-stall garage, narrow entry space, kitchen directly off the entrance, living room just beyond, short hallway linking a couple of bedrooms, couple of baths. The furniture appeared to be placed randomly, the floors were strewn with unopened packing cartons. "Forgive the mess," she said, adding by way of explanation. "I'd hoped to get all the dishes out today, but I wanted to clean the cupboard shelves first. That's when I discovered there wasn't any hot water."

Norman nodded, said nothing. His nostrils pinched against a trace of an acrid scent he was certain he detected in the air.

The lower level was simply a basement, nothing more, no access to the out-of-doors, a bare concrete slab for floor, exposed pipes on the cobwebbed ceiling, part of one cement wall covered with blond panelling, otherwise unfinished. Leading him through it, she remarked, only partly in jest, "What do you think? Needs some work?"

"Maybe a little," he said. As recently as four years ago, it would have seemed to him palatial, this basement. He hadn't forgotten.

They passed through the door to the utility room and stood before the cylindrical water heater. "This now," she said, grimacing at it in mock indignation, "this is what's giving me grief. Here, let me show you." She reached into a pocket of her shirt and removed a lighter and struck it.

Norman thrust out a hand and snuffed the flame with his cupped palm. "No!"

She jerked back, startled. "You *burned* yourself."

"There's gas in here. Don't you smell it?"

"Well, no, not really."

"Trust me."

He stooped down and examined some copper tubing at the base of the heater. Came to his feet and said, "I can't pretend to know much about these things, but I think the coupling may be loose. Potentially very dangerous."

"So what should I do?"

"Call the gas company. Better yet, a plumber."

"Could I, uh, use your phone?"

"Of course."

"What about your hand? Let me get you something for it."

Norman looked at the raw blister spreading like fungus across his palm. "It's fine," he said. "I won't laugh, then it won't hurt."

BACK AT HIS SON'S CONDO, Norman got out the phone directory and laid it on the kitchen counter. "So which will it be," he asked, "gas man or plumber?"

"Which do you suggest?"

"Plumber, as I said. That is, if you want it done today. The gas jockeys aren't famous for promptness around here. Or solicitude."

"Can you recommend one?"

He could. He did. He handed her the phone. And while she placed the call and made the arrangements, Norman found himself watching her again, studying her face, collecting its details as if to commit them to memory, God knows why. It was slightly squarish, inside that swag of hair, the forehead broad under the dangling ringlets; pale brows curving in a wholly natural, quizzical arc. Her eyes were a vivid blue, deeply socketed, eerily perfect circles, like a doll's eyes, as though all the energy and intensity in that slight frame were squeezed into them and funnelled through them. She had a fine, straight nose, a wide, mobile mouth, skin innocent of paint and drawn tight over sculpted bones, remarkably structured bones. And while she spoke he discovered himself listening again to the melodies in the voice and following the battery of expressions animating the features: anticipation, misgiving, may-I-put-you-on-hold exasperation, let-me-transfer-you despair, finally a cheering-news elation. And then she put up the phone and turned to him, and a fresh smile flowered across her face, a joyous relieved smile, and she exclaimed, "They'll do it! Be out in about an hour, they said."

"Piece of luck for you, with the holiday weekend coming on."

"God watching over fools, huh."

"Also are you lucky you didn't blow yourself up over there."

The smile went rueful. "Blow us both up. I can't tell you how sorry I am about that. And about your hand."

He put the unseared one in the air, brushed away her regrets impatiently. "All right, you've told me, enough said."

A trace of hurt flickered in those extraordinary eyes. It had come out harsher than he'd intended, and to soften it some he said, "Maybe you should play the lottery, all that luck. Meantime, you'd better wait here till they arrive. Don't want any asphyxiation victims in this placid little slice of Americana."

"I think I've caused you enough trouble for one day."

"It's no trouble."

"You're sure?"

"I'm sure," Norman said. But he had no idea what you say next. Seriously short on practice with these neighborly dialogues. As in a couple of decades short. For a moment he stood there awkwardly, a bumbling sand-kicker, still gawking at her. In that moment he was acutely aware of the elfin size of her, the side-to-side narrowness, the slender limbs, the exquisite fore and aft molding, small, almost adolescent spheres of breasts and slightly rounded hips in exact proportion to a waist so microscopic he was convinced he could enclose it in the grip of a single hand. For a woman like this one, Norman thought, anatomy is surely destiny. He asked her if she wanted lunch. It was something to say.

"No, thanks. I had a big breakfast. Moving day, you know."

"Some coffee, then?"

"Coffee would be nice."

"We can take it into the sun parlor. Watch for your plumber there."

He poured two cups, handed over hers, and led the way around the counter and through the living room into the sun parlor, which, true to its name, captured all the available light through its brace of windows.

"What a beautiful home you have," she said, a ring of sincerity in the reflex remark.

It was too. At least by any measure he had ever known. Spacious, airy, decorator-designed, and expensively furnished (the way Michael wanted it), with lush silvery carpeting throughout. A solid-oak dining suite stood at one end of the living room. There was an enormous crescent-shaped couch patterned with a sprinkling of pale green leaves on a field of eggshell white, pair of matching easy chairs, each with ottoman, huge glass-topped coffee table, hutch full of antique glass. And in the sun parlor, salmon-colored rattan furniture, another couch and glass table, both of them smaller, cozier, and two more chairs. He motioned her to one of them, took the other. "It's not mine," he said. "It belongs to my son."

"But you live here?"

"Yes."

"How do you like the neighborhood?"

"It's not for me to like or dislike. It's a place to live."

"There's just the two of you?"

"Yes. He's not married."

"What about you?" she said, half teasingly. "No wife either?"

In a voice utterly empty of tone Norman said, "Not anymore."

Her eyes fell to the cup clutched in both hands. It occurred to him he'd neglected to provide a saucer. Or to ask if she took milk or sweetener. Too absent of those amenities. Again. And after a protracted pause, astonishingly, in apologetic whisper, as though their thoughts were somehow in concert, she replied, "Lately I seem to have mislaid all my social graces."

"That's all right. So have I."

"I really didn't mean to pry."

"Don't worry about it."

"It's just that it's such a large place. And so . . . orderly. For two men."

"He has a cleaning lady in every week."

Now her eyes lifted and roamed about the room. "You know, the only thing I'd change—out here, I mean—is I'd have plants. Lots of plants. And a terrarium."

"He's not much on greenery, my son. Obviously, neither am I."

"You collect glass instead. One of you, anyway."

"No. No hobbies, either of us. The glass was his mother's."

"Oh," was all that she said.

A moment of stiff silence. Not comfortable. Norman got to his feet and went out to the kitchen and returned with an ashtray and a pack of Marlboros. He shook one loose, lit it, inhaled deeply, expelled a thin gust at the ceiling. All the while conscious of her watching him curiously. "Is something wrong?" he asked.

"You smoke?"

"You find that surprising?"

"Well, I can't help but notice you're wearing sweats. And when you first came to the door it looked as if you'd been working out."

"So I had."

"You exercise and still smoke?"

"Everyone's entitled to one irrationality. Of course, Michael doesn't believe that. Or approve."

"Michael's your son?"

"Yes. He belongs to the sanctimonious generation. Yours."

"Not all of us are quite so sanctimonious."

"What are you saying? You want one of these?"

Her smile blossomed again, as though a secret little joke had passed between them. "I left mine over at my place," she said. "I was hoping you'd offer."

Norman pushed the pack across the glass table. He couldn't remember if you were supposed to light it for them anymore. Didn't matter. She produced her own flame from the same lighter that had, a short time ago, nearly scrubbed them both.

"Your son's not like you, then?" she said.

"Afraid he is. In many respects."

"Then he can't be all bad. What does he do?"

"He's a management consultant."

"Sounds important. What does it mean?"

"I'm not sure. Ministers to ailing businesses, I think. He travels most of the time."

"And you? Are you retired?"

Norman massaged the crevice between his eyes thoughtfully. It took him a moment to reply. "You might say."

"I'm doing it again," she said.

"What's that?"

"Prying. Can't seem to stop myself. I'm sorry."

"You can leave off the apologies. No harm in questions."

"I could tell you about me. That might stop them."

"All right, what about you?" he asked her. "Husband?" Might as well start at the top.

She shook her head vigorously. "Same as you. Not anymore."

Hardly the same, Norman was thinking, but he said, "What's your work?"

"I'm a teacher. Elementary school."

"Here in Hinsdale?"

"Yes. I was lucky enough to get a job here, a last-minute opening. Well, lucky for me, I guess. Not so for their special-ed teacher. She was killed in a car accident last week."

"What did I say about that luck of yours? Every person's death has a way of smoothing life for someone else."

She looked at him steadily, solemnly. But there was neither

shock nor reproach in her voice when she said, "You're a very curious man, you know that?"

"So tell the curious old man what it is that a special-ed teacher does. Work with mongoloids? Retards?"

"That's not a very kind way to put it."

"How do you educators put it?"

"We call them learning disabled or emotionally impaired."

"Nice euphemisms. Tell me, how do you go about disimpairing the emotions?"

"You're making fun of me, aren't you," she said quietly, not exactly injured, but not a question either.

"Not at all. I'd really like to know."

"You would?"

"Tell me."

"Well, you have to understand these are extremely hyperactive children. Very disturbed, most of them. So to begin with we try to provide an environment where they can learn to control their behavior through rigid structure and setting and through a system of consequences and rewards."

"Sounds to me very much like modern life," Norman said. Or prison, he might have added, though he didn't. Instead he let her roll on, interjecting a polished query here and there. He presented an attentive sympathetic face, its wall of irony momentarily breached, nodding sagely now and again, as though he comprehended fully the opaque jargon learned by rote at some dismal college of education, as though all its laughable, circuitous puffery addressed the central issue locked in his original question: *Child or man, how does one undertake to heal the fractured heart?*

But it mattered not that she had no answers. Watching her there, a flawless cameo quickened by breath and sprung miraculously to passionate life, and entranced by the harmonic rhythms in her voice, Norman felt something opening in his chest and throat. It was not unique—a man of sixty years couldn't call it unique—but something so remote, so distant, it defied definition. Something like joy came to mind.

She talked. He listened. Both of them smoked steadily, thinning the deck of Marlboros, a pair of miscreants in wicked league.

And then her glance strayed to the window. She broke off midlesson and said excitedly, "They're here."

Norman walked her to the door. She hesitated an instant, said, "How can I thank you for all your help?"

"None required."

"You know, you never did tell me your name."

"It's Woodrow. Norman Woodrow."

"Thanks for saving my life, Norman Woodrow."

"It wasn't me. The eye of the Father records every sparrow's plunge. If the Good Book tells true."

A corner of her mouth turned up in baffled smile. Her head moved back and forth slowly. "Curious man," she murmured. "I hope we'll have a chance to talk again, Norman."

"Perhaps we will."

She scampered off down the street, hair swirling around her shoulders, arms flagging. And when she was no longer in sight, the something that might have been joy was replaced by a desolate sense of bleakness, and the bewildered, helpless melancholy that will sometimes settle over the faces of old men who unwisely allow themselves to contemplate the mystery of all that's lost-finished-wasted-gone settled over the face of Norman Woodrow.

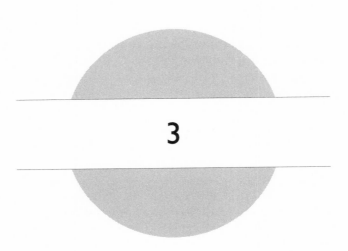

3

Victor Flam had spent the better part of the morning watching women weep. First the mother, then an aunt, then the best friend. They all began bravely enough—the way people will do, conditioned by seeing their cinematic selves in numberless overwrought dramas and, in his experience, not totally unhappy to have a role, however small, in this one; the universal appetite to be in on the action—but as their respective angles on the victim and on the grisly tale unfolded, all three of them soon dissolved in bitter tears. With the mother he had been obliged to present a properly mournful face (she was, after all, the one paying the freight), but by the time he got to the best friend his patience was wearing thin, and it was all he could do to restrain himself from muttering, "All right, all right, enough with the waterworks."

Mrs. Roland Swales had phoned the day before and asked if he could stop by the following morning. Why, she didn't volunteer. Which wasn't unusual, in his line of work. *Swales.* The name sparked a dim recollection. He agreed. Nine-ish, say? Nine-ish would be fine with Flam. Fine. They rang off.

Victor Flam was the sort of man who always did his homework,

liked to come prepared. It was that close attention to detail earned
him the jacket for top tracker on Florida's Gold Coast, bar nobody.
He operated out of his home in Palm Beach Gardens. (When you're
the best you didn't need an office and you didn't need to advertise,
clients found you), and he got work from all over the state and even
his share of the Hebe trade down from New York. He wasn't rich,
but at forty-five he could live pretty much the way he wanted, which
was well, and he could pick his jobs. Twice divorced, self-sufficient,
his work was his life. His card read:

VICTOR FLAM
RESEARCH, FACT-FINDING, CONFIDENTIAL INQUIRIES

Purposely vague.

But he had the connections, twenty-two years in the business
worth of connections. And so after he'd put up the phone yesterday
and searched the Rolodex of his memory for the name Swales, he
tapped one of them, called in a favor from a Palm Beach County sheriff's deputy of his acquaintance, and got a look at the file on one Shelley Russo, née Swales. Murder victim.

And a most brutal slaying it had been: some twenty-seven shank
wounds, box and boobs badly mutilated, throat slashed so deep to
the spinal cord the head very nearly severed. Serious whacking. Body
discovered in a grungy no-tell motel up in Juno Beach. Cuckolded
husband (many times over, it developed) with a vacuum-sealed alibi,
same as all the boyfriends of record. Robbery not a motive, nor drugs.
After six dead-end months, the file had drifted to the back of the cabinet; six more, and it was collecting dust, still "open," but in name
only. Which doubtless prompted the Mother Swales call.

So this morning he'd dressed in one of his finer linen suits,
tooled his Caddie across the Royal Park Bridge into Palm Beach,
pulled up punctually at 9:00 A.M. in the circular driveway of the opu-
lent Swales estate ("compounds," they like to call them over here),
and was greeted at the door by a little spic girl who ushered him into
the elegantly appointed living room and the presence of the lady of
the house. Mrs. Swales was a chubby, sun-leathered woman (about
seventy, his best guess) with champagne-colored hair, bulldog face,
and the blunt-edged, spare-the-pleasantries manner of up-by-the-boot-

straps bucks. She launched right into her story, a good share of which he already knew, though he listened carefully anyway.

From her he learned that Shelley was a beautiful girl (to call her a girl, age forty-two at death, was something of a stretch, but Flam didn't remark on that), and kind, generous, warm, trusting to a fault— all the things mothers, even the monied ones, want to believe about their daughters. But also was she fiercely independent, he was told. There was absolutely no reason—no *need*—for her to work at that awful industrial laundry, even though her position there, executive secretary to the president, was of course lofty and responsible. Nor should she ever have gotten involved with that *Eye-talian* husband (number three, Flam knew, but again he elected to remain silent).

A wall of what-might-have-been tears formed in the eyes of Mother Swales. To hold them off, she showed him photos: Shelley, the diapered newborn; the child in frilly pink dress; the shapely adolescent in briefest of majorette outfits, lots of spangles and beads, caressing a phallic baton; the first-time-around bride in gorgeous gown of stainless white; the mature responsible woman standing in the entrance to the Sanitary Laundry Services Company, dressed for success. At a recent shot of Shelley and Daddy, the dam burst and Mrs. Swales's doggie face collapsed in sorrow. For it seemed Daddy Swales, a hit-it-rich developer, was no longer with us either, passed away last spring, overdose of grief, she implied, at the loss of his angelic only child.

Flam studied the photograph while she composed herself. It revealed an attractive brunette with good features, though nothing extraordinary, a clever knowing smile, hint of a naughty glint in the eye. What he would call a seasoned face, been there and back, more times than a few. The kind you'd look at twice, not for its beauty but its lush promise.

Finally Mrs. Swales was ready to get on with it. She told him of her outrage with the police, their callousness, indifference, general incompetence. She offered him the assignment: find the monster who had taken her daughter and, indirectly, her husband, and bring him to justice. Flam spelled out carefully what an investigation of this magnitude could cost. She didn't blink (and by now the tears were long gone). She wanted blood. Blood for blood. Seemed only fair. He accepted. An agreement was struck.

Victor Flam was an orderly, methodical man. Whenever he com-

menced a new job, the first thing he liked to do was construct a profile of the subject. Penetrate the character, penetrate the mystery,
was his theory. So he got from the mother the names and addresses
of Shelley's aunt, the only other living relative, and of her best friend.
He drove back across the bridge and paid them each a visit, the aunt
first, up on Singer Island; then the friend, over in North Palm. Each of
them offered a history of Shelley Swales Powers Wick Russo not dis-
similar to the mother's, though each with a slightly different slant,
skewed differently, and filtered through goggles slightly less rose-
tinted. Also was he forced to suffer through more blubbering, both
places, particularly with the best friend, a woman who'd known Shelley, in her words, "since Adam" and who was given to such broad
histrionics she might have carved out a nice career for herself on the
daytime soaps.

So it was something of a relief to discover the widower (whose
current address, a doublewide up in Jupiter, Flam had taken from the
police file) not exactly grieving. And not exactly communicative either, at least not in the beginning. Said he wouldn't speak a word, not
word one, without his attorney present but then went ahead and did
anyway. Many words. Flam could have that effect on people, when
he wanted to: a kind of soothing folksy quality, made them want to
confide. It was one of the things you learned in this business.

Sal Russo (a sometime toy and novelties salesman and a full-time
gambler of the low-roller variety; deep into the forties; thickening but
still handsome in a woppish way; blissfully remarried to a blond beach
bimbette parading around the trailer in string bikini, looking an easy
fifteen) bitched about the heat still leaning on him, year after the, uh,
incident, dicking him over strictly because of his ethnic origins, like
he was *connected* or something, maybe hired a shooter to blitz Shelley. Whined about his mounting legal bills to defend himself against all
these patently false insinuations, all the rousting. About the departed
wife he had plenty to say, none of it charitable. Flam listened quietly,
let the grouching roll and the venom spew, thanked him, and left.

From the four of them, from the case file, and from his own
thoughtful conclusions on the fallen state of humankind, Flam was
starting to patch together a profile of a pampered little rich girl with a
will of her own, outlaw streak, grown into a flashy fluff who, married
or not, was no better than she had to be and who never hesitated to
indulge her erotic tastes for some strange, especially the younger

ranks of strange. Like her libido, which was never quiescent, had gone into hyperdrive when she hit the big four-o. Badges were crowding Sal just for the exercise, give the impression they were still flogging the case now and again. Of course they knew better. Aside from the painfully obvious fact a sleazoid like Sal couldn't possibly have any ties to the Life, not even in his dreams, not in a thousand years—aside from that, they knew no pro would ever do a number like the one done on Shelley Swales (which is how Flam thought of her now, with the wop clearly out of the suspect picture). Which left a mighty upset sack partner. Or a world-class psycho. If the latter, it would be his first. Could be interesting. Also potentially hazardous, solo player like himself. Step light, Victor.

The next place he stopped was the last place Shelley Swales had been seen alive. A sprawling enterprise, the Sanitary Laundry Services, Inc., was a gigantic wash-o-rama, as big as a tractor factory, but with a pleasant sudsy smell about it. Like your neighborhood laundromat on steroids. Did a thriving business with all the major hospitals and hotels and industries in the area, Flam had taken the time to learn. He talked his way past the gate and into the management offices, but none of the executives had any time for him, so he cornered a typist who'd worked directly under Shelley, and it was out of her he scored his best buzz yet.

"I already *told* all this to the cops," said Ms. Bridget Vatchek in that pert, sassy, take-no-shit tone and manner some plain women will affect with prying strangers, a kind of veiled vamping—flirtatiousness stood on its head. *You want the goods? Try me and we'll see.*

They were sitting in facing chairs in the secretaries' lounge, where she'd agreed, half grudgingly, half coyly, to meet after he'd displayed his card, explained why he was there. Flam's mouth was arranged in smile, affable and warm, but his drill-bit eyes watched her steadily, took in everything. He was practiced that way. To call Ms. Vatchek plain, he'd decided, was to put it most kindly: pumpkin-colored hair so wiry and thin you could see right down to the scalp in spots; sharp, witchy face with hollow, freckle-washed cheeks and too much nose; gangly, shapeless body afflicted by the premature shoulder stoop and obscene little tummy pouch that come of hunching over a keyboard eight hours a day. Late thirties maybe, maybe more. The sort of girl who spent prom night playing gin with Grandma, grown into the sort of woman who studies other, more fortunate women, with that sour mix of envy and spite that occasionally makes for penetrating insight. Like the widower, she had no tears to spill over the victim.

"Yeah, I understand that," Flam said, pitching his voice low and smooth and suasive. "But it would help if you could tell it to me. Anything you remember about Mrs. Russo."

"Like what?"

"Oh, your impressions of her, say. Kind of person she was."

"Kind of person, that covers a lot."

Flam started over. "Was she an intelligent woman?"

"Guess she knew her job okay, but outside of that I wouldn't call her real bright. No rocket scientist, that's for sure."

"But she was good at her work? Efficient?"

"I suppose you could say that."

"Just *suppose?*"

"She got by on a lot of dazzle, you want my opinion."

"How do you mean, *dazzle?*"

"Oh, you know, hairstyles, makeup, jewelry, clothes. Shoulda seen her clothes. You can bet they didn't come off the dog racks."

Unlike your own, Flam was thinking, running his eyes over the bargain-basement blouse and skirt hiked up just enough over crossed legs to reveal knobby knees and a peek of stringy inner thigh. But he said, "Was she, y'know, well thought of here? Well liked?"

"Oh, yeah, I'd say well liked, if it's the men you're talkin' about. They were all of 'em sniffin' around her."

"Would you say she, ah, encouraged this attention?"

Ms. Vatchek snorted at that. "What do you think?"

"What about affairs? Any that you knew of?"

"Only one I knew for sure was with a kid in the mail room. Nineteen-year-old kid. Course, everybody knew about that one. They were goin' at it hot and heavy for quite a while. Their nooners was the big joke around here. You know what I'm sayin', *nooners?*"

"I think I follow," Flam said dryly.

"But the cops ran the kid downtown and talked to him. He was clean. You hear about that?"

Poor Ms. Vatchek. Too much late-night TV infecting her speech. "I heard," Flam said.

"Nobody could ever figure what she was doin' here in the first place, her folks got all that money."

"Why do you think?"

Ms. Vatchek shrugged. "Beats me. Get away from her old man maybe. She never talked about him much, but the word was he was a real loser."

Flam already knew that, so he said, "Anything you can tell me about that last day?"

"Wow, that's a toughie. Been over a year now."

"I know. But anything you can remember. Anything out of the ordinary."

Ms. Vatchek looked blank.

"Phone calls? Visitors? Upsets?"

She tossed her head negatively.

"Anything unusual in Mrs. Russo's behavior? Any break in her normal routines or patterns?"

"Only thing I remember about that day is she was spendin' a lot of time down in the bird room."

"What's that, bird room?"

"Where the consultants were."

"Consultants?"

"Yeah, they had 'em in here, shape up the operation. Gave 'em this room to work out of. Y'know, keep their stuff, huddle."

"These consultants, where were they from? Around here?"

"Oh, no. This was a real heavy-duty outfit. Out of Chicago, I think, or New York. Someplace like that."

Flam's interest in the thoughts, opinions, and observations of the unlovely Ms. Vatchek had been rapidly waning. Now it picked up again. He asked her to tell him something about this heavy-duty outfit.

"Not much to tell. There was four or five of 'em. Real serious dudes, all business."

"What exactly did they do?"

"Y'got me. They were always nosin' around the facility, askin' questions, snoopin' in the files. All's I know is everybody was scared spitless of 'em. Good reason, too. On account of them, forty people got axed. Me, I was lucky."

"So these consultants weren't winning any popularity contests."

Ms. Vatchek rolled her eyes heavenward. "Hope to shout, they weren't."

"Were these older men? Young?"

"Whole range. Guy in charge looked, oh, fifty maybe. Other ones were thirties and forties, I'd guess."

"How long were they here?"

"About three months, must've been. Seemed like forever."

Flam was silent a moment. He rubbed a temple thoughtfully.

"Listen," Ms. Vatchek crowed, "you think you got some heavy clue here, forget it. They finished up that day, were outta here in the morning. Cops checked on 'em."

"Expect they did," Flam said, though he couldn't remember anything on a consulting team from the file. If in fact there'd been a routine follow-up, it must have been written off as another of those blind alleys leading nowhere. For himself, now, Flam wasn't so sure. He had an instinct about these things. Tracker's unfailing instinct. Never hurt to find out more. "You remember any of these consultants' names?" he asked her.

"Unh-uh. They weren't the kind you cozied up to."

"How about the name of the company?"

"Can't place that either. Been a year, remember."

"I remember. Think you could get it for me?"

"Might be I could turn it up. Not right now, though. I gotta get back. Pile a work."

"Later today?"

Ms. Vatchek gave him her best impression of a coquettish look. "Maybe. If I did, how'd I let you know?"

Flam reached into a pocket, removed one of his cards, and handed it to her. "You could call me," he said. "The number's on there."

"Tonight?"

"Tonight would be good. I'm not there, leave a message."

She rose up out of her chair, flashed him a mouthful of crooked teeth, wiggled her bony fingers in farewell. "Be in touch."

VICTOR FLAM WAS A BIG MAN, big-boned, big-shouldered, barrel-chested, thick-waisted, broad-hipped, square and solid as a chain-locked gate. He stood three inches over six feet, went about two-forty when he was watching his weight, which he hadn't been lately, there being a couple weeks downtime since his last job. He had one of those wide-margined faces, full but not fat, uncreased except for the deepening squinters around the dark, spiked eyes, generous of mouth, firm of jaw. Still had all his hair, though most of it was

gone slate-gray. The kind of face and frame that, along with his bearing, projected an aura of authority with just an undertone of quiet
force, contained but ever at the ready. Some women still found him
attractive. Enough, anyway, so he never lacked for tender companionship when he wanted it. And in point of fact he had a dinner date
that very evening, with a busty manicurist he'd been seeing off and
on—mostly off, given the nature of his work—the past six months.

But for now it occurred to him, driving away from the laundry,
that he'd eaten nothing since breakfast, and here it was, middle of the
afternoon. He was due for some nosh. Anyway, he thought better on
a full stomach, and after the several conversations of the day, last in
particular, there was some heavy thinking to be done.

And so he stopped in at the Parnassus up on PGA Boulevard, just
down the road from where he lived. He lunched there frequently,
since he seldom had the time or inclination to fix anything at home.
The owner, a happy-handing second generation Greek who went by
the name Nicky, out of Nicopolous, invariably greeted him as "Mister
Victor" and liked to trade the latest local gossip: who's stiffing who,
who's boffing who, things like that. But Flam had a lot on his mind today. Some of the rush he always felt at the outset of a new job (particularly a lucrative and dangerous one, as this held every promise of
becoming) was beginning to build. So he gave Nicky a quick, passing
salute and very conspicuously made for a booth in the back. He ordered a beer and a gyro, enough to hold him till dinner, and started
mentally piecing together everything he'd gathered so far on the
luckless and maybe not-so-saintly Shelley Swales.

So intent was he, so inward-focused, all this pondering, what he
failed to see was a pair of hostile eyes glowering at him through
the narrow slit of a portal opening from the kitchen. Nor could he of
course hear the string of muttered obscenities escaping the lips of
the cook, a lanky fellow with spindly arms and legs, blotchy skin, and
feedsack paunch, hired by Nicky only the week before. As it happened, in one of those curious quirks of chance, this cook, Lester
Cobb by name, was the same man Flam had tagged on a child mo-
lestation rap, tracked him after all the authorities—heat, social services—had given up, and nailed him dead in the act, a six-year-old's
dick in his mouth. It was Flam's evidence (he had the damning Po-
laroids) and testimony that earned Lester a nickel jolt. Cost him wife,
family, reputation, big job as manager of a Barnett bank, and reduced

him now to fry cook in a Greek restaurant. Not surprisingly, Lester figured he had a little payback coming, though what it could be he wasn't quite sure. Nothing too extreme, seeing as how he had a P.O. yet to answer to. Something innovative, creative.

A masterful inspiration came to him. He had an unseasonable case of the sniffles, and so what he did when Flam's gyro order arrived at the kitchen was summon a mighty breath, lay a thumb over one nostril and fire a glob of snot through the other, squarely into the pocket of a pita bread. Then he shaved the slivers of lamb off the slowly revolving spit and stuffed them, along with some diced cheese and onions and tomatoes, and also a lump of moist greenie extracted from the undischarged nostril, into the bread pocket, slathered it over with yogurt, set the plate on the portal counter and called, "Order up." And then, giggling manically, he watched and waited.

Nicky, still hoping to get some chatter out of his favorite customer, brushed the waitress aside and delivered the plate himself. Uninvited, he slid into the booth and said with labored heartiness, "So, Mister Victor, whaddya hear?"

Flam held off a frown, but he wasn't cheered by the company and he didn't want to encourage it. "Not much, Nicky. Nothin', in fact."

Didn't slow Nicky any. "Know that blond cunt, works in the card shop next door? Word is she's talkin' to the mike on Mr. Hallmark there, runs the place."

"No kiddin'."

"Bet your ass, no kiddin'. Gets even better."

Swarthy face opened in a nasty grin, voice a confidential whisper, Nicky went on to describe in graphic detail the blond cunt's sexual proclivities and appetites. Flam listened, but not very carefully. He had an appetite of his own to appease. He took a healthy bite of gyro, chewed and, sadly for him, swallowed part of it before its viscous consistency and full acidic flavor stung his taste buds. Once it did, he blew the remaining morsels onto the table and, with a sudden exodus of his habitual cool, bawled, "Jesus! Fuck's *in* this?"

Nicky looked stunned. "Whazzit? Wha's matter?"

"There's some kinda shit in the sandwich."

"What? No. I get all my food fresh today. This morning." Now he looked hurt, his professional integrity called into question.

Flam sliced open the bread with his knife and picked through the filling gingerly. Probed it. Lifted a twining, gluey ladder of phlegm. His mouth twisted in disgust. "See this?"

Nicky moved his head up and down.

"Know what it is?"

Nicky's head went the other way.

"Unless I'm mistaken, somebody's honked some nose sauce in here."

"No. Can't be."

"Who's your cook?"

"New fella. Just come on."

Nicky started to glance in the direction of the kitchen portal.

"Keep your eyes on me," Flam said.

Nicky brought his baffled gaze back to Flam.

"Okay. You wait here. I'm gonna go have a word with this new cook, yours."

For a large man, Flam could move fast when he wanted to. Now he wanted to. He bolted out of the booth and charged into the kitchen, catching up with the fleeing Lester before he could make it through the rear door. Flam seized him by the collar, spun him around, and slammed him against a wall. "You put that gyro together?" he demanded.

When he'd seen Flam coming, Lester realized, suddenly and with an agony of fright, the consequences of his spontaneous mischief. Now, with his back pinned to the wall, his terror-struck eyes darting wildly, searching floor, ceiling, anywhere but the hard, vindictive Flam face, he strained to find a voice, but all that emerged was a wordless squeak.

"Askin' you a question here, Cookie."

"I made it," Lester mumbled at the floor.

"Speak up."

"Said I made it."

"Okay, that's good, we got that established. Now you can tell me why you added that special gourmet ingredient."

"What ingredient's that?"

"Why is it I get the idea you already know."

Lester, cornered, said, "I got a real bad cold. Been sneezing all day. Ask anybody. Ask Nicky. Could be something got, uh, well . . ." He trailed off, unwilling or unable to complete the thought.

Flam finished it for him. "Got in the sandwich? Something like your nose dew?"

"If it did, it was an accident."

"Accident," Flam repeated.

"Yeah, right, accident. Could've happened to anybody."

Flam had one of those encyclopedic memories, the kind that warehouse, file, and compartmentalize every scrap of useful information and relevant experience. And because there was something vaguely familiar about this quaking miserable worm, something about the skittish eyes and craven mouth and abnormally red, damp lips, he ransacked it now. To speed the process along, he grasped a hank of oily hair and jerked the lowered head up and back, and stuck his own face in close, peered at him. "I know you from somewhere," he said.

Lester tried to shake his head no, but it wouldn't move in Flam's iron grip.

"What's your name?"

Lester's mouth began to twitch. He couldn't speak. It occurred to him to wonder now, too late, why he'd ever yielded to the crazy impulse. Melancholy story of his life.

"Name!" Flam barked at him.

"Lester."

It was all the spark Flam's compendious memory required. "Lester Cobb," he said, snapping the fingers of his free hand. "Lester the Molester. Mr. Short Eyes. Back on the pavement again. Tell me, Lester, you been suckin' any kiddie cock lately?"

"Lemme be, Flam. Please. I didn't mean anything with the food."

"I understand, Lester. It was an accident, right? Like you said?"

"I'll fix you another one. Good one."

Flam made a thoughtful face, like he was actually entertaining the offer. But he didn't let go of Lester's hair. "Yeah, well," he drawled, "you could maybe do that, slap together another one. But what about that one you already fixed? Can't let it go to waste now, can we? Think about all the starving niggers in Africa or India or wherever it is they're starvin' these days."

Flam didn't wait for a reply. He jerked Lester away from the wall and dragged him across the kitchen. At the portal he called out to Nicky, instructed him to come on back. "And bring along the gyro," he added.

Nicky, bearing the plate of shredded gyro, appeared in the doorway.

"Set it on the floor," Flam said.

Nicky did as he was told. He knew Flam. And the tone of voice he was hearing, you don't argue.

Flam released Lester's hair, motioned at the plate. "Chow call, Lester."

Lester didn't move. He glanced over at Nicky, whose gaze was locked on the floor. No help there. So he shaped his mouth in a ghastly, pleading grin. Like it was all maybe just a little joke he was privileged to be in on.

Flam widened his eyes, a look that on anyone else would have been guileless, innocent, but on him managed to be somehow menacing. "Y'got shit in your ears? Said it's time to eat. Better get down there."

"C'mon, Flam—"

"You know all about goin' down, Lester. Comes natural to you."

"Look, I'm sorry about—"

"Down!"

Lester got down on all fours, his head over the plate.

"Let's clean it up now," Flam said. "Every last bite."

And though he produced some wretched, gagging noises, Lester did it. He cleaned the plate. Every last bite. And when he was finished, Flam said amiably, "Okay, Lester, you did good. Real good. Now all you got is a little KP duty, and then you're done."

"Huh?"

"The floor there. Want you to clean that too."

"How?" Lester groaned. He didn't dare look up. He had an idea how.

He was right. "With your tongue," Flam said. "What else? Way I remember it, you used to be pretty slick with that tongue of yours."

"Please," Lester whimpered.

"Scrub the floor, Lester."

Lester's scrawny shoulders quivered and his face was streaked with tears, but he did that too, crawled across the filthy kitchen on his hands and knees, licking the grease-spattered floor, Flam above and behind him, prodding him now and again with a sardonic word of encouragement or, when he faltered, with a tasselled loafer applied to his buttocks or the back of his neck. When they arrived at the opposite wall, Flam said, "Sensational job, Lester. You keep that up, and the place be all spic and span next health-department inspection."

He swaggered away. Nodded a farewell at the dumbstruck Nicky. Lester's shuddery sobs trailed him through the kitchen door. So his day seemed to be ending as it had begun, on a weepy note.

Well, not quite. The phone was ringing when he came through the door of his house. He got to it before the machine kicked on, said his name into the receiver.

"Mr. Flam? This is Bridget."

For an instant it didn't register, this bright, expectant female voice. "Bridget?"

"Yeah. From over at Sanitary."

"Oh. Yeah. Ms. Vatchek."

"Bridget," she corrected him.

"Right. Bridget."

"I got the info you wanted. About that consulting outfit."

"Terrific."

"Picked up quite a bit on 'em," she said, her voice lowering to conspiratorial pitch. "Y'know, company's name, where they're out of, guy in charge of the job. That kinda stuff."

"Listen, I appreciate this."

"No problem. I could get it to you after work. Maybe we could, uh, meet for a drink."

Flam remembered his dinner date. But also did he remember his priorities. He said, "Great idea, Bridget. You name the time and place."

She did. Time and place, both of them. "See you then," she said, voice chirpy now, eager. "Bye bye."

Flam replaced the phone. He thought about his buxom manicurist, about the forfeited evening of soft companionship. But not for long. It was astonishing sometimes, what you sacrificed for your work.

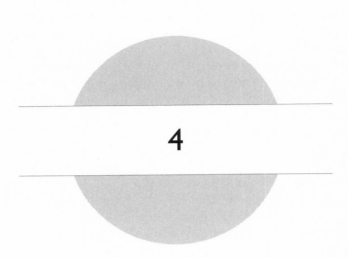

4

Norman had been sitting in the sun parlor most of the afternoon, reading from an edifying text. Rereading, actually. For another of his projects was to slog through the classics again, once more before he croaked, if only to uncover what he might have missed the first time around, something overlooked or never understood. Some nugget of wisdom that might have made a difference, changed things.

But it was slow going. Anymore, concentration came hard for him. Prison, with its primal focus on survival, had sapped his brain cells, turned them to mush. Especially after the little contretemps with the education director, which earned him a lengthy hole holiday and consigned him to a mess hall steam table for the remainder of his hitch. Also cancelled any prayer of an early parole. Unlike Spinoza, crafting a recondite metaphysic as he polished away at his lenses, Norman had taken no inspiration from the bubbling vats of chili and shingle shit he presided over. Even now, years after—planted in an easy chair in the comfort and security and silence of this elegant shelter, the slanting bands of sunlight warming his grizzled flesh and soothing his creaky bones—even yet could he feel the ghost of a whirlwind stirring in his chest at the thought of that ignorant, fatuous, bullying oaf. For all the grief it cost him, Norman wasn't sure he had any regrets. Served the hemorrhoid right.

Better not to think about any of that. There lies madness.

By an effort of will he brought his wandering attention back to the text at hand, *The Canterbury Tales.* A couplet in "The Pardoner's Prologue" caught his eye, spoke to him, and he copied it in the pocket notebook kept for just that purpose:

> For though myself be a ful vicious man,
> A moral tale yit I you telle can

A possible epigraph for his own opus, should it ever be seen through to completion.

He read on. Most curious, this dark fable: the three would-be slayers of Death, themselves slain, each betrayed by a wickedness within. Fate and chance and character converging beneath a tree heaped with gold florins. Destiny finding you. A cautionary tale filtered through the mouth of a sotted, arrogant, self-loathing scoundrel. Which meant—what? Hope for himself? Absolution? Pardon? Either that or, all the fawning critics' paeans to his "humanity" notwithstanding, the sly old Chaucer had to be, at bottom, infected by the bleakest cynicism. No way to know. Norman put aside the book and thought about it awhile.

But not for long. Shortly before six, a jangling shattered the perfect, contemplative silence. He got out of the chair, crossed the living room, picked up the phone, and said into it that which he always said: "Michael Woodrow residence."

"Norman? It's me. I'm at the Cypress. Why don't you pop in the car. Come on up. We'll have dinner here."

His son's words came tumbling through the wire, a peculiar breathless urgency to them. "You're sure that's what you want to do?" Norman said. "I could fix us something."

"No, let's bag the cooking for tonight. Think of it as a small celebration. San Antonio's a wrap."

Sounds of prattling voices, jolly whoops of laughter, rose in the background, filled the line. A muffled dissonance. Unwelcome. Norman had no great affection for crowds. Been enough jostling in his life. More than enough. Yet he also understood he was where he was only at the sufferance of his son. Decisions, choices, they belonged to Michael, not to him. So he said, "Whatever you like."

"Good. I'm in the Pub Bar. See you suddenly, huh?"

"Yes. Suddenly."

"Oh, and, Dad, you remember it's pretty much coat and tie here."

Dad. From his son that fond conventional appelative emerged almost a stutter, as though its bracketing consonants had all the consistency of glue. Seldom was it trotted out and then only when he wanted something. Which, in fairness, Norman had to admit wasn't often. "Not to worry," he said, somewhat stiffly. "I won't embarrass you."

"Come on, Norman."

"See you shortly."

Norman owned two suits, one for each season. Like all his wardrobe (all his possessions, for that matter), they came courtesy of his son. He put on the summer one, knotted the alien, strangulating tie, hopped in Michael's Nissan Maxima, and pointed it north on Madison, then east on Ogden. The clotted Friday night traffic inched along, slowed by the interminable road repairs, which, as far as Norman could tell, repaired nothing. Fully forty minutes after the telephone summons, he swung into the Cypress lot. Forty minutes to change clothes and cover a little over three miles. Best he could do.

He came through the side entrance and hesitated a moment in the doorway of the redundantly designated Pub Bar, searching for his son. A flagging arm hailed him. Norman skirted the festive gaggle congregated around the bar and approached a table near the center of the long, rectangular room. Michael got to his feet and, grinning crookedly, arms uplifted and swinging wildly, in simulation of an inept, punch-drunk fighter, snarled, "Find an opening, find an opening."

It was their ritual greeting, a remnant salvaged from across the distance of the ruptured years. Ordinarily reserved for privacy, he invoked it now, Norman assumed, in oblique apology for the brusque dress-code reminder. A no-hard-feelings gesture. Norman balled his fists, did an easy bob and weave, grinned back at him, and said, "I'm looking, I'm looking."

The little ceremony done, they took their seats. A waitress appeared, inquired after Norman's drink preference.

"What's that you're having?" he asked his son.

"A Gibson."

"What's a Gibson?"

The waitress drummed a foot, spun her eyes.

"Martini with a cocktail onion," Michael said quickly. "Try one."

Norman shrugged.

"That what you want then?" said the waitress, her impatience thinly cloaked behind a tight, commercial smile.

"Yes. One of those."

She hurried away.

"Charming woman," Norman remarked.

"They're busy tonight."

"So it appears."

"It's the holiday."

"Of course. The holiday."

Michael told him about the limo ride from O'Hare, the godawful traffic. About his flight, his day, his week, his work. The things you tell. Spiking his rambling account with anecdotes by turns droll and serious. Filling the space between them with words. He sat hunched forward in his chair, a knot of barely contained energy, pulsating twitch of nerves. He gestured broadly. His animated features were lit by a bright, camera-ready smile. The peculiar vocal rhythms Norman had detected earlier on the phone persisted. They were, if anything, more pronounced: a kind of swirly, manic intensity, as though he were trying, through the torrent of words, to outrun the interior of his head. Norman dropped in a polite query now and then, but mostly he listened. At an appropriate juncture he said mildly, "Is anything wrong, Michael?"

The smile collapsed. "Wrong? What do you mean, *wrong?*"

"Only that you seem a bit, well, jittery."

Michael glanced around the room, into his lap, his drink. Uncertain where to put his gaze. "It's been a long day," he mumbled.

A silence opened. At that fortuitous moment, the waitress returned and set Norman's drink in front of him. She asked if they were ready to order, the question directed at Michael around a flirtatious smile. Not just yet, he told her. Once she was gone, Norman lifted his glass in a toast, "Here's to the end of it."

"End?"

"Your long and arduous day."

"Oh. That. Yes."

Perfunctory clink of glasses. More of the dead air.

Michael pretended to study a menu. Norman lit a red and regarded him thoughtfully, a measuring look. The lean body, thick dark hair, Anglo-Saxon chiseling of features—all of it pure Woodrow strain, all but those emerald green eyes, which, even lowered, as now, never failed to disquiet him. His mother's eyes, her only legacy, though with a perpetually startled cast to them and with none of the hard glitter. All the same, looking into them, for Norman, was rather like looking at some fantastic twisted image refracted off the warped and not-so-funhouse mirror of time. But apart from the eyes (which others, women in particular, found striking), his son's face was, by Norman's estimate, one of those faces totally handsome and totally empty. Not in the way of intellect (for he had the solid credentials and early achievements to authenticate that) but rather of feeling, a face normally undisturbed by any but the most surface of emotions. Which made his behavior now, tonight, the more curious.

A plume of smoke drifted across the table. Michael looked up, grimaced, shook his head slowly. "Another of those ounces of death?" he said, less question than judgment.

"Better these ounces and a quick exit than five years drooling in a nursing home."

"What happened to your hand?"

Norman glanced down at his blistered palm, laid open on the table in a defensive gesture. "A small mishap. Nothing serious."

"Looks serious to me. Did you burn it on the stove?"

"No."

"How, then?"

"Actually, I was helping a neighbor. A woman who's moving into the unit behind yours."

"Ours," Michael amended. "You live there too."

"All right. Ours."

"Well, however it was done, you ought to put something on it. Band-Aid at least."

"I'll be sure to do that."

The initiative regained, and with it a share of his composure, Michael said, "Do you know what you want for dinner?"

"What do you recommend?"

"The filets are decent here."

"Is that what you're having?"

"Probably."

"Then that's fine with me."

"You could look at the menu," Michael said, a skirr of annoyance edging his voice. "There are other choices, you know."

"Filet will do. I've got a peasant's taste in food. Always had."

Michael sighed. "Have it your way."

That's how it was between them. A corrosive seesaw: amity, abrasion; harmony, discord; concern, indifference; affection, aversion; devotion, distance. The baffling, inspiriting, dismaying, confounding lineaments of love.

Michael beckoned the waitress and ordered for both of them. That done, he turned his attention back to his father, revived some of the smile, clasped his hands on the table as if to immobilize them, and said, "So. And how was your week?"

"It was uneventful."

"Everything under control at the house?"

Norman nodded.

"Were you able to get the car serviced?"

"I did. But they charged nearly thirty dollars."

"That's what you pay these days, Norman."

"For oil and filter? It's criminal."

His infelicitous choice of words effectively arrested that line of conversation. Michael steered it down another avenue. "What about that book you're working on? Any progress?"

"A little. It goes slowly."

"It's a biography, is it?"

"Yes, a biography," Norman said. Because he didn't want to follow that topic, he added quickly, in non sequitur, "The new neighbor is a pleasant-seeming young lady."

"Really."

Norman described his afternoon encounter with the pleasant-seeming woman.

Michael chuckled, a little patronizingly and without much mirth. "For you to spend an hour with someone, she must be pleasant."

"It wasn't a full hour."

The muscles in Michael's face tightened against a yawn. "Whatever," he said.

"She's interesting enough. You might like to meet her yourself."

"I doubt that. I was never much into neighboring."

"Also she is an *attractive* woman. In the best sense of that tired, slippery word."

Michael looked at him narrowly, and behind that steady gaze and the synthetic amusement in his voice there was just the barest shade of hostility, shadow of a shadow. "Spare me the matchmaking, Norman."

"Nobody's making matches. I merely said you might care to meet her."

"I'll be the judge of that."

"I'm sure you will."

Their dinners arrived. And as they ate, the talk, under Michael's direction, turned to inconsequential matters, the safe, vacant puffs two strangers will produce to fill the vacant air. Michael spoke knowledgeably, voluminously, on the upcoming presidential election, its potential impact on the business community, and, by natural extension, on his own career. Norman had little to contribute. He knew nothing of the candidates, cared even less about the so-called "issues." What did any of it have to do with him? If he could have chosen a subject it would have been "The Pardoner's Tale," that strange, chilling story of all the covetous human souls lost out there, floundering in the nightmare dark. But he knew better than to bring it up. So instead he attended to his son's sober political analysis, not so much to the words emerging from that earnest face, but to the face itself; and as he did he caught himself wondering about the mystery lurking just beneath the surface of the informed, engaged, food-masticating, good-citizen faces we show the world, all of us, and about all the other urgent appetites and greeds, the assorted desolations and horrors and bottomless griefs. Another subject best left untouched. But he could wonder about it, and he did.

IT WAS WELL PAST EIGHT when the Nissan, Michael at the wheel now, pulled up outside the condominium. Norman helped with the luggage and then disappeared down below. As soon as he was unpacked, Michael removed his coat, loosened his tie, and went directly to the room he called his office. He was knocked out, wasted. But the report, neglected on the plane, remained to be written and wasn't going to be wished away. Possibly he could get a start on it, at least put his scattered notes in order, maybe even prepare an outline or part of a draft. If he set his alarm for an early enough hour, he could finish in the morning, have it faxed off before noon. So he sat down at the tidy desk, opened his briefcase, and got to work.

But in a moment his concentration was broken by a rustling behind him. He glanced over his shoulder, and there stood Norman in the doorway, changed now from the fashionable suit into worn, shapeless chinos and sport shirt. "Yes?" Michael said.

"Sorry to disturb you, but I thought I'd let you know I'm going for a little walk."

Michael stared at him puzzledly. The shabby outfit came as no surprise; the walk, though, that was something else. And that's what he said: "Walk? You don't take walks."

"Tonight I will."

"Not another new resolution?"

"No. Simply a need for some air."

"Well, don't go far. It'll be dark soon."

"You're suggesting it isn't safe? Even in peaceful Hinsdale?"

"Not even here, Norman. There's nowhere safe anymore."

In about an equal mix of irritation and irony, Norman said, "Then I'll be certain to take serious care." With that he was gone.

Michael turned back to his work. The taunting voice in his head was utterly silenced now. Maybe it was the immense fatigue, or the drinks at dinner, or the security of familiar surroundings. Didn't matter which, any or all would do, as long as it stayed hushed.

He laid out a folder full of loose sheets accumulated over the course of the Jiffy Jack project. What he liked to do was transfer the salient facts, figures, observations, analyses, and ideas randomly recorded on those sheets onto three-by-five cards arranged in strict chronological sequence. Impose an order. He searched the drawer of the desk reserved for supplies. No note cards. Stalled for the lack of some three-by-five cards. In a sudden fit of exasperation, he banged the drawer shut. Uncharacteristic for him. Must be the exhaustion catching up. Maybe he should let it go, start fresh tomorrow.

But then it occurred to him that Norman, with that absurd biography of his, or whatever it was kept him occupied, would surely have note cards. He descended the stairs, entered the room, and began rummaging through the impossible clutter on his father's desk. It was mystifying to him how anyone could work in such an appalling mess. Everything disordered, everything reeking of smoke. He turned up no note cards, but a thin sheaf of typewritten pages peeking out from under the calendar caught his eye. A mild curiosity overtook him. He scanned a few paragraphs, paused, shook his head in a baffled way. Very perplexing, very odd.

Beyond the window a fat, plum-colored sun squatted at the edge of the world, poised for its plunge below the horizon. A soft amber light settled over the room. Somewhere off in the distance a siren shrieked. He dropped into the chair, switched on the desk lamp, and read on.

And this is what he read.

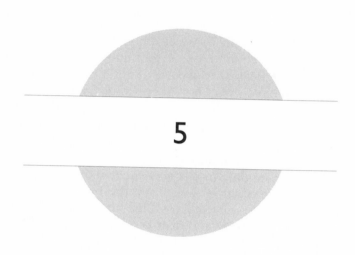

5

was born the biggest baby ever hatched out of St. Mary's, Long Beach, California. That is to say, the heaviest (for that time anyway) on record there: twelve pounds, seven ounces. Maybe I exaggerate. Maybe it was eleven, or only ten, seven. No matter, I was the biggest. When I was young, my mother liked to tell how the sisters carried me up and down the hospital corridors, occasionally popping into the rooms of the hopelessly ill to show me off. "Over twelve pounds," (or eleven, or ten) she claimed they announced proudly, "just about the biggest baby ever." She seemed to find a pleasure for herself in the telling, as though my squawking, rubbery-red presence, unwittingly deputized to dispatch her universal and naive goodwill, might some-how have brought solace to those wasted figures down the hall.

All the same, the delivery must have been hell on her, fragile slip of a woman that she was. Rather like, as they're given to say, shitting a watermelon, though of course my mother was far too decorous ever to refer to it that way. "A hard birth," was how she put it, re-treating behind the wounded, accusing look of female sorrow that crept over her pale features before she turned bravely away.

But then she was all her life a delicate creature, ill equipped for this harsh world. ("Nervous," Aunt Grace would say, "your mother's a nervous soul.") After my mother's untimely death at age forty-seven, I found a picture of her in one of the neatly stacked cigar boxes full of family mementos in the attic of Grace's house. It was an early photo, taken perhaps for a high-school annual or shortly before her journey to California, the single great adventure of her life. It shocked me, that photo did, for like most sons I had never conceived of my mother as capable of youth. My image of her was static: desiccated skin crinkling over good, even bones; hair gone early gray, frizzy, splitting at the ends, doggedly resisting order; a long, straight, noble Anglo-Saxon nose; quivery mouth and mineral-blue eyes forever on the edge of tears. And so it was startling to discover she had once been dewy and lovely and young. Especially young. Even the prim choke collar and ruffled blouse, and the austere "do," the then-thick, tar-black hair drawn severely off the brow and over the ears into a wadded bun in the back—even these could not obscure the gentle slope of moist skin off the elevated cheekbones and the dignified inward turn of the nostrils and the melancholy trust in the eyes. If anything, they served only to magnify her loveliness. Such clouded fragility was made to melt the cynic's heart. Little wonder then, my father, by all flimsy accounts a hustling cynic of the first order, was smitten.

Of him I know next to nothing, and that filtered through a memory by turns bitter or sentimental. Except for what Grace had to say, and she was never sentimental. She nursed a venomous grudge against that shadowy discomposer of her methodic spinster schoolteacher's life, that dark specter she had never seen who materialized magically, diabolically, to keep a malevolent destiny with her guileless younger sister in a gaudy, grungy oceanfront carnival known as the Long Beach Pike. The man who set in motion the chain of events that led inexorably to this oppressive burden she now bore.

"Clean yourself up good," she admonished, scrubbing me down herself with a harsh alkali soap, perhaps in the wan hope of scouring away whatever vestige of paternal taint might be revealed on my flesh, "or you'll end up looking like some circus gypsy."

Whenever she felt moved to exorcise the demon certainly lurking in my blood and bones, it was the hapless gypsy got his comeuppance.

Because it was Grace's house and because she had taken us in when there was nowhere else to go, my mother most often found it politic to cluck an approving reinforcement to the tart scoldings. "Listen to Auntie now," she would enjoin me. "She's had a hard time of it. She knows what it's all about." (The *it* presumably yet another region from which my maleness excluded me forever; like childbearing, a mystical country accessible only to injured Woman, tested and proven in the white heat of transcendent experience, enduring and suffering Woman.) Or she'd remove herself altogether, sit dreamily at the upright piano (sole legacy of their destitute departed parents) in the living room, pounding out "The Robin's Return" while the redoubtable Auntie, armed with shaggy dustmop and locked in a running battle with dirt and disorder, scurried through the house, bearing steadily toward my room, searching for symptoms of my corrupt and fallen nature. One morning I woke to find her examining the seat of my drawers, as though a fecal stain might offer the first clue to my predestined depravity.

Yet my mother could be charitable too, and tender in her reminiscences. It was that upright piano was the catalyst, for if "The Robin's Return" was Grace's favorite, "Ciribiribin" had been *his* (scourge the name!). There were times when the two of us were alone, she used that tinkling melody to spark her softer sensibilities and to pick at the scab of lost love. Had it been playing the night they met? Surely it must have. By gramophone or radio or in jangly accompaniment to a spinning carousel, somehow those tinny notes must have come floating through the fishy saltwater air as she, alone and friendless in the alien city, stops at a lunch counter on the dazzling Pike (nothing like this in Charles City, Iowa—*nothing!),* counts from her dwindling change just enough for a bowl of livid chili, and discovers on its serving . . . discovers . . . the chili bowl flanked by plates of red hots and beans and salad greens. The counterman brushes aside her bewildered protests and her money both, nods in the direction of an adjacent shooting gallery *(plop* go the ducks under a marksman's keen eye, *plop plop plop).* A lean, blade-faced, squinty-eyed fellow smiles at her thinly and touches two fingers to a brow in an acknowledging salute. Gilbert Ray Mercer, as I would eventually learn: carny barker, grifter, seeker—without success—after the main chance (as I would put my own construction on it, also later).

I suspect they lived together after that, though I have no way of knowing this for sure. Chronology got muddled in my mother's recollections. Those early years were, I gather, the happy ones. Nations founder, institutions collapse, all the old verities crumble, shooting galleries and other assorted enterprises fail, but who's to worry while there's youth and spirit and adventure and sweet, sweet love? Who's to fret in California, where all good dreams come true? Secure between lovers' sheets, thumb the nose at calamity and at time. Yet the Depression did come; yet she did get pregnant.

The rest of this reconstructed history is purely my own conjecture, pieced together from the things she let fall, and from Grace's endless, fuming plaints. They went to San Bernardino, to do what, I never learned; whatever it was came to nothing. They tried their luck in Los Angeles, and it was just as bad. They returned to Long Beach, and it was here, I think, shortly before my birth, that her spirits sagged utterly, and I fear the black bile of her melancholia oozed through my nourishing placenta and crept along my cord to smirch my blood forever. Here, belly swollen, adventure gone, romance gone, money gone, everything gone—here she must have conceived the germ of the notion that Iowa was not so bad after all; the vapid, neighborly faces—curious, prying, malicious, sly—a comfort after all. And it was here, I'm certain, she took to conjuring childlike visions of snow, immaculate purifying snow settling quietly over the streets, lawns, and houses like spilt milk seeping into the clefts and fissures of a colorless linoleum floor. Ideally, for my story, there would *be* no milk for this pitiable, soon to be parturient woman, but to the truth of this I cannot speak. Perhaps I could had I weighed a trifle less at birth or grown up consumptive.

But the fact is I was a remarkably healthy infant, born, it seems, without a trace of complication. What remains a puzzle to me is the place—St. Mary's—and my mother an uncompromising Lutheran and Grace the more ossified in her faith. Oh, they could be a pair, those two. One of their fondest memories was the week they spent at the Camp Alpine Bible Conference on the shores of Clear Lake near the teeming metropolis of Mason City. They were in school then, and had somehow scrimped and saved to get together the money to attend. Neither of them ever forgot it. Many an evening the three of us sat in the living room, I with a worn and dated *National Geographic* for amusement, they with their bundles of mending, Grace moving efficiently through hers, Mother dawdling and dreaming over a single sock, till out of those dreams might come a faint, slightly off-key humming, followed by a timorous rendering of the lyrics:

I've got that Camp Alpine en-thew-zee-az-um down in my heart,
Down in my heart,
Down in my heart.
I've got that Camp Alpine en-thew-zee-az-um down in my heart,
Down in the bottom of my heart.

And Grace, eyes still fixed on the clothes in her lap but catching the spirit all the same, began her own contrapuntal trilling that grew like a groundswell to merge with Mother's warbling, in a rhapsodic ode to their divine illumination:

I've got that Martin Luther Ref-or-may-shun down in my heart,
Down in my heart,
Down in my heart.
I've got that Martin Luther Ref-or-may-shun down in my heart,
Down in the bottom of my heart.

Finally, as if by design, they laid aside their mending, came to their feet (singing all the while), and joined in to work out their own spontaneous variations, like a stiff song and dance team on amateur night:

MOTHER: *I've got that luv-a-Jee-zus, luv-a-Jee-zus down in my heart.*
GRACE (explosively, with a clap): *Where?*
MOTHER: *Down in my heart!*
GRACE: *Where?*
MOTHER: *Down in my heart!*
IN UNISON: *I got that luv-a-Jee-zus, luv-a-Jee-zus down in my heart.*
GRACE (hand cupping ear): *Where's that now?*
IN UNISON (fortissimo): *Down in the bott-uum of . . . my . . . heart!*
GRACE: *One more time!*

And so they did it again, and more than just once. If I looked up from my magazine, I did my best to produce a smile, but ordinarily they were too taken by the rhythm and the beat to notice or care.

We went to church too. Grace hauled us along in defiance of the mean, prying eyes (though invariably we found seats in a back pew of the balcony), and she bellowed out the hymns and prayers as though her fallen sister's shame had in no way sullied her own God-fearing reputation, as though the mark of sin (personified, I suppose, by me) had not been plainly engraved on my mother and so, osmotically, on her. Mother was meeker, more cowed by her guilt. When the preacher, an iron-jawed Hun, greeted us at the door after services, she nodded humbly if he found it in his heart to clasp her hand and mumble, "Mornin', Miz Woodrow." And if he chose to take passing notice of me, as he sometimes did, she beamed gratefully.

"Gonna be a big fella," he liked to predict, chucking me gingerly and somewhat distastefully under the chin. "Football player, I bet."

I fooled him though, and every other adult given to such fatuous pronouncements. I grew to be of quite average size, and a football has always been fumbly in my hands.

So how was it I was born in St. Mary's? To this day it mystifies me. My mother scrupulously avoided the issue, and Grace's sour, pinched features twitched at the very mention of the Catholic faith. "Papists," she would snort, "all they know is their idols and their beads and making babies. Virgin Mother!" she would sneer, casting a meaningful look my way. "Those gypsies—"all Papists, I learned, were gypsies—"couldn't find an honest virgin among their own kind over six."

Was the gypsy Gilbert one of those reviled Papists? Sadly, I shall never know. But it's at least possible he was proud of me, mostly, I expect, of my size in those days. For a time anyway, he might have been proud. Maybe he even made vows to get on, accept the crushing weight of responsibility, now he was a father. Stranger things have happened.

He opened another shooting gallery on the Pike, and the three of us moved into a cramped, rented tin trailer directly behind it. *"Plop!"* my mother could mimic the sound of the ducks biting the dust, but only when her bottled-up memories of this gloomy shard of the past grew too oppressive, demanded ventilation; and I, bastard child, objective correlative for all her ignominy, all her woe, was the only available auditor. "All day and all night long. *Plop* went those ducks. Till I thought it'd drive me clean out of my head." And with the total recall of a fleetingly lifted repression—sudden, vivid, precise—other sounds came back to her too: the barkers' bawling exhortations ("Step right up here, Lay-deez and Genemum, try your luck!"), the tinsel carny music ("Ciribiribin" soured?); the keening, piercing whistle of a teakettle on a grease-spattered burner of the furnished trailer's hot-plate version of a stove; and other smells, like the acrid stench of gunpowder, sticky sweet perfumes of caramel corn and cotton candy and elephant ears; and the odors he brought home with him as well: nickel cigars, hair slickum, sweat, beer—or worse—on his breath. And hungry, he came home. "So hungry," she euphemized. "It got so I hated to hear his step at the door. Every noon and every night, so hungry."

Winter set in. Even to California, winter must come. Black nights and gray days. Stone-cold carnival, entombed in rain and mourned only by the occasional lonely sailor keeping forlorn watch at the silent carousel; trailer lashed by winds scudding in off the ocean; drizzle beating a steady, maddening tattoo on the tin roof; kettle boiled over and cupboard bare; squalling child; penniless, callous, surly stranger with nothing but time on his hands, and hungry, hungry. Misery on misery. What's a poor woman to do?

The gallery failed, of course, its failure as certain for that luckless, inept scammer as if foreordained. And from here my chronicle is hopelessly shrouded in utter darkness. Neither of them, neither Grace in her bitterest moments nor Mother in her most bathetic, could be coaxed or tempted to reveal the details of that time immediately after the gallery folded its shutters for good. Not my most odious misdemeanor (noisily lapping soup, say, or neglecting to lower the cover of the stool), not the lilting strains of "Ciribiribin" and the mawkish memories kindled by that dulcet measure . . . Nothing, in fact, could unlock the secret of what finally moved her to pack a bag, shoulder an infant (no small burden, you remember), and board a drafty train for Charles City, Iowa, to be met at the depot by Grace in her Apple Annie garb. Grace of the wrathful eyes empty of forgiveness and the sallow, indoors complexion and the tight, prim lips unacquainted with smiling; cadaverously thin Grace doubtless wondering aloud how we would make it, three of us, on her schoolmarm's pittance. Whatever it was moved my mother to this—for her—rash, desperate act must have been dramatic in the extreme. A battering? It's possible, though from the snippets I gathered of Gilbert's character I rather think not. Other women? Perhaps. A sexually sparked man like that—there were times when she hinted darkly. Or maybe I'm mistaken. Maybe it was nothing more than the interminable rain pelting the trailer. Maybe the conjunction of his latest failure with her recently discovered affinity for snow was enough to inspire a moonstruck frenzy that worked itself out in flight.

But it's possible I do her an injustice. Possibly it was he who abandoned us, likely even, since we never saw him again. Left to follow his own restless itch, swallowed up by some shabby itinerant carnival, presiding over an endless chain of sacrificial ducks, lifelong mark himself, scamming the marks.

Part

TWO

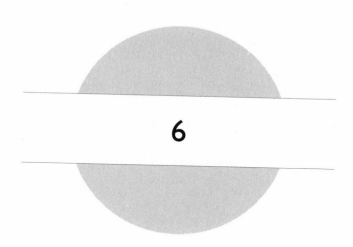

6

At 5:00 A.M. the next morning, Michael was seated at the desk in his home office, gazing at the Jiffy Jack folder in front of him. *No more stalling,* said the exacting voice in his head (the familiar one this time, that other alien voice seeming to have vanished in the night, smothered in a dream-riddled sleep). He opened the folder, picked up a pen, centered his attention, and set to work on the report, twice suspended in the past twenty-four hours *(by your own sloth and fantastic delusions,* the pitiless voice reminded him), but no more.

Half an hour later, he heard Norman stirring down below, and for a moment his focused thoughts strayed to those curious, oddly touching, oddly disturbing pages he'd read the night before (and discreetly returned to their place on the chaotic desk and fled the room before Norman got back). For a moment he wondered what his father could be up to. Only a moment. No time now for trifling riddles. Later. He'd think about it later.

By 9:00 A.M. a longhand draft of the report was completed. He typed it into the PC, ran off a hard copy, and spent another hour revising and editing, taking pains to ensure that every paragraph, every line, was clear, precise, succinct. Unlike his father, he wrote in a spare, terse style, absent altogether of any mannered verbal embroidery. He had been told his reports set the standard at AS&A, models of directness and clarity, and he was convinced they had contributed in no small share to the IM title affixed to his name (*never mind it was "acting,"* the voice assured him, its confidence rapidly renewing; *wouldn't be "acting" for long*). When he was fully satisfied with his work, he scrolled the text up the monitor, keyed in a few last revisions, and printed a final copy. And then he switched off the computer and went to the head of the stairs and called out Norman's name.

An acknowledging grunt floated around the corner and up the stairs.

"I've got to fax off some material. You want anything from town?"

"No."

"Want to come along?"

"No."

The invitation was a formality, a courtesy, nothing more. He knew that Norman didn't welcome any interruptions in his lockstep routine. He understood that, respected it. But a grunt and two curt nos? Questions and replies delivered down and up an empty flight of stairs like cryptic radio signals beamed across a continent or an ocean. The measure of the distance between them. So he merely said, "I'll be back soon," expecting no response and getting none. Finally, he supposed, it didn't matter.

He steered the Nissan out of the condominium complex and pointed it north on Madison. The morning sun was tacked to a bright, stainless sky, the air dazzlingly clear. Beautiful morning, beautiful sky, even though off in the east, on the periphery of his vision, a gray smudge hung like a motionless cloud of soot over the city. But that didn't matter either. He liked it here, Hinsdale, liked the pastoral *dale* in its name; the quiet residential streets, elm lined; stately old houses, brick, many of them, many with collonaded entrances, and the newer frame ranches, upscale family homes with basketball hoops over the garage doors and ten-speed bikes on the walks and kids and dogs chasing joyously through the yards. He liked the manicured lawns, green shrubs, and flower beds, riots of natural color—all the timeless, stable traditions preserved in this tranquil little pocket of refuge and peace. He liked it.

Also did he like it for the more practical reason that he and his father were perfectly anonymous here, knew no one. Which was why he'd settled on it three years back, shortly before Norman's release (that, and its proximity to O'Hare). It's true, the traffic had thickened over the course of those years, clogging the major arteries running through town; and elements less than desirable were seeping in from the surrounding burbs. But that was a headache for another time, not this morning. Too good a day to fret over that kind of worry.

He swung over past Grant to Lincoln (presidentially christened streets, yet another quiet satisfaction), crossed the Burlington tracks, and parked in the Grant Square lot. From there he walked two short blocks to a faxing station located in the renovated depot's mini-mall, moving briskly, weaving as best he could through the leisurely knots of shoppers and browsers who thronged the streets and seemed to amble along at about a mile-a-month pace. Wrap reports were expected, without fail, at the Bunker no later than the end of the day following a project's completion. Max was notorious for testing the boundaries of that deadline, but as long as this one was going to bear the Michael Woodrow signature, he was determined to have it in New York by noon, eastern time at that. It was a point of pride (not to speak of ambition).

But once inside the Commuter Secretarial Center, he discovered the single employee, a fish-lipped young woman, occupied with an elderly spectacled lady agonizing over a choice among various shades of copy paper ("But don't you think the Brilliant White is a bit, oh, stark?"). Saturday morning, holiday weekend—who could have anticipated this? Nevertheless, he should have factored the delay into his timing. Too late now. So there he stood, heating his heels for ten minutes or more (felt like ten, anyway), not patiently, and silently resolving that his next purchase would surely be a fax machine of his own. At last the fussy bluehead arrived at a decision and, with the solicitous clerk's ongoing help, ran off a seemingly endless stream of some monumentally critical document (a garage sale announcement, no doubt). When the transaction was finally concluded, he stepped up to the counter, handed over his sheets and the New York number, and at precisely 11:52, their time, narrowly within his self-imposed target deadline, the report was delivered.

But out here in the heartland, there was an hour of morning left, and probably thirty-six after that before the word came through on his next assignment. Then, depending on its location and flight arrangements, another twelve or so, maybe more, before he'd be packed and off to O'Hare. And so while he felt good—better than good, actually, mildly euphoric—with another project successfully wrapped, the prospect of forty-eight idle hours was almost intimidating. Ordinarily a weekend at home flashed on by, the single free day filled with all the catch-up details and obligations of the onerous business of living: bills to pay, errands to run, market investments to review and ponder, possibly a certain amount of what they liked nowadays to call "quality time" with Norman. And while those things remained to be done, of course, all the looming extra holiday hours sapped some of their urgency. For reasons unclear to him, unvisited, he felt vaguely restless too, twitchy even, as though a persistent vexing insect, too microbic to be seen, buzzed at the portal of an ear.

Probably nothing more than tensions too suddenly relieved, or caffeine-charged nerves, breakfast forsaken in the morning's flurry of activity. That had to be it, breakfast to attend to. But first he strolled down Hinsdale Avenue to Washington, crossed the street, and doubled back toward Grant Square, deliberately curbing his stride and filling his lungs with the clear air, to settle himself, glancing incuriously through the windows of the multiplying and determinedly quaint specialty shops—luggage repair, antiques, travel consultants (everybody a consultant these days), hairstyling, tailoring, a place given over exclusively to the grooming of pets and known coyly as the Velvet Touch—thinking how pampered we've become, how undisciplined, effete.

The square's single eatery was crammed with diners. Three years in town, and he'd never once been inside its doors. No occasion. Now he waited behind a group of smartly suited merchants, feeling just a trifle self-conscious in his casual Dockers and Polo shirt, like a laggard soldier caught out of uniform, till it came back to him he was unknown here, invisible. Though not, evidently, to the bustling hostess, who advised him of an empty seat at the counter, "If it's just yourself, sir, or you're in a hurry." No hurry. He'd wait.

And while he did, the consultant in him reflexively studied the layout. The room was large, brightly illuminated, with an abundance of greenery (a nice decorative touch) and long columns of booths separated by panels of frosted glass and snaked brass tubing polished to a high gloss, catching the sparkly light from the ceiling. Counter situated along the back wall, unwisely, in his judgment, for it contributed to the gridlock in the narrow aisles. Reception area too small, too congested at peak business hours (like now). If it were his project, he'd eliminate the counter altogether (a haven for unprofitable coffee dawdlers and long-winded loafers anyway), widen the aisles a bit, to accelerate customer flow and waitress efficiency, expand the receiving space, streamline the entire operation. And the lights, he'd soften the lights some, and get rid of the brass. Convince management that less is often more. That's part of what he would do, if it were his assignment. But then nobody here had solicited his professional opinion, and it was, after all, a day off.

Eventually a booth opened, and he was ushered to it, seated, and further, if absently, advised to enjoy his meal. Sizzly odors of other meals drifted on currents of cigarette smoke through the thick air. Conversational murmurs and ribbons of laughter reached him from adjacent booths. Waitresses whisked on by, identically clad in beige skirts and forest-green blouses with the restaurant's logo, underscored by the names of community and state, block-lettered on the backs. Ventilation would be improved, in his hypothetical plan, and the acoustics as well. And the logos would have to go. Presumably, one knew where one was.

A scurrying waitress braked at his booth, produced a steaming pot. Barely in time (and at considerable risk to himself, poised as she was to pour), he covered the cup with a flat hand.

"No coffee?" she demanded, brow lifted, smiling quizically.

"No, thanks."

"All coffeed out, are ya?"

"Something like that. No menu either. I can tell you what I'd like."

"Now what'd that be?" she asked, and he thought he detected the tiniest gleam of worldly mischief in her eye. She stood beaming at him, strenuously cheery. If he'd had to guess, he'd put her at about his own age or a few years older, a full-figured woman, borderline dumpy, mouse-colored hair with a conspicuous, rather brazen, blond streak in it, plump cheeks pitted, under the heavy war paint, with vestigial acne craters. Acned or not, she'd stay on in his plan: cheery would be absolutely essential, a place like this. Part of the ambiance.

He recited his order: small orange juice, vegetarian omelet (the eggs a concession to the holiday and to the real project done, and done well), whole wheat toast, unbuttered, no jam.

"No meat?"

Catching the by now unmistakable mischief glint, he declined meat.

"Comin' right up," she chirped and scooted away.

He'd keep her, yes, but conditionally, and only if she could learn to sound her *g*'s and tone down the familiarity. A certain decorum was required too, even here.

The "right up" was, by his exact clocking, fourteen minutes later, a little too long a wait, high-volume hour notwithstanding.

"Breakfast is served," the woman announced brightly, setting plate and juice glass before him. "Getcha anything else?"

He said no. Off she trotted.

He inspected the food. Eye appeal was adequate, portions ample, maybe a bit too generous. A slight scaling back, imperceptible to all but the most gluttonous of diners, would boost the profit margin appreciably. He took a tentative bite. Eggs were undercooked and not as warm as they might be, probably from languishing on a counter in the back, overlooked and unserved. Toast as coarse and brittle as weathered shingles, doubtless for similar reasons. And while he had no expectation of freshly squeezed juice, this had the tinny smack of the canned variety, wasn't even chilled. Certainly there'd be some drastic kitchen shake-ups in this speculative exercise of his.

But in the tangible, sensory, unspeculative world he inhabited just now, the breakfast, flawed or not, waited to be consumed. And he supposed he was hungry or ought to be. And so he ate, chewing each bite slowly, thoroughly, the way Aunt Grace had always insisted. "Bolt your food, and you'll get the belly cramp for sure," her shrill, eternally cranky voice nagged at him from across the years and the wider gulf of the grave. And this fleeting unwelcomed thought of her (normally suppressed by censors ever at the alert), fussy, choleric old woman, scourge and savior of his wounded youth, led inescapably to thoughts of Norman's account of his own melancholy childhood, its distressing echoes. And from there to uneasy conjectures on his father's intentions with that profitless incursion into the murky country of a remote past better left unexplored. Where was it leading him, that peculiar zigzagging fragment of exhumed private history? Maybe it was nothing more than a fanciful aberration, excited by some fugitive memory; or a break, maybe, from the tedious scholarly study of a dusty, forgotten poet. Still was unhealthy, near to neurotic. And it troubled him, thinking about it. He worried about

Norman. Ultimately he'd have to deal with it (like all problems, it would yield to analysis, deliberation). But not today. The weekend was long. Tomorrow maybe, or a future time, or—

"Somethin' wrong with the eggs?"

The waitress materialized at the table, yanking him back to the here and now. "They're fine," he lied, a harmless fib. "Why do you ask?"

"Notice you wasn't exactly inhalin' 'em there."

"I'm a slow eater."

A trace of a lickerish grin scampered across the pocked face. "Slow's always best, I hear, comes to eatin'."

He said nothing. She sauntered away, putting a little hip wiggle in it. He watched her, frowning slightly, decided he'd been wrong. Cheery was one thing, transparent vulgarity quite another. In the interests of even a baseline propriety, she would surely have to go. In that wholly imagined consulting plan of his, that is. He nibbled at the remains of the omelet, but his appetite was gone. He pushed the plate aside. Waited. Soon she was back.

"All done?"

"Yes."

"Sure you won't have some coffee?"

"Just the check, please."

She got out order pad and pencil, tallied the numbers, and then paused for a moment, during which she gave him an appraising look, very direct, very bold. "You from around here?"

"I live here, yes."

"Well, you be sure and come again now," she said, lingering suggestive stress on the *come,* a voiced leer. With her left hand she tore off the sheet and fluttered it expertly onto the table. In that nimble motion, he caught a glimpse of stubby fingers bedecked with gaudy rings, wedding band among them, and a work-thickened wrist looped with faux-gold bracelet. And something terrible awakened in a distant recess of his head; he sealed his eyes, but beneath the tightly squeezed lids a tumbling rush of images unreeled at seeming photosynthetic speed—rings, bracelets, chains, spiked heels, ankles, fleshy naked hips, skimpy bras, rubbery breasts, assorted body cavities—and blood too, unstopped gutters of blood. A memory surfaced from some swamped sunless place within him, fate-ordained, where nothing existed, nothing endured, but unspeakable horrors.

When at last he opened his eyes, she was gone. But a reflection of himself, queerly distorted in the curve of brass tubing along the border of the booth, regarded him curiously. A funhouse mirror reflection, its features swollen, prognathic, its eyes bulging. His heart clubbed. Stomach pitched and yawed. He lurched to his feet and, moving stiffly, erect and rigid as a nightwalker, made for the men's room in the back.

Mercifully, it was empty. He pulled the stall's door shut behind him, sank to his knees. A convulsive tremor, commencing in the deepest trenches of his viscera, spiraled up through his chest and throat and erupted in a geyser of thick glutinous fluid, pea green and speckled with mushy lumps of undigested toast, unrecognizable vegetables, and saffron-tinted egg. He gagged once, spewed another, thinner stream. Purged, he rose, tottered through the door, bent over the sink, splashed his face with cool water, rinsed his mouth. Took a towel from the dispenser, dried himself carefully. There was a mirror above the sink, and he cast a cautious glance in it, half expecting to discover a gargoyle there, the biblical beast unleashed and revealed for all the world to see. Yet it was merely his own familiar likeness, a little blanched, a little haggard, that peered back at him. But penned in a precise hand on the wall by the mirror was a comic, dreadful graffito, mocking reminder of who he was, what he might have done: "Wherever you go," it read, "there you are."

7

The Undertaker and the Ultimate Warrior, each in his alloted turn, hurled taunts and insults and sneery challenges into the camera's eye, while the announcer, a tubby, mustachioed, cleanly bald little fellow, miniaturized alongside these goliaths, elevated the mike deferentially and arranged his features in an attitude of awe. The Undertaker's performance, in Norman's considered judgment, was good—eyes blank, face expressionless and ashened by powder, voice a gravelled whisper, funereal monotone befitting his persona—but not nearly so accomplished as the Warrior's. Lunatic intensity of glare; dramatic pitch variances, now thundering, now muted, vocal italics to clenched-fist jeers; manic swirl of mighty arms in the air, as though their freakish size and titanic strength were somehow, miraculously, empowered to orchestrate the whole of nature, excite tempests, generate whirlwinds, unloose the primal savage within. He had it all down nicely, Mr. Warrior did, all the artful moves. But in a real-world scuffle, no clowning, Norman's money would go with the towering, knob-knuckled Undertaker to administer a serious touch-up, dust the ranting muscleman.

The Warrior called to mind a joint iron-slinger, Bettybop by tag, whose brawn was no less puffed and proud but whose mincing lisp gave away her queenly inversion. Timid jailhouse lady in a Godzilla suit. Of course, he might be mistaken too. Prison maxim had it that dingers were always dangerous, best wide-berthed. And Warrior, behind all the histrionics, had a certifiable bughouse stamp on him. So maybe it could go either way, that imagined back alley down and dirty.

It was the only television Norman watched with any consistency. He enjoyed it, pro wrestling. He admired those brutish Calibans, their gymnastic agility, programmed theatrics. Equally did he fancy their pendulum swings in fortune, champ this week, chump next; and their unforseen and blithely unexplained character shifts. (Thusly did our happy-go-lucky Tugboat finger-snap himself from valorous, lovable simpleton into truculent lout, rechristened Typhoon, and remorseless now like his new name, as bestial as a Scythian.) The unabashed foolery engaged him. It was, in a curious way, much like life itself, or a reductive version thereof, voluted morality play wherein arrogance often as not trampled humility, duplicity outwitted decency, evil routed good. Life as choreographed by a rascally prankster, stripped of its subtleties, hyperbolized, spoofed.

But even as he managed a feeble smile at the comic-opera pageant of a tag-team bout unfolding on the screen (the Natural Disasters trashing a pair of hapless sacrificial buffoons), his thoughts, guilt-pricked, wandering, reprised the lost day. Another one lifted out of his rapidly dwindling store. Squandered, more accurately, if truth were told. Six hours of impotent gaping at a blank page, head flitting with words, unstrung, as elusive as fireflies in the night. Followed by forty sweaty minutes on the treadmill, a Sisyphean march to nowhere; followed by shower number two, solitary tinned sardine lunch, and then two more hours back on the Canterbury trail, still destitute of attention, for all the bawdy company of the Wife of Bath, and finally surrendering to wrestling's low burlesques.

But mostly was he thinking now, as he'd been all day long, puzzledly, and for the first time in longer than memory served without rancor or bitterness or smoldering fury, about a woman. About Ms. Lizabeth Seaver. About her fragile beauty, her winsome charm, forthright and guileless as a child, the honeyed music in her voice. And as though by some telepathic sorcery, the phone at just that moment sounded. He muted the television, padded over, and lifted the receiver, pronounced his routine salutation into it, and the voice coming back to him, winged by the occult force of his durable thoughts, was surely hers, none other.

"Norman?"

"Speaking."

"It's Lizabeth. Lizabeth Seaver? Of gas leak fame? Remember?"

"Would I forget a brush with Lord Death?"

After the slenderest of pauses she said, "Is something wrong?"

"Wrong? No, nothing wrong."

"I'm calling at a bad time, aren't I?"

"I can imagine none better."

"But there's *some*thing wrong."

"Why do you say that?"

"Your voice. You sound, well, sort of gruff. Irritable."

"It's my natural wheeze. Nicotine-abused larynx, you know, and smoke-blackened lungs."

She giggled softly. Most fetching giggle.

"Don't laugh," he said with a touch of mock severity. "It'll happen to you one day. Unless you mend your wicked ways."

"It's not your voice I'm laughing at."

"What, then?"

"The words that come out of your mouth. You talk like a philosopher or a judge. Or a college professor."

Very quick, this Lizabeth Seaver. He reversed the conversational direction with an abrupt bootleg turn: "So, are you settled?"

"Getting there. Pretty close."

"No more noxious fumes, I trust."

"No, everything's under control that way. Thanks to you. At least I'm still alive, last I checked."

"That's always comforting, another day above ground."

"And it's part of the reason I'm calling. To ask if you'd like to come over for dinner tomorrow night."

"Me? A dinner invitation?"

"Think of it as a small token of gratitude. For saving my life yesterday. Will you come?"

"Well, actually, I, uh, don't know," Norman said, acutely conscious of his stammering speech. He took a shallow breath, added, "I'd have to check with Michael."

"Your son's home?"

"He got in last night."

"Then it's easy. Bring him along. He's invited too."

"I'll see what I can do."

"Is that a yes?"

On an impulse neither examined nor understood, he said, "Consider it a yes."

"Good. Tomorrow night, then? Seven?"

"Seven it is," Norman said in what should have been a confirming closure. But another impulse, equally opaque, perhaps because hers was the first human voice he'd heard all day (apart from the curt muttered exchange with Michael and the stagy, trumpeted, scarcely human harrangues issuing from the imbecile box, neither of which counted), impelled him to put in quickly, "And the other part?"

"What?"

"If I remember rightly, you said the invitation was part of the reason for your call. Which leaves at least one other. Reason, that is. If the laws of arithmetic still hold."

"Oh, yes, that. Well," she said, affecting a teacherly scolding tone, "I think you ought to know I'm *very* unhappy with you."

"And why would that be?"

"I saw you walking by the house last night. Twice, I saw you. Why didn't you stop in?"

"Strictly, it's a condominium."

"You're dodging the question."

"I had an errand to run."

A block of silence filled the line, dispatching skepticism's perceptible communiqué.

He tried again. "I was in something of a hurry."

More of the accusatory silence. Till finally she said, quietly and with all the teasing affectation gone, an earnestness approaching plea in its place, "If we're going to be friends, Norman, we've got to tell the truth."

"The truth," he repeated, striking, oddly and against his will, a note of contrition. "All right. I assumed you were occupied with your unpacking. Could do without visitors. A natural assumption." It wasn't quite the truth, but it was close, reasonable.

"I hope next time you'll stop," she said, sounding somewhat mollified now.

"If that's what you want."

"Next time being tomorrow night."

"Promptly at seven. We'll be there."

"See you then. Bye, Norman."

He put down the phone. Stood there a moment, shaking his head slowly, sorting through the tangle of his feelings, among which was an unmistakable exhilaration, absurdly adolescent and so all the more preposterous in a battered old fossil like himself. Just as confounding was the recognition, long forgotten, buried under the weight of the womanless years, of how adroitly they wrest control of a situation, women do, how effortlessly they gain the upper hand. But most of all did he feel a mounting anxiety over how the invitation, unilaterally accepted, would be received by Michael. Not well, he expected. Michael preferred to maintain an unbreachable wall of domestic privacy, and it was safe to predict he'd be less than cheered by the news. Too late now. Deal with that when the time came.

Which time arrived all too soon. In a little under a quarter of an hour, he heard the door swing open, footsteps crossing the floor above, descending the stairs. He glanced up from the grunting grapplers on the screen. "Business attended to?" he asked, elaborately casual.

"It got taken care of," Michael said, flopping onto a cushion of the sectional couch, opposite end.

Oh, oh. Quarrelsome edge to the voice. Fatigue's sullen slump. Not auspicious signals. Not for what he had yet to announce. Give it a while.

Michael removed his shoes, laid his legs across an ottoman. He looked morose, depleted, eyes pink-rimmed and inward turning, skin as gray as slate. He swept an impatient arm at the television. "You enjoy this foolishness?"

"Switch channels if you like."

"That wasn't the question."

Norman sighed. Everyone a Socratic hairsplitter today. "It's diverting," he said.

"But you're not interested in sports."

"Some might say there's a certain athletic grace to the figure-four leg lock and the flying dropkick."

"I'm talking about real sports."

"Then you're right. I'm not."

"So how do you rationalize this?"

Norman held up surrender palms. "Call it an aberration."

"Were you ever? As a boy, I mean."

For all its brittle crust, the question had an undercurrent of genuine curiosity. A curiosity in itself, since by unspoken contract they had always scrupulously sidestepped any mention of the past.

"Interested in sports?" Norman asked back.

"Yes."

"No."

"But you exercised. I've got a dim memory of you lifting weights. In a basement somewhere."

That would be De Kalb, Illinois. Norman could have pinpointed it for him but didn't. Instead he said, shrugging, "Another aberration, I suppose."

"Did you begin it when you were young? The weight lifting?"

"Quite young, yes."

"How old?"

"About fifteen."

"Why? It couldn't have been fashionable in those days."

"Adolescent bid for attention, I expect. Showy muscle in lieu of acceptance. I was never what you'd call a popular youth."

"Did you keep your weights at the house there? In Charles City?"

"In the garage, actually."

"What did your mother think of it?"

"She was too addled to notice."

"How about Aunt Grace?"

Something going on here, Norman wasn't sure what. Very baffling, very discomforting. Maybe it was nothing more than the patronizing sounding out the young will now and again inflict on their elders, bored and boring queries posed with a fraudulent display of interest. An obligation, exercise in mutual feel-good, not unlike that commonplace squealed endorsement of a dolled-up, dried-up bonebag in Sunday best: "Why, don't you look *nice!*" Yeats's pathetic tattered coat on a string, or however that line went. Had to be the same thing at work here. What else? Draw out the witless old fool, let him babble on, human sedative, about his pedestrian, lusterless life. Norman had no desire to be a party to it. And if he was wrong, if it was something else, even less did he care to probe it. All that was strictly between him and the elusive stranger who came to call—or didn't come—in the solitude of morning. So he said bluntly, "Why do you ask me these things, Michael?"

"No particular reason. Just curious, I guess. No hidden agendas."

His eyes were averted, mouth twisted in mangled facsimile of an amiable smile, smile of the man protesting too much.

"Maybe we should find another topic. If we're going to talk."

"No, honestly, I'd really like to know."

"About Grace?"

"Yes. Grace."

"Well, predictably, she didn't approve. Waste of time, in her jaundiced eye."

"But you went ahead anyway."

"Yes, I did. It was a way of expression. Almost a need. And by then I'd discovered there was very little Grace approved of. Outside of her Bible walloping, of course, and even that came heavily qualified. If she ever made it to heaven, I'm sure she's pecking away at God right now."

Michael chuckled at that, but softly and without a trace of amusement. "She pecked at you too?" he said, part question, part rueful recollection.

"All the time. This was an irascible woman. Whoever named her Grace must have had a keen sense of irony. Not a charitable bone in her body."

"Well do I remember," Michael said, inflection flat now, freighted with desolation.

"Are you looking to compare notes here?" Norman said, aware of his own voice rising, thorny catch in it, nettled, defensive, and cold, cold. "Is that it? Is that what these questions are all about?"

"Maybe. I'm not sure. I don't know what I'm asking."

"Because it's pointless, you know, these self-pity contests. Worse than futile. Everyone's victimized by his past. Some more than others. If you're bitter about what happened, where you got dumped, what I did, the disgrace I heaped on you, on all of us—if that's it, you can say it."

"It's not that, Norman."

"What, then?"

"I don't know. I've been feeling, well, strange lately. Not depressed exactly, more, oh, dislocated. Like this morning. After I finished up in town I was—" He lifted a cupped hand as if to pluck the precise word from the air and, failing, settled for "at loose ends. So I went for a drive. No place in particular. Aimless drive. Imagine that. Me, of all people."

"Driving without destination, that's not like you," Norman conceded.

"That's the point."

"Where did you go?"

"Out the East-West Tollway. West on it. Past the Fox River, I think. Possibly even farther. Haven't been that way in God knows when. Months, years maybe. You should see it out there, all those industrial parks and plants and homes and suburbs sprung to life." He hesitated, stared at his hands, both of them in his lap now. "All those people," he said, voice trailing away wistfully, "busy, innocent, simple, normal people."

"That's what you discovered on this excursion?" Norman prompted, making a little joke of it, but softer now, watching him, attending to the peculiar rambling monologue. "A world filled with uncomplicated people?"

"But it was *more* than that! Don't you see? The engine was humming and the sun was glaring on the windshield, and the cars and fields and towns and people zipped by. It was—how can I put this?—almost hypnotic. Like time blurring. The past, now, whatever's ahead—all of it blurring. It was like driving through a dream. Not a pleasant one, either. Do you know what I'm saying, Dad? Does any of this make sense to you?"

Dad again? Twice in twenty-four hours? Something indeed going on, this fractured, oblique recitation. Something resembling a groping confessional, almost as though he were the one stained with guilt. Very curious, very odd. Norman gazed at him steadily, this grown man with features strong enough, perfect enough, to be embossed on a coin, a sage proverb scrolled in Latin beneath the likeness. This luckless young man who, by fate's for him cruel stroke, happened to be born Norman Woodrow's son. Murderer's son. He watched him. And studying him that way, he seemed to see behind the troubled face the anguished, abandoned child; and he was swamped with sudden grief, helpless against the current of the vanished years, flooded with sorrow for all the forfeited moments, nameless, precious things vaporized between them then and now by one rash, irreversible act. He fumbled for a cigarette, tapped it vigorously on a palm, lit it, pulled smoke into his lungs, exhaled. The ritual of buying time. Finally he said, "Is there something you want to tell me, Michael?"

His head jerked up and back, and he looked at his father, startled, wary, and he said, "Tell you? What do you mean? I *am* telling you."

"Then I have to confess it's not clear."

"Forget it then," Michael said, all the supplication abruptly gone out of his voice, displaced by the annoyance perpetually riding near the surface. "It's nothing. Probably just nerves. The jitters that come with the end of a project. You know how that goes."

"Afraid I don't."

"Well, trust me, that's all it is."

"You're sure?"

One of his arms chopped the air emphatically. "Look, let's forget it. All right?"

For a considerable patch of time they sat silently, feigning an interest in the parodic conflicts racketing from the screen. Norman welcomed the silence. He was weary of all the dodging, weaving, sparring. All the verbal smoke. Exhausted of words. Till a gesticulating brute filled the screen, vowing to have some upstart challenger for lunch, "chew 'im up and spit 'im out." Then it came back to Norman there was one thing more to be settled, and that's what he said, "Ah, there's one other thing I should mention."

"What's that?"

"We've been invited to dinner. Tomorrow night. Both of us."

"Invited by who?"

"Whom."

"By whom, then?"

"The young lady I told you about. Just moved in. The condo across the street behind here."

"And you accepted?"

"I did."

"Do you think that's wise?"

"Probably not. But it's done."

Michael steepled his fingers. Contemplated them a moment. Astonishingly, he appeared unmoved by this intelligence. "Well, why not," he said. "You're alone here all week. Maybe you could use a friend."

"Maybe we both could."

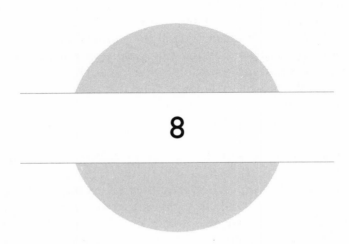

8

Among the many useful lessons Victor Flam had learned in his three years as a jarhead MP was what you see is almost never what you get. Take that suntan he'd smoked up at the Portsmouth Naval Correctional Facility back in, oh, '67, '68—couldn't place exactly when, somewhere back there (sitting now in the quiet of his living room and smiling to himself as the murky memory emerged from some whimsical conjunction of deep past and last night's mercy fuck with Ms. Bridget, vividly recollected). Or the crazy spade's name, couldn't remember that either, or what he looked like even. Spade, that's all. Only that he was a model inmate, joint-whupped, never gave you any grief. Till the day they nailed him on a random bend-over inspection, fished a torpedoful of smack out of that black ass. So Flam and another guard stick-marched him down to the Therapy Room (little sixties joke of theirs) for a tell and tell-some-more session.

Now you know we can't be bringin' controlled substances into a government facility, Flam explained to him patiently. *Goes against rules and regulations and the law of the land. You just tell us who you're mulein' for, and we'll go light on you.*

Gimp like that figured to be an instant rollover. Should have been baby food, right? Wrong. He gets it in his head to be a hard case, snitch on nobody. Seen too many movies. So they corner-slam him into the steel bulkhead a few times, which is a nice procedure for both parties concerned, seeing how it dings the chimes but leaves no marks, bleeding's all internal. Coax most anybody.

Not this tar baby. After about the fourth slam, he comes bouncing off the wall and backswings a scrawny arm and rakes something sharp across Flam's chest, draws a bright seam of blood. Turns out he's got a razored sheet-metal shaving taped inside his sleeve, and it carves a zipper Flam wears to this day.

They haul out their billies and maneuver him into a corner, and he's jabbing his make-do shank with one hand and goading with the other, squawking, *C'mon, muthafucks, c'mon.* What a hoot. Like he's got a hell prayer, this splinter-skinny spookadoo, up against the two of them. For sure he's been seeing too many movies. Death by cinema.

They circle in on him. Signal with their eyes. Other guard waits his moment and then whacks him upside the head, shatters a cheekbone. Flam steps nimbly (he was forty pounds lighter, those days, lightning in a bottle) inside the shank arm, lays on a lock, and snaps it at the elbow. Down he goes, jelly-kneed, groaning.

And then they go to work on him in earnest. Patented USMC disciplinary barracks tune-up. Make some chocolate-cherry pudding. Five, ten minutes into it both their arms getting heavy, so they take a quick breather, and damned if he don't lift that bashed black skull— must've been made of concrete—and spit out some blood-washed teeth and growl, gaspy little growl, *You better be fraggin' me, Flam. Ain't gonna be good enough, bust me up. You better be fraggin' me while you still can.*

Well, Flam drawls, *I expect we can do that too.*

So they did.

Afterward, they waited till lights out (it was a Sunday, Flam remembered now, no brass around except a weenie lieutenant sleeping off his Saturday night—funny how those details come back to you) and then dragged what was left of him onto the block and chucked it over a rail, three-flight drop. Inquiry ruled him a flyer, didn't trouble to explain what he was doing out of his house that hour. Nobody gave a fuck. One less porch monkey.

But for Flam, twenty years old, it's a most valued lesson. Here's a meek little ankle biter gets a sudden case of the stiff nuts, thinks he's

King Kong, opens you up, and puts his permanent seal on you. Who'd've ever guessed? Which goes to prove that life and all the people in it just one long go-figure. Which also proves when you see one thing, you'd better be goosed and ready for something else. Something altogether else.

Same with Ms. Bridget (where all these vagrant recollections and reflections first began). Now here you got this buttly twat, travels by united broomlines, looks like somebody gave her a fierce thump with the ugly stick. And what does she do? Just turns what's supposed to be a charity pump into a balls-out bang bang, is all. Best boink he's had in recent memory. Acrobat's elastic limbs, ass powered by non-stop piston rods, quicksand pussy. And all the right moans. Real goat fuck. Compared to Bridget, his manicurist, herself no sack slouch, seemed almost rigor mortissed.

You never know. Never. Night like last one puts a twist on the old saw: Sure, most times the bear eats you, but once in a great while you're dining on grizzly filet. Add to the start-up buzz she gives him, free for nothing except the price of dinner and a Victor Flam tube-steak dessert, it's like a Christmas bonus.

His smile widened, thinking about it. He hauled himself up and shambled into the kitchen, legs a little stiff yet from all the pretzel positions, a pleasant, satisfied ache in his crotch. He got a bag of pistachio nuts and a Bud Dry, brought them back to the living room, settled into the BarcaLounger, and waited for the New York call, which ought to be—damn well better be—coming through soon. And while he waited, popping pistachios and shocking the brewbie, he went over everything he had so far, as gathered in a looseleaf note-book coded SSI, for Shelley Swales Investigation.

Okay. Here's what he's got. Got a thumbnail bio on Shelley from Mama Swales and a sketchy profile drawn from his nosing-around conversations yesterday. Got a pirated copy of the police report on her whacking, along with some crime-scene photos. And courtesy of Bridget, he's got the name of the consulting outfit, Alexander Stoltz and Associates, and where they're headquartered, which is New York. And also the name of the guy who honchoed the Sanitary job, one Max Stroiker. That's what he's got as of last night.

But since he don't know from dick about management consulting, and since his mind is always busy, even when he's getting the old drain snaked, and since by nature and experience he's a meticulous man (got to be, his business), what he does first thing this morning is slip quietly out of Bridget's bed. She's still soundly crashed, honking like a moose, nostrils being about the only holes on her gone un-plugged, he's thinking now, the thought sparking another grin. He takes himself over to, of all places, the Palm Beach JC library. Now, your colleges and libraries are not exactly Victor Flam familiar turf; Corps was his college, street his post-graduate degree. So he collars a shusher and tells her what he's after in the way of information. She's a spindly twig of a girl, dwarfette, stands about even with his joystick, about the same looks department as Bridget, sub-basement. She runs her eyes over him, says not a word but makes this sniffing sound, like she's downwind a blotcher fart, then leads him back to some refer-ence shelves, and with an exaggerated flourish and a you-poor-dumb-fuck expression on her coyote-ugly face, points him to a thick volume and sashays away. College cunt. Book smart, like all them people. That's okay, though. He's got the large man's genial contempt for the little folks of this world, all of 'em, either gender. Nothing ruffles him, long as he gets what he's come for.

Not that he gets all that much out of this fat volume. It's a direc-tory of management consulting firms, and it gives him some bare-bones data on the Stoltz company: New York address; names and brief background on the principal officers; skimpy corporate history (founded in '49 by the now-departed Alexander Stoltz, started out in Chicago, moved east in '61, grown to world's eleventh largest con-sulting firm in its forty-plus years in the business, lot of "management declined issuance of" stonewall in the account, indicating a pretty tight organization, bunch of lawsuits, all satisfactorily resolved); some stats on the current number of employees and recent years' billings (loose estimates, but both figures substantial enough to suggest a thriving operation); some mumbo jumbo on their areas of special ex-pertise, incomprehensible to him. Pretty thin stuff, most of it, but he takes notes anyway and then reshelves the book and gives the pygmy bitch a broad, lewd wink on his way out the door. Little token of grat-itude for all her generous help.

Yeah, some help. He's going to need a whole lot more than just that directory fizz, and it comes to him immediately where he's going to get it. So he goes straight home from the library and puts in a call to Nathan up in the Bad Apple. Nathan's a clever Jewboy, not too tightly wrapped but a genius on the computer, tap into heaven's own data bank. They've done some business in the past (most notably tracking down a Manhattan insurance executive who got into the cookie jar and then into the Caribbean wind with a bagful of company loot—nice score for both of them, very profitable), and Flam figures he's got a professional courtesy coming. He tells Nathan what he needs and when he needs it by, and squashes the protests ("Tonight! I seriously doubt that's possible, Victor. It's a holiday weekend, you may recall.") with an affable "You'll come through, Nathan. I got faith in you."

But as of this moment, six o'clock Saturday night, that's all he's got: some meager notes and faith in a fussy Hebe's keyboard wizardry. Sum total. Not much. Which is why he's beginning to feel a little edgy, sitting there washing down pistachios with beer and watching a phone that stubbornly refuses to ring.

Two hours later it does.

"Victor?"

"Yeah, speakin'."

"Nathan here."

Like he's not going to recognize that sinus-clogged whine? Sure. "Hey, Nathan," Flam said, pitching his own voice hearty, casual. "Glad you called back."

"I've been working on your problem all day. Not an easy safe to crack, I might add. You're going to owe me one, Victor."

"Any time. All you got to do is ask."

"Perhaps you'd like to hear what I've uncovered."

"Was hopin' you'd have something for me."

Elaborate throat clearing. "Alexander Stoltz and Associates," Nathan began in the clipped, by-rote tone of a precocious schoolboy delivering a classroom report. "Founded in the late forties. Namesake trained in the mail-order line. Refined a productivity-enhancing technique called short-interval scheduling and adapted it to a variety of other businesses. Successfully. Said to be a brilliant man, but reclusive, controversial, and, I gather, somewhat mean spirited. No longer with us. Company now in the hands of his protégés. A good-sized enterprise, multinational. Billed over $375 mil last year, employs somewhere in the range of a thousand personnel. Exact figures impossible to come by, even for me. However—"

"I know all that already," Flam broke in on him. "Gimme something I can use."

"Do you know their reputation in the consulting industry?" Nathan said, a little testiness riding the nasal whine.

"No."

"I thought not. It's really rather interesting."

Expectant pause. Flam waited. Nothing. Pause lengthened. Then, humoring him, remembering how he got off on these displays of natural superiority, Flam filled it with the obligatory question, "How's that, Nathan?"

"Well, my impression is they're consulting's bad boys. Strictly hatchet men. Head cutters. They'll come into a client firm, search out the fat, and trim it right down to the bone."

"Thought that's what consultants are hired to do."

"Some of them, yes. But the Stoltz people are known to take an unseemly delight in their work. Something of a no-prisoners approach. Quite ruthless actually, though evidently it gets results."

Flam was scribbling notes in the SSI book. "Okay," he said, "that's good. What else?"

"Internally, they're a very secretive organization. Also very authoritarian. Almost paramilitary."

"How do you mean?"

"The employees live in terror of their jobs. And the pace is killing. Brutal hours, perpetual travel, constant surveillance, and ongoing evaluation of their performance. A kind of mercantile Darwinism, one might say."

"You wanna talk straight, Nathan?"

A sigh came down the line. "Survival of the fittest, Victor. You've heard of it?"

"Yeah, I heard," Flam said.

"Turnover, I learned, is about fifty percent annually. But for those who last, the rewards can be sweet indeed. Rapid promotions, six-figure salaries, generous expense accounts. And a healthy year-end bonus. Slice of the melon, in their quaint jargon."

"These survivors, they all of 'em located up there?"

"Oh, no. They're scattered all across the country and abroad. Work out of their homes. Assignments come by fax or phone from the headquarters here. Everything's centralized. Keeps the overhead low, you see."

That wasn't what Flam was hoping to hear. Complicated matters for him. But he said, "This is some good buzz you're giving me, Nathan. Now what about this Stroiker? What'd you get on him?"

"Rather a good bit, I'd say."

Another dangling silence. Flam's turn to sigh. "Like what?" he asked dutifully.

"Max Edwin Stroiker. Forty-eight years old, Chicago native—Winnetka, to be precise—Northwestern MBA, came with Stoltz in 1978 after a series of forgettable middle-management jobs. Rose quickly to section chief, a responsible enough field position, but stalled there. Outgoing, gregarious, considered bright, but clearly a man with problems."

"Like what?" Flam said again.

"Marital, for one. Recently he went through a stormy divorce. Sauce, for another. Apparently he's something of a lush. Also a satyr, it seems."

"Huh?"

"A womanizer, Victor."

Wiseass yid, Flam was thinking, but he let it go. Dealing with Nathan, there was some shit you just had to swallow. "So how'd he do on that laundry job down here?" he asked.

"Not well. Near as I can tell, one of his underlings carried him. File's a bit vague on it."

"You get the names of the other people worked that job?"

"Most of them, I think."

"You 'think'?"

"The low-level consultants come and go, Victor. That turnover I mentioned? A couple of them were terminated during the course of the project."

Flam didn't want to hear that either. More snarls to untangle. "You get them names to me?" he said.

"Fax them off tonight, if you like."

"That'd be good. Okay, back to this Stroiker. He still in Chicago?"

"Not anymore. The ex got the house and the better part of the bank accounts in the settlement."

"So where could I find him?"

"Well, right now he's between assignments. The last one was in San Antonio. In point of fact, I intercepted his final report on that project this very afternoon. Subordinate's report, more accurately. He didn't write it."

"What I'm askin' here is how I'd locate him."

"This weekend?"

"Right."

"I'd try Atlanta. Seems he keeps a little love nest there."

"You got this Atlanta address?"

"I do."

"You maybe wanta pass it along?"

Nathan recited it, enunciating deliberately, the way one speaks to a particularly dull child.

Flam recorded the address in his notebook. "Fuck'd you get all this?" he asked him, truly impressed.

"From his confidential file, of course. Where else? Very devious, these Stoltz people. Very sophisticated intelligence network. I told you this was a fascist organization."

"Yeah, I remember you sayin' that."

"Let me advise you to get to him quickly, Victor, if that's your intention. His file looks grim. Last evaluation—done August third, by the way—strongly hints of an upcoming axing."

"Appreciate the advice."

"Anything else I can assist you with?"

"No, that about covers it for now. Listen, want to thank you for your trouble. You been real helpful."

"Always a pleasure, Victor. Perhaps you'll be able to reciprocate one day. Should the occasion arise."

Flam chuckled. Trust a Jew, let you know he's holding your marker. "Like you said, Nathan. I owe you."

He had two more calls to make that night. The first secured him a seat on an 8:00 A.M. flight to Atlanta. The second, to Mother Swales, was in the nature of an update, show her he was earning his keep. Also to get from her a recent photo, preferably the shot of Shelley at the laundry. Mrs. Swales, eager to help, said she'd have a driver bring it over tonight. Flam expressed his thanks and a guarded optimism— things you say, things the client wants to hear. Promised to keep her informed of his progress. Rang off.

He went back into the kitchen and returned with another bag of nuts and a fresh brew. No sooner was he settled again than the doorbell chimed. Curious. Not even a Palm Beach cash cow got the laser express, last he heard. He crossed the room, swung open the door. Blank-faced kid standing there holding a large brown envelope, one of those interoffice mailers. Local courier-service van parked in the drive. "What can I do for you?" Flam said.

"You Victor Flam?"

"That's right."

"Supposed to give this to you," the kid said, handing over the envelope.

"From who?"

"Some lady. Didn't give no name. Just said make sure you get it. Nobody else. Need you to sign."

Flam scrawled his signature on the sheet. He took the envelope inside, peeled away several layers of clear tape, and extracted an eight-by-eleven photocopy. Of what, he wasn't just sure. He had an idea, but he wasn't sure. He held it to the light, tilted it at various angles, turned it upside down. Couldn't be what he was thinking. No way. Couldn't. He turned it over. There was a tiny inscription at the bottom, written in a precise hand. It read:

A little remembrance of last night. If you'd like some more
of the real thing, give me a call. I'm home now. Waiting.
B.

Flam laughed out loud. He was right the first time. Loopy broad had photocopied her goddam crotch, f'chris'sake, beaver and all. Twat had imagination, give her that. And broomhilda or not, it was a temptation. But there was the Shelley photo yet to be delivered and Nathan's fax yet to arrive. Eight o'clock came early, and tomorrow promised to be a busy day. Have to take a rain check on this one. Work comes first.

9

Fifteen minutes short of the appointed hour the following evening, Lizabeth Seaver sank into an easy chair in her living room, glass of white wine in one hand, cigarette in the other. It felt good to be off her feet. All day long she'd been scurrying about, readying the house, the dinner, finally herself. Now, far as she could tell, everything was in order. The place looked, to her vigilant eye, immaculate (upstairs anyway; down below, well, that was another story). The shrimp Florentine steamed in the oven, timed precisely for an eight o'clock serving. Salad was tossed. Appropriate wines chilled. Bottles of scotch, bourbon, vodka, gin—one each—stood sentinel on the kitchen counter, in case these Woodrows were drinking men. Table was set with her finest china and silver, legacy from her parents, salvaged, along with some skimpy personal belongings and an unequal share of the furniture, from the split. *And that was about all was salvaged,* she thought, less with bitterness than immense relief.

She was herself casually outfitted in denim skirt, midnight-blue silk blouse, smart saffron vest with an abstract beading design, and sueded leather loafers, cactus-colored. A study in contrasting golds and blues, to set off her eyes and rich corona of hair. Apart from a touch of rose lipstick and a light dusting of eye shadow, not a trace of brass or shine to either, her face was absent of makeup. No need for any: Its remarkable bone geometry relayed a message better left understated and unadorned. She wore her beauty carelessly, like a familiar old sweater, but she was not entirely unaware of it either. For well over half of her thirty-four years, she had witnessed its peculiar effect on people, men in particular, but always from within some central core of herself, a chaste and incorruptible space of her own creation, and always the slightly bewildered observer, utterly unacquainted with artifice or cynicism or guile. By now she accepted it for what it was, a gift of nature, but a gift weighted with mixed blessings: distrust of women, target for men, tool of both. If it opened doors, they were, in her experience, invariably the wrong ones.

And so while everything, herself included, appeared to be in place for the little soiree upcoming, she was nonetheless anxious, almost fidgety. The wine helped some, and the smoke, but not much. She was out of practice, these things. It had been a while, close to— what?—six months now. Longer even than that, actually. After the first few years with Rick—when his career was getting underway and he wanted her on ready display, like the sleek Corvette or one of those golfing trophies lining a shelf in his den—after that, the formal entertaining dwindled, more or less in direct proportion to the steady unraveling of their fragile union. Often as not, there'd come a late call and the clipped announcement he wouldn't be able to make it for dinner. ("Heavy case tomorrow, Liz. It's midnight oil time for me. Don't wait up.") And toward the end, no calls at all. So much for beauty. And fidelity. And trust. And all the old virtues. So much for dinner parties.

So what was she doing here, barely settled and already inviting a couple of perfect strangers into her home. Inviting more tangles, complications, and potential griefs. Madness.

No good to think that way, she reminded herself. Nothing served by it. Anyway, madness or not, she was certain she knew the answer, or pretty certain. Instinct told her there was something about this eccentric man, this Norman Woodrow, that struck an empathetic chord, some instant . . . affinity? . . . bond? . . . connection? . . . impossible to loop it with words. Whatever it was, she trusted her instincts, this one anyway. In a curious way he called to mind her father, dearly loved (maybe, if she were ever to own up to it, the only man she'd ever really loved), recently passed on, sorely missed. Maybe that was it, her father. She was equally certain Norman was drawn to her. She could tell. Another of those doors opening. She'd seen it before, many a time. About the son, some kind of business consultant, she couldn't begin to guess. But she was braced for disappointment, men of business being not all that far off lawyers. That was all right. It was a friend she was looking for, not a lover. Looking not to be used again. For a change. Nothing to do now but wait and see.

Punctually at seven, the bell dinged and the waiting, along with all the wandering reflection and speculation, was abruptly over. She set her glass on the end table and hurried to the door. The Woodrows, father and, presumably, son, stood on the porch, their faces partly shadowed in the softening light but sporting tight social smiles, both of them. "Norman, you made it," she said brightly, beckoning them in.

"Would I fail you?"

"And right on time too."

"You said seven."

"And here you are."

He turned to his son, announced, "Lizabeth Seaver, Michael Woodrow," identifying each with a crisp toss of a hand. In the other he held a small package, clearly gift-wrapped.

"I'm happy to meet you," said the son.

Standing now, the three of them, in the lighted entry, she could see he was a little taller than Norman, leaner, slighter build. And handsome. No, that wasn't right. More than just handsome. If it was possible to link the notion of beauty with a male, his was a face of such perfect symmetry it could be called beautiful. She wasn't the sort of woman given to studying men or, she liked to think, judging them by appearance, but his features were so extraordinary, so arresting, so, well, flawless, it was hard not to gawk. So she murmured an acknowledgment and fastened her eyes deliberately on Norman, who was just then thrusting the package at her.

"For me?"

"You. Open it."

She peeled back the wrapping, unsealed the carton, and removed a lead crystal ashtray, as heavy as a rock. She held it up to the light. "Norman, it's beautiful. Thank you so much. But you really shouldn't have, you know."

"A small token. In celebration of your new digs."

"A gift wasn't necessary. Or expected."

"Nevertheless, there it is."

She sensed, at a corner of her vision, the son looking on with an attitude of mild amusement. To Norman she said, "Then we'd better break it in, right? Couple of addicts like ourselves."

"Straightaway."

She ushered them into the living room. Norman took one of the chairs flanking a lamp table; the son the facing couch. She laid the ashtray on the table, picked up her empty glass. "I've got a little start on you," she said. Explaining the obvious. Settle down, settle down. "What can I get you to drink?"

Beer for the father, a martini, gin, for the observant son, whose nimble eyes (vivid green, she noticed, stunning, disturbing) were taking in the room and who volunteered diplomatically to mix his own.

"Trust me, I know how to make a martini," she said (remembering the ex and his finicky tastes, and thinking, *Oh, oh, not another one, not a good sign),* but jokingly and with a big disarming smile at him, her first. All he did was shrug.

Some quick, fluttery moves in the kitchen—prepare the drink, get the beer (fortunately, she'd thought to lay in a supply of Heinekens), and a glass for Norman, fill her own glass of wine, peek in the oven (the pungent aroma of exotic spices assuring her everything under control there), and a moment later she was back, dispensing refreshment all around. The efficient hostess, even on this miniscale. She settled into the chair by Norman, who allowed, "Your home looks considerably different from two days ago."

"It's still pretty bare bones yet."

"Looks orderly to me."

"You wouldn't want to see the basement."

"Well," he said, ignoring the glass and hoisting the bottle, "here's to bare bones and new beginnings."

"Especially those new beginnings."

She lifted her glass, smuggled a glance at the son, who elevated his sightly, dutifully, like a man forever on the fringe of things, and took a cautious sip. Brow-knitting sip. So she looked at him dead on and asked directly, "Is the martini okay?"

"Fine."

"You're sure? You can say. My womanhood's not at stake."

"No, you were right. You know how to make the perfect martini."

A smile, guarded but genuine-seeming, scampered across his face. Her first assessment was accurate, absolutely: beautiful smile, beautiful face. She felt oddly twitchy. She lit a steadying cigarette, turned away. Norman had set the bottle on the table between them and was pulling at the knot in his tie. "I almost didn't recognize you at the door," she said, grinning at him.

"What do you mean?"

"Out of your sweats."

"I don't recall you mentioning a dress code."

"You're right. I forgot."

"The suit was my best guess," he said, somewhat stiffly. "I don't get many dinner invitations."

"It's a joke, Norman. You look smashing."

"Oh, yes. Positively dapper."

It felt easy, right, twitting him, this determinedly austere man. Calming somehow. So why then was her gaze tugged irresistibly back to the son, sitting there casually elegant in linen slacks, open-neck sport shirt, knockabout mocs, watching them both with the same amused tolerance she'd detected earlier? Why? "At least you look more comfortable than your dad," she said.

"Informal was my guess. A neighborly thing."

"I'd say neighborly. Did he tell you how we met?"

"Yes, he did."

"How he got that burn on his hand?"

"That too."

"It was very . . . heroic. What he did."

"Oh, Norman's always been something of a hero," he said, faintly ironic.

The object of all this flattering endorsement tilted the bottle to his lips, took a long swallow, blew the smoke from a third Marlboro at the ceiling, said, "I wonder if you two would care to refrain from talking about me as if I weren't in the room."

She swung her attention back to him. "You were right about that loose coupling. Plumber told me the smallest spark could have sent the place up in flames."

"A lucky guess. Luckier, evidently, than my choice of garb tonight."

"Don't change the subject, Norman. Face it, you saved the day. Which makes you a hero."

He swatted the air with the back of a hand, a sharp whisking motion. "Enough, maybe, with the reflex expressions of gratitude?"

"Well, when someone saves your life, you'd better be grateful."

"Duly noted. And accepted."

"How *is* the hand, by the way?"

"The hand is fine."

"Sure. Fine like Michael's martini there." She looked back and forth between them, her features arranged in ersatz reproach, to show it was simply more of the twitting. "You're bad liars, you know. Both of you. Very transparent."

The son cocked his head, put up disclaimer palms. The father said, "All right then. It's perhaps the greatest pain known to medical science. Is that better?"

"A little."

"How about, 'I fall upon the thorns of life! I bleed!'?"

Now she looked at him blankly.

"Shelley," he said. "Trust a long-suffering romantic to produce the proper words."

"You have to be patient," Michael said, filling the instant of silence that followed this last pronouncement. "Norman reads a lot. He's a warehouse of quotes."

Norman thrust an arm overhead and shook it vigorously, the way one of her pupils might evidence knowledge of the answer to a difficult question or signal an urgent need. "I'm still here, Michael," he said, and though he was smiling, there was a prickly edge to his voice too.

Again she looked at them. Each in turn. And slower this time, long, measuring stares. Something going on here, impossible to tell what. So she said that which struck her as a penetrating insight: "You know, no one would ever mistake you two for father and son."

Norman arched a brow. "That's a dubious compliment for this young man."

She glanced over at Michael, then back at him. "You think so? I don't."

Michael leaned back on the couch, shook his head slowly. "You want to know what I think?" he asked, the question directed at her.

"What's that?"

"I think I see why you and Norman got on so quickly. And, obviously, so famously."

"Why?"

"He cuts right to the chase. So do you."

"You may be right."

"I'm sure I am."

"The only thing I'm sure of," Norman said, extending the empty bottle, "is that I could stand another of these excellent tonics. If they're still being offered, that is, after all this recondite talk."

"Does that mean he wants another beer?" she said, her eyes fixed on Michael.

"That would be my interpretation."

"What about you? Another?"

"Why not."

"Maybe you want to come along. Fix your own this time."

"I like yours."

She shot him a skeptical look.

"No, really I do."

"Really?"

"Hand to heart," he said, laying one over his chest in that approximate location and smiling that gorgeous, enveloping smile. Straight at her. From somewhere beneath her own breastbone she felt the first rumor of an ache, and her hand trembled slightly when she took his glass.

They finished the second drink of the evening (three now, for her), backing off, as if by unspoken agreement, from the touchier topics, dealing the commonplace banalities. They subjected a week's worth of weather to minute analysis (eventually congratulating one another on today's fine day). They deplored the Hinsdale traffic, the soaring costs of suburban living, speculated on the Bears' prospects, segued naturally from there to the presidential election campaigns swinging into fast gear. The things strangers, testing the murky waters of friendship, will say. By the third drink, they were laughing easily. Making small jokes. Now and again Norman delivered a sententious line, but with the practiced self-mockery of the man who understands it's expected of him. By the fourth, it seemed clear they all felt good together.

Eventually Lizabeth wearied of it, all the white-bread talk. She had been parceling her attention evenly between father and son, but now, loosened by wine, she turned to Michael and said, "How old are you, anyway?"

The blunt question seemed to startle him. "You're asking my age?"

"Yes."

"Why?"

"I don't know. Curiosity."

"I'm thirty."

"You look closer to twenty-one. Don't you think so, Norman?"

"I think he looks much younger than his years, yes."

Michael shifted on the couch. Rearranged his hands and feet. Looked uncomfortable over the close scrutiny and the sudden corkscrew twist in the conversation. "I suppose that's kind of you to say, but in my work youth is not necessarily a virtue. Or any particular advantage."

"What exactly is it you do?" she asked him.

"Management consulting."

"I know that. Norman told me that. But what does it mean?"

"It means we go into floundering organizations, assess their problems, and find solutions."

"But *how?*" she persisted. "In practice, how?"

"Through the application of a variety of broad-line analytical skills," he said vaguely.

"I don't understand any of that. What you just said."

"Well, we use a refinement of a technique called short-interval scheduling. Sort of a contemporary spin on the old time-and-motion studies. Which, at the simplest level, translates into watching and evaluating employee performance. Ensuring they do an honest day's work."

"And if they don't?"

"Oh, there's any number of ways to motivate them."

"For instance?"

"Dismissal, for one. You'd be amazed at how a few strategically placed termination notices will enhance an operation's productivity. Any operation."

"Isn't that kind of . . . harsh?"

"You have to remember that's why our services were engaged in the first place. To cut costs, increase profits. Ordinarily it's easier for an outsider to make the less than popular decisions. We can look at things more objectively. Dispassionately, you might say."

Lizabeth had to think about that a minute. Finally she said, "So what you do for a living is fire people."

He smiled again, thinner this time. "We prefer to think of it as weeding out the incompetents. And the slackers."

"By firing them."

He gave a helpless shrug. "Just another dirty job."

Norman had been peering into his bottle as though he found something intensely interesting there. Now he said wryly, "What a poet once called salvation for pay. Something like that."

"What did I tell you?" Michael said to her. "About the quotes? That one's for me."

"No," Norman corrected him, "that one's Housman. Loosely."

"But meant for me. Norman's very much the intellectual. You have to get used to it."

Lizbeth's gaze shifted puzzledly from father to son, then back again. "Why is it you two address each other so, well, formally?"

"You mean by full Christian name?" Norman said.

"Yes. That."

"Diminutives do just what they're intended to do: diminish the man. Shrink him. It's a theory of mine."

Michael chuckled tolerantly. "That's another thing Norman's got," he explained. "An abundance of theories."

"Test it on your schoolchildren sometime," Norman said, ignoring him. "Reduce your James to Jimmie, Thomas to Tommy. Consider what happens to an Edward when he becomes Eddie. Observe the subtle behavioral differences."

"Or Norman to Norm?" Lizbeth said. "Michael to Mike?"

"There you are. Hear it?"

"Don't encourage him," Michael said, still chuckling, but without much mirth in it.

She put a hand to a temple, shook her head. "What a pair you two are."

"Don't listen to him," Norman said. "And don't just take my word for it. Try it yourself. You'll see."

Now she laughed too, but kindly, to lighten things. "I've got to tell you, Norman, I think it's a crazy theory. Especially with kids."

"You're a teacher?" Michael asked her, clearly a topic-turning maneuver.

"Yes. Elementary. The one over on Oak."

"You enjoy it?"

"Too early to tell. I just started last week."

He looked at her curiously. "This is your, uh, first job?"

"Oh, no. I'm sure you noticed I'm not exactly fresh out of college. I've taught before, but I've been away from it for several years. I was married for a while. Didn't Norman tell you?"

"No."

She watched him. He seemed to be sorting this intelligence out, deliberating his reply. "Well," he said carefully, model of tact, "now that you're back, what do you think of public education?"

"Here in Hinsdale it's very good. At my school we have all kinds of innovative programs."

"Ms. Seaver repairs the emotionally impaired," Norman put in.

"You can call me Lizabeth, Norman. I won't feel diminished."

"All right. Lizabeth, then. And is yours one of those programs you'd call 'innovative'?"

Her head felt light, inflated, as if it were miraculously severed from the rest of her somehow, floating toward the ceiling. But not so light she missed the vocalized quote marks bracketing her word. Perfectly decent word, *innovative.* Nothing wrong with it. So with just a touch of defensiveness, she said, "It's one of them, yes."

"And there are others?"

"Lots of others."

"What, for example?"

"What is this, Norman? Humor the hostess time?"

"It's a simple question."

"Okay," she said, and was about to say more, something expert, polished. Nothing came to her. "Ah, what was the simple question again?"

"Your other innovations?"

"Okay, there's gifted and talented. We've got a terrific gifted-and-talented program. One of the best in the state, they say."

"Gifted and talented," he said in echo. "Whatever could that mean?"

"Just what it says."

"Help me out anyway. Explain."

She took a time-out. Glanced over at Michael, who presented an attentive face, deeply interested. Unless she was mistaken. Still a beautiful face, interested or not. The ache in her chest, submerged in all the drink and talk, resurfaced. She drained off the last of the wine in her glass, said, "I was right. It's bait the hostess time."

"Wrong," Norman said. "I'd like to hear more about this. What a notion. Gifted ten-year-olds."

"You think we don't have them here? A town like this? All these professional people?"

"How is it you identify them, these gifted children?"

"There are different performance measures."

"And once identified, how do you instruct them?"

"We challenge them."

"How, exactly, is that done?"

At the year's first faculty meeting, someone, some stuffy little man who spoke in decidedly feminine accents and with the hint of a lisp, had delivered a windy report on the progress of the program she was being quizzed on now. She had listened, but only at the edges. Enough, though, to appropriate some of his words (as best she could bring them back, words like *enrich, creative, learning, outcomes, compacted curricula, restructured classrooms*—substantial-sounding words), seize on them shamelessly, and fashion them into a rambling answer to the question, a defense. She extemporized. She was rolling now, confident, animated, barely conscious of leaning forward in her chair, hands stabbing the air. But on one of those expressive punctuating stabs she caught a glimpse of her watch, and a sudden alarm went off in her head. She read the time and broke off abruptly, midrecital. Her jaw dropped. "Oh, my god!" she exclaimed. "It's after nine! The dinner!"

She bolted out of her chair, sprinted to the kitchen, yanked open the oven door. And discovered a seething blackened mess. Some unrecognizable reek—charred fish, scorched spices—assaulted her nostrils. "Oh, god," she said again, dismal groan this time, and to no one but herself and the bubbling remains of her elegant meal.

She felt a gentle touch on her shoulder. Turned, lifted her eyes, and met the mild, composed gaze of Michael Woodrow. "I've ruined everything," she said, voice softened now to no more than a plaintive whisper. "The dinner. Evening. Everything." Her eyes filled. Reflexively, she laid her head against his chest. The soothing hand stroked her hair. Soothing voice, soft as her own, said, "Nonsense. No great harm done. We can all go out. Or better yet, order something."

"This is so humiliating."

"What about pizza? You like pizza?"

"Pizza!" she moaned.

"But do you like it?"

"I guess so. You?"

"Norman and I would have it for breakfast if we could."

"More charitable lies."

"Tell her, Norman."

She disengaged herself from the pacifying half-embrace (but slowly, reluctantly . . . how long had it been since she'd felt a tender male touch? . . . couldn't remember). Norman, gone unnoticed in all the calamity, stood behind Michael and slightly to his left. Unlike his son, he looked tense, distracted, almost agitated. "He speaks the truth," he confirmed, but he was edging for the door all the same. "None for me, though. I must get back."

"You're leaving? Why?"

"Something I have to do. Before it slips my mind."

"It's the dinner, isn't it?" she said miserably.

"Not at all. Food has nothing to do with it."

"I'm sorry, Norman. I did so want things to go right tonight."

"And so they did. Believe me when I tell you it's been a most enjoyable evening. And most instructive."

SHE WATCHED HIM PICKING at a steaming wedge of pizza, carving it into tiny, manageable bites, and maneuvering them around his plate like pieces in an intricate puzzle. She watched. Anyone else would be eating this stuff with his fingers. Not him. Knife and fork, if you please. She wasn't sure what to make of it. Nothing. Make nothing of it. The fastidious Woodrow boys.

Now and again he speared one of his puzzle pieces, brought it to his mouth, chewed slowly, thoroughly. Followed it with a sip of beer (from a glass, of course—what else?). They had switched to beer, and her head was weightless now, as buoyant as a weather balloon soaring off into deep space. *I can fly! I can fly!*

Maybe not, though. Actually, she was sitting across from him at her small dining table, earth-anchored. With Norman gone, the talk, what there was of it, had drifted back to bland ordinaries, safe social-speak. The kind that always made her restless. So at a convenient breach in it (of which there were many, for without the buffer of his father he seemed uneasy, almost shy), she said (taking pains not to slur her words), "You really don't like it, do you?"

He glanced up from his absorbing edible puzzle. "What? The pizza?"

"Yes. The pizza."

"Of course I do. It was my idea. Remember?"

"Tell the truth, now," she said good-humoredly, hoping it would evoke that entrancing smile.

No such luck. "The truth," he said solemnly. "All right, I suppose it's not my absolute all-time favorite. It seemed like an easy solution."

"I thought so. Same with Norman, right?"

"Norman eats whatever's in front of him. I doubt he even notices."

"Noticed enough to make a fast exit. Invited to dinner, go home hungry."

"Norman operates on impulse. That's the way he is. If he'd been hungry, he'd have stayed."

"I still feel guilty."

"About what?"

With a sweep of an arm she took in the whole room, whole evening. "Everything."

"You shouldn't. It was kind of you to invite him. He hasn't many friends, you know. None, in fact. And I'm gone most of the time."

"It's not kindness. Your father's a fascinating man. I like him." She hesitated, but only a beat, and then on an ungovernable impulse of her own, plunged on. "I like you too. More than that. I'm enormously attracted to you."

He put down the fork, clasped his hands on the table, stared at them woodenly. "Are you sure you want to tell me that?"

"I just did."

"Do you always say exactly what's on your mind?"

"Just like Norman. You said it yourself."

Thinking about it later, head unfogged and properly balanced on the rest of her, she would explain and justify it to herself not so much as momentary aberration or drink-driven impulse as compelling need, dizzy with longing. For the very next thing she heard herself saying was, "Maybe you'd care to stay the night." Before he could reply, she came to her feet and glided around the table, leaned toward that startled, beautiful face, and kissed it full on the lips. Long, searching kiss laid on lips pressed tightly together, resolutely unparting.

She backed away. Eyes swimming, nerves twitching, cheeks scalded. What am I doing? Ladies don't proposition guests. No more flying. "I'm sorry," she murmured. "Believe it or not, this is not the way I normally behave."

"And I'm ... well ... flattered. A little surprised maybe, but flattered."

"But not interested."

"No, no, it's not that. But I don't think it's such a good idea. Not just yet."

"Why?" she asked, trying without much success to erase the wavery note of pleading in her voice. Ladies don't plead either.

"For one thing, we both may have had too much to drink—"

"Unaccustomed as I am to public drinking," she broke in on him. Salvage what you could with a joke.

"For another," he went on patiently, "I have to leave in the morning. Early."

"Tomorrow's a holiday, Michael. You don't have to spare my feelings with a lie."

"For me it's no holiday. That's the nature of my work."

"Where is it you're going?"

"Michigan."

"How long will you be gone?"

"Hard to say. A month. Maybe longer."

Stop, stop, stop. Stop it right now. Ladies don't pry. Don't proposition, plead, pry, and not necessarily in that order. The three *P*'s. Rules to live by. And all three violated. "I suppose this happens to you all the time," she said.

"What's that?"

"Wanton women throwing themselves at you."

"Not all the time."

"I expect I won't be seeing you again."

"Why do you say that?"

"After a night like this one? Making the perfect fool of myself?"

"That's where you're wrong. I want to see you again. Very much."

That's what he said. She heard it. And the look he gave her was so tender, so earnest, so—stricken? Could you call it stricken? She was all but swamped by another wave of longing. Unless she misread it. Once the fool ... But not twice. Not in one night. So she said lightly, "You've got elegant manners, Michael. Very gentlemanly. Your mother must have taught you well."

He lowered his eyes. And in a voice subdued but as chilly as a polar draft, he said, "No, not my mother."

•   •   •

APART FROM THE EERIE YELLOW GLOW cast by the lamp on his desk, the room was utterly dark. From where he sat he could see a pale seam of light in the bay window of her condo, and above it an immense black sky spattered with stars. Breathclutching sky. Heartbreakingly lovely night.

He smoked. Occasionally he sipped from a mug of nuked instant coffee, black, very strong, to sweep the beer smog from his head. (And recalling, irrelevantly, when he did, a routine line of jailhouse wit: Coffee in here's like the best fresh fish in the house—hot, black, instant, and free. Haw, haw, haw. Stateville wit.) Memory's perversity. Over there, at the source of that thin light, things had come together—or seemed to come together—with the sudden radiant purity of a celestial vision. Over here, nothing.

So he summoned the lofty stranger, who came strolling leisurely out of the dark and whispered in his ear, *What are you doing here, Norman? It's night. You work—if it can be dignified as such—only in the morning.*

I know, I know.

Maybe you should sleep now. The prison of habit can be comforting too. Secure.

Are you mocking me?

Call it what you will.

I call it mockery.

If you say so. Now, what is it you want from me?

Guidance. Help.

With what? Be explicit.

I don't know. I was onto something a moment ago. Something the girl said. Now it's gone.

Something? You'll have to do better than that.

Something lost. Buried. Maybe significant.

Or maybe not?

Maybe not.

Remember the hole?

If I have to.

Remember all the teeming mindlife went on there, in the silence and the blackness and the stink? All those endless internal dialogues, stark images, tumbling memories, capricious arousals, bizarre hallucinations, fantastic dreams? Remember any of that?

Only too well.

In there it was easy. Elementary.

That was there.

Same thing here.

Look around you. It's not the same.

I'm trying to help, Norman.

Then you're the one who'll have to do better.

All right. Try this: "And the way to look for a thing is plain,/To go where you lost it, back again." Remember that one?

Now that you remind me.

Whose is it?

I forget.

Bret Harte, brain dead!

So? I've already done that. Gone back. It's the Day I'm after. Trying to snare. The Day.

You're not ready, Norman. Listen to wise Bret. Go back again.

Where?

Ransack the past. Get it right.

How?

It's your tale, not mine.

Obediently, he picked up a pen and began to scribble, slowly at first, prying loose a word here, another there, chasing down the scattered images and shaping them into thought chains, letting the words lead him. Soon he was writing furiously, the memories flooding in on him, the stranger looking over his shoulder.

And this is what he wrote.

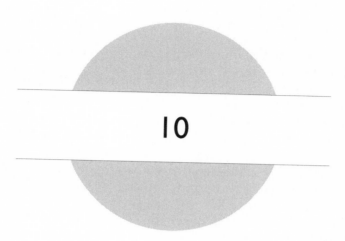

10

Now and again, one is privileged to hear of the latest enthusiasms of our professional pedagogues. It appears that after a couple of decades of ministering to the needs of the economically deprived and intellectually disadvantaged—what you and I would call the poor and the dumb—they have, in this age of the achiever, refocused their glaring light of wisdom on a group they call the "gifted and talented." Now, I know nothing of the art of instructing the very young, and the very notion of a roomful of impudent squirrels weaned on the comic-strip world of television fills me with unutterable dread. Still, I am bold enough to presume to recommend an alternative approach, one that is far less costly, considerably more direct, and, I am convinced, vastly more effective.

Admittedly, it is unorthodox. It requires no federal monies (as they are pleased to call such ill-gotten gains), no new technologies, not even a brace of schoolmarms armor-plated in the zealous recti-tude that comes with certificates of renovated erudition. Yet to my thinking it is tailored perfectly to the needs of that select fraternity of the favored young. Though I can boast of no such native endowment, I was lucky enough to stumble upon it during my own formative years and it has, I see now, served as cornerstone for my peculiar metaphysic.

Education, like life, was simpler in those days. Where I grew up, the community's public-school campus consisted of three buildings set in triangular pattern on an oversized city block. A child began, as I did, in a boxy three-storied elementary building, with his promotion passed across a playground to a larger junior high, and from there angled back to a long, toaster-shaped high school. Thusly were a dozen years of one's life spent describing the three points of that geometric figure, scaling that sometime hurdle of intellectual challenge, more often mastering the arts of stealth and cunning.

Such mastery was absolutely essential, simply for survival's sake. Early on, I grasped that hard truth, perhaps the most cogent lesson of all. As a first-grader I found myself assigned to the "Y" room, a kind of limbo located somewhere between the Olympus of the "X" room and the academic Slough of Despond appropriately alphabetized "Z." In that less altruistic era, such pigeonholing was based as much on a child's socioeconomic rank (as we would have it nowadays) as his native wit, and not surprisingly Z rooms were disproportionately populated with brutish urchins from the wrong side of the tracks.

It was not much better in the Y. Our instructress was a petulant old maid (a colleague of Aunt Grace, which association, by the way, earned me not the slightest leverage) who went by the improbable Dickensian name of Doris Bugbee. Thoroughly persuaded of the hopelessness of her charge, she ran the class like a drill sergeant, slapping a chunky thigh with a swagger-stick ruler and striking fear in the heart of any young scholar guilty of some innocuous infraction. Nor was there any relief at recess or after school hours, for bands of Z-roomers roved the playground like packs of wild beasts, expropriating swings and slides and monkey bars at whim and at will. Merciless as Salvadoran death squads, they terrorized anyone luckless enough to stray across their path.

Even in my day, the elementary building was superannuated, a tinder box waiting to ignite. Years before, the local planners had wisely erected a fire escape, a funnel-shaped metal tube affixed by a trapdoor to our own third-floor classroom, and from there depending like a limp member to the ground. By the time I arrived, it had fallen into desuetude and its upper entrance was boarded over. By then, fire drills were conducted in much the same manner they are today.

An alarm sounded, Miss Bugbee stood us at attention by our desks, and, after we had an unconscionable wait for our turn to come, marched us smartly down the stairs and out the doors to safety—this in about the span of time it would have required to parboil us all.

But the fire escape, obsolete though it was and strictly forbidden as a play site, held a potent fascination for me. Better than any grudging recognition from Miss Bugbee, any peevishly delivered syllable of faint praise, can I remember my sense of achievement at finally shinning up to its very summit. Spine pressed to the nailed-shut door, limbs quivery with the effort of bracing myself against the cool steel, I perched there like a fetus in that cylinder black and silent as a womb, suspended for a joyous instant before surrendering to the fearsome plunge toward the speck of light below.

The fire escape was my initiation into the proscribed secret places (available at most school campuses) that, I contend, offer another, less traditional means of educating our more promising youngsters. Once, concealed halfway up it, I observed a pair of high school lovers locked in steamy embrace. Peering downward as though through an inverted spyglass, I caught my first miniaturized glimpse of bare tit and heard my first groans of passion. That was instructive.

Another time it was equal to its name and helped sharpen the survival skills alluded to above. The pithecanthropine cream of the Z room was represented in the persons of the dreaded Heath twins, Delbert and Duane by given name, but for reasons best known to themselves dubbed respectively Buck and Bingo. Say their names. Hear the menacing plosives break against the serpentine hiss of surname. Now you have a remote glimmer of the terror those very utterances inspired, never mind the monstrous corporeal presences that all too often followed close in their wake. ("Jesus, here comes Buck"—or Bingo, take your pick—"Run!")

On this occasion, that Scythian pair, school-yard scourge, was after me, god knows why. Maybe I had the lunatic temerity to hold my place on a Z-room-annexed merry-go-round. Or maybe, as is so often the case in life, they were merely the agents of a random evil luck. Whatever the reason, I had incurred their wrath and it was an awful thing to contemplate, as I had sufficient leisure to do from recess till the sounding of the final bell. I had been warned. One of them, Bingo I believe, had thrust his face in mine and advised me of the "ass pounding" in store at day's end.

Squirmy with fright, I divided my remaining hours between anxious speculations on the limits of pain and frantic hatchings of all manner of reckless and utterly unworkable flights. None of the latter, I was obliged to conclude, had any merit whatsoever. The hands of the clock ticked a steady, remorseless beat, sounds of time running out. My invention was exhausted. I was trapped. Until, providentially, it struck me that, as with so many conundrums, the key to the answer lay in the question itself. How to escape? Through the means provided, of course. What could be plainer?

You can fill in the rest for yourself. But unless you have shared the experience of a thirteenth-hour deliverance from some private cataclysm, there is no way to convey the exhilaration I felt, the triumph, closeted at the top of the tube while the Heath brothers and all their cretinous minions sweep-searched the school and playground twice over, their fuddled growls ("Where's he at?—fucker—kick 'is fuckin' ass—find 'im") an intoxicating symphony rising up the funnel and settling in my delighted, not to say immensely thankful, ears.

Tell me: Can any drab textbook or simpering schoolmarm, fussy little old lady of either gender, offer a keener lesson in the dynamics of problem solving? The answer is self-evident. Allow me, then, to move along in time and place to another illustration, in this case a budding comprehension of what we commonly call human nature.

With my promotion to junior high there came, quite by chance, a simultaneous progress in the alternative instructional mode I propose here as a matter of deliberate course for the contemporary educator. Fire escapes of the sort I have described are manifestly out of architectural fashion. But every modern school comes equipped with heating tunnels, narrow and dusty passages that weave like constricted arteries through the corpus of a building and dispatch tiny tributaries to each room, conduits for the flow of dry institutional air. And these, really, are all the enterprising pedagogue needs.

In junior high, those of us who packed a lunch were banished at noon hour to a dungeonlike boiler room, I suppose on the administrative assumption that anyone unfit for a home-cooked or cafeteria meal would certainly exhibit barnyard manners best removed from public display. So there we fed, squatted on the floor, backs to a carbonized cinder-block wall, eating in the cowed silence that comes with a child's morose recognition of his place on the bottom rung of the social ladder. Sour garnish, that insight, to an already juiceless meal.

On a far wall of this sorry, sooty room was a mysterious aperture, dark and gaping like a wide-open mouth. Courage, even elementary curiosity, had been so wrung out of most of us that no one ever approached it. No one till I. Like the off-limits fire escape, it emitted its own magnetizing tug, and inevitably, in solitary, quaking, after-hours probes, I found myself within it. Not far, you understand; I was not that valorous. A few feet into it was like a descent into another element, total immersion, the blackness stroking every pore.

Naturally, at the times I chose for these tentative explorations the basement was empty, but one afternoon I heard a terrifying fall of footsteps at the stair, hard bass voices preceding them. Abruptly and surely, my all-fours stance lent new meaning to the term petrification. From where I crouched, a yard or so deep in the tunnel's enveloping darkness, it was impossible to see who was there, but soon enough their voices gave them away. It was the janitors, two avuncular old farts who, at lunch hour, liked to josh and tease us after the fashion of adults sunk to servile station themselves, and left with nothing to torment but curs and kids. My petitions to heaven went unheeded, for in a moment I heard the sound of fat rumps settling onto creaky chairs. There was nothing to do but wait. And eavesdrop. And what I overheard I could scarcely believe:

"Get a peek at Lyman up there in the lounge?" (Miss Jeanette Lyman was the dewy young lady who taught us civics. Fresh from normal school, she was a curious anomaly among her nursing-home candidate colleagues.)

"Boy fuckin' howdy, did I."

"See her skirt ridin' halfway up her ass?"

"Bitch can't be wearin' no panties. Think I saw some gash."

"*Think!* If that ain't gash, a cat ain't got no ass. Looked like somebody took a ax up there."

"Haw."

"Christ, I'd like to thump the livin' shit right outta her."

"Hear she's bangin' that science teacher."

"Elliott? That needle-dicked little bugfucker? Nah."

" 's what I hear."

"Nah!"

"Tellin' ya what I hear."

"If that's the truth, then there ain't no justice, this world."

"Maybe you could coax her down here sometime. Give her a tour a the tunnels." (As you might imagine, this suggestion, even tendered in obvious jest, brought on a reflex spasm I had to struggle to contain.)

"I ever did, she'd find out quick what bangin's all about. Make her walk bowlegged for a month. Elliott! Jesus!"

And so on, for an hour or more, in similar poisoned vein. Eventually, Miss Lyman's indiscretions and lamentable tastes exhausted, they departed and I was able to make a cautious exit.

I was grateful, of course, for my luck in going undiscovered. And I was properly relieved. But after that first glimpse of the underside of human nature, a view markedly different from all we were conditioned to expect, there was not enough of either, not of gratitude or relief, to keep me from my now established post in the tunnel, hazards notwithstanding. There was too much to learn, too much by far. And as those astounding revelations and sour fancies unfolded, filtered though they were through the eyes of that spite-ridden pair, I began to see first my mentors, then all the adult world, through new and more discriminating eyes of my own. No longer could I listen to a Lyman monologue on civil law without reflection on the uncivil lawlessness of her baser passions. No easier was it to sit through an Elliott lecture on microorganisms without an image of his alleged micro-organ springing unbidden to mind. Nor was it possible anymore—particularly after spying one of the janitors in an act of desolate boiler-room onanism over the girdle section of a Sears catalog—to feel anything other than a cool contempt for those two pathetic, taunting chin-chuckers.

If the junior-high tunnel served for my undergraduate training, then the high-school heating ducts were the equivalent of a postdoctoral education. They were not, however, so easy to find, and I was well into my sophomore year before I discovered, during a rehearsal for some gaudy Easter pageant, a ladder bolted to the wall behind a tattered back curtain on the auditorium stage. From where I stood, it appeared to lead to nowhere. I was wrong. Like the fire escape, its summit was capped with a tiny, barely negotiable portal, but this one was unboarded and I managed to squeeze through.

And found myself in a spectral world of night, peopled by disembodied voices, queerly resonating, rising on the parched air of connective-tissue passages leading to every room in the building. I was no more courageous than I had been three years before, but without a doubt I was hopelessly addicted. By groping on hands and knees through the dark, I could make my way to each room's flue and, with sufficient attention, distinguish the sounds and voices issuing from it. The tunnels, I would ultimately discover, were like a shadow that described in perfect outline the building's contours. Soon, by touch and by measure of my awkward four-points crawl, I had internalized a map that led me unerringly to whichever room or office I cared to eavesdrop. And thus commenced an apprenticeship that was itself a shadow of the more conventional wisdoms dispensed a level below.

What did I learn from those vigils? Well, at least a dim perception of that which our subtlest philosophies and finest literatures attempt to unveil: the oftentimes startling distinction between those two imposters, appearance and reality. Once, echoing up out of a girls' lavatory were the unmistakable moans of two young ladies, cheerleaders reputedly the easy playthings of varsity heroes, locked in forbidden amorous games of their own. And more than once did I hear the squeals of barely pubescent girls as the band director, one Arne Carson, "fitted" them out in the uniforms closet. ("That tickle, little sweetheart?") Carson was a dwarfish man whose minikin skull linked by thin cord of neck to a swelling convex figure gave him the odd appearance of an upended exclamation point. He bore an uncanny resemblance to Napoleon, right down to the wisps of lank black hair laid over a twilighting forehead, and he was vain of the likeness. His most exalted public moments were in lead of the marching band, strutting out ahead in a glittery uniform festooned with silvery piping, lustrous brass, scarlet sash, a martinet with the absolute power to transform blissful silence into godawful din, deafening counterfeit of a Sousa march, with the snappy flick of his baton. But for me, after the secret watches above the uniforms closet, it would be forever impossible to uncouple the public and private man, to erase a vision of those nervous musician's fingers playing the nubs of girlish breasts like keys of priceless woodwind instruments.

Novel schooling, those tunnels afforded.

Most extraordinary of all, though, and easily most enlightening was a tangled little psychodrama unfolding around two rooms and three players—four, actually, with me as silent witness. The first actor, the catalyst, was a classmate of mine, Ronnie "Grunt" Slocum, a youth so hulking and with bones so knobby, and brows and jaw so prominent, he seemed to fall just this side of acromegaly. Farm bred, he was impoverished of any but the earthiest talents and appetites. He openly acknowledged a predeliction for bestiality, defending his tastes on the inarguable grounds that "cows don't tell." He was called Grunt, admiringly, because of his fabled ability to break wind at will and in a variety of pitches, or, some maintained, because of the peculiar sounds emanating from the bathroom stall he occupied for his punctual midmorning whack-off break. Equally admired was his ponderous size and strength, truly a Krakatoa of enormous latent force that evoked a cautious respect from his peers. Even the teachers skirted him warily, and his deportment, normally undomesticated anyway, nudged the frontiers of open defiance.

Once, in the faculty parking lot, I heard Grunt boldly announce the approach of Coach Finn, a habitual cigar chomper, with the homespun aphorism: "Must be gonna rain tonight. Here come a hawg with a shit cob hangin' out its mouth." Coach, who governed his athletes with the same iron authority Arne Carson did his tunesmiths, slunk on by. My acquaintance with Grunt flowered during our junior year, for we had adjoining seats in the classroom of Miss Samantha Quill, teacher of literature, poetess of some local renown, and second player in this drama.

Miss Quill was a fortyish spinster shackled, it was said, to a cranky, ailing, ancient mother perennially overlooked by death. Somewhat horsey-featured, with great accordion rows of stained teeth (rumor had it she smoked cigarettes) and leathery dun-colored skin, she was nonetheless trim and, in fact, rather well turned out. As teacher she was subscriber to the pebble-in-the-brook theory of pedagogy, the circular ripples of her high-minded idealism reaching on to infinity. She seemed to understand literature solely as a vehicle for moral betterment, and each day we were favored with a worthy excerpt from a poem or an uplifting fiction. For a good share of the period, we anatomized the passage earnestly. "What does this *mean?*" she prodded us, forehead furrowed in missionary zeal. "How can we apply it in our daily *lives?*" Tennyson's celebrated admonition to strive, seek, and so on was translated into the lesson of more effort on our homework. The clash of Arnold's ignorant nocturnal armies came to her, and thence to us, as an antiwar message. In her hands the Truth of Keats's noble equation became the doctrine of the

Methodist Church, the Beauty whatever happened to appeal to her pedestrian tastes at the time.

Those two, Grunt Slocum and Samantha Quill, were on a collision course unsuspected by either, the shock of which would have a lasting and, I believe, salutary effect on me, a mere spectator at the impact. We had spent the better part of a term in close exegesis of one of Miss Quill's favorite works, *The Lady of the Lake,* and now the moment had arrived for examination. While she sat smiling dreamily into a volume of Romantic poetry, we sweated over the sheet of incomprehensible questions, panic mounting at the blank pages of our blue books and the accelerating hands on the clock. One of the more inane questions, the full thrust of which has mercifully escaped me, concerned a plotting element, what the Lady was actually engaged in doing at some given point in the narrative. Grunt, I noticed, had been busily scribbling, and after a moment I felt an insistent tug at the elbow and turned to see him hunched over, mouth a widening hole in his face, beefy torso shivering in mirth. He slipped me his blue book, held up the number of fingers correspondent to the question on the Lady's activities, and shuttered an eye in the broadest of winks. In pencil he had written: "She fingerfucked herself."

That was the answer convulsed him so. I mustered up an appreciative grin (he was something of a friend, after all), returned the blue book, and thought nothing more of it. Later, leaving the room I again felt Grunt's hand on my elbow. This time it was damp with sweat. "Holy fuckin' gawd," he groaned. *"I forgot to erase it!"*

The next day, Miss Quill's manner was studiedly frigid, and her eyes never once fell on our corner of the room. At the bell Grunt made a desperate lunge for the door, but well before he could reach it a voice uncommonly stiff-spined for addressing the likes of him declared, "Ronald, you are to report directly to this room after school."

For the remainder of the day, he speculated tiresomely on the reckoning to come, growling threats and averring he was not of a temper to "take no shit." I, along with his other cohorts, attended to these bellicose outpourings with the stupified fascination of onlookers at a runaway blaze. But it was hard to square the menacing tones with the chalkiness that appeared to have invaded his ruddy cheeks and with the trace of a quiver in the meaty red lips even as the slurred warnings spilled off them. At the ordained hour, he set out down the hall in his undulating, north-forty roll, jaws bunched, scowling, fists clasping and unclasping at his sides. I waited till he was out of sight and then made for the auditorium, scrambled up the ladder and through the tunnel to my post at the airshaft above the room.

Enter the final player. By name: Lester A. "Doc" Corrigan; by title: high-school principal; by station: this production's star. Doc Corrigan was known to a handful of us on the outlaw fringe of the school as Pruneface, a name inspired by an unfortunate resemblance to a comic-strip villain of the day. The bone structure of his face was narrow, the line of chin weak, and from it a series of terraced fleshy folds depended in ripply waves to a withered neck. Hence Pruneface. At that time he was deep into middle age, still slender overall but with scrawny shoulders and disproportionately wide hips. He had taken a degree at a teachers college somewhere, come directly to the high school as track coach and social studies instructor, labored for countless summers over a master's degree, and at the conclusion of this academic odyssey, arrived at last at the Ithaca of his principalship. Established for life. He was known as a stern disciplinarian and an indefatigable social climber, perhaps natural reflections of his narrow schooling. Married to a woman as ambitious and indelibly ugly as he, they lived in a modest home befitting their means but strategically located on the same street reserved for attorneys, physicians, dentists, bankers, prosperous haberdashers—persons of substance. He belonged to the Episcopal church, that charmingly noncommittal faith; the Elks, country, and Rotary clubs, the latter of which he once addressed on the somewhat capacious topic: "The Future of Education in America Today." I had learned all this, you understand, not so much by calculated investigation as by natural osmosis, the way one learns any and every thing in a small town.

On this afternoon of Grunt's tribunal (to which I could only be auditory beholder, imagination summoned to plug the visual gap), I heard a door swing open, footsteps, then Doc's suitably melancholy greeting to the injured custodian of the good, beautiful, and true. I heard her get-right-down-to-brass-tacks reply: "Lester, I don't think I have to *take* this sort of thing." A rustle of paper, the wicked blue book, no doubt. Some harrumphing. Some prefatory throat-clearing. Out of Grunt, nothing yet.

"Well," began the inquisitor, disarmingly mild, "what are we going to do with you, Ronald?"

"All's I wanna say is—"

"You just hold your foul tongue," Doc barked (and I intend the verb quite literally, for there was an explosive guttural quality to his voice, reminiscent of a riled hound). "Shut up that filthy mouth. I'll tell you when to talk. You're in big trouble, young fella, whether you know it or not."

If he was intimidated by Grunt's fearsome aspect, there was nothing in that combative bawl to give him away. For an instant, dim misgivings plucked at me but I shook them off. Grunt was merely biding his time. Soon enough his turn would come.

"I don't think I have to put up with that kind of . . . of . . . *slime,*" Miss Quill volunteered, a trifle redundantly it seemed to me.

"No, you most certainly don't," Doc affirmed, spacing each word for maximum abhorrent effect. "Disgusting things like that . . . that . . . well, you can bet your bottom dollar we're gonna do something about it. And pronto."

They both appeared to be circling wolfishly around the forbidden word, eager to pounce but wary too, as if voiced it might be possessed of some demonic power.

"It would be different if it was a wrong answer," she bore on, "or a difference of opinion. I could take that. But this *filth.* . . ."

Words failed her, and I would not have been at all surprised to hear next the sounds of a crumply swoon. Instead came some deep-throated sympathetic gurgles and the gentle advice, "Sam, why don't you just wait for me down to the office. I'll handle things here. Run along now. Be there in a minute or two."

I'm sure I caught some dolorous whimpering before the door shut behind her.

Apart from his aborted exordium, Grunt had uttered not a word. *Now,* I thought, breathless with anticipation, *now it comes.* I could picture the two of them alone, man to man, glaring at each other, the hostility a third presence thickening the air in the room. But it was Doc the first to resume, his voice modulated in a curious blend of ice and pity.

"Way I see it, Ronald, you just don't care. Don't care about that fine woman out there cryin' her heart out. You don't care what you've done to her. Do you?"

From the pause that followed, it was clear the question was not rhetorical. He expected an answer, and so of course did I. The pause lengthened. I yearned for an occult power to unseal those liver lips, animate that slab of tongue and set it to fashioning a reply capturing once and for all our sublime collective scorn for that misshapen worm and all he stood for. Have at it, Grunt!

I was rewarded by a sound of the sort cattle make under a branding iron, toneless croak of injury and astonishment. Grunt was weeping. Great, heaving sobs. I trembled myself, but in confounded disbelief. Grunt? Weeping? A corner of my world began to topple.

After a time the sobs dwindled to a breath-sucking whinny, and then he gave vent to a sniveling confession the more bewildering to me for its ring of sincerity. No one liked him. He had no friends. His rural upbringing inspired sneers, his disastrous appearance derisive hoots. He lacked grace, charm, even a rudimentary wit. Girls shrank at his approach. Dogs bayed at his passing. He was, in sum, unloved and alone.

Throughout it all, Doc kept a wise silence, and when it was finally done I heard some thoughtful pacing. Then some jowl-clucking. At last he said, "Ronald, in my thirty years in the education business I've seen a lot of things. Some of 'em good, some not so good. I picked up a little bit along the way 'bout human nature. Got its good side and its not so good one. Sorta like life. We got to expect some bad in it, but thank the Lord there's a whole lot more that's good." (Where, I wondered, was this contrapuntal wheeze leading?)

"We're all of us a little like that, 'specially your male of the species. What we got to learn here in school, us males of the species," (obviously enamored of the word, he pronounced it in rhyme with *feces*) "is not just our ABC's—course they're mighty important too—but some self-control too. We got to learn to show some respect for the weaker sex. Y'see, they're not used to some of the things we are. They're more what you call sensitive, more, more—" (his vocabulary manifestly so far beyond Grunt's puny grasp, he groped for just the right communicative term)—"ladylike, y'might say. They get hurt real easy. That's the way of nature.

" 'Nother thing—and a real good sign I see in you, kinda keeps my faith up in human nature, which is a wonder I haven't lost, all the things I seen these years. Anyway, 'nother thing we got to learn is when we done something wrong to feel sorry. And to say it. And mean it. When you're sorry," he explained patiently, "shows you got some human feelings left in you. That's all that counts, long run. Human feelings."

From its rambling quality it was plain this monologue came unrehearsed, though it had the empty peal of something delivered in variant form many times over. For a good quarter of an hour it maundered along, and its upshot, the bottom line for Grunt, was an atonement so boneless it must have staggered the repentant offender with its saintly charity. Grunt was to compose a formal apology to the wounded Miss Quill. As further penance he was to serve a six weeks' janitorial servitude scrubbing out johns after class hours. ("Get a fella down on his hands and knees," he was advised, "workin' up an honest sweat, he's got some time to think over what's right and decent and what's not.")

"Now," Doc concluded, "I'm goin' to the office and tell that heartbroken woman down there how it is you feel—way you're sorry and so forth—and what you're gonna do to make it right. Meantime, you scat on down to the basement and find Ward. Tell him what's up, how you're gonna be workin' for him and so on, and tell him I'll talk to him 'bout it later. Sound fair to you?"

Grunt produced a sound in echo of his name. A chair scraped the floor. Feet shuffled. The door opened and fell shut. Court, it seemed, was closed. And though I felt sick with disgust over Grunt's lickspittle performance, I had no leisure just then for disenchanted reflection. There was a denouement remaining and I didn't want to miss it. Fast as four limbs could propel me, I scuttled through the tunnels to the shaft opening onto Doc's office.

And arrived in time to catch that heart-sundered woman's fervent wish: "Well, I sure hope and pray you put the fear of God in that dimwit's dirty brain."

"Oh, you can bet I did," was the silky, if somewhat evasive, reply.

"What he needs is somebody to take a strap to him," she said, her *s*'s hissed in passionate outrage.

Doc struck an atonal chord: "Hmmm."

"Well, Lester, *did* you take a strap to him?"

"Sam, believe me I gave him just exactly what he had comin' and then some. I know how to handle these country boys. Ought to. Reared on the farm myself, y'know." (A tolerant, mellow chuckle here.)

"But did you read that awful—that des*pic*able—word he wrote right there in his blue book? Bold-faced . . . just shameless . . . not a shred of decency in him . . ."

Persistent woman, Miss Quill. She was after some blood, would have been happiest wielding the bastinado herself, I believe. And that word! Odious, mesmerizing, poison word! It was all I could do to restrain myself from enunciating it for her delectation, projecting it syllable-spread through the shaft like a ghostly, demon-driven reminder of all the hot lawless appetites loose in the world: *fin-ger fuck! Finger fuck!*

Firmly, in tones of closure, Doc said, "You're not gonna have any more trouble with that boy again. You got my guarantee on that one." Then, softening, almost playful: "C'mon, Samsie, cool down. Relax a little. You're all tensed up."

"I don't know how anybody could relax. After what's happened."

"Sure y'can. Sure. Sure."

His voice was as thick and viscous as melting wax, as though the hole it leaked from were sinking into the chin, and the chin into the rubbery folds beneath it, the whole bottom half of the face vanishing like a ship on a far horizon fading into sky and sea. I had never heard that voice from him, never. Something very odd was going on down there, unforeseen in my most lurid imaginings, something wondrous, and it occurred to me suddenly just how lucky I was, how favored by fortune and chance to bear witness to it.

First there was a series of movements whose peculiar sounds defied visualization, then the unmistakable click of the lock on the door turning. And then—mirabile dictu!—zippers unzipping, stays unstaying.

"Doc, no, no, we mustn't."

"Please, Samsie . . . it's okay . . . c'mon . . . please . . ."

Some more of this, some urgent moans, and then the gaspy, cinematic yielding: "Oh, yes, Doc. Yes, yes, yes!"

THE NEXT DAY GRUNT REPORTED to his retinue of admirers. We were treated to an elaborately embroidered fantasy: his towering courage, reckless insubordination, the feeble force of his antagonists. He reprised the scene for us, declaiming all three parts: Doc's and Miss Quill's in high-pitched, lily-livered squeaks, his own in low Bogart snarl (". . . an' he sez . . . an' then I sez right back at 'im . . ."). On the fringe of his worshipful circle, I said nothing.

Miss Quill continued her relentless pursuit and dissection of elevating sentiments. Later in the year she took a fancy to the work of Thornton Wilder, and one day we chipped away at the banal concluding line of *The Bridge of San Luis Rey* that purports to link love and death. Not trusting myself, I kept clear of that discussion too (perhaps just as well, for if I remember correctly she read it as incentive to regular church attendance). There were, you see, more episodes in Doc's office of the sort I have described. Many more.

As for Principal Corrigan, he carried on presiding magisterially over his school. He delivered inspiriting addresses at pep rallies, and more thoughtful ones—though still spiced with a dash of irrepressible humor—at general assemblies. By year's end I heard he was elected secretary-treasurer of the Rotary.

None of the players had changed in the slightest, none but I, the witness. Nothing was the same again. Life and all its curious pageantry came to me now through a different prism, crimped and canted, as if it were reflected off a pool of stagnant pond water shimmering under a hard, angular light. Sneers rode the fluid crests of smiles. At the snap of a finger, sorrow masks dissolved into gargoyle grins. On second glance, a solemn, inturned air might slide over into vacant gape, or righteous smirk, or fierce glare. Everything was aslant, nothing quite the way it seemed. But with this private dawning of wisdom came also the genesis of a loneliness, an unbreachable apartness from others that shadows me still and will, I fear, for the remainder of my allotted days.

Which is not to say any of it was occasion for adolescent weltschmerz or a precocious cynicism. Quite the contrary, the priceless gift of the tunnels kindled in me everything the purest pedagogy hopes to arouse: curiosity, persistence, patience, concentration, memory, an ardent thirst for knowledge (albeit of a somewhat skewed variety) tempered by a healthy respect for all of life's dark and convoluted mysteries, coiled as the tunnels themselves and locked in a blackness so final no eye could ever hope to penetrate. Isn't that, finally, a definition of the fashionable phrase "learning experience"? And if it is, that is the reason I present myself as their staunchest advocate.

To all our educators—teachers on the firing line, administrators hatching tactics, school boards, concerned citizens' committees, legislative task forces, presidential commissions, all busily plotting grander strategies—I offer this advice: Take your gifted young and point them in the direction of the tunnels. Turn them loose. But if you do, a humble caveat. Don't be dismayed at what they uncover, for it may include the regrettable truth that there is more in our nature to despise than ever to admire.

Part

THREE

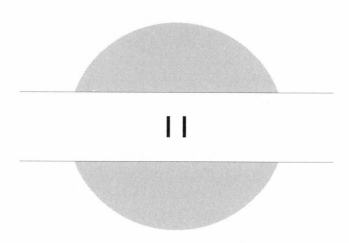

11

9:00 A.M., CST, Monday, September 7. Labor Day.

For Michael, skull throbbing, eyes bleary, mouth gin-scorched, stomach moiling, the day's labors commenced with the alarm's 6:00 A.M. wake-up jangle. One shower, two aspirins, four ounces of V8 juice, three coffees, and ninety minutes later an airport limo whisked him toward O'Hare, and thirty minutes after that (the holiday traffic being relatively thin at this hour) deposited him at the United gate. Another hour, and here he was, twenty thousand feet in the air, winging north and east, a Michigan course. Beyond the sliver of window, the sun laid a glaze rich like orange marmalade across a perfectly cloudless sky. Down below, the lake shimmered like a vast sheet of polished glass. The plane was passenger-sparse, the seats around him blessedly empty. Absolved for this brief moment of the burden of gratuitous chitchat. Fortune's charity.

He was feeling a little better, but not much. God, where was his head last night? Multiple martinis, pizza, beer—what was he thinking? He couldn't be sure, couldn't say. A muddle of thoughts, images, impressions, even—yes—emotions crowded in on him. He tried to sort them out.

Beginning with this curious, contradictory woman, this Lizabeth Seaver. About her, he conceded, Norman had been right, or at least partly right. Attractive, without a doubt. Which established nothing. The world was full of attractive women. More than enough of *them* to go around. This one, though, seemed somehow different in a slippery way he could neither grasp nor define. Maybe it was her manner, delicate as lace. Or her voice, soothing as an herbal tea. Or the madly innocent smile. Or the gleam of childlike trust and wonderment he believed he detected in those star sapphire eyes.

Unless, of course, he was mistaken, and she was just another hormone-charged tramp looking for a partner to heat her mattress, and he happened to be handy. He hoped not. And though he had no evidence to the contrary other than instinct (which, as a consultant, he knew was no evidence at all), he didn't think so. For she seemed to project an aura almost of (could he call it chaste? All right, call it that) chaste spirituality, in spite of and in stark contrast to the blunt carnal offer. That offer struck him now, on sober reflection, as the spontaneous outpouring of a generous, genuine tenderness that had nothing to do with appetite. Entirely natural surge of a rare, natural electricity. Heart-stitched appeal for a linkage more spirit than flesh.

Either that, or these were merely fanciful imaginings, adolescent daydreams, romantic delusions, and he the greater fool for entertaining them. It was baffling. Troubling. Outside the range of his experience, all of it.

So in the tiny block of unoccupied time remaining to him, and by a deliberate effort of will, he shifted his thoughts and reflections to Norman. Mostly were they vexed, those thoughts, at Norman's abrupt ducking out last night, leaving him to shoulder the awkward weight of commiseration, conversation. Abandoning him. It wasn't *his* responsibility. *He* wasn't the one invited.

Equally bewildering—maybe even more so—was his discovery this morning of Norman (normally long since up and bent to his desk, wrapped in a noxious swirl of cigarette smoke) soundly sleeping. When Michael descended the stairs for the perfunctory parting words, that's exactly how he found him, sprawled across the bed, facedown, arms and legs spread-eagled like a drowning victim, head buried under a pillow. He tiptoed over to the desk, scrawled a farewell note with a number to call if an emergency arose, laid some bills alongside it. His glance fell on a stack of typed pages. He stooped over, skimmed them hastily, turning each page noiselessly, one cautious eye on the slumbering figure on the bed, puzzled and deeply disturbed by what he read.

Confounded by all the riddles of all the events of the past twenty-four hours. Wearied of following them too far, parsing them too closely, tracking the alien landscapes of alien emotions.

And so it was something of a relief to see the orderly files of whitecaps breaking on the Michigan shoreline below, to feel the familiar popping in the ears, to hear the announcement of the plane's imminent arrival at Grand Rapids' Kent County Airport and the cheery reminder of the time, eastern now, an hour vanished. He set his watch accordingly. But on the long, slow glide to earth, he caught himself thinking of the elastic nature of time, warped by invisible and wholly arbitrary boundaries capable of thrusting you magically into the future or dragging you back to the past, annoyed at himself for indulging in the kind of profitless meditations his father was, evidently, so fond of.

Soon the plane was on the ground, and all such dreamy thoughts were dispatched in the bustle of collecting bags, securing a rental car, getting directions to the Hilton, locating it, checking in, unpacking, going over his slender notes scribbled during yesterday's characteristically terse phone instructions out of the Bunker ("Be in Grand Rapids, Michigan, tomorrow . . . Hilton, noon, no later . . . doing a college up there . . . Russ Marks contact you, fill you in . . ."). The comforting sense of attending to business. And by the time the call came through, 12:10 by his adjusted watch, he felt revived, recovered, himself again. Eager to get to it. He said his name into the phone, and a booming voice came back at him: "Mike, Russ Marks here. You been waitin' long?"

"Not long. I just got in."

"Same with me. I'm in their coffee shop. Whyn't you pop on down."

"Be right there."

"Attaboy."

Michael had never met this Russ Marks, but he'd heard about him. Manhattan-based, a VP, top gun on the sales force, legendary closer. And he knew the type: shrewd, purposeful, hurried, aggressive, but glib and easy and earthy too, when the occasion demanded. A Stoltz cheerleader, machine-stamped from the original drummer mold. Peddler arrived at the pinnacle, kind who's learned to call a used car a pre-owned vehicle and watched his career soar from there. Kind whose card doubtless read *Russell "Russ" Marks* ("You can call me Russ, pal"). Still very heavy-duty, for a project of this obviously limited magnitude. Michael wondered what was up.

No problem whatsoever, picking him out of the lunch-hour crowd. A barrel-shaped, fiftyish man in flashy Euro-cut suit that camouflaged the paunch not at all, boozer's bloated, blistery cheeks, pouchy eyes, shock of midnight-black hair suspiciously absent of even the slightest fleck of gray and slicked back off a meager shelf of brow—exactly as he'd pictured him, extrapolating image from voice. Also a relentless grinner, as Michael soon discovered, still grinning at him long after the reflex hand clutch, the reintroductions, the routine pleasantries; at the waitress who appeared to take their orders (coffee and English muffin for Michael, his stomach marginal yet, plate of eggs, sausage, and hash browns for himself, and in studiedly casual afterthought, a "Mother Mary," as he called it, with the winked vindication, "Too much holiday whoopee"); and, when she was gone, at nothing in particular, the entire room perhaps, sanctioning it with a sweep of his all-purpose grin.

And then he fixed it on Michael and said, "So, Mike Woodrow. Been hearin' a lot about you lately, out at the Bunker." Adding, after a theatrically timed beat, "Most of it repeatable," and favoring him with another broad wink.

"That's always good to know."

"Word is you're a hitter. Got a real flair for this racket."

"That's even better," Michael said carefully. Something going on here, this needless stroking. Tread cautiously.

"Gets better'n that. I got the good news bean to drop on you." Another studied pause, pleasured grin widening to the very portals of his ears.

"What would that be?"

"Been authorized to tell you scrub the "acting" off your IM. No more chicken colonel. You're the straight goods now."

Marks stuck out a congratulatory hand, and Michael took it, second clasping in under a quarter of an hour, pumped it, and thanked him. He was pleased, of course, and gratified, but not terribly surprised. He figured it was coming, though maybe not quite this soon.

"You're on the escalator goin' no place but up, Mike."

"Thanks for the vote of confidence," Michael said. "And the welcome news."

"Hey, nothin'. That's the best part of this job. Easy part. Hard part's the work." This homely sentiment delivered with a big, chesty guffaw, to go with the trumpet voice and durable grin.

Their food arrived. Marks took down half the Bloody Mary in a fast gulp, then fell to his steaming plate with a vengeance. A big eater, fiercely focused. Michael nibbled at the muffin, sipped the coffee, and waited. Not patiently. Good news was fine, but in this business you were only as good as your last project, and what he needed now were some particulars on the present one. Eventually, around a mouthful of sausage, Marks got to them.

"Okay, here's what we got here. Place called Hobbes College. Private, church-funded, good rep. But runnin' in the deep red, leakin' money. Racked up a two-mil-plus deficit last year alone, and the deacons gettin' a serious case of the chapped ass. I promised 'em we could develop a plan, get 'em well inside three years, tops."

"Off two mil in ink? That's pretty optimistic, wouldn't you say?"

"Don't mean shit. This one's a throwaway. Strictly analysis and recommendations. Toast without the jam. Tellya the truth here, Mike, surprise the hell outta me if it ever got to implementation."

Marks had disappeared the last of the sausage, moved on to the hash browns. Watching him, Michael was fascinated by his ability to fork in food, chew, swallow, stifle a rising burp, speak—all the while maintaining the slick grin. He wondered idly if they'd bury him one day with that smarmy grin stubbornly pasted on his chilling face, the cosmetician's best efforts at a solemn departing dignity all for nothing. To smother such whimsical thoughts he asked, "Why do you think that?"

"It's the president. Broad. Name of Hilda Rostovich. Dr. Rostovich, to you'n me. Your basic iron maiden. Y'know—cobwebs in the pussy, good fuck croak her?"

Michael looked away, smothering disgust now, in place of the whimsy. As far as he could tell, there wasn't the slightest redeeming quality to this coarse, repugnant man. Which is probably why he was a Stoltz VP. "Yet she agreed to the analysis," Michael said.

"Yeah, kickin' and clawin' all the way. Listen, it was about as hard a sell as I come up against in years." The memory of its difficulty was punctuated by a fork stabbing the air. "It was the board finally laid it on her: shape up or haul ass. See, she got it in her head they can heal themselves. Y'know, study committees, task forces, that kind of featherhead professor shit. Like those weenies could find their way out of a phone booth."

Remembering his father, Michael said, "I know what you mean."

"So Dr. R. could end up bein' her own dragon."

"What are the project parameters?"

"Maintenance, custodial, grounds, food service, dorms, support personnel. It's all in the file."

"Instructional staff?"

"Unh-uh. Teaching's a no-no. One of her conditions. Any payroll but that."

"And we're supposed to salvage two mil out of *that?*"

Marks shrugged. Not his problem.

"All right. Who's the team?"

Marks rattled off three names, all of them unfamiliar, one identified as a green pea. They weren't making it easy. "And who's chiefing?" Michael asked him. "Max?"

Plate cleaned, Marks put down the fork and toweled his lips with a cloth napkin. Behind it, peering over it, eyes atwinkle, he said, "As of this morning, Mr. Stroiker's no longer with us."

"Max got his card pulled?" Michael said, referencing the commonplace AS&A firing procedure: a home office executive materialized out of nowhere to demand your air travel card, often as not at the airport, on your way to what you assumed was your next assignment, to add a touch of ignominy to the dumping.

Marks folded the napkin carefully, replaced it on the table. "We prefer to think of it as leaving to pursue other interests," he said. He paused, let the grin take a nasty upward tilt. "Like a job."

"Sorry to hear that," Michael said, and he supposed he was, though not enough to feel anything other than a mild, detached pity, the kind you'd feel at the news of the passing of a distant cousin you never much liked anyway. It was the nature of their profession. Came with the territory.

"Don't be. Stroiker's a loser. We been carryin' him too long as it is. So this one's all yours."

Marks reached down, unlatched the briefcase at his feet, removed two bulging manila folders bound with rubber bands, and handed them to Michael. "There's the skinny. Everything you need to get rollin'. Your people be in by six. Give you a chance to bone up on it before you boys huddle tonight." He glanced at his watch, made a tuckered-out face. "Well, gotta run. Catch the puddle-jumper to Milwaukee. Over there we got us a real jackpot, I can close it."

"What's the project?"

Marks looked momentarily distressed at the breach of company protocol. Ask us no questions, lies we'll supply in abundance. He said, "C'mon, Mike. You're an IM now. You know better'n to ask." There was a hint of a threat in the patched grin, but he softened it with a confidential wink and added significantly, "Tellya this much, though. You do good here, and it'll be your next one."

And remembering now Norman's sardonic, oddly prophetic "salvation for pay" remark from last night, Michael said, "Then I guess I'll just have to do some good here, won't I."

THE FIRST JARRING SCREAK was incorporated effortlessly, instantaneously, through the subterranean mind's gift for quicksilver improvisation, into that particular moment's production of the antic theater of dreams, and the fractured drama took an abrupt and altogether different, though no less surreal, turn. But when it sounded a second time, third, the gift faltered, failed him, and the curtain fell, the playlet evaporated, lost to the impenetrable chambers of sleep.

Simultaneously startled and dazed, he rolled over onto his back, groggy-eyed, disoriented (no underside of a bunk directly overhead, no bars at the door, no cellblock bawl, none of the sweat, smoke, urine, lingering flatus, and other assorted perfumes of massed male stink), blinked the fiction of the world outside his head back into being. He swung his legs over the side of the bed. Chinos and T-shirt lay in a heap on the floor. He pulled them on and climbed the stairs, tracking the source of the grating screak (transformed now to waspish buzz broken by micro-measures of silence, aural water torture) to the front door. On the other side of which stood Ms. Lizabeth Seaver, none other, finger on the bell and sporting a smile strained and half-apologetic, but only by half. Outfitted all in white, jeans and sleeveless linen blouse both dazzlingly white. Enchanting vision in the soft morning light.

Norman knuckle-ground his eyes, motioned her in. "Let me guess," he mumbled. "This time the sky really has fallen."

"I woke you, didn't I," she said, voicing flatly what he supposed was so painfully obvious it nullified any notion of denial.

"What time is it?"

"Little after nine."

"Yes, to answer your implied question. And a good thing too. I never sleep this late. Never."

"Even on holidays?"

"Even then," he said and, the day coming back to him and with it a shard of his wits, added, "Even on this patently misnomered one. Which by rights should be called Leisure Day. Or maybe Sloth Day."

Some of the tightness seemed to ease out of her smile, gentling it. "Then you're not too . . . upset? My getting you up? Being here?"

"Gratified. Cheered. Honored. But hardly upset. Tell me, what can I do for you?"

"You can come to breakfast with me. Talk to me. I need someone to talk to, Norman. I'll drive. I'll buy."

An unmistakable urgency frayed the edges of the normally silken voice. She stared at him anxiously. Were the eyes misting? He couldn't be sure. To lighten things (for what did he know of a woman's tears?), he said, "Free food, free transportation, charming company—who could refuse an offer like that?" He was conscious now of his own voice emerging rasped and gravelled, informed by the three decks of reds vanished in the solitude of night, torched and sucked absently and forgotten, dwindling to ash-heavy stubs in the ceramic tray as the memories embalmed in a tiny pocket of the heart sprang to life, miraculously reanimated in a torrent of words. Conscious too of his rumpled clothes, sour breath, the general fetid bouquet of himself. So he said also, "That is, if you're willing to wait a few minutes. While I clean up."

"I'll wait."

Half an hour later they were pointed west on Ogden Avenue, Lizabeth behind the wheel of her sleek Camaro, Norman gazing through the windshield, unfailingly wonderstruck by the mercantile blight framing the street, by the architectural wilderness of taverns, eateries, fueling stations, bowling palaces, roller-ramas, stop 'n shops, cut-rate emporiums, factory outlets, and by the marquees with their cryptic messages calculated to incite a feeding frenzy of purchase, acquisition, consumption. *Buy! Drink! All-U-Can Eat! Cheap! Wholesale! Nothing Down! 90 Days No Interest! Guaranteed! Hurry!* Out of that thicket he spotted on a corner up ahead a bold block-lettered sign announcing the Garden of Eatin', and in scrolled subtitle the coy assurance of Heavenly Food and Beverages. "There," he said.

"There?"

"There."

"You're sure?"

"Absolutely. Any place that bills itself as paradise can't be all bad."

"You're the guest," she said, executing a deft cross-traffic turn and swinging the car into a narrow lot fronting the Garden's weathered frame exterior which, up close, bore the suspect look of a converted residential dwelling. Its interior was as murky as a cavern; its conditioned air clammy and condiment-rich; its dining space, gradually emergent to their adjusting visions, a long rectangular-shaped room crammed with oilcloth-draped tables, a couple of them occupied by sullen-looking patrons, the rest empty. They took a table near a small, windowed alcove, to catch some of the splinters of outside light. A gum-chomping waitress ambled out of the gloom, produced menus and coffee pot from which, unbidden, she splashed their cups, inquiring, "Know what ya want?"

"We'll need a little time," Norman said. "To look over your fare."

"You got it."

Predictably, the Garden's menu was replete with all manner of inventive wordplay on the presiding motif: Adam's Ribs, Serpent's Sting Red Hots, Eve's Own Apple Dumplings, and, under beverages, a Tree of Knowledge Margarita. Scanning it, Norman remarked, "Biblical comestibles. Unbearably clever."

"Maybe we should have stayed in Hinsdale."

"No, this is right. It's always instructive to discover the latest enterprise zones of the merchant soul."

A small, indulgent smile creased her troubled face. "What a trip you are, Norman."

No response occurred to him. Fortunately, none required, for the waitress reappeared and took their order, and only moments later the chef, apparently possessed of chefly powers of prescience, delivered it. "Getcha anything else?" the waitress asked, gum wad temporarily suspended, though still visible along a fang of molar. They shook their heads, negative unison. Back into the murk she went.

"Can't fault the service," Norman said.

Lizabeth regarded his matched pair of red hots and sides of slaw and fries doubtfully. "Peculiar choice for breakfast."

And Norman, memory serving up one of the numberless Stateville breakfasts of slightly rancid powdered eggs, Froot Loops, tepid milk, lime Jell-O, white bread untoasted (the toasters forever down) and with the consistency of a damp sponge, savoring it all again in memory, merely replied, "A gastronomic quirk."

"I imagine you're hungry, though. After last night's disaster."

"Somewhat," he said truthfully and, indicating her skimpy muffin, "Clearly you're not."

"No."

"Is that what's behind this morning's invitation? Atonement for last night?"

"Partly."

"You shouldn't worry about it, you know. Accidents will happen, as the comforting old bromide assures us. For myself, I had an excellent time."

"It's not the ruined dinner bothering me."

"What, then?"

"Well . . . ," she began. Hesitated. Lit a cigarette. Emitted a funnel of blue smoke at the water-spotted ceiling. Shifted nervously in her chair (to Norman a curiously sensual motion, as if she were employing those slim haunches to buff its surface). Lowered her eyes, for certain moistening now at the corners, prelude to some painful revelation. Yet none came.

"Yes?" he prompted.

"After you left I . . ." Another hesitancy.

"Yes?"

"I acted the perfect fool."

"And just how did you do that?"

She told him, the account of her brash nocturnal proposition spilling out in a purgative rush, shame's aphasia suddenly routed, the narrative rich in detail, annotation, in "he saids" and "then I saids," as if its meticulous reconstruction might somehow illuminate motive, vindicate conduct, expunge guilt, concluding at last, defeatedly, "Worse than fool. Perfect slut."

Norman had listened, saying nothing, face composed in an attitude of patient commiseration. Listened, thoughts straying, behind that sympathetic veil, to the plate of red hots before him, resisting the urge to lift one to his mouth (how long had it been since he'd eaten?—twenty-four hours, the routine tin of sardines at that), tear into it chomping, gnawing, teeth grinding. The way the waitress assaulted her gum, the prison way, without regard for manners or breeding or decorum, if anything a brutish defiance of all the civilized conventions forsaken that side of the walls. Confidant with mouth bulging with weiner, lips streaked with mustard, bead of relish glistening on the chin. Listened, but discomfited by all such confessionals, having lived too long by the joint caution to dodge, twist, fabricate, manipulate, but always, always hold your mud. And now it was his turn to deliver some comforting advice, some fraudulent pap, duck-billed platitude. Staring into his plate as if the wisdom sought could be extracted from two rapidly chilling hot dogs, he said, "Who among us has not behaved badly. One time or another." Best he could do. Words to say.

"But I'm not *like* that, Norman. Never have been."

"I'm sure you're not."

"It must have been the wine."

"Doubtless the wine."

"I'm not used to drinking. Hardly ever drink. Lately, though, I've been, well, manic."

"Why is that?" he asked, picturing himself in medical whites, the wise healer, pipe sucker, jaw stroker, calmly peeling away the mysteries layering the disturbed psyche. Dr. Sigmund Woodrow, answer man to the bruised spirit, the wounded heart.

"Oh, the divorce, Rick—that's my ex—all the time hounding me, my dad's death. Everything. It hasn't been a good year."

"Maybe you want to tell me about it."

She wanted to. She did. Another lengthy recital, wandering, innocent of chronology, rent with multiple digressions, illustrative anecdotes, fragments of remembered humiliations and deceptions and griefs. The genesis and evolution of an ill-starred, decade-long union, its gradual corrosion, final acrimonious dissolution, six months ago. Abrupt leap to the present, the faithless former spouse overtaken by remorse, tardy second thoughts, pleading for reconciliation. Bootleg turn, unsegued, to the recent past again, the cherished father's long, slow agonized passing, cancered rot invading the farthest outposts of tissue and marrow. She, the anguished witness to its steady progress, while the marital storm swept around her. Conjunction of calamities.

Norman, attending to this chronicle, here and there introducing the neutral query ("And this was when, now?"—"Who was it said that?"—"Where, exactly, did all this happen?"), fitted its fractured pieces together, imposed on them an order sequential and geographic, best as he was able. To his thinking and from his lofty perch of age and tarnished experience, these private cataclysms seemed less than monumental. Not quite trivial, to be sure, but near to mundane. Divorce, after all, a commonplace failure; and death with its own subversive logic, minor confusions, a passage, at fate's crapshoot, more painful for some than others (the fleeting recollection here of a snitch cornered by a pack of savage homeboys in a kitchen storage room, eyes punctured, anus broomhandle-penetrated preparatory to disembowelment, muffled shrieks echoing off the shelves and shelves of institutional-size cans of spinach, beets, beans). You want catastrophe, grief? Come to me for the advanced schooling. Who's more gifted and talented than I?

And yet, listening, nodding gravely, watching her, the head backlit by bands of sunshine filtering through the dust-streaked window and haloed in a nimbus of gold; the hair, sunstruck, recast in soft amber, rich as syrup; the sorrow-congested face, subtly permuted by light and shadow and sparking, perversely, the thought of how near the contortions of sorrow are to the intense inner focus of passion— watching her this way, this fragile, gorgeous, grieving creature, Norman felt priviliged to be elected auditor to these confidences, and reason, for the first time in longer than he could remember, to be glad he was not himself dead.

Eye-dabbing time-out. Long, beseeching look. His turn for the sapient commentary come around again. Because he could think of nothing else to advise, and because the fancy of death still lingered, he said, "Are you familiar with a certain drill practiced by the samurai warriors?"

"Who?"

"The Japanese samurai."

"No, I'm afraid not."

"In this drill," he went on, unfazed by the look's widening bafflement, "a samurai, first thing on waking, takes a few moments to envision his own death. Very bracing exercise. Concentrates the mind, restores balance, perspective. A kind of stoic serenity, you might say."

"What are you telling me, Norman?"

"A way to get through bad times. I recommend it to you."

"From experience?"

"Mostly hearsay."

"You've had them too, haven't you. Those bad times."

"Live long enough, and they'll find you."

"You've heard mine. Tell me yours."

"Maybe another day."

"Don't you trust me?"

"It's not a matter of trust. One melancholy tale at a time. Anyway, my troubles are behind me. Yours are immediate."

"Do you think he'll ever want to see me again?"

"Who?"

"Michael."

Evidently they were back in the present again, last night's negligible disaster. Not easy, following the zigzag trail of her many distresses. "Impossible to predict," Norman said.

"He said he did. But he may have been trying to spare my feelings. Leave me something."

Remembering his son's peculiar behavior just the other day, the halting attempt to reveal some nagging inner distress of his own, Norman said, "Understanding Michael is rather like searching for the theorems of Euclid in a plate of undercooked spaghetti."

Now her look was perplexed, as though uncertain if she were supposed to find this funny or not. Not, it appeared, for she said fretfully, "I can't imagine what he must think of me."

Norman took from a pocket Michael's note, spied among the bills on the desk when he came out of the shower this morning, and slid it over to her. "There's the number where he can be reached. Why don't you test it?"

"You think I should?"

"Nothing ventured . . ."

She copied the number on a napkin, folded it carefully, and put it in her purse. Then, brightening some, awarding him with a wistful smile, said, "You're the eternal optimist, aren't you?"

"Optimist without delusions."

"You've been awfully kind, Norman. I appreciate it."

He gave a dismissive shrug.

"Listened patiently. Answered all my questions."

"To the best of my limited ability."

"May I ask you one more?"

A faint alarm sounded in his joint-seasoned head. "You can ask," he said. "No guarantee of an answer."

"What about his mother? Your wife, I assume."

A stiffness entirely involuntary overtook him, tightening the muscles of his jaw, neck, torso, limbs. "What about her?" he said.

"Why is he so . . . touchy, when she's mentioned?"

He gazed thoughtfully at his plate. The red hots, slaw, fries were uneaten and all but forgotten in the convolutions of memories, sorrows, afflictions, guilts, the braided chain of words weaving circuitously but surely, inevitably, as all words must, back to the cardinal stain of his life. "That's the one better left unasked."

FOR VICTOR FLAM IT HAD BEEN, already by nine, a long, uncomfortable, and, so far, less than successful morning. Better make that twenty-four hours' worth of unsuccess, he was thinking dourly, running those hours by in his head, wondering if Nathan could have fucked up, steered him wrong. It was a way to pass the time, get his mind off the muggy heat pouring down out of a sun-bleached Georgia sky.

Began promising enough. Plane on time, Sunday traffic up the South Expressway manageable, apartment complex (situated off Peachtree Road and inaptly named Rolling Hills, its gentle, wooded slopes some cracker developer's inflated idea of hills) easy to locate, old map decipherer like himself. Downhills be closer on the money, far as he was concerned, seeing that's how everything went after that.

First was the goddam speed bump, shook the shit out of him and the rental Merc, both. Then the daunting size of the place. Rat's maze of streets (the tank-trap speed bumps every hundred feet or so) snaking through hollows, winding up grades, often as not leading you down some blind cul-de-sac. Flanked by grainy redbrick buildings set back in dense clusters of trees, their numbers nonsequential, far as he could tell, and all but unreadable through all the greenery. Complex from hell, laid out by a fugitive from a wig factory. Which left him no choice but to pull up by a finger-popping suntan strutting along with audio vines twining out his ears (told you something about the clientele here) and get directions to the manager's office. And from there, out of a grouchy cunt studying a *Glamour* magazine (and desperately in need of such instruction, by the skaggy looks of her) further direction to Building 14C. All this occupying the better part of an hour.

So it was going on one o'clock when he finally hit the bell on Number 11, 14C (as pinpointed for him by Nathan the night before). He got only silence. He pounded the door. More silence. Tried the adjoining apartments. Nobody answering, either side. Drove back to the office and asked Miss Glamour Queen if by chance she'd seen Mr. Stroiker or knew of his whereabouts. He was told, "Christ, there's six-hundred-plus units here. How would I know?" His request for Stroiker's phone number (unavailable from Nathan) was summarily, not to say rudely, denied ("We don't give out that kind of info on our residents."). So he drove over to Peachtree and stopped at a spic diner and checked a directory dangling from the pay phone in the entrance. No listing for a Max Stroiker.

Now it was half-past one. His hopes of catching a break—wrapping this Stroiker business today, getting a late flight back to PBI, maybe paying the eager Ms. Bridget a friendly call—were fading fast. After killing another thirty minutes over a couple of tacos, couple of drafts, he returned to Downhills and 14C (the route committed to memory now) and tried Number 11 again. Nobody home. Nothing to do but wait.

Four long hours he waited, sweltering in the hotbox of a car, fierce sunlight glinting off its hood like a blade in the eye. Sweat pooling in the pits. Jockeys creeping up the royal gorge. Like an afternoon spent in your basic tropical rain forest. Four hours of it. Nothing.

Back to Peachtree, where he found a sleep cheap (the happy notion of a quick and easy wrap long since abandoned . . . so much for those good thoughts), checked in, showered, got into fresh laundry, popped back three more brews and a microwaved fishwich in the bar and, feeling a little better but not a whole helluva lot, resumed his watch outside 14C. A few people, not many and all of them young, none even remotely resembling a fifty-pushing business executive, came and went. The sun settled behind the crest of a slope, cooling the gluey air scarcely at all. Building gradually blackened in the night. Here and there a light winked on, but not in Number 11. Around midnight, shoulders sagging, ass turned to stone, thoroughly cashed, he gave it up. Fuck it, life's too fucking short.

All that was yesterday. Not exactly a primo day for your Victor Flam. And this one shaping up not much better. First thing on arriving, seven sharp, he'd tried the bell again, case Mr. Invisible Man dragged in late off some pussy patrol (womanizer, that's what Nathan had called him). Same story. So here he sat again. Squinting into a shimmery blaze of sun again. Oozing beery sweat again, every pore, scalp to the balls of his size thirteens. Shorts drifting north again. Entertaining smoldering doubts about the fabled expertise of his Jew York confederate, and thinking maybe it's time to regroup, Victor, come at it a different angle.

When, a couple clicks past nine, up pulls a cab and out steps a large, portly gentleman, tall and square as an outhouse, silver hair, pink puffy face, suit, lugging bag and briefcase. In a bunch-shouldered, battering ram stride, all business, he makes straight for 14C. Got to be his man. Flam climbs out of the car and cuts across a patch of sun-frazzled grass, intercepting him at the door. "Mr. Stroiker?" he said, smiling easily (you always start out smiling).

"That's right."

"My name's Flam. Victor Flam."

Stroiker looked him up and down coldly.

"Wonder if I could have a minute of your time."

"For what?"

"I was hopin' maybe we could talk inside. Get out of this steambath."

"If you're selling something, I'm not—"

"Nothing to sell, Mr. Stroiker." Flam held up empty palms, as if in evidence.

"Talk about what, then?"

Voice was low, froggy, practiced in dispatching orders, snuffing protests, but with a small tremor in it too, like he was restraining, with some difficulty, an urgency of emotion. Face, at this near distance, not so much pink as salmon-colored, chum variety at that, stitched and worked and gratified, splotched with purple broken veins under the thickened skin. Visible pulse beat in the coiled ones at the temples. Worried cast to the rheumy eyes. Trace of a tic under one of them. Eyes of a man seriously distressed over something. Or maybe just seriously hungover. Something, anyway, going on here with our Mr. Max Stroiker. "A job you supervised," Flam said. " 'Bout a year back. In Florida."

Face puckered in the effort of recollection. Eyes turned inward. "Sanitary Laundry?"

"That's the one."

"What about it?"

"Sure you don't want to step inside, Mr. Stroiker? It's hotter'n hell's own kitchen out here. And that bag of yours lookin' awful heavy."

A tiny glimmer of expectancy ignited those watery eyes. "You wouldn't be with Burns and Nye?"

"Who're they?"

Sudden as it appeared, the glimmer flickered, flamed out. "Another consulting firm," he said dully.

" 'Fraid not."

"Then get to the point. I've got a lot of things to do today, calls to make . . ." Trailing off, the weighty burdens too numerous to tally, or momentarily escaping him.

"The point," Flam said mildly. "Okay, point is an employee of this laundry, lady, got herself hurt right around the time you people were on that job."

"Hurt? How?"

"Well, worse even than hurt. Killed. Murdered, in fact."

The face registered a kind of labored shock, but he said, very carefully, "What's that got to do with me?"

"Oh, I'm pokin' into it. For the family, y'know. Seein' what I can turn up. Any help you could give me be much appreciated."

Stroiker looked at him narrowly. "You a police officer?"

"No."

"Private detective?"

"More a consultant, you might say. Sorta like yourself."

"You got a card?"

Flam produced one.

Stroiker set down his bag, took the card, scrutinized it closely. "A private detective," he said, flat this time, no question mark tagged to it.

Flam shrugged. "Whatever."

"Then I don't have to talk to you, do I." Also delivered flat, more challenge than question.

"No, you sure don't," said Flam, accommodating, deferential, ever amiable, wry little tuck at one corner of the mouth, folksy good nature relaying its own special brand of menace. "Not if you don't want to. Or if you got some reason not to want to."

"Well, I suppose we could go inside. For a minute."

Flam allowed the corner tuck to spread across his mouth in another big smile. Amiable carried the day, every time.

Number 11 (the Stroiker lovenest, in Nathan's fanciful description) was one of those assembly line efficiencies, cramped living room dominated by hide-a-bed couch (unhidden this morning, its tangle of sheets testament to nights either frisky or restless); galley kitchen with grease-streaked counter and sinkful of food-crusted plates and saucers; closet of a head whose open door revealed a tiled floor strewn with towels and clothes stepped out of and forgotten. And over it all, saturating it all, a thick, almost tactile air that somehow managed the impossible feat of blending dry and sticky, ripe with lingering and not quite identifiable aromas of take-out eats and assorted bodily functions. Some lovenest.

"Sorry about the mess," Stroiker said (reading his thoughts?). "I don't spend much time here."

"Expect not, your line of work."

"Place to crash, that's about it. Have a seat."

Stroiker indicated the single armchair, went over and hoisted the legs of the bed and vanished it back into couch, a tail of sheet dangling at a corner. From there he went around the room-divider counter (Flam watching him, noting again the lumbering, big-guy step, self-conscious eyes-on-me gait of the onetime athlete, noseguard maybe, second stringer at best), foraged through a cabinet, and came up with a bottle of V.O. "Pour you a tightener?" he offered.

"Short one be good."

Stroiker brought him a water glass three-quarters full, his take on short, and sank onto the couch. Lifted his own glass, not in the least short, took a long, Adam's-apple-bobbling swallow, expelled a lip-smacking wheeze, and said, "Little pooch hair."

"Big weekend, was it?"

"I'd say big. Me and the girlfriend had ourselves a party hearty getaway." Adding in prideful afterthought and with a lewd, tells-it-all wink, "She's a stew."

Flam had to wonder if he had any idea what a pathetic figure he cut, this graybeard playing at frat boy on spring spree. Probably not. "Sounds big, all right," he allowed affably, still in Mr. Charm gear.

The civilities exhausted, Stroiker loosened his tie, a get-to-business signal. "So. What's this all about, Mr. . . ."

Flam supplied his last name again.

"Mr. Flam."

"Well, like I was sayin' outside, there was this unfortunate incident down in Florida—"

"This 'incident' being a murder?"

"That's right," Flam said evenly. "A murder."

"And in what way can I help you?"

"It happened, this murder, the same day your consulting team finished up the laundry job. Thought maybe you could tell me what you remember about that day."

"Nothing."

"Nothing at all?"

A triumphant smirk played across the broad, jowly face. "I wasn't there the day of the wrap. Was in Baton Rouge, steering another project. You can check it out. Which establishes what people in your profession call an ironclad alibi, correct?"

Flam was more than a little wigged at this intelligence (which had the confident ring of verifiable truth) and was cheered not at all. But he said, still even, still cool, "You were never a suspect, Mr. Stroiker." Oh, no. Perish the thought! "We're just chattin' here."

"Doesn't appear to be much to chat about," Stroiker said, smirk perilously close to sneer now. "So if—"

"Maybe you could help fill in some background on the victim, then. Lady name of Shelley Russo. That ding any bells for you, that name?"

"No."

"Might be a picture jog your memory."

Flam removed the Shelley photo from an inside pocket of his jacket, handed it over. Stroiker studied it a moment, brows knitting thoughtfully, head moving back and forth. "Afraid I don't recognize her," he said, passing it back. "Sorry."

"That's okay. Been over a year." Flam took a small sip of the V.O. Arranged his features in a puzzled expression. "Kind of surprising, though. You not recognizing her, I mean. Seeing she was executive secretary to the president there."

"Not if you understand the role of a section chief," Stroker said smoothly. "Which is what I was. At that time."

"How's that?" Flam asked, showing an interested face now, eager to learn. "That role?"

"A section chief is something like, oh, a plant foreman," Stroiker said, his tone instructive, deliberate; patient tutor, bonehead charge. "Responsible for three, four projects, sometimes more. Simultaneously, you understand. The Sanitary Laundry was just one of several I had going then."

"So you weren't that involved with the job?"

"Hardly at all. Got down there, what? Maybe half a dozen times. I had a strong crew working it. Didn't require much supervision."

Flam gave his chin a pensive stroke, part of his bag of moves, automatic, after all these years in the business, and all but unconscious. "This crew," he said, "you tell me a little about them?"

"Such as?"

"Oh, kind of guys they were. Personalities, quirks, habits. Things like that."

Stroiker had been pulling steadily at his drink. He drained off the last of it, heaved himself up off the couch, glanced at Flam's glass, said, "Another splash?"

"I'm still good."

Around the counter he went, step slowed to a stiff shamble now, the sauce catching hold, mellowing him out. Returned with his own glass properly splashed (as in spilling over the rim splashed), settled onto the couch. Gazed at his guest, the smirk-smile coming back into his face, but with a joyless and decidedly untriumphant twitch in it, like he was struggling to contain a commotion of fears. Exactly like he'd looked outside. Finally he said, "Tell me, Mr. Flam. You want me to respond to all these questions of yours as private citizen, or Stoltz employee?"

"There's a distinction?"

He loosed a harsh, bitter laugh. "There is now. Because I'm no longer the latter. Seems I got shitcanned this morning."

"Sorry to hear that," Flam said (though not surprised, recalling Nathan's prediction: score one for the sheenie).

"Hey, don't be. I can pick up the phone and get me another position like that." *That* symbolized by a sharp fingersnap. "Fact, when I asked if you were with Burns and Nye—outside there?—thought maybe the word had already leaked out. They been after me for years."

Voice was big now, rising with hollow bravado, but one of the hands, glassless one, described agitated circles in the air. Flush showing in the baggy cheeks. Undereye tic accelerating. Clearly a panicked man. Tough luck for him, nothing to Flam, who had his own agenda. And who, pushing it, before it got lost in some rambling juicer whine, said, "Guess it'd have to be as private citizen, then. Gettin' back to that issue we were discussing."

Stroiker looked at him blankly.

"Your crew down there? Florida? Sanitary job?"

Stroiker sighed a long, expiring sigh, heavy with injury and self-pity.

But once launched on that issue, he was generously forthcoming (himself safely off the suspect hook now, one small solace in an otherwise disastrous day), releasing all his choked-up bile, funnelling it through spited assessments of his former subordinates. A mix of fact, conjecture, gossip, mean-spirited innuendo, rich in revelation: one, Ivy League boy, bright enough but a little too girlish for the manly Stroiker tastes, very likely a closeted swish; another, talented consultant, gifted even, but with an old man who'd done time, some dark scandal, didn't have all the scoop; couple of them, slackers, bumblers, not pulling their weight, dumped late in the project and never replaced; last one, a piece of chickenshit, a back-stabbing corporate snitch, for certain. Cloaked in the righteous mantle of keen student of human nature, shrewd interpreter of human failing, he wore on. Soiling them all.

Okay by Flam (attending closely, taking mental notes, matching this freely offered catalog of traits and taints to the Nathan-supplied list of names recorded in his head). Oftentimes, in his experience, out of pure dog-ass meanness—like this miserable shitsack was dispensing right now—come the most useful and penetrating insights (though what they might be he couldn't begin to speculate just then, have to sort it out later). So he was grateful for any dish he could get, what with the Stroiker name almost for certain scrubbed from that list. One down, five to go.

". . . and that's about as much as I can tell you." Stroiker concluded his character analyses and assassinations, emptied, it seemed, of malice and information both.

"You wouldn't happen to know where these fellas are now? What jobs they're on, I mean?" Flam couldn't resist adding, "Ones still with the company, that is." Get in a little reminder needle. Asshole like that (talk about your scummy snitches) had it coming.

"No idea," Stroiker said desolately, his personal calamity, momentarily swamped in the wash of venom, now resurfacing. "I'm out of the Stoltz loop." He looked at Flam, who watched him with a lizard smile, then declared stoutly, "Well rid of it too."

"Bet you are, at that."

"Goddam right I am."

Flam got to his feet, crossed the narrow space between them in three strides, one hand extended, the other upheld in a restraining gesture, saying, "Want to thank you for your help, Mr. Stroiker. Don't you get up now. I'll find my way out." Like he was going to get lost in this birdcage.

The Stroiker hand was damp and a little trembly. The mouth slack at the corners. Eyes glassy with dread. "Glad to help," he said.

Equally glad not to have to haul his lard ass up off the couch. At the door Flam paused, cocked his head, like he'd forgotten something, glanced over his shoulder, and drawled, "Oh. Yeah. Write if you get work, huh."

AS NUMBED AS KNIGHT and boistrous Host by the Monk's interminable litany of woe, Norman followed, line by line, the seriocomic ramblings of Chanticleer and Dame Partlet and the cunning, pride-snookered fox, their leisurely digressions on the portentive powers of dreams, on love and treachery and the terrible mysteries of fate and free will. Followed the godly Sir John's fable to its decreed happy ending, an ambiguous mix of amusement, buried resentment, remembered private sorrows and vague forebodings stirring in his head. Occasionally, struggling with the Middle English, he glanced up from the text and out the sun parlor windows, watched the burnished glow of late afternoon folding softly into dusk. Dusk, at next glance, into dark, a yellow rind of moon stuck on the black sky.

Another tale finished, he doused the lamp and stood at a window, his gaze drawn across lawn and street to the light in the Lizabeth Seaver condominium, his thoughts straying to this morning's dialogue. Monologue, more accurately. Her Monklike chronicle of everyday misfortunes and defeats; the dilemma of her instantaneous attraction to Michael, ingenuously disclosed, bungling advances and all (and for which dilemma he had, in truth, no ready answers, no foolproof solutions, the sensibilities of his son as enigmatic to him as to her); the ominous question on the mother (impossible for him to shape, even in the stillness of mindlife, her name), bluntly forestalled, but only for the moment, ill-omened question augering no good and, should this curious, unlikely, and now, evidently, tri-cornered connection tighten, ultimately to be reckoned with. Thoughts finally giving way to an abstract, wordless, unsettling perception of himself clenched in the iron fist of time, the past squeezing in, present paralytic, future collapsing toward him.

AND IN THE LIGHTED CONDOMINIUM across the lawn and street, Lizabeth sat rigidly at the dining table (same spot from which, less than twenty-four hours back, she'd played the fool). The numbered napkin laid out before her, mentally rehearsing bright opening lines, editing them, rejecting them—this one was too flippant, that too forward, another far too desperate—and inventing new ones, staring at the cradled phone on the wall as though the lasered focus in that fixed stare bore the magical power to activate its ring, deliver a soothing voice to solve her nagging indecision, erase her humiliation, heal her distress.

And in time, magically, it did. Rang, anyway. But the voice coming down the line—drink-sloshed, syllables strung together, by turns weepy and sulky—was the least welcome and absolute last she wanted to hear. Rick again, begging forgiveness . . . one more chance . . . just one . . . make it up to her . . . make things right again . . . she'd see. . . . Voice swaying from remorse to bitterness to belligerence, underlined with the veiled hostility of the petulant child, inconsequential toy discarded, demanding it back, threatening a tantrum.

She listened. An hour or more she listened, phone tacked to her reddening ear, pacing, twirling, twining and untwining herself in its rubbery cord, exasperation's unquiet waltz; fretting through half a pack of cigarettes; filling the infrequent silences with clipped, distancing monosyllables; till finally, at one of the acid bursts of bitterness, slamming down the receiver. Exhausted by all this oppressive emotional leakage, too dispirited for anything now but sleep, she switched off the light and started for the bedroom.

When the phone worked its clattery equivocal magic once again.

•   •   •

AND ON A PLANE pointed in a southeasterly direction, Flam slouched in a wide, cushy, first-class cabin seat (why not? Mother Swales footing the bill—only way to fly unless, as the old joke went, it was united); thoroughly wasted from a nine-hour wait (this late flight the only one available, or so a surly clerk informed him: "End of the holiday traffic, sir. You should have booked early." Flam thinking, *Yeah, yeah, book this big one down here, geek);* gut and bowels burning under the blockage of two days' worth of road-kill chow and a variety of doctors (yesterday's brews, this morning's V.O., a few pass-the-airport-hours tonics, the brandy and water on the tray table in front of him right now, alongside his opened SSI notebook)—all of it was fueling his already dyspeptic vision of the world and all its buttlick inhabitants as he reviewed, listlessly, his notes and tried to put a figure on his next moves.

First one, of course, was obvious and inescapable. Back to the temperamental Nathan, confirm the Stroiker alibi, and nail down the current whereabouts of the five leads. Heavy challenge in the cases of the two got axed, but neither of them to be discounted or scratched. With a schiz, how you gonna know? And while he had faith in the Jewbie's computer wizardry, he knew also that sooner or later (probably sooner), one way or another, Nathan would be there with his hand out to collect. Nothing free, this sinkhole world.

After that, though, it got soupy. Starting once more at the top and running down the alphabetized list of names, he could find nothing in all the schmuck Stroiker-supplied dirt that leaped out at him and said, *This one, Victor, this is the one to lean on.* Except for the dude with the old man who'd done time, your felons always of professional interest to Flam. Still a stretch, seeing how the son got nothing but high marks out of Stroiker. Maybe worth peeking into, maybe not. Have to see how the tracking shook down, the geography of it all.

He let it go for now, closed the notebook, bottomed the brandy, racked the tray, and settled back in his seat, eyes shuttered, sleep pressing in. Time enough tomorrow, when the head was screwed on straight and the belly Pepto-Bismolized, to look it over again, all of it, see was there something he'd missed. And if not, if he still came up zip, then nothing left to do but tick them off the way they fell, one by one, alphabetical order.

• • •

AND IN A SECOND-FLOOR ROOM of the Grand Rapids Hilton, Michael sat with his back propped against the headboard of the bed, legs outstretched, television remote in hand, idly grazing the channels, engaged by nothing he saw. Now and again he sipped from a can of ginger ale, fast losing its chill, and then replaced it by the phone on the nightstand. Though it was 11:00 P.M. (by eastern time) and though it had been a long, arduous, and eventful day (with tomorrow promising the same, or more), he was wearied not at all. Rather, he felt charged, restless, but also a curious sense of discontinuity, as though something had been overlooked or forgotten, left undone. Doubtless nothing more than the familiar stresses he always experienced at the onset of a new project, exacerbated now by the promotion and the ponderous weight of full responsibility (and, perhaps, by the news of Max's dismissal, a cautionary lesson in the disastrous consequences of neglect and weakness and failure). Doubtless it was that. Had to be that.

After the meeting with Marks, he'd brought the project file back to the room and studied it thoroughly, taking careful notes, memorizing key names and backgrounds, outlining a tentative course of action. By 6:00 the team members had arrived and settled in and made phone contact. By 8:00 they were convened in his room for a preliminary strategy session, himself presiding. For two hours he passed along all he had gleaned from the file, explained the parameters and his opening tactics (subject, of course, to ongoing revision as the project unfolded), made initial assignments, fielded questions, throttled the occasional cavilling objection. All three—even the green pea—seemed competent enough, but they all had a few years on him, and it was vital to establish from the beginning his absolute authority. AS&A, in the wisdom of Max Stroiker, late and only scantly lamented mentor, was many things, but democracy it was not. Accordingly, accepting the lonely truth of the familiarity-contempt equation, he declined an invitation to join them for a loosener at the bar after the session was adjourned.

And so here he sat, not displeased with his performance, not in apprehension of tomorrow's challenge, yet somehow vaguely uneasy, oppressed by his own company, the source of his discontent unknown, untraceable. Unless it was the twangy voice issuing from the hole in the used, weathered face filling the screen just then, a

whiney country singer moaning something about "lonesome standard time." He punched the mute button and immediately another
voice—thrilled, rushing, velvety—crooned in his ear. And another
face—framed in a cascade of golden ringlets, serenely smiling, displaying nothing but purity—unveiled itself behind his eyes.

He checked his watch. 11:10. In Illinois, 10:10. Late, but not too
late. To soothe his throat, scratchy from two hours of nonstop
speech, he drank off the rest of the warm ginger ale. It seemed to
help some. He picked up the phone, got the information operator,
obtained the number. Pecked it out quickly, before doubt could set
in, nerve falter.

Busy.

He gave it ten minutes. Tried again.

Same thing. Busy.

For another quarter hour he sat scowling at the still muted television. Jaws clenched and horseshoe rigid. Throat gone dry again. An
anger—powerless, smoldering, visceral—swept through him. The
face in the vision took on a mocking, libidinous cast.

Once more he tried. This time the line was clear. Fourteen rings,
by his close count. Then a greeting: curt, guarded, edged with hostility.

"Uh, this is Michael," he said. "Michael Woodrow?"

And the windsong of the Lizabeth Seaver voice—exactly as he'd
heard it in his head, all the wariness gone suddenly out of it, all the
hostility—came back to him. "Michael. You called. You called me."

12

About Dr. Hilda Rostovich (Michael was thinking, 7:00 A.M. on a Saturday morning, pajama-clad, frowning into the stacks and stacks of printouts, graphs, flow charts, preliminary studies—daunting to any eye but his—spread out across the hotel room table, sorting them out, imposing an order, the genesis of a plan), that grinning oaf Marks, with his shifty peddler's nose for trouble, had been absolutely right. Three weeks into the project and the woman had given him nothing but grief—stalls, evasions, needless roadblocks, cunning duplicities. Grief. Clearly no friend to this undertaking.

Case in point: Yesterday's meeting, a Friday afternoon ritual insisted upon by the redoubtable Dr. R. ("To keep our staff apprised of your progress," she'd directed early on, imperial plural, the *progress* set off by insolent vocalized quotes.) Enthroned grandly at the head of the table, hands serenely clasped in her lap, she was mistress of all she surveyed (all being a spartanly furnished presidential conference room, its chief appointment a line of portraits of past Hobbes College helmsmen adorning the wall behind her, witnessing all present proceedings with stern, judgmental eyes). Flanked by toadying vice presidents and deans, she listened as he delivered the weekly update on their activities and uncoverings. A tall, big-boned, square-hipped woman, downside of fifty, wake-outfitted in funereal black suit and ruffleless ivory blouse, asexual oddity (never mind the rumored husband, trotted out only, it was whispered, on ceremonial occasions), she listened impassive and unsmiling, regarding him out of wrinkle-nested eyes coldly skeptical, eyes in training against the day they'd join that austere crew on the wall. Heard him out, not a word escaping the thin crease of mouth, fissures ascending from its bloodless upper lip like hairline cracks in plaster (a total image of her returning to him now, the whole inquisitorial scene, still rankling), broad cheekbones tapering to a witchy needled chin, skin powdered a startling geisha white, startling contrast to the helmet of black hair framing the face in anachronous windowpane do, Prince Valiant bangs squaring the steep forehead. Not a word, not a query, not an objection.

Till he was finished. And then, after a moment's grave silence during which she gazed at him steadily, as though examining a most curious bug under glass, narrowing in on a small but symptomatic cost-cutting measure, one of the many he'd introduced for their consideration, she said, "You're suggesting we *charge* our students for clean towels in the gymnasium?" Brows lifted in simulation of stunned disbelief and remaining in that attitude, while he pointed out said fee would save the institution something in the neighborhood of three thousand dollars annually. To which irrefutable evidence she replied, "It is not in our tradition, Mr. Woodrow, to extort money for simple hygenic services. Ours is not a bottom-line philosophy." Brows relaxed now but shoulders drawn up haughtily, voice low-pitched, even, studied in condescension, an easy reading of ten on the sanctimony scale.

One of the deans, jug-eared bootlicker with the sad, seamed face of a wise old bear, ventured solemnly, "I'm afraid I have to agree with Dr. Rostovich . . . ," the agreement swelling into a windy, winding, metaphor-maiming ("You see, there are times, Mr. Woodrow, when, in the best interests of the college, one must be blunt even to the point of being sharp") sermon on the noble mission of Christian-based higher education. Thus emboldened, the band of sycophantic vassals charged in, each with a seconding opinion, and there followed an hour or more of earnest sharing of views (the eyes of the dragon, glittery with malice, fastened on him through it all).

The Great Towel Colloquy. Democracy in action. Not a productive meeting.

Nevertheless, in the restorative stillness of his room, Michael
was neither discouraged nor intimidated. In spite of her worst efforts
to sink the project, he was gathering the goods on the ball-breaking
Dr. R., the mounting and incontestable evidence of her appalling mis-
management laid out before him. Give it another two weeks and he'd
be armed and ready. See who did the ball-breaking then.

Two more weeks . . . three down, two to go . . . only two . . .
thoughts willfully straying from the urgent business at hand to the
nightly phone conversations with Lizabeth Seaver, by now the
summit of his otherwise colorless days, bewildering aberrations
in his measured, cadenced life. Rambling, unfocused, marathon
length, those conversations, filled mostly with spontaneous accounts of her day, her new job, her flowering friendship with
Norman (who was, he learned, helping panel the walls of her basement; the same cerebral Norman who loathed household chores of
any sort, recoiled at hammer and nails. And he the cautious auditor, always vigilant, though night by night, at her gentle prodding,
opening up, peeling away the outer layers of his life, experience,
mind-sets, dreams. Lowering his guard. Revealing himself, or a di-
mension of himself.

Phone pals, she'd called them ("That's what we're getting to be,
Michael, phone pals") though just the other day he'd found in among
his business mail a greeting card (softly scented, was it?, or merely an
imagined fragrance), its canned Thinking of You sentiment lightened
by a weak gag. But semantically plain, wholly unimagined—a
woman, *this* woman, thinking of him—and signed "Gratefully, L." He
had to wonder if it weren't veering off in a strange new direction,
strange to him anyway, unfamiliar country, his quickened imagination lending an almost tangible substance to the disembodied voice
reaching out to him from across the miles, a presence lingering in the
silence of the room long after the phone was recradled, the voice
stilled. Wondered, at this secure remove and with a mix of anticipation and doubt, what it would mean to lay eyes on her again, put face
and flesh and form on that spirit voice again.

For an instant he allowed himself to entertain the notion of
phoning her right now, this very moment, 6:00 A.M. in her weekend
morning. He toyed with the idea, rejected it, and returned his wan-

dering attention to the stacks of drab papers in front of him, waiting
to be analyzed, organized, marshalled.

Two more weeks.

Four hours later, head reeling with numbers, neck and shoulders
stiffening from the protracted clerical stoop, stomach running on
empty, he put aside pen and calculator and slumped back in his
chair. Time for a break. Past time. Hit it again after lunch.

He went into the bathroom, showered and shaved, discovering,
exasperatedly, the can of shave cream expelling its last limp worms
of foam, and the blade, also his last, dulled, scraping his skin, drawing
here and there a thin streak of blood. Annoyed, he dressed (casual
slacks and shirt, for he intended to see no one today, stay with the
work, get a handle on the data, and call a team strategy session tomorrow night), walked down the corridor to the lobby and solicited
shopping advice from a pathologically cheerful woman at the desk.
Was told, "Oh, you'll want to go to Meijers, they got everything, you
name it." (Which he already had: the blades, cream, sundry other personal articles, to carry him through those next two weeks.) Was
given directions (the boundaries of his Grand Rapids universe hereto-
fore circumscribed by the seven miles between Hilton Hotel and
Hobbes College on the outskirts of town). Was dispatched with the
reflex injunction to "Have a super day, now." Out to the parking lot
and the rental Olds, and from there a short drive to the fabled store
that had everything (driving under a low, mean sky roofed with lead-
colored clouds dense with the promise of yet another day of rain, the
weather in this corner of the world as consistently gray and dismal as
any he'd experienced, anywhere).

Its interior was armory-vast, awesome in its assemblage of com-
modities and wares. He paused just inside one of its many entrances,
dismayed by the maze of customer-clogged aisles, from which there
rose a steady, hornet swarm hum punctuated by infant wails, the
Muzak of the retail trades. The smile button desk clerk was certainly
right: Meijers sold everything. The problem was how to locate his
small scrap of everything. Better he'd asked directions to a neighborhood pharmacy, if any such existed anymore.

He approached a greeter, a portly, apple-cheeked, silver-haired,
red-jacketed (as indeed were all the Meijer minions, a mobile bustling
blur of red) elderly man stationed by clusters of shopping carts accor-
dioned into long, linked files. Jolly as Santa (everybody forcedly jovial

here, perhaps a means of staving off climatic-induced despair, fore-stalling a regional depopulation by mass suicide), he ho-hoed a "Welcome to Meijers" and, in answer to Michael's question, pointed him to Cosmetics in the rear of the store and supplied him with a cart un-yoked from the nearest file.

Off he went, confidently steering his cart down the adjacent aisle. And was immediately lost, the aisle leading him through Menswear and dead-ending at a counter fronting a block of fitting booths. He bore to the left, found himself first in Shoes, next Toys, after that Home Fashions. A scurrying redcoat, buttonholed, listened to his plea, then flung an arm in a diagonal direction, assuring him, "Y'can't miss it." But he did. Wound up in Groceries generally, Cereals specifically. It occurred to him to wonder if they'd ever considered engaging the services of a consulting firm or, perhaps more aptly, a cartographer.

Eventually, though, through the good offices of a kindly granny (who allowed she too, after years of Meijer loyalty, had trouble finding her way around), he was escorted, childlike, to the perfectly-secreted Cosmetics Department. By then he was so thoroughly irked he plucked the sought-after items off the shelves with scarcely a glance, dumped them in the cart, and through some near miracle made it back to the checkout lanes. Cooled his heels at the end of a static line of shoppers, docile as sheep, in a lane designated, with cruel irony, Express. Paid his money and was about to flee through the handiest exit when he discovered, too late, he'd picked up the wrong brand of shave cream, the one peeking out of the plastic bag a gooey green gel that, experimented with once, long ago, softened his whiskers not at all and left his face raw and chafed. Wouldn't do. Back to the cashier, who said cheerily, "Exchange? Sure, no prol'um. 'Cept y'gotta take it over to Customer Service, seein' it's already been rung up."

All this for a simple transaction. Toiletries, at that. He took a place at the end of a line trailing back from the Customer Service counter. Gradually it inched forward, its progress glacial as the last one. He waited, not patiently, watching out of habit the directionless dashings of the clerks on the other side of the counter. Definitely in serious need of some consulting advice, even an elementary time-and-motion study. A full six minutes, as testified by the clock on the wall, elapsed. Finally his turn arrived. A beamy clerk beckoned him over,

inquired how she could help. Displaying the can of shave cream, he
explained his non-problem. "No-o-o prol'um," she confirmed (a
folksy, slurry, consonant-swallowing articulation seemingly in vogue
here). But a search for the appropriate form produced nothing, and
with a breezy "Be right back" she scuttled away.

So he waited some more. Outwardly calm, inwardly fuming. Directly to his right an exchange similar to his own was being
processed by another of those clerks, a woman, unnoticed before, of
such arresting, exotic appearance that, observed closely now, he
found it impossible to unfasten his gaze. Not a young woman, not
particularly shapely, certainly not beautiful. More a sultry Mediter-
ranean quality, or maybe it was south of the border, hard to tell. Skin
smooth, glossy, slightly oleagenous, slight olive cast beneath the several strata of powders and paints. Her full lips were lacquered a brilliant cherry red; dark, sleepy eyes shadowed in startling dahlia
purple; shoulder-skimming spill of hair so profoundly black it
seemed, like some dreaded galactic hole, to sponge up all the light
around her. Abundance of trinketry, gaudy hoops, chains, bracelets,
and rings (in among the latter, of course, the wedding variety) adorning ears, neck, wrists, stubby, crimson-taloned fingers. Figure, what
he could make of it under the baggy red jacket, flattering to no one,
round but not fat, a certain overripe fleshiness to it, breasts a pair of
plump trophies brushing the surface of the counter as she pressed
herself into it, languidly examining the product in question, a bottle
of cheap perfume. Altogether, in his estimate, the flashy, slutty look
of a woman dogged in the pursuit of carnal pleasures.

And gazing at her that way, he recognized something loosing in
him, some satanic warp in his head, starting small, the barest stirring,
but coiling slowly upward out of the darkest recesses of a savage, inventive imagination, out of memories blotted, buried, sealed. He tried
to remove his fixed stare, turn away. Couldn't, or didn't. Continued
to gawk, against his will, against all reason, as she lifted her eyes to a
scruffy, acned youth, fluttered her lashes, fondled the phallic bottle,
and murmured in a husky whisper rich in implied intimacy, "Didn't
get the job done?"

"Huh?"

"She didn't like it? The perfume?"

"Who's that?"

"Why, your girlfriend, course. Who else?"

The young man shifted awkwardly. "Uh, no. Said it ain't exactly, y'know, her style."

Her lips opened in a lazy smile, part teasing, part dreamy. "Oh, I dunno," she said. "I can remember some steamy nights, that perfume."

A flush deep enough to match the cherry on those parted lips or the crimson on the nails came into the young man's pitted face. She scribbled some numbers on a form, pushed it across the counter. Without a word he scooped it up and got out of there fast.

She giggled softly. Glanced over and discovered him watching her, apparent witness to the entire little scene. She met his gaze, looked him up and down boldly. Bold, measuring look, unflustered, unacquainted with shame. "You bein' helped?" she asked, turning the lazy smile on him, notching up its heat.

Michael said *Yes,* shaken by the peculiarly thick sound of his voice, the monosyllable emerging as though from a mouth coated with shellac.

"Wanna swap?"

"Pardon?"

"The shavin' cream. You wanna trade it in?"

"Yes."

"Darla run outta exchange slips again?"

Darla, evidently the clerk, pledged to be right back. Where was Darla? "So it seems," he said.

The smile enlarged, lifting at the corners in a knowing U-shaped grin, full of promise. "I can take care of you," she said. "Got everything you need right here."

A sudden shrill chorus of voices pealed through the contracting corridors of his head, sang to him. No, that wasn't right—assailed him, boomed at him. There was his own prudent, rational, drilled voice; and another—darkly familiar, taunting, wicked, spiraling up out of that kinked imagination and spawning, out of the crypt of memory, rapidly unsealing, a confusion of others, scarcely recognizable, voices with no faces to put with them, muffled, pleading, screeching, every one of them. And there was Norman's, by turns prolix, clipped, ornate, blunt, freighted always with irony. And, more distantly, Aunt Grace's, pettish and scolding. But most predominant of all, come like a fragile lifeline flung across the miles of phone wire, was that feathery spirit voice offering the wondrous gift of new beginnings, seeming to carry with it the magical power to mend the tattered fabric of his secret life, brake the rush of bestial impulse, decelerate time, possibly even reverse it, miraculously erase the stains of the past. And it was the force of that voice salvaged him now.

Aloud, he said, "No. I've . . . changed my mind. I'll keep it."

"You sure about that?"

"I'm sure."

"Well, you change it again, come back and see me. Ask for Melanie."

"Melanie."

"There you got it," she said, staring hard into his eyes. "Melanie."

"I won't. Change it, that is."

"Yeah, well, we'll see."

He seized the can, dropped it in the shopping bag, spun on his heels, and made for the exit, muttering to himself, *I won't,* repeating it, the conviction lessening as he crossed the parking lot, moving stiffly, like a man treading through wet cement, while one of the many clashing voices, the taunting one, ascended above all the rest to whisper in his ear, *Yes you will, you'll be back.*

AT ABOUT THE SAME TIME Michael was driving, directionless, down a busy Grand Rapids street, Victor Flam was standing at the door of the Woodrow condominium in Hinsdale, Illinois, his finger on the bell. He'd spent the past couple of days in Hammond, Indiana, ticking off another of the names on his list, another dead end. Though he knew for a fact this Michael Woodrow wouldn't be home, was up in Michigan someplace, he was still a little curious about the old man who done the time. Figured no harm, looking in on him. This close, why not?

And on the other side of that door Norman was just then climbing the stairs, muttering darkly under his breath. Something about goddam unwelcome, unwanted, unsolicited, unpardonable intrusions. He'd spent an entirely nonproductive morning gazing at a blank sheet of paper, and the rest of his day was pledged to Lizabeth Seaver. The great paneling project. Your all-purpose Mr. Fix-It, wall boards to bruised hearts.

And so he was not in the mellowest of humors when he swung open the door and discovered a tall burly fellow, thick in the neck and the chest and the middle, bulging his natty suit, ruddy face lit in a wide Rotarian grin. Norman looked at him coldly, stiffened, framed the word *yes* into sleety question.

"Mr. Woodrow?"

"Norman Woodrow. Yes."

"My name's Flam. Victor Flam. Wonder if you could spare me a minute of your time."

"If you've got something to sell, it's my son you'd want to speak with. He's the owner. And he's not here."

"Got nothin' to sell, Mr. Woodrow. Word of honor."

"Really. Then what's your business?"

"Well, you was to ask me to step inside, be glad to fill you in."

"I'm not in the habit of inviting strangers into the house."

"Hey, I hearya. Ordinarily that's your best idea. Can't be too careful nowadays. Here, lemme show you my card."

He produced one, handed it over. Norman pretended to study it. Stalling. He had him made for heat, one species or another, the instant he cracked the door. It was the eyes gave him away, a polychrome of shades, one for taking the measure of the world, another for probing weakness, yet another for calculating risk. Chameleon eyes, stippled with venom. Kind you never want to show your back to. No mistaking heat. And the card, for all its artful linguistic dodging, merely confirmed it. Norman gave him back his card, said, "And what exactly is your area of inquiry, Mr. Flam?"

"Beg pardon?"

"Your card says you're a researcher. What do you research?"

"Well," Flam drawled, "this particular case it's your son."

"My son?" Norman said, doing his absolute best to smother the ripple of shock in his voice. Give heat nothing. "I'm afraid I don't understand."

Flam let the grin sag, posted a thin tricky smile in its place. Watched him levelly. That piece of news sets him back a little, lowers him a notch. All that fancyass talk cuts no shit with Victor Flam. He'd've spotted him for joint through a mile of ground fog. Written all over him. Even old, he still got the wiry, rope-muscled build comes of all that heavin' iron, nothing better to do, pass the years. Also the narrow seamed face, hardcase zipper in it. But the real cincher, trademark seal, is the dead-behind-the-eyes stare. Flam's seen it before, many a time. "Michael Woodrow," he said, "he's your son, right?"

"That's right."

"Then he'd be the party I'm researchin'. Indirectly, y'might say."

"You've got something to tell me about him?"

"Tell some, ask some."

"I'm listening."

"Kinda damp out here. Sure we can't talk inside? Only take a minute, and I think you find it real interesting, what I got to say."

Norman considered. Like all heat, he looked about as trustworthy as a bottled scorpion. But if it was grief he wanted to give, he'd have done it by now. And the Michael angle was truly puzzling. Worse than that, vaguely alarming. "A minute," he said, and motioned him in.

A couch cushion exhaled softly under Flam's weight. He glanced around the room, allowed affably, "Nice place you got here."

"It's not mine. Remember?"

Flam snapped a finger, made an *oh, stupid me* face. "That's right. You told me that. Belongs to your boy, correct?"

"Correct."

"But you live here with him?"

"Also correct."

"He must do pretty well for himself, the consulting business."

"Well enough."

"Bet you're proud. Young fella like that."

Norman settled back in his chair. Lit a red. Composed his features in an attitude of wintry distance. "Let's see now," he said. "So far we've covered ownership, living arrangements, Michael's profession and approximate age. Clock's ticking, Mr. Flam. Your minute's running down."

Now Flam displayed the helpless exasperated face of the man conscious of his own verbosity, but powerless to contain it. "I tellya," he said, "I get to jawin' and the time just scoots away. Sorry about that. Can see you're a busy man."

Norman let that last little shot go by. Made no reply.

"Y'see," Flam pushed on, still in good-humored rube persona, "what I'm researchin' is an unfortunate incident, happened 'bout a year back. Down in Florida. Same place your boy was workin' at, one of his consulting jobs. Which is what brings me here."

"And what was the nature of this incident?"

Employing essentially the same rap he'd used with Stroiker

and the three names already scrubbed from his list, Flam laid out the Shelley story, but padding it here and there, stringing it out, softening some of the details. Explaining patiently, respectfully, the way you'd talk at your everyday seniors, but watching this one carefully all the while, looking for a reaction. Nothing. Just sits there pulling on his weed, listening, saying not a word. No comments, no questions. Never even asks is Flam the law or solo or what his stake is in it, like all the others done. No, not this one. Too much street in him. He knows.

". . . so that's pretty much it," Flam concluded, easing back on the couch and turning over summary palms.

"I see. Sad story."

" 's truth, it's a sad one all right."

"And what exactly is it you hope to get from Michael?"

"Well, what I'm tryin' to do here is chat with anybody might of known the victim. See can they help me out with some background on her, kind of lady she was. Habits, friends, things like that."

"Shed light on her character?"

"Something like that, yeah."

"A profile?"

"There you are."

"And you came all the way from Florida for that purpose?"

"Oh no. I been talkin' to a lot of people knew her. Anybody I can turn up. Was in the vicinity and thought might as well stop by, chance he'd be here. It bein' weekend and all."

"But as you see, he's not."

No offer of his whereabouts either. Tough old bird still operating off joint code, volunteer nothing. "Yeah, I can see that," Flam said dryly. "Shame."

"Isn't it, though."

"Well, was just a wild shot anyway."

Norman stubbed out the cigarette, glanced at his watch. "Anything else, Mr. Flam?"

"Guess that about covers it."

Norman ushered him to the door. On the way Flam said idly, "Oh, you wanta mention to your boy I was here, that's okay too."

"Perhaps I will."

"Maybe I'll give him a ring sometime. Let the fingers do the walkin', like they say."

"You do that."

Flam paused, tilted his head quizzically, gave it a beat. "Y'know," he said in tones of trivial afterthought, "there's one thing strikes me a little peculiar, Mr. Woodrow."

"What would that be?"

"You never troubled to ask what capacity it is, I'm doin' all this research. Mind my askin' why?"

"I think I can make an educated guess."

"Bet you can, at that."

A look of chilly shared recognition crossed the hostile gulf opened suddenly between them. For a breath of an instant neither one spoke. Then Flam stuck out a meaty palm, flashed his big grin. "Sure do wanta thank you for all your time."

"Nothing," Norman said. "Forget it." But he didn't reach for the hand either.

Flam shrugged, turned, and strode toward his car. Over his shoulder he called, "You have a super day now, Mr. Woodrow. Y'hear?"

"I hear," Norman said, staring at him. And he continued to stare as the car backed into the street and pulled away, a ragged nameless desolation rising through his chest, bunching in his throat. Call it doubt. Or confusion. Or fear.

"MICHAEL?" SHE SAID, HEAD COCKED, squinting into the waning light. Then she said it again, "Michael!"—astonishment shifting accent, pitch, tone, investing his name, this second uttering, with the mingled resonances of wonder and joy. The lifeline voice he had travelled two hundred miles to hear firsthand, unfiltered by wire and distance and the gloss of solitary reveries.

"None other."

"Where did you . . . come from?"

The very edge, he might have told her, but he said simply, "Michigan."

"I *know* that. But I thought—"

"I decided to take a day off."

"What a marvelous surprise. I was going to call you tonight."

"This is better."

"I'd say better." Her face beamed in a smile of such genuine warmth, genuine sweetness, he felt an odd stitch in his chest. She pulled open the screen door, motioned at him. "Come on in. Your dad's here."

He hesitated. "Norman's here?"

"We just finished the basement. That paneling I told you about? Remember?"

"I remember."

"Come in, come in." She reached out and grasped his arm, a gesture of easy intimacy, almost proprietary. Led him through the door and into the living room, released the arm, and went to the head of the stairs. "Norman," she called. "Guess who's here."

"I've no idea." Voice floating up from below.

"Well, come and see."

Footsteps on the stairs. Norman's head appearing between the wooden banister rails, level with the floor, the curious look of decapitation. "Michael," he said, one eyebrow lifted, as much as he'd ever give away of surprise. "And out of familiar context." He mounted the remaining stairs and approached him, fists doubled, arms upraised, wide flung, windmilling the air. "Find an opening. If you can."

Reflexively Michael crouched, ducked, made a cross of forearms above his head. "I'm trying. God knows, I'm trying."

Lizabeth, standing off to one side, watched them puzzledly. "What's all *this?*"

"Our version of the ceremonial handclasp," Norman said, arms lowered now, grinning.

"Very civilized," she said, schoolmarmish mock severity. "But if the bout's over, why don't you battlers sit."

Norman took a chair, Michael the couch. Lizabeth remained on her feet. "Basement finished, Michael back, Saturday night—I think the occasion calls for something. Don't you agree?"

"Inspired thought," Norman said.

"What would you like?"

"Beer would do nicely."

"Michael?"

He nodded, to signify the same.

She started for the kitchen, paused, looked over her shoulder at them, a trace of remembered chagrin clouding her features. "But this time soda only, for me."

"You're permitted to join us," Norman said drolly. "All past gaffes, real or imagined, forgotten and forgiven. Right, Michael?"

"Absolutely."

"Oh no. I've learned my lesson, around you two."

Michael looked at Norman, looking at her. His eyes, normally remote and brooding, were full of fondness. There was between them, in their easeful bantering, their interplay of glances, a kind of relaxed and casual . . . what could you call it but domesticity. And for a moment he felt like a lumpish interloper, welcomed of course, but somewhat disruptive, a presence to be tolerated, endured. Felt for a moment a wrenching loneliness. Wondered why he was here.

Till she returned bearing a tray of drinks and, after serving Norman, came over and sat next to him on the couch, assuming that place naturally, as though it were the only place in the room she naturally, rightfully belonged. She set the tray on the coffee table, handed him a bottle of Heineken, lifted a can of Pepsi in salute, and, her face opening in a pleasured smile, said, "Here's to the prodigal's return."

"You're starting to sound like Norman," he said.

She slapped her forehead with an open palm. "Manners like him, too. I forgot to offer you a glass."

"This is fine."

"So what brings you home unannounced?" Norman asked him.

He shrugged. "A whim."

"Whim," Norman repeated, skeptical edge to it. "Job proceeding satisfactorily?"

"Project, Norman. We don't do jobs."

"Project, then."

"It's coming along."

"It's a college, isn't it?" Lizabeth's question.

"Yes. A college."

"Public or private?" Norman again.

"Private."

"Church affiliated?"

"Afraid so."

"Worse luck for you."

"Why do you say that?" Lizabeth asked.

"Because all of those scripture-manglers, academicians in particular, take their greatest joy in watching people squirm."

"That's not very kind, Norman," she said.

"The truth seldom is."

"In this case," Michael said, "you may be right. I've been getting a certain amount of resistance. From the president. A woman."

Norman snorted. "Small surprise."

Lizabeth shook an admonishing finger at him. "And *that's* not exactly a nineties attitude, Norman."

"Endless apologies. But I've never experienced the many uplifting benefits of a consciousness raising."

"You dad's still living in the fifties," she said to Michael, touching at his knee lightly, to show it was a joke, a gentle brushing motion, no more than that, the more meaningful for its delicacy.

"Forties would be closer," Norman said. "Or possibly even the thirties, the child being father to the man."

Neither of them appeared to be listening.

"When will you be done up there?" she asked Michael. "In Michigan, I mean."

"Another two weeks."

"And when do you have to go back?"

"Tomorrow."

"Early?"

"Pretty early."

Norman cleared his throat, said, "How did you get here, by the way?"

Michael lifted his gaze from her, looked over at him blankly. "I'm sorry?"

"Your means of transport?"

"Oh, that. I drove."

"Did you stop at home?"

"No, I came here first."

A silence opened, small but tight. Lizabeth put a question into it. "Would you like to have a look at the basement, Michael?"

"Sure. Why not."

"Your dad's become quite a carpenter."

"I'd never have guessed."

"The master craftsman," Norman said. "Put a Phillips in my hand and I'll construct you another Taj Mahal. Or the Cologne Cathedral."

"You're such a twit, Norman. Come on, let's show him."

She took Michael's hand, pulled him to his feet. Somewhat heavily, Norman rose out of his chair. "You do it," he said. "I must be getting back."

"Getting back? What do you mean?"

"Just that. I must be going now."

"But why? It's early yet. Michael just got here. And we have to show off your work."

Michael, for his part of it, said nothing.

Norman looked at them, both of them, standing there, hands linked. He smiled. Charitable, benedictory smile. "You do it," he said again.

AFTER HE WAS OUT THE DOOR and gone, they remained in that posture, still standing side by side, the tips of their shoulders brushing, hands still joined.

"Well," she said finally, "do you want to see the basement?"

"If you like."

But neither of them moved.

"I'm so happy you're here, Michael."

Happy. Her word. Not pleased or glad or delighted or cheered. *Happy.* He watched her, studying the many particulars of her lovely face, listening for the subtle colorings in her voice. The stitch came back into his chest, sharper now, a stinging, yearning ache. The seed of the hope of the possibility of deliverance. Was that happiness? Impossible to know. "It's good to be here," he said.

"So. The basement?"

"Maybe another time."

Wordlessly, she switched out the light, and they turned toward her bedroom.

AND ACROSS THE STREET and the stretch of lawn, Norman stood at a window watching the darkness settle through her condominium. He rejoiced for his son, sorrowed for himself, overtaken by a hopeless wanting, the universal wanting in the heart to fold back the years, begin again, get it right this time.

And mingled with that sorrow was the disturbing recollection of this morning's curious encounter, buried these past hours in the comforting normalcy of sweat work. The tale of a murder trailing halfway across the continent to this serene shelter. The sly, oafish teller of that tale, who just happened to be "in the vicinity." Sure.

Worst of all, too appalling to cinch with words, the dreadful possibility of a poison passed along in the blood.

He looked up at the cold glitter of stars spattering the black sky. Listened to the sigh of a small wind. Rise and fall of the wind. First breath of the icy grip of winter in the heart.

13

1. BABCOCK, BRUCE
2. CASSIDY, GARY
3. POMFORD, LEONARD
4. TATE, CHARLES
5. WOODROW, MICHAEL

Numbers 1, 3 and 5 starred, signifying the ones still on the Stoltz payroll; 2 and 4, the dumpees, starless; check marks behind 1, 3 and 4 (2 as yet unlocated, for all Nathan's artistry with the show-and-tell screen), to indicate they'd been reached, interviewed, eyeballed, read, more or less accounted for, scratched.

Flam, late that same Saturday night, sitting hunched over the table in a spacious, elegant room at the O'Hare Hilton, staring at the list of names. Lost track of how long he'd been at it. Too long. Continued to stare at the names anyway. Fixed, stony glare of concentration. Didn't help. Anybody was capable of murder. Fuck, make that *everybody,* Mother Teresa not excepted, given the right set of conditions, right button punched. Of that, he hadn't the slightest doubt. But the Shelley Swales wasting—that, now, required a special brand of bughouse, and none of the three he'd connected with so far had enough kink in them for it. Or enough stones.

Take the first one, Babcock, for sure a closet case, the gossipy Stroiker (his own Baton Rouge cover confirmed by Nathan with the peck of a key, alibi while-u-wait) square on the money there, absolutely. Caught up with him in Cincinnati (more of Nathan's professional courtesy) where he was part of a Stoltz team doing a grocery chain; concluded ten minutes into their talk this was not his man, no way. Little fudge-packer got no use for women, that much was plain, but no spine for a Shelley-style whacking either. Not in Flam's considered judgment, which was always reliable enough for him, there being no substitute for experience and a shrewd tracker instinct.

Just to be sure, though, cover all bases (for he was nothing if not thorough), he'd dropped by the public library and with the help of another one of them library wimps, male this time, done a microfiche check of all the newspapers of all the cities Babcock had worked the past year. Looking for accounts of similar types of homicides. Looking for a pattern, a trail. Came up jack, just your everyday waxings: drug deals gone bad, stickups munched, drive-bys, gang punk paybacks, mom and pops. Which didn't, of course, rule out the possibility of a single-bagger, a one-shot explosion of rage. He didn't think so. Not from what he'd seen of little Bruce.

Same drill with the other two. Tate, eventually and with no little Jewboy pissing and whining ("You realize this is consuming an inordinate amount of my time, Victor") traced to Connecticut, gone solo after the Stoltz axing, doing a few five-and-dime consulting jobs, scrambling to put something on his plate. And Pomford, the last one, a fussy bean counter, climber with his eyes on the corporate prize, busy with a foundry over in Hammond. Both of them pass the Victor Flam eyeball test just fine, flying fucking colors. And nothing in the newspaper files to suggest any follow-up mischief, either one.

So where was he at? *Nowhere* was where. Handful of zip. Three weeks gone by and already Mother Swales starting to crowd him, wanting to know what he's turned up, clues he's uncovered, what he's got to show for all the cush she's laying out. Wanting *progress* reports, for chris'fuckin'sake. Like it's the goddam Federal Bureau she got in her employ. So what he's got to do is try and explain to her (but gently now, nice and easy, lots of woolly words, lots of smoke, this being one deep well you don't want drying up on you too quick) all that apprehending your perps through scientific crime detection, all those coordinated efforts by your law enforcement agencies, your behavioral science units, labs, eggheads in white coats—all of it so much ass gas, movie scheisse. Real-life tracking more like the military, like a military campaign: Confusion, guesswork, hunch-playing, automatic reacting, general fuckups, couple steps forward, you get lucky, least as many back, you don't. The ass covering, that part he don't tell her. Or that sometimes you lose. Not that he liked to, not with the mondo-class jacket he got, this business. But sometimes you did.

Which was exactly what was going to happen, sure as God made little brown turd balls, he didn't catch a break soon. Nothing in the photocopied p.d. file to go on (been over it more times than he could count), and only two names left on the list and one of them still in the wind. The little sitdown with Woodrow senior this morning was interesting but inconclusive. Old joint dog too seasoned to give away anything of himself. For all Flam could tell, he could've done his stretch for some diddlydink white collar scam. Talked like a cookie-pusher, all that wiseass foof. Which left no option but to swing on over to Michigan and have a word with junior, by all accounts a by-the-books player, workaholic, on the Stoltz fast track. Your basic straight arrow. Didn't look promising.

Nothing else in the ideas and inspirations duffel, so Flam was about to haul his bulk out of the chair and put in a call for a morning flight to Grand Fucking Rapids when the phone rattled on the nightstand, and he stepped over and picked it up and said his name into it and got back a nasalized "Nathan here, Victor."

"Nathan. What's up?"

"Your spirits, perhaps, after you hear what I've discovered."

"What'd that be?"

"This Gary Cassidy whose whereabouts you were inquiring after? Seems I've located him."

"Hey, nice goin', Nathan. Where's he at?"

"Phoenix, Arizona."

"You got an address?"

"Of course."

He recited it, same deliberate tone of voice he always used, like he was talking to a retard. Flam copied it onto a notepad, waited.

"Interesting fellow, your Mr. Cassidy," Nathan said, letting it hang there, adding nothing.

"Yeah, how's that?"

"Appears he's something of a chronic ne'er-do-well."

"Like how?"

"Oh, numerous job dismissals, a few drunk and disorderlies in his past, some check-kiting. Things of that sort. None of it in his Stoltz file, incidentally. Serious lapse in their screening process."

"So how'd you come by it?"

"I have my ways, Victor."

Yeah, yeah, yeah. Yid games. Still, Flam's interest was picking up a little, not much. D&D's, airborne paper—sidewalk-spitting stuff. Better than what he had, though. Better than zip. "Okay," he said, "so how you suppose he got on with 'em, first place? Stoltz, I'm sayin'."

"My guess is he falsified his resume."

"You think so?"

"Educated guess, Victor."

"He get away with that?"

"Evidently."

"This is pretty good, Nathan, what you're tellin' me here. Anything else on him? Anything heavy?"

"Depends."

"On what?"

"Your definition of 'heavy'."

Flam suppressed a sigh. "Like time, say. He do any time?"

"No."

Now he sighed. "Not into Twenty Questions, Nathan. You got anything or not?"

"Quite possibly."

"You maybe wanta share it?"

"First I have a question for you, Victor."

"Fire."

Throat-clearing pause. "Very well," he said. "Over the past several weeks I've done what I think you'll agree is a goodly amount of research for you. All of it uncompensated, by the way."

Another little pause in there, to let the message settle in. Flam thinking, *Oh, oh, here it comes, the touch.* But saying nothing. Make him spit it out for himself.

"But that's all right," Nathan went on. "That's fine. Always happy to be of assistance."

"The question, Nathan."

"You realize you've never confided in me, Victor, regarding the nature of this investigation. Had you done so at the outset, I rather expect it, i.e., said investigation, could have been expedited considerably. Conservation of mutual effort, you know, to say nothing of our valuable time."

"Still waitin' on that question, Nathan."

"Question? Yes, the question. Question, Victor, is why the shroud of mystery?"

For Flam that one was easy. You let a Hebe in on what's shaking down here and, worse, who's picking up the check, and he's for sure gonna want a cut of the action. See a nice piece of the old green gabardine in it for himself. In his fuckin' dreams, he'd see it. Comes to the Palm Beach cash factory, Flam's not big on any fifty-fifty arrangements. So he says, very carefully, "Just a routine track, is all. No mystery."

"Routine. Really. I'd never have suspected."

"Yeah, why's that?"

"From your obvious preoccupation with it, Victor, this 'routine' track. Almost obsessive, one might say."

"Yeah, well, I got a rep to maintain, same as you."

"That's certainly understandable. Your good name at stake."

Flam was getting mightily sick of it, all the waltzing. Getting a gutful. "Look, Nathan," he said, "you after some of that compensation I heard in there someplace, why not just drop to the bottom line. Spare the dickin' around." Flam hoping to wring a number out of him, flat fee, then kike him down, maybe slide some of it in on the next expense statement, cushion the blow.

"Oh, I'm confident we can work out something equitable, Victor. For both of us."

"So you wanta gimme a figure?"

"We'll discuss it later. When the time is right."

Yeah, right, later. Flam could see it now. Great moments in crime fighting: presenting the bill. For now though, Israel and his magic box got him by the short hairs, and they both knew it. He said, "Your call, Nathan. Whenever."

"Later will do. In the meantime, getting back to your Mr. Cassidy, perhaps you'd be interested in another item of biographical information I've come across."

"Anything you wanta pass along, I always got an interest."

"Seems he's a bit rough on the ladies."

"Rough? What kind of rough?"

"The physical kind, Victor."

"Just how rough we talkin' here?" Flam asked, keeping his voice even, cool, close to neutral as he could pitch it.

"Assault-and-battery rough. Two instances of record. First one on an ex-wife, more recently a live-in companion."

"Charged, was he?"

"Dropped, both cases. However, he was slapped with restraining orders on both. Which is partly how I managed to discover them. Along with some other creative burrowing, of course."

"How far back these go?"

"With the ex, four years. The girlfriend just last month."

"You got an age, this dude?"

"Just turned thirty-three. His Christiad year."

"Huh?"

"Never mind, Victor."

Probably some Jew zinger, that Christiad shit. Flam let it go by. He didn't give a fuck. Too wired. All he wanted to do was get off the horn, get his rushing thoughts slowed down, ordered.

"I hope this intelligence will prove to be of some use to you," Nathan said smugly. Like he'd just cracked the nut for him.

"Well, I'll sure take it into account, Nathan."

"Most prudent. And I trust you'll keep me updated on your progress."

"I'll do that."

"I'm beginning to feel something of a personal involvement in this little—how shall I put it?—puzzle of yours. You've got my interest piqued."

"Appreciate all the good buzz, Nathan. We'll be talkin' again soon."

"I look forward to it impatiently, Victor."

Flam put down the phone. Bet your sweet Jew ass, impatient. No way around it, this one gonna cost him some heavy juice before it's all wrapped. Worth it, though, this Cassidy live up to his jacket: loser, history of fucking up, lady swatter, and about the right age, given Shelley's documented tastes in bangin' partners. Could be the break he was looking for. The big bingo.

From his wallet he removed a crime scene photo and stared (as he'd stared many times over the past weeks) at Shelley's nude, hacked body, sodden with blood, entrails spilling, the look frozen on her face not so much terror or even pain as bewilderment, utter incomprehension. Lately he'd taken to carrying it with him, a reminder of the shadowy figure he was tracking. He thought about something Nathan had said, a word he'd used. Obsessive. Wasn't that, exactly. Nothing to him, apart from the job itself, what had happened to Shelley. All he knew, she might've had it coming. Life got a way of balancing things out. Live long enough and you get pretty much what you deserve. But no denying either, there'd be a certain satisfaction—kind that goes beyond loot, even—in nailing the bent scumbucket put that look on her face.

So it's scratch Michigan for now, leave it on hold, and off to sunny Arizona, first flight out. Pay a little visit to good-time Gary. Have a friendly little chat.

14

The capricious stranger was surely gone. Vanished into that murky ether of wayward fancy and willful self-deception we choose to call the past. Sauntered away with an insolent shrug and not a glance backward. Gone, it seemed, for good.

And Norman could pinpoint exactly his departure date: Saturday, September 26, two weeks ago this very day. Day of the disquieting visit by the crafty Victor Flam. Even more precisely could he trace it to the moment of Michael's sudden and altogether unprecedented appearance at the condo across the street. Ever since then this woman who in five short weeks had come to fill his thoughts and his days with the wholesome numbing normalcy of the present (paneling walls, for God's sake, not to speak of installing carpet, shopping for drapes, sharing dinners and idle chatter and evenings spent gaping at her television, the classics forsaken), this Lizabeth Seaver had, since then, presented the excited, radiant glow of a woman with a new man in her life. In her bed. Invited him wordlessly, through gesture, act, bearing, movement, expression, secret hushed smile, the unphrasable dispatches of the delirium of romantic love—invited him thusly to share in her renewal, her joy. And ever since that mo-

ment Norman's feckless guide had deserted him. Abandoned him to
his blank pages, as though the calamitous and unresolved past had
lost all its perverse fascination, its liberating promise, its relevance.
As though to say: If that's your choice, my deluded friend, then so
be it.

For something over six hours he had been staring at the pad of
paper in front of him. It remained resolutely blank. He fidgeted. His
nerves twanged with caffeine and nicotine. The tip of his ballpoint
was gnawed to a gummy stub. He set it down, lit another in the procession of cigarettes. Lifted his gaze from desk to window, to the
patch of grass beyond it, fading a drab autumnal brown, to the sky
above it, overlaid with a sheet of gray clouds. If there was a sun behind them it was nowhere to be seen. A damp, bleak October morning, showers in the air. Nature in collusion with his confounding
vacancy of memory and imagination. Baffling, if you wanted to think
about it, explore it. Which he didn't.

Didn't have to, for his glance was drawn just then to a sleek,
bone white Corvette wheeling around the corner and lurching to a
stop outside Lizabeth's condo. A man stepped out, marched purposefully to the door, laid a finger on the bell, and left it there. An instant
passed. The door swung open, and over the man's shoulder Norman
could see her standing in it. Appeared to be blocking it. The man began gesturing, subdued motions at first, then picking up animation,
heat, arms semaphoring, chopping the air. Agitation's dumb show.

The door slammed shut. The man's head jerked back as though
he had taken a blow full in the face. He turned stiffly. Tramped toward his car. Halfway there he stopped. Planted himself in a wide-
legged stance, hands on hips, jaw outthrust, eyes elevated, glowering
at the heavens like some necromancer summoning a lightning bolt,
or the philosopher issuing his imperious command: *Sun, stand thou
still!* No sun visible anywhere, in all the leaden sky.

Abruptly, he spun around and strode back to the door. Ham-
mered it with a fist. A rhythmic pounding. Tireless. Kept hammering
till it opened again, and this time he shoved her aside roughly and
charged on in.

One of the first things you learn—you'd *better* learn—is a respect for space, yours and everybody else's. And the natural corollary
of that joint axiom was you back off from their private beefs. Going
to be enough of your own to keep you occupied. More than plenty.

And so Norman's conditioned impulse (friendship, fondness notwithstanding) was to do nothing, stay out of it, stay put. And for a moment that's what he did. Nothing. Sat there watching, deliberating. But only for a moment.

And then he took a last steadying pull on his cigarette and snuffed it out, came to his feet, and left the security of his room and the larger sanctuary of his son's dwelling, and started across the lawn. Well before he got to the street, a clash of voices reached him from the wide-open door, one of them harsh, bellowy; the other, shrill and pleading, dissonant symphony of domestic discord; and a familiar, distant echo, arriving from across the gulf of years, sounded in his head; and he quickened his pace, thinking, *this is senseless, what you're doing here, worse than madness,* but doing it all the same, drawing a series of shallow breaths to slow the tempest rising in his chest.

Lizabeth saw him first. She was backed up to a kitchen wall, penned in by her visitor's wildly gesticulating arms. He caught something in her eyes and turned slightly, just enough to follow their stricken gaze to the narrow entryway where Norman stood. "Who the fuck is *this?*" he demanded.

"A friend," she said.

The flagging arms fell. He glared at her, then at Norman, then back to her. Fierce pendulating glare. He expelled a scornful grunt. "Robbing the grave now, are you, Liz?"

"A friend," she repeated.

"Well, tell your friend to butt out. Go on back to his shuffleboard or Chinese checkers or whatever it is they play at the nursing home."

In a voice quavery, absent of conviction, she said, "Maybe you'd better, Norman."

Norman said nothing. But he didn't move either.

"You want to turn up the hearing aid?" the man spat at him (quite literally, Norman noted, for the sneered query came winged on spittle). "This is a private conversation we're having here. Personal matter. I'm the husband."

"Ex-husband," Lizabeth amended, barely a whisper, barely audible.

He ignored the emendation. His mouth stretched open in a wicked smile, displaying a curiously shark-like prominence of teeth. "So you just scoot along now," he advised. "Time for your meds and a nice little nap."

And Norman, for his part of it, disregarded the advice. Remained where he was, taking in all the particulars of the scene, the width of the entry, the distance between them, Lizabeth's position against the wall. Taking, also, silent measure of this man, this truculent ex. Late thirties, forty at the most. And tall, maybe half a head taller. Not good. But spindly-limbed, scrawny in the shoulders, broad at the hips, soft in the tummy. Weekend golfer look to him. Basic pencilneck. That much was good. Still, could have one of those colored belts certifying his invincible martial artistry. Anymore, you could never be sure.

So what you do is stare him down. Dinger's stare: vacant, wintry, void of expression or emotion, empty behind the eyes. Nobody fucks with a dinger, everybody fears him. Jailhouse wisdom.

But the ex, evidently unschooled in that arcane lore, cupped his hands at his mouth, no longer smiling, and bawled, "You stone deaf? Said run along home now."

What he'd discovered was that each of these confrontations had its own unique rhythm, its singular choreography, a time to keep silent, a time to speak. And in this one that precise psychological moment to speak had arrived at last. But the words had to be right, and the inflection, and the delivery. Had to draw him over here, into this cramped entry, where his height and reach lose some of their advantage. "I don't think so," Norman said, mild but flat. As flat as the stare he continued to level on him. "Think I'll be staying."

"What! What did you just say?"

"Staying. You're the one who's leaving."

The ex advanced on him, stooped his shoulders, and stuck his scowly face in close, as if presenting it for inspection. If so, it wouldn't pass. Coarse-pored, angular, slightly lopsided (though to be fair that could be due to a corner of the shark-toothed mouth tucked back in a suggestion of menace), rodent eyes, dark and tiny and set in puffy pouches, bluish-black stubble of beard, breath a sweetish reek of scotch and ineffectual Tic Tacs, cinnamon flavor. No, never pass.

"Listen up now, gramps, and listen good—"

"*Well,*" Norman cut in.

"Huh?"

"*Good* is the adjective. You want the adverb *well.* Listen *well.*"

"Good, well. You'd better be listening—"

"Oh, I am."

"—because I don't know what movies you've been watching lately—"

"*Valdez Is Coming.* Classic western. Saw it just the other night. Right here, in fact. In the company of your ex-wife. Heavy on that *ex.*"

The shoulders lifted. The stubbly jaw projected grimly. A warning index finger (left hand, Norman noted and recorded in a memory cell) stabbed the air. "Don't push me, old man."

From behind those squared shoulders came a voice wretched with distress and supplication. "Rick, please. . . ."

"Shut up, Liz."

"Rick's your name, is it?" Norman said, phrasing it rather like a sociable question.

"Richard to you, asshole." Hauling up to his full intimidating height now, an easy six-four, towering over Norman. "Richard Charles Nagel. And you are?"

"The way I see it, Richard, you've got two choices. You can leave quietly, like the reasonable man I'm sure you are. Or you can accept graciously what's going to happen to you."

"What is this? Some kind of joke? Let me see if I've got it right. *You're* threatening *me?*"

"Hardly a threat. Think of it more as a pledge."

The rodent eyes spun heavenward, or as much of heaven as the low ceiling allowed. An open palm thwacked the brow, elaborate show of disbelief. "Jesus, somebody needs to give Father Time here a reality check."

"I guess that means you're rejecting option A," Norman said, putting a little note of sorrow in it. He took a step toward him. The palm flew off the forehead, clenched instinctively in a fist, and the arm swung in a wide looping arc, like half a hug. Norman ducked inside it, and aimed and delivered a short solid punch at a point low on the stylish Sans-a-Belt trousers, drove it into the spongy underbelly, jacknifing him, reducing him to manageable height. Then he crooked his right arm at the elbow joint and swept it under and up, hooking it squarely across the throat in a wrenching, clotheslining motion, pivoting on the balls of his feet, all his weight and force behind it. Enough, anyway, to butter the legs and drop Mr. Richard Charles Nagel gasping and gagging to the floor.

Norman was doing some of that gasping himself, his share,

maybe more. But he had the momentum now, and in brawls as in physics you never want to give away the momentum. So he got down on one knee and, in precaution, laid the other laterally across the reddened stalk of a neck. He took a second—several seconds, actually—to recover his breath and decelerate his storming pulse to something short of hazardous range. When he felt sufficiently composed he said, "That was B, Richard. If you ever come bagging on this lady again there's option C yet. Not in your worst nightmares can you imagine that one. Not even while it's happening. You follow what I'm saying?"

There was a movement of the head, scarcely perceptible, more on the order of a twitch.

Norman let up a little, not much, on the knee-to-neck tensity, eliciting a strangulated gurgle. "That mean yes? You follow?"

The head bobbed affirmatively.

"Better say it. So it's on the record."

"Yes. Follow."

Norman removed the knee, rose, and positioned himself between Lizabeth and her ex, glancing quickly between them, she with a trembly hand held at her mouth, face streaked with tears, thin shoulders quaking, and he still on the floor, curled up tightly and clutching his punished lower abdomen, producing the bubbling sounds of a colicky child. After a while he unfolded the long planks of legs, the slowest of motions, testing them, glacially slow, then rolled over and staggered to his feet. Not quite so belligerent anymore.

Or was he? Standing there, swaying precariously, features twisted in the shifting attitudes of shock and amazement and gradually receding pain and a monumental, impotent rage, he nonetheless managed to sputter, "You sonbitch. I'm not finished with you. This isn't over."

Norman took another step toward him, pure bluff, fully aware of everything expended, not an erg of force left in him. Nor was he unaware of the preposterous figure he had to be cutting there, baggy shapeless clothes, face grizzled and scarred and embroidered with the stitchings of age, ragged timbre of his voice, gone croaky from so brief an exertion. Most of all the theatrical posturing, the low burlesque of it all. But come this far there was nothing to do but play out his assigned—or assumed—role: fair lady's champion, in hoary dress.

"Looks of you," he said, affecting, as best he could, a hardcase growl, "I'd say it's over."

"See about that. We'll see."

Pronounced defiantly, but backing away and with a restraining hand in the air, backing through the door and off the porch and toward the car; and Norman in cautious pursuit, but only as far as the door, transported with relief, silently blessing whatever gods stood watch over doddering fools. But on a reckless impulse, the flush of triumph perhaps, perhaps further to assay the favor of those gods, he called after the retreating figure, "You know, Richard, one of the first signals of a civilization's decline is a loss of respect for its elders." Without success, he struggled to contain the flicker of a smile crossing his face.

"Think that's funny, do you? Cute? You'll think cute when I bring you up on charges." He climbed into the Corvette, fired the engine, thrust his head out the window (perched at the end of that stringy craning neck, it looked oddly like the head of a turtle peeked out from under its shell) and announced, "I'm an *attorney!*" This afterthought delivered in tones of fearsome portent, as though the grave mantle of The Law cast a new and ominous shadow over an incident otherwise forgettable, a mere scuffle.

As indeed, for Norman, suddenly destitute of a ready mockery, watching him squeal away, it did.

"YOUR FRIENDSHIP IS MY THANKS," he said in reply to the weepy wash of gratitude. He had her calmed now, more or less, sunk in a living room chair and swiping at damp eyes, himself on the facing couch, slump-shouldered, clocking a heartbeat dwindled to something approaching normal.

"I'm sorry, Norman. I never cry. Well, almost never."

"You're sure you're all right?"

"I'm sure."

"He didn't swat you around?"

"No, but he might have, if you hadn't come by."

"This sort of thing, does it happen often?"

"Right after the divorce it did. Not so often anymore. When he's drinking, mostly. He's got a nasty temper."

"Not your happiest attribute. Particularly in a lawyer."

"Only with me. With everyone else he's a model of lawerly cool. It's like one of those Jekyll and Hyde things."

Most of the daze had gone out of her eyes, all of the tremble out of her voice and limbs. And so, gently steering the talk to matters for him considerably more nagging and urgent, he said, "Remember when you first told me about your difficulties with him?"

"That morning we had breakfast. In that cafe on Ogden."

"You realize you, ah, neglected to mention his profession?"

"I did? Guess it must not have seemed important."

"Do you see how it could be to me? If he elects to make good on that threat?"

"Which one? He was doing a lot of threatening."

"To press charges."

"Oh, that. Not a chance. That was just bluster. He's got too much macho vanity. Be too humiliating for him."

"Bested by a senior citizen?" he said, mustering a wry smile, but stung in spite of himself. Speaking of vanities.

"I didn't mean it that way, Norman."

"Doesn't matter. About those charges, I can only hope you're right. Because, you see, it wouldn't do for me to—" he paused, debated how to put it, settled on the fuzzy—"become entangled in a lawsuit."

"Won't happen. I know Rick. Trust me, I'm right."

Hoped to Christ (or to any of those fickle gods who'd deign to listen) she was. Sounded confident, just enough airy dismissiveness in it to be convincing. And he wanted to be convinced and so—for the moment anyway, worry about it later—he was. On to that other issue, more immediate and no less vexing, maybe even more so. "By the way," he said, off-handed pitch, "when Michael gets in tonight it would be better if we, uh, didn't speak of this unfortunate little episode."

She looked at him puzzledly. "But Michael's not coming home today. Didn't you know?"

"No, I didn't."

"He called last night. They're finishing today, in Michigan, but something's come up in Texas. San Antonio, I think he said. He has to go down there for a few days."

"I see."

She continued to stare at him. "You shouldn't feel hurt, Norman, or slighted. He probably just assumed I'd be seeing you today. Let you know."

"Very likely," he said, uncertain whether it was hurt he felt at getting the news secondhand, or relief, at the purchase of time. He added quickly, before the message got lost, "In any case, I'm sure you'll agree there's no need to trouble him with it, whenever he arrives."

"But why wouldn't we tell him?"

"Your turn to trust me. It's better left unremarked on."

She rolled over acquiescent palms. "If that's how you want it."

"That's how."

"But you know he'd be proud of you, Norman. *I'm* proud of you. What you did, it was, well, heroic."

"More like histrionic."

"It was heroic, Norman."

He shrugged. "You supply the sand, I'll do the kicking."

"It was all so fast," she said, the sally unacknowledged, "so . . . sudden."

"Good thing, too. Another thirty seconds and you'd have been summoning the EMS unit. For me, that is."

"How did you do it, anyway?" she asked, voice small but charged with wonder, genuine curiosity. "You don't strike me as the brawler type."

"Mens sana in corpore sano."

"What?"

"Sound mind in a sound body. Semi-sound, both places."

"Be serious, Norman."

"I am. It's all a matter of the head you're in."

"Where'd you learn that? Those Japanese warriors you were telling me about?"

"There, and elsewhere."

"Where, elsewhere?"

"Elsewhere."

"Tell me, Norman. I want to know."

"Why? It's over now. Let it rest."

"Because it's all so . . ."

"Improbable?"

"Yes. Exactly. Improbable. Like something out of a movie. One of those Clint Eastwood movies."

"No . . . it was Burt," Norman mumbled under his breath, his gaze turned suddenly inward.

"What?"

"Burt," he murmured again, nerves taut, scalp tingling, mouth gone dry, squinting off into some distant interior horizon.

"Burt who? I don't know who you're talking about, Norman."

"Burt Lancaster. Another actor. Leading man. Famous in his day. You wouldn't remember him. Before your time."

"Of course I do. We saw him just the other night. That movie you mentioned to Rick."

"Valdez Is Coming."

"I've seen a lot of his movies. On the late show."

"The late show," Norman said ruefully.

"There's *Elmer Gantry*. And that bird one. About the prison."

"Birdman of Alcatraz," he said, screening it again inside his head, fast forward speed, thinking how different Burt's cinematic prison was from his own.

"But what about him? What's the point?"

A shimmery figure appeared on that inner horizon, seemed to hail him from across the arid wastes of the past.

"Norman?"

He came up off the couch, saying, "If you're all right now, I must be going."

"Going? Now?"

"Yes, if you're all right."

"I'm fine," she said, confusion in that small voice. "It's you I'm worried about."

"Don't be."

"You really have to leave?"

"Yes."

"Will you call me later?"

"If you like," he said, somewhat brusquely. Had to hurry now, before the beckoning figure was lost to sight, vanished again.

She walked him to the door. Put a tentative hand on his arm. "Norman?"

"Yes?"

She leaned toward him, laid a light brushing kiss on his cheek. "Thank you," she said.

•   •   •

Rewarded with a kiss. How sweet.

So you're back.

Never really gone, Norman.

No? You had me fooled.

Small achievement, fooling you.

Back to insult me, are you?

To compliment you, actually. You handled that one rather well. Very heroic, to borrow the lady's words.

It's a belief in the heroic that makes heroes. Somebody said that, or something like that. Disraeli, I think.

A bit melodramatic, of course, by your own testimony. A trifle overwrought. Borderline farce, some might say, for a man of your advanced years.

Yes, well, I'm not yet quite ready to settle for the wreckage of age and death's long goodnight.

What a sententious gasbag you are, Norman.

That's the sum of your compliment, is it? Many thanks.

It was intended sincerely. On balance, an admirable performance. All things considered.

Your praise overwhelms me. I swoon with bliss.

Too bad all those others were so botched.

Others?

Don't be disingenuous, Norman. It doesn't become you. You know the ones I mean. And you do agree they were messy, to put the most charitable construction on it.

I'm a slow study.

I'd say, slow.

Is that why you're here? To rub my nose in bygone shit?

Whew! Not only pompous, touchy as well. Not to say crude.

The question is why you're here.

You solicit my help, I come to help.

How, exactly?

Well, for a start, you did recall Burt.

So?

He was a poseur, like you.

This is your notion of help?

You certainly are a slow study.

So instruct me.

How many times must I say it, Norman. It's your story.

But where does Burt figure in?
That's for you to discover.
I suppose I could try.
Stout fellow! Pick up your pen now and trace the progress of *your celluloid hero.*
Do what I can.
Best of luck.
Oh, and by the way—thanks.
Don't thank me yet, Norman.

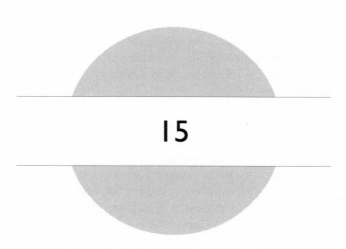

15

Like a good many men of my generation, I've had a movie going in my head the better part of my life. Actually, a series of movies, fantastical adventures of my own creation, impossibly romantic, featuring of course myself. Or, in the formative years, the man I hoped to become. For many of us, you see, particularly the fatherless, coming of age during a narrow window of time, the decade of the forties and maybe a year or two into the next, no further—many of us, all but the dullest, took no small share of our character from those heroic figures that loomed so vastly in the Bijous of our vanished youth. By this I do not mean simply our dated fashions and quaint, mannered slang, though they were a part of it, too. I mean the way we apprehended the world, fit our faces to it, confronted it.

The same is not true today, I think, for all the fretting talk of television's pernicious influence. Those incessantly running micro-screens are too accessible, live-in guests we have come to tolerate. Familiar, passionless, incapable of surprise, and therefore deserving of nothing more than our wandering attention. Watching them is like submitting resignedly to a garrulous drunk: so earnest, so much to tell, and all of it tattered by so many tellings.

Not so, I maintain, in that earlier time. Then, screen and self were isolate, disjoined by a chasm much too wide for breeching. But in the recognition of that gulf and the effort to transcend it lay our deepest impulse to private mythologizing. Perhaps our finest impulse, for we were reminded of elevations that towered somewhere out above the fog shrouding our own drab lives, and they beckoned us, those peaks, they lured us.

Meanings, as we all know, are hard to come by in life, but after the lapse of six decades certain detectable patterns are bound to emerge. Burt Lancaster has exerted a profound sway over mine. Burt himself and not merely the mythic figures he portrayed, for like so many actors of his era he slipped into a character as easily as you and I slip on and discard our clothes: different duds, same man. I have sat in a hundred darknesses watching his image flicker across as many screens in as many simpleminded scenarios. Pirate, prisoner, acrobat, soldier, outlaw, sheriff, pioneer, Indian, scammer, preacher, prophet—he was always the same man, which, I suppose, is no compliment for an actor but which in Burt's case is part of the measure of his enormous appeal. I have watched him age, seen the sharp planes of his face settle, the impregnable fortress of his physique crumble. It didn't matter. The man was unchanged, the man within. If the acrylic smile lost some of its luster, the hard fearless eyes retained their capacity to clean out a saloon with a single piercing sweep, and the voice to resonate, on call, with aggression, fire, vulnerability, world-weary resignation, a detached amusement, even with, yes, a kind of nobility.

And over the years I came to identify with him, do yet. Though he is close to twenty years my senior, our lives seem to have opened and folded together, in tandem, like time-lapse studies of two flowers budding, blooming, fading, shrivelling; his, on those luminous screens and mine peering at his, palely reflected out in the dark. How could a more than mortal Burt Lancaster have any bearing on the uniformly monochrome gray of my life? Only as I willed it, with whatever puny force I could muster, aspired to be not like him but to *be* him. And if with the passage of years my own weakness and sloth and ruinous choices and bungled, amateurish performances made a shortfall inevitable, still I had something to measure myself against, even if it were measured only in mounting calamities and griefs.

Out of all the images of Burt that crowd my memory, the one

most vivid and insistent comes, curiously, from an obscure forties movie with the spectacularly unambiguous title *Brute Force*. It comes on summons, readily: The young Burt Lancaster of the immense shoulders and thick swag of hair and hard chiselled jaw, staggering up the steps of the burning guard tower, the prison break miscarried, carnage and flames and death everywhere; and the ringleader Burt mortally wounded but still resolutely stalking that slithery embodiment of evil, Hume Cronyn (he of the waxy skin and pinched ferrety features and Joseph Goebbels eyes; he of the jackboots and clubs and perverse taste for swelling Wagnerian strains as backdrop to his sadistic torture of helpless cons); and Burt bent on a higher justice, instrument of divine reckoning, cornering him in the tower, hauling him shrieking overhead and in a final mighty expiring heave flinging him into the arms of a mob of howling convicts whipped to a murderous frenzy.

That image, noble and tragic, touched some emphatic nerve and buried itself in the farthest reaches of my head. And there it stubbornly remained through my initiation into an arid bookkeeper's world that smirked at notions of adventure, and dreams of valor and high drama. Experience would not budge it. Education, the desiccated, hand-me-down wisdom of effete and corrupt little men (the Doc Corrigans, you remember, and all his ilk) could not dislodge it. Periodically throughout my life I found occasion to reenact it, recreate it for myself in suitable guises, and each time with more serious consequences.

But in the beginning, after I saw that exhilarating film and passed through the doors of the theater and back onto the dreary streets of Charles City, Iowa, the afterimage danced behind my eyes and enticed me with extravagant visions of what I might myself one day become. Inexplicably, and for all the promise of a jumbo infancy, my adolescent growth had stalled at a couple of inches under six feet and a runtish 140 pounds. So I bought a set of York barbells and, unknown to anyone (excepting of course a scowling aunt and twittery, preoccupied mother—impossible to keep anything from those two), labored over them slavishly in a gritty garage, shivering or sweltering by season's turn. Within a year my body, with the compliance of youth, sprouted flashy muscle everywhere. I let my hair grow long, in imitation of Burt, long for that time, swept up and back and over the ears and collar but with a thick forelock dangling rakishly across the eyes. Those eyes grew steely and the voice low, hinting of secret sorrows. I cultivated a moody air, tough and brooding, befitting the transformed appearance.

The effect was magical. Presto! I stood in the glare of a new and alarming celebrity. More accurately a notoriety, for everything about me was anomalous to the place and time. Like Burt striding through his chummy Hollywood prison tall (in my own case as tall as five-ten allowed) and aloof, I was an enigma now. I played no sports, tootled an incongruous clarinet in the nimble-fingered Arne Carson's band, was an indifferent scholar, avoided all clubs and activities, haunted the tunnels, hung on the sidelines at school dances, a solitary, mocking observer.

I soon discovered the new persona strapped me with obligations and impelled me on new adventures. Burt seemed always on the move, a tireless wanderer, and so whenever I could I rode my thumb to exotic destinations up and down and across the Midwest. At one of them the money ran out, squandered on a butcher's daughter (no sultry Yvonne DeCarlo or husky-voiced Lizabeth Scott, but she would have to do) who vigorously dry-humped me midnight till dawn. Yet she determinedly shielded her treasure and left me limp and aching with stone balls, slinking home broke and still virginal.

But the journeys made me believe in my luck. I toyed with the notion of dropping out of school and joining the Marines. Evenings I took to hanging out in our local pool hall, and in time developed a keen eye for snooker. I liked the precise geometry of the game and the feel of the heavy cue in my hands. I liked the figure I cut at the table, a package of loose, big-shouldered skill. Now and again I was able to cadge a beer, the watery variety they served off the tap in those days. It was vile-tasting stuff but I quaffed it with a robust air (Burt, after all, put away shots of whiskey with a virile manliness). Some nights I got my hands on actual booze, swilled it recklessly, and went reeling through the streets, head brimming over with prodigious dreams. More often, with a handful of friends, I scouted the reaches of town, searching out whatever experiences might later, through the magic prism of imagination, be transformed into tales of epic adventure: hunting savage squealing rats at the city dump with Wham-O slingshots; blasting turds that floated across the muck of the sewage plant with twenty-twos; firing ripe tomatoes into unsuspecting passing cars. Arrogant, devil-may-care, circling the borders of trouble. It was inevitable I cross them, and eventually I did.

"YOU WANNA FINISH IT?"

I was looking into a pair of mean expectant eyes, black marbles pressed into a spherical lump of dough. Glaring out of a cast iron skull rooted by bull neck to a bunched, draft horse body, a body nicely suited for the limited function it served: plugging a hole in the line of the varsity football team.

"You wanna finish it, he's waitin' in the alley. 'Less you're too chickenshit."

The invitation was couched in a just about equal blend of malice and contempt. And hearing it I was not at all certain I cared to accept. A battered nose (whose deviated septum remains with me yet) and split upper lip still leaked blood. My chest and shoulders ached from the solid punches I had absorbed in clumsy efforts to deflect the heavy fists that had pummelled my face. Real world fights, I was discovering, were nothing like those choreographed brawls on the screen. The "he" who waited so eagerly in the alley stood four inches taller and outweighed me by forty pounds, and though he sported nowhere near the showy muscle I did, he was acquainted with violence. Like his emissary, he was a tackle on the football squad. I had made the monumental blunder of taunting him with the name Bluto, after the Popeye cartoon villain (to whom, by the way, he bore a remarkable resemblance), and he was spoiling for revenge, much of which he had already exacted.

I looked to my small circle of friends, fading into the shadows, volunteering nothing. No counsel there. I looked back into the hard black eyes, glittery with scorn. And then, with a swaggery assurance I felt not at all, I said, "Okay, let's go on back." Burt at the tower, nothing left to lose.

Bluto stood in the dark by a brace of lidless trash cans spilling over with fetid garbage. He was flanked by cronies, teammates, and when he saw me he sneered contemptuously and doubled his fists. He had good reason to feel confident, burly as he was. But none of his accumulated combative experience could ever have prepared him for the graceless maddened lunge that brought him first to his knees, then onto his back, legs twisted wickedly beneath him, gagging and choking from the arm that cinched his throat, and blinded by the blood that squirted from his nose and mouth, streaking across his face under a fist that rose and fell like a furious hammer.

A cop appeared and disentangled us. Bluto lay by the trash cans, facedown in an assortment of orange rinds, eggshells, and coffee grounds, moaning. All his friends had scattered. I leaned against the arsenic-colored wall of a shed, quaking with rage. We were booked on disorderly conduct, released, and the next day reported to the station to hear a windy lecture from the police chief. Formal charges were dropped (it was football season, though Bluto sat out a game), but were were required to shake hands. We did, avoiding eyes. And we left through separate doors.

A couple of my own friends waited outside, eager to hear the outcome of an encounter with Authority grander and more absolute even than a Doc Corrigan. And so I shrugged toughly and, shameless as that craven scribbler of forbidden words, Grunt Slocum, fabricated a bluff tale of defiant insolence, a tale calculated to preserve my image intact. Whether it did or not I couldn't tell. It troubled me some, but not so much as the recollection of the alley, the sensations of wild, animal fear and an ungoverned rage that stormed like a hurricane through my head. It was just that, a hurricane, nothing less, but a queer sort of hurricane, utterly lacking in calm eye.

SOME YEARS PASSED. Burt began to move away from the one-dimensional roles that had made him famous, the raw-edged ruffian of *Kiss the Blood Off My Hands, I Walk Alone, Rope of Sand,* misunderstood and with a seething potential for violence, often outside the law but at bottom a fundamentally decent man. He undertook the character of the beaten husband in *Come Back, Little Sheba,* and though they padded his hips and whitened his hair, had him walk with a loser's shuffle, there was no mistaking the fierce young battler inside that shapeless sweater. It was impossible to believe in him as weakling. Burt, a chiropractor? May as well try to pass him off as haberdasher or shoe clerk. We knew better and he must have too, for in *From Here to Eternity* he was himself again.

Well, yes and no. As Sergeant Milt Warden he was himself—all those early heroes badly used by a harsh world—but grown up now, shrewder. Adaptable to, if still scornful of, life's abundant swindles and deceits, with most of the moonstruck lunacy of youth gone. Or gone undercover. For Warden was not unwilling to risk it all for the captain's wife, all but his integrity when it finally turned on that. And as ever, he was absolutely without fear, whether facing down the brutish, knife-wielding Fatso Judson or holding the Imperial Japanese Air Force at bay.

Eternity appeared in 1953. Coincidentally, I was in the army at the time (though, unlike Burt, no valiant infantryman, rather a lowly PFC in the Transportation Corps, whose ship's wheel insignia was known in service-wide sneer as "the wheel of shame"). But I count it no coincidence that three days after its screening at a post theater I was once again drawn into an episode that, with some small variation, might have been lifted intact from the film, a quintessential example of life echoing art.

It was very sudden, that episode, and very brief. Visualize it: a craps game conducted on the floor of a barracks communal john reeking of ammonia and red sweeping wax; fog of cigarette smoke haloing the semi-circular knot of crouched players; bottles of cheap wine flanking their knees. One of those players, a Corporal Wendell Nobody (last name escapes me, censors-blocked forever; what I recall is a barrel-shaped West Virginia hillbilly, mole-flecked face the color of spoiled meat, mouth-breather with an enormous purple tongue too thick for that perpetually gaping cavity), cupping the dice in hands wide as spades, petitioning them with such uninspired appeals as "C'mon, bones, baby need new combat boots"—preface to flinging them against the base of a commode with the repetitively boomed "Drop poop, pick up luck!" Which luck, sad to say, had been consistently going his way. Everybody was getting mightily sick of Wendell, myself not least among them.

The dice came out. But on this particular roll one of them, fate-propelled, missed the stool altogether (Wendell's coordination somewhat impaired by a jug and a half of Gallo), tumbled across the floor, and came to rest a few feet from where I knelt. "No play," somebody called, and Wendell, irked, tossed his head at me and snapped, "Woodrow, off your ass and gimme the dice."

"Die," I heard myself correcting, and I didn't move.

"Huh?"

"One is a die."

"Fuck you talkin' about?"

"Die is the singular, *dice* refers to two or more."

I should own up here that I have since discovered the word at issue, *die,* can be used either way, plural or singular. But at the time I was thoroughly convinced of my grammatical infallibility, a classic example of a little learning's potentially grave hazards. For Wendell, I saw, was glowering at me darkly. "Whadda you know?" he snorted, and then supplied his own answer. "You know shit. *Die* means y'croak."

"No, *die* is also a noun, signifying one cube. Not two."

"Wiseass college fuck—" this in reference to my three semesters at the University of Iowa, rudely aborted by an unsympathetic draft board—"gimme the dice."

"It's a die, Wendell. Why don't you look it up in a dictionary. You know, that fat book? One with all the words?"

"You ridiculin' me?"

Another player, exhausted of patience, muttered, "F'chrissake, Woodrow, give 'im the dice—or die—or whatever the fuck it is. Let's get on with the game."

It was a temperate suggestion, but it came too late. Wendell had hauled himself to his feet, growling, "No, no, hold up just a goddam minute. This wiseass pokin' fun here and I got me a bellyful his shit. No more."

The hill country face boiled up crimson. The outsize tongue drooped over a spittle-damp lower lip. More alarmingly, one of those shovel hands clutched a wine bottle, which he swung suddenly against the commode, shattering it, staining the floor a claret red. I rose (with some haste, as you might well imagine), and because I was too startled to think to reach for a bottle, went for my belt instead, unclasped it, yanked it off, doubled it. Feeble defense. All I had.

And so there we stood, squared off and fiercely glaring, hoping (both of us, I suspect, certainly myself) someone would intervene, invoke the soothing balm of sweet reason. "What a couple of shitheads," an anonymous player, spear carrier in this unfolding drama, allowed, but along with all the others he was circumspectly backing away. Who needs grief?

You remember the scene now? The variant here is that I, as Burt, should have been grasping the jagged bottle, and Wendell, my Fatso, a switchblade. Nor did it end, as in the film, in a standoff. Wendell advanced on me, making the c'mon, c'mon gesture with his free hand, weaving like a spooked rattler and hissing through bared and badly yellowed teeth, "Y'want die, I'll giveya die." Getting deep into his role. And I, for my part of it, backpedaling, swinging the belt wildly, overtaken by a terror raw and primal. And overtaken eventually by Wendell himself. Spine pressed against an unyielding wall, last avenue of retreat blocked, I watched (as in a dream one watches, freeze-framed, catastrophe's relentless approach) him closing in on me, grinning triumphantly. This was not the way the scene was scripted.

He charged. I ducked, but not nimbly enough. A spike of glass, razor-keen, raked my forehead, narrowly missing an eye and ornamenting me with a zipper I wear even today. The bullish rush carried him into the wall, and in the splinter of a second before a wash of blood erased my vision I pivoted, looped the belt around his throat, dug a knee into the lardy small of his back, jerked the belt and with it his head, and tugged with all the force in me. A feral voice in my head chanted *kill kill kill kill,* while a gaggle of alien voices, no more audible or real, squawked *Jesus, Woodrow, let 'im go, you're killin' 'im.* Sightless, I kept on tugging.

Finally they stepped in, pinned my arms, and pulled me away. Someone staunched the gush of blood from my lacerated brow and, blinking, I caught a parting glimpse of the hapless Wendell/Fatso, crumpled on the floor, retching, shuddering, comically lolling tongue plum-colored, swollen as a lynching victim's and much too dilated now to fit the mouth around it. The galvanic surge of rage I'd felt but a moment ago receded suddenly. Poor Wendell, born to the villain's role (for he had, I knew, seen the movie too, must have identified with his Fatso character at some dim preconscious level). And I wanted to reach out to him now, take him aside, compliment him on his performance, exchange helpful suggestions. For what I could not shake was the eerie sense of screen and spectator blurring, no longer quite so distinct, and it was a revelation to discover there were others who manifestly felt as I felt, believed as I did, and, more significant, ordered their lives accordingly, careless of all risk.

SOME OF THAT SAME SENSE was rekindled for me, though far less dramatically, a couple of years later and on the other side of the continent. For the vastly successful *Vera Cruz* Burt had accepted the villain's role and second billing to Gary Cooper's pursed-lipped and rather phlegmatic hero. Naturally, Burt strutted away with the picture, flashing his fabled teeth like marmoreal neon and advancing a world view so hyperbolically amoral it came off as parody, perilously close to spoof, and he as unlikely comedian. Recalling it now, I am convinced that is exactly what he intended: a comic western, conceived and executed well before its time. Particularly is it hard to escape this conclusion when one recalls the climactic shootout, the fatally wounded Burt literally dead where he stood, but with his character's passion for control completing a dextrous six-gun twirl and reholstering before sinking to his knees, electrified smile still plastered across his face. One of the great howlers of film history, supreme test of willing suspension of disbelief.

But when I first saw the film disbelief was the last notion I entertained, I and the rest of a like-minded collection of itinerant beach bums and body worshipers who were by instinct and experience as amoral as Burt's villain. Shiftless hustlers all, we were gladdened by that magnified image of ourselves dominating—right up to the sanctimonious windup at curtain fall—a predatory fantasy world that, apart from its quaint other-era costumes, mirrored closely our own. We sauntered out of the theater and onto Santa Monica's smog-poisoned streets sporting grins lopsided and sardonic. And for weeks after, those streets, beaches, bars, and gyms served as display case for our now-crystallized conception of lovably wicked rogues.

More years passed, and with them a share of the frantic delusions of youth and just about all its spirited vision. Eventually, options dwindling, emptied of cash, I drifted back to the Midwest, to Iowa City, and enrolled once again in college, funding this latest scam courtesy of a benevolent G.I. Bill. A twenty-six-year-old anachronism, lugging books, cramming for quizzes, attending to pedantic priggish wheeze and giving it back in what they were pleased to call "papers" (which term always, for me, conjured cinematic images of an intrepid American undercover agent—an Errol Flynn, say, or an Alan Ladd—on hazardous mission behind enemy lines, detained by a brutal SS trooper demanding "Your papers!"). It was not inspiriting, but for someone with an almost preternatural aversion to work it beat a job hands down, no contest. Yet astonishingly I did rather well, perhaps because those waning options, never wide anyway for a five-and-dime hustler, were reduced now to none. So if one framed certificate of arcane and utterly useless knowledge was salutary, why not two? Three?

Burt, meanwhile, had gone on to a series of ill-chosen parts that for a time baffled and distanced me by their strange inaptness. What did I, a born-again heartlander, know of or care about his caustic, be-spectacled New Yorker of *Sweet Smell of Success?* What could I possibly take from the enervated sot of *Separate Tables,* and what was he doing anyway in that bloodless English setting? That was for the Nivens and Masons, not the man who had made it up the flaming tower. Worst of all was *The Devil's Disciple.* Burt a gloomy parson? Had it come finally to that? The estrangement widened. And then came *Elmer Gantry* and all was healed.

As rendered by Burt, the corrupt evangelist is recognizably human. He is the scoundrel who endears through rascally charm. A drummer with booze on his breath and holes in his socks, and a satchelful of worthless geegaws to peddle and bawdy tales to tell, but with a sure grasp of all our secret urges and longings and fears, and a kind of pity for us for harboring them. He is the archetypical artist of the burn who, at the push-shove hour, holds steadfast and firm, who might abscond but would never flee, a crucial difference. A man with a healthy and unappalled sense of the absurdity of the human condition. In short, an American original. It is inconceivable not to root for him, especially when he confronts the thug swatting poor Shirley Jones and, before evening the score, delivers that line unforgettable in its menacing simplicity: "Don't you know that hurts?" This was the Burt of another, more valorous time, an either-or time, agent of celestial vengeance, returned at last.

A year or so later those laconic words of his would echo in my head as I stared down a slighter, paler, life-sized version of the rude bully outside a campus dormitory. Though I was fast approaching thirty and desk-bound, skidding into woeful shape, I nonetheless undertook the role of defender of a coed (delicate wisp of a girl in the first blaze of beauty, inky of hair, creamy of skin, emerald of eye. . . . Enough of this—a girl eight years my junior, hitherto unknown to me but who, ten short months later, big with child, would become my wife) enduring the same physical abuse as the trollop Shirley. Who could sidestep such an opportunity? Certainly not I, Burt-tutored and full of my own gallantry. What a moment it was for me, and how much was I in debt as I uttered my own ominous, if somewhat less terse, line: "You're a real badass with women, let's see how well you do with men." And then I fell on him with the same blind, delirious rage with which I'd fallen on Wendell a few years back, and on Bluto before that, but with nowhere near the force.

Like the girl, he was much younger, and for all his seeming scrawniness a wiry bundle of ferocity. Also a raver, bawling such predictable threats as "Butt the fuck out, asshole" and "None your goddam business" and, in aside to the girl, a malediction whose bitter message I would have, as things turned out, done well to heed: "Cheater! Cunt! Fuckin' tramp!" But I was too occupied dodging his flailing fists, and not at all unhappy when someone broke it up. And while it was gratifying to see some blood on his face, I emerged with a finger so badly sprained it is gnarled and misshapen to this day.

The widely acclaimed *Birdman of Alcatraz* was released in 1962, but it would be another decade before I saw it (ironically enough, in realworld prison, presumably screened for an audience of surly inmates on a Corrections Department assumption the legendary Birdman's exemplary character would serve as inspiration to us all—and greeted, I should add, by that same audience with derisive hoots and raspberries). For life, you see, and its cumbrous baggage—wife, infant, dog, debt, duty—had crowded in, revealing all its gas company essence, all it had ever threatened to be. Harried, destitute, an overage schoolboy sadly out of place in that sea of fresh young faces, I no longer had time or patience (or spare funds) for such frivolous and extra-scholarly pursuits as filmgoing.

The seasons came and went and came again, misting into years. Eventually I was graduated, a string of initials tacked to my name tesifying to the expanse of my learning: Dr. Woodrow, if you please. We U-Hauled across the state line, to Illinois, to a position I'd found at a warmed-over normal school, now self-proclaimed university with pretensions to academic eminence. De Kalb, Illinois. Its very name evocative of seed corn and silos. Dismal town (scarcely larger than the Charles City of my boyhood, and no less bucolic), dismal institution.

Nevertheless, freshly minted Ph.D. and Assistant Professor of English Neo-Classical Literature, I embarked on a belated career with noble vigor and fixity of purpose. In the classroom I offered up windy pronouncements, an ambulatory pleonasm, gasbag weighted with the gravity of the wisdom of the ages. I served dutifully on departmental committees charged with the moronic task of identifying and, in tortured teacherly prose, defining our murky "mission." I published opaque, prolix articles in drab scholarly journals. Verbal Sominex, all of them, read (never mind understood) by no one. Once

I was invited to address a faculty colloquium on the ponderous issue of the current state of literary education in America, and with the ghost of Doc Corrigan cackling in my ear advanced my own numbing, didactic wheeze. In due course I was promoted, tenured. Settled.

At home I was settling just as easily into the role of responsible husband and father, practical, sensible, a checkbook balancer and counter of pocket change, thoughtful peruser of *Consumer Reports,* soundly middle class, outwardly quite rational and in splendid control. Inwardly, the kind of man I despised. For a faint image of Burt accompanied me still, nagged me with blurring memories of youth's soaring dreams, and mocked that man I'd allowed myself to become. And so, perhaps in reaction, I bought another set of barbells and sweated over them as grimly as I'd done two decades earlier (and just as secretly: a weights-heaving professor? Perish the notion!), our clammy basement a small step up (or down) from the gritty garage, and with an orb-eyed son looking on admiringly, if a bit puzzledly. Now and again my wife would come to the head of the stairs, inspect me wordlessly—this grunting, aging buffoon, thinning hair, thickening middle—with appraising, glinting eyes and increasingly lip-curled smirk. Her unuttered scorn spurred me to mightier efforts, though to what end I could not, in my wildest imaginings, foresee.

By the time *The Swimmer* and *The Gypsy Moths* appeared, late in the sixties, my marriage, as you've doubtless already concluded, was crumbling, and with all the anguish and fury only the bitterest of such dissolutions can arouse. I understood failure and betrayal (hers of me, mine of myself) at a fundamental level now, and Burt's aquatic journey across a Connecticut countryside, his gradual unsealing of Neddy Merrill's bankrupt integrity, botched ambitions, and ripening madness seemed apt metaphor for the chaos I found myself in. A condition, I see now, I had been sliding toward all my life. There were vestiges yet of the fierce pride and indomitable spirit I had once shared with a younger, bolder Burt. But there were darker things to share too, untriumphant, uncinematic: an innocent, terrified child caught in the furious heat of marital dueling; aspirations, puerile or not, collapsed like antique buildings under a wrecking ball swung by the power of one's own hand; years frittered away, squandered as casually as the loose change I habitually tallied. And so, after that final lunatic and irreversible act, its stormy violence a kind of primitive poetry more eloquent than words, it was not at all difficult for me to understand and symbolically identify with Burt's taciturn *Gypsy Moths* skydiver declining to release the chute on his last jump, passion-poisoned moth drawn by the seductive flame of death; though for me without his success, as I realized on waking out of a sleep not of death but narcotic stupor, self-induced, in a joyless funhouse where the doors were barred and bolted and the caretakers brutish and the—no!—no more of this!

> *And why not, Norman?*
> *You again?*
> *None other.*
> *So? What is it now?*
> *You don't know?*
> *Would I ask if I did?*
> *Very well, then. I'm sure you'll agree this is awfully murky.*
> *Murky? How so?*
> *You don't see it? Look again. Talk about opaque. Reveals next to nothing of that turbulent Day you persist in agonizing over. Mewling, some might say.*
> *You could do better?*
> *I like to think so. Were it my story. My mystery to unravel.*
> *I'll come back to it another time.*
> *What better time than now?*
> *I said another time.*
> *Very well. Too bad, though. You were getting close.*

TO PROCEED, THEN.

Two years into my incarceration and five short of a chance at parole, I saw *Valdez Is Coming* for the first time. Pulse quickening, I watched them (*them* being a ruthless arms trader, an Anglo, and his scruffy hirelings) lash Burt, Chicano peace officer aging and deferential (the Joe Collins of *Brute Force* miraculously grown old, and his rash heroics, time-churned, reduced to their proper place in the proper order of things), to a makeshift cross and drive him ignominiously from the rancho, to which he had come on an errand of simple justice. Bloodied, humbled, staggering under the weight of the cross, he makes his way across a sun-scorched desert. But once released, he retrieves from an ancient trunk the portentous symbols of the man he was before caution, politic discretion and time ensnared him: musty uniform of a cavalry scout and rifle powerful enough to bag elephants. He sets out again, a curious anachronism, riding tall this return visit. Almost gently, he tells the first victim of his deific vengeance to go quickly (for life is leaking fast) and advise the others "Valdez is coming."

One man, greater by far than the aggregate force of all the world's insolent villainy, craftier, vastly more experienced, immeasurably more courageous, he storms the rancho and wreaks a righteous havoc. My temples pounded, a thickness clogged my throat. Outnumbered but never outgunned, he is finally ridden down. To no end. At the moment of confrontation even the scrofulous gang members recognize in Burt something superior, better than most, and they fall away from their leader, exposing him for the coward he is. And Burt, who initially wanted only to collect a minuscule sum owed a wronged widow, reminds him simply he should have "paid the hundred dollars."

The next morning one of those sudden, unforseeable incidents that will periodically convulse a prison lockstep chanced to erupt at my work station. Had it happened a week or even a few days later, after that blood-kindling image of Burt had cooled some, who can guess at what its upshot might have been? Perhaps no different. Perhaps the incident I'm about to describe to you was for me, as for the cross-bound Burt, a divinely ordered test, a last opportunity to atone for the glossy shambles we'd made of things, last grasp at an elusive piece of redemption. On reflection, I can see it was possibly the second most senseless thing I ever did, but at the time it felt the most unsullied, pure. Whatever the case, one is left to ponder the waggish vagaries of chance and to wonder, in the dimming hindsight of age, far too late, if there is anything in life worth forfeiting everything for, a conundrum that baffles me yet.

My job was inmate assistant to the Stateville education director, a natural assignment (how many Ph.D.s, after all, did they have?) and, on balance, cushy enough, as cushy was measured in there. My duties consisted of scheduling the largely vocational instruction, selecting and ordering texts from a skimpy book budget, conducting some of the high school completion classes (strictly meat-on-the-seat learning, in prison parlance, good-conduct points that, the vine had it, upped the odds with parole boards, otherwise useless), writing the director's self-serving "progress" reports and generally relieving him of any tasks beneath his rank of master of education, of which dishwashing chores there were an abundance and of which exalted degree he was inordinately vain. It was mind-numbing work but routine, undemanding, and, not the least of its virtues, relatively safe (if, as with cushy, one could put a measure on safety in a violent ward). A couple of furious initiatory scuffles, reprises of the Bluto/Wendell episodes though with considerably more at stake, had earned me a dinger jacket (probably deservedly, given the walking catatonia of my first few months behind the walls) and, temporarily, some small space. But I discovered early on there was finally no sanctuary in a madhouse. Best you could do was keep your head down, your back covered, and your eyes ever on the prowl.

We were warehoused in the basement of a cellblock, a grim chamber, poorly lit, dusty, neglected, unpartitioned but for the director's screened-in office situated at the foot of the stairs and from which imperial vantage point he could survey areas arbitrarily designated study and instruction, the former identified by files of grafitti-scarred wooden benches, the latter by portable blackboard, rickety podium, and a dozen or so desktop chairs (come late and you were rewarded with a seat on the stone floor). One of the windowless cinderblock walls was adorned with inmate art—chimerical land- and seascapes, mostly, or birds in flight; here and there an abstract, color-splashed rendering of a schizoid imagination—and with a bulletin board tacked with telegraphic announcements of upcoming enrichment opportunities (e.g., "Small-Engine Repair I—startup 9-15-73—8 wks—max enrl 20"). Taped to another was a collection of inspirational thoughts (the director's motivational strategy), among them the inevitable desiderata advising the reader to "Go placidly amid the noise and haste" and all the rest of it, and one that began: "If you're going to work for a man, in the name of heaven give him your best," and wore on interminably in that asinine vein, one of those exhortations to diligence and duty reminiscent of the welcome posted, with similar ham-fisted irony, above the gate of a Nazi death camp: "Work makes you free." Towers of Styrofoam cups, flanking a squat rusted coffee urn, rose from a small table in a corner. Ashtrays were everywhere, for in the keep, you see, cigarettes served not only as currency but equally as insulation from the glacial rhythms and day-to-day horrors of waking life. Often, in the early morning hours, when the place was empty and silent, it reminded me curiously of a small town railroad depot after the trains no longer passed that way: abandoned, desolate, unspeakably lonely.

"SO HOW THEY HANGIN', DOCTOR?"

The invariable greeting of my lord and education master (its "doctor" a vocalized sneer dispatching the clear message those titles cut no shit with him), to which I just as invariably replied, "Hanging just fine, sir" (my "sir" no less insolent).

"Fine, fine. You remember we got that voc pref test to give, nine bells?"

I said I'd not forgotten.

"Well, you got 'em ready?"

I nodded at the test booklets neatly stacked on his desk.

"How 'bout the number two pencils?"

The properly numbered pencils, I told him, were also ready.

He regarded me narrowly. "Looks like you're way ahead of me this mornin', doctor."

I said nothing. There was a contentious edge to his voice, a man searching for a gotcha and not at all pleased to find none. You learned to listen for such tonal colorings.

"Okay, okay. We're gonna have a gang of 'em in here, so maybe you better give the floor a quick sweepdown."

"Whatever you say, Mr. Pike."

That was his name, Pike, though with those slack piscatorial lips and watery bulging eyes it might as easily have been Bass, say, or Trout, or Smelt. But it was Pike, Otis Pike. He was, I'd guess, about my own age, but with the smooth, pink, absent face of a man unacquainted with possibilities, untouched by griefs or joys or enlarging intellect or hard-won wisdom, as though time and experience had left not a trace on him. Stout and untall, the exaggeratedly forward-leaning tilt of his upright posture betrayed the very real likelihood of lifts in his heels. He wore, that steamy August morning, a bilious green sport shirt with vertical stripes in it (sadly, of small help with the height problem) and polyester trousers the color of dull rust. While I navigated a broom, he sank into his swivel chair and busied himself with a manual on dog breeding. A hobbyist and bachelor, his rumored sexual inversions were the subject of endless lewd speculation. And because jailhouse jest had it the luckless mutts were bred for purposes other than show, he was commonly referred to by in-

mates and hacks alike (both of whom held him in supreme contempt) as Oat-ass the dog-fucker.

Shortly before nine the scholars came shuffling down the stairs,
carrying with them blasts of torrid cellblock heat and the gamey stinks
peculiar to men restricted by draconian rule to twice weekly showers.
About their numbers Pike was right. Chairs were quickly comman-
deered, the floor soon covered with bodies crammed in elbow-to-el-
bow. No way can I capture for you the dizzying stench rising from that
constricted space. Sweat, flatus, assorted hair gels and pomades, the
sweetish scents of chippie queens . . . well, you had to be there. Yet
for all of it they were in a playful humor, and when Pike assumed his
place at the podium some simulated doggie woofs and yips issued
from the floor. He drew himself up to full angled height, cleared his
throat, and, pitching his voice severe and low as it would go, com-
manded, "Awright, men, knock off the diddlyshit and listen up here."

A sullen hush settled over the assembly.

"Awright, what we got here is a vocational preference test,
which is a test gonna help you find out what interests are, kinda work
you're cut out for. Plain English, help y'get your shit together. Which
right now it's not, or you wouldn't be here, first place. Y'don't need
me tellya when you're out on the bricks y'gotta have a skill, trade.
Otherwise it's *G'bye freeworldin', hello Stateville* again. Y'with me
so far?"

Their silence seemed to express understanding, if no great ap-
preciation for his pathetic stabs at joint lingo. He pressed on:

"Test takes two hours. No more, no less. Finish late, it's tough
titty. Finish up early, y'stay put right where y'are. Everybody got that?"

Continued silence. Everyone, evidently, had it.

"Awright. Good. Now, doctor here—" my booklet-bearing presence a foot or so to his rear acknowledged by curt head jerk—"gonna
monitor. Any questions, flag an arm. Otherwise be no gum-flappin',
no dickin' around." And turning to me: "Doctor, y'got any prol'ums,
sing out."

"In dulcet tones," I said.

"Huh?"

"I'll be certain to consult you, sir. Should the need arise."

A suspicion of mockery clouded his dull features. "Yeah, you be
sure'n do that," he said, and when I offered no response (the limits of
his clearly foul temper sufficiently probed), added, "So whatcha

waitin' on—parole?" This delivered with a spiteful chortle. "Let's get 'em movin'." And having so directed, he retired behind the screen and resumed his study of the Weimaraner, or whatever the breed that currently caught his fancy.

As that whimsical chance alluded to earlier would have it, there was among this sorry, sweaty band of misfits, rejects, sociopaths, and certifiable lunatics an inmate known by prison tag as Buckwheat. Massive, jolly, kindly by nature, awesomely strong, he had the mind of a ten-year-old stuck in the body of an ape. His crime was rape-murder, though if the vine told true he was, penniless and confused, merely the victim of a ball-busting hooker whose teasing jibes he mistakenly interpreted as genuine invitation.

It was this man-child's evil luck (and mine as well, I suppose, as it turned out) to be floor-seated that morning alongside a squirmy, restless rowdy. Another simpleton, a maker of mischief who persisted in nudging him and delivering comedic remarks sotto voce behind a cupped hand. Buckwheat, stolid and earnest, sat hunched over his test booklet, number two pencil clutched like a dagger, simian brow pinched in the agony of brainwork, doing his best to ignore the distractions. As did I. None of my affair.

But eventually, inevitably, one of those whispered quips sparked a huge sunburst grin. And at just that moment Pike glanced up from his manual of canine lore.

In a flash he was out of his chair and his office and looming over the fuddled Buckwheat like some anointed angel of heaven's own wrath, bellowing, "Awright, Buck, on your feet. You're outta here."

"What? What I do?"

"Warned ya 'bout the dickin' off. Won't tolerate it, my classroom. Gimme your test book."

"Wasn't doin' no dickin' off."

"Don't try'n job me. I saw it."

"Why you juggin' on me, man? I didn't do nothin'."

Pike wagged a thumb in the direction of the stairs. "Said gimme the book and get your ass gone. Now!"

Buckwheat didn't rise, didn't move. Seemed to deliberate a moment. And then he shook his head slowly, and with a quiet outlaw dignity said, "No. Ain't goin'. Didn't *do* nothin'. Gonna finish my test."

Pike looked stunned. Confounded. Nobody challenged a master

of education. The pink in his face deepened. Pudgy hands clasped and unclasped. A snigger rippled through the room. He hesitated, conscious of every hostile eye in that room on him, conscious perhaps for the first time of his own potential peril.

At last he said to Buckwheat, "Okay, okay. That's how you want it, that's how you get it. But what you just done here is buy yourself a Seg ticket." And then to me, hanging off to one side, watching the scene unfold, keeping out of it: "Woodrow, go call Ceese."

Ceese (full name an unlikely Cecil Figg) was the hack stationed at the head of the stairs, a man whose feedsack gut, twangy voice, buckled teeth, baggy face, and mean, canny eyes called to mind the late Slim Pickens. And Seg was joint shorthand for Segregation, itself a Corrections Department euphemism for the hole. Not a desirable place to do time. Not for a blameless grin. Unaccountably, an image of Burt appeared to me and I heard myself saying, against all caution and prudence, "Let it go, Pike. He was smiling to himself. Probably at one of those inane test questions." (Joint code forestalled any fingering, mine or Buckwheat's, of the true instigator.)

"Don't wanna hear no fuckin' *probablys,*" Pike shot back. "Tellin' ya go call Ceese."

"Let him finish," I said coldly. Burt's Bob Valdez had taught me a thing or two about the virtues of succinctness.

He fixed me with a furious glare. "You're diggin' yourself a deep trench here, Woodrow. Ask you one more time. You gonna get Ceese or not?"

"The latter of the two."

"Huh?"

"Not."

He snorted, wheeled around, and began picking his way through the crush of bodies on the floor, stepping carefully, quickly. I followed, caught up to him at the stairs. Tapped him on a fleshy shoulder and said again, "Let him finish," appending to it now, "dog-fucker."

His jaw fell. His eyes, normally protuberant anyway, bugged. *"What? Say what?* What'd you call me?"

"What you are, Otis. A miserable little despotic browneye fucker of dogs."

The jaws reclenched. Mouth twisted into a wicked sneer. "Dog-fucker, is it? Awright, awright. You just done the goddam dumbest thing in your stretch, doctor. Pissed away a soft job and earned yourself a Seg holiday in the bargain."

Was it the sneer? The "doctor" taunt? The recognition, stark and final, of everything I'd forfeited? The goading memory of Burt at the tower (in my case a subterranean version thereof)? Who can tell. Perhaps all of them, in confluence. For I said to him, "And this is what you've earned, Otis," *this* being a driving lunge that chop-blocked him into the wall, whacking the wind out of him and sagging him to the floor. I straddled his plump torso and, with that surge of savage joy that is, I expect, what we mean by catharsis, battered his head against the cool stone, drenching it with blood (and, by the way, permanently incapacitating him, though I would not learn this till later).

From behind me rose a raucous chorus of cheers; from the widening hole in Pike's face, shrieks. On the stairs the urgent clomp of Ceese's heavy boots. Then his sapper stick whooshing through the air in roundhouse swing, connecting thuddingly with the back of my neck.

An explosion of light burst behind my shuttering eyelids and was instantly gone, swirled up in darkness. But in that flickering instant, on the wide screen inside my head, Burt smiled his dazzling enigmatic smile, and it was meant for no one but me.

Part

FOUR

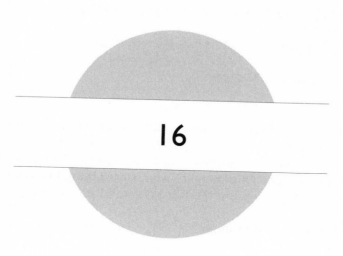

16

On any given Saturday night, as this is, the store is thronged with tardy weekend shoppers. Aisles are jammed, checkout lanes clogged. Cash registers hum. A lengthy line of customers, disgruntled in one way or another with their merchandise, snakes back from the service counter. Behind it the red-jacketed clerks bustle about, relentlessly sunny, as they're trained to be here. Among them is a woman chipper as all the others, but weary too. In her feet and the small of her back, and the muscles of the face that generate a glued-on smile, she can feel the weight of every slow-ticking minute of every interminable hour of her working day. One of those fleeting thoughts of life's tedious repetitious bleakness enters her head. She pushes it away. Her watch reads 8:45. Only fifteen minutes till shift's end.

She processes another customer complaint, files the appropriate form and, absently and without looking up, calls "Next." A figure appears at the counter. She hears her name pronounced with a slight lift to the final syllable, a partial question: "Melanie?" Now she looks up, squints at the unfamiliar face and, placing it, thinks, *Holy shit, that gorgeous stud from a couple weeks ago.* But she doesn't allow the thought to show. She remains cool. Her lacquered lips part in a practiced lazy smile. "So," she says, "you come back after all."

"Yes."

"So what can I do ya for? Got somethin' to swap?"

"No."

"Got a prol'um?"

"No."

"What then?"

"I thought perhaps you might care to join me for a drink."

"Join ya for a drink," she repeats, a trace of mimicry in her voice. None of the dudes she knows—and she knows plenty, her share—ever talks that way. "Now why'd I wanna do a thing like that?"

"Maybe you wouldn't," he says mildly. "It seemed like a good idea."

"We talkin' about tonight?"

"Yes."

"Kinda short notice."

He merely shrugs.

She tugs at her chin. Gesture of deliberation. Schooled in flirtation, she understands its precision timing. Then she looks him full in the eyes, full steady gaze (beautiful eyes he's got, so serene, so remote), and says, "Well, might not be such a bad idea at that."

"Good," is all he says. Like it don't much matter either way.

"Tellya what. I'm off at nine. Whyn't you wait out front, main door there. Gimme about twenty minutes."

"I'll be waiting."

She watches him saunter away. Tight, beautiful buns on him, too. She feels a charge of excitement, anticipation. All her weariness is miraculously gone. The melody of an old Elvis tune flits through her head. She supplies her own modified lyric: "Well it's Saturday night and I'm gonna get laid. . . ." Better'n just laid, she's gonna take this boy home and *abuse* him. Except it can't be home, she remembers, not with Carl there. Oh oh, got a little prol'um here. So she does some fast calculating and the solution comes to her while she's finishing up with her last customer gripe.

At 9:00 P.M. she punches out. She puts in a call to the house, tells numbnuts there her and a bunch of the girls gonna take Jeanine ("You remember Jeanine, one gettin' married next week?") out for a little celebration. Girls night out, like, could get late, she'll maybe stay over to Darla's, okay? Like she figured, he just grunts. Soon as he hangs up the phone pro'ly gonna haul his fat ass down to Sensations, drool over the prancin' pussy. Fine by her. About all he's good for anymore anyway.

That taken care of, she ducks into the ladies' room and puts on some fresh war paint. Fluffs out the abundant black hair, her best feature, easy. She remembers this one guy, liked to get his gun off in it, but he was pretty weird, pretty kinky, and a pig too. She checks the goods in the glass. Not bad for a lady lookin' at forty in the rear view. Little heft in the hips and middle but that's okay. Men like that, gives good bounce. Clothes she's not so happy with: jeans, plain pink blouse, bomber jacket, her regular go-to-work threads. She'd've known she was gonna get lucky, woulda worn something slinky. Don't matter though, won't be in 'em long.

He's waiting under the drive-up canopy outside. It's a chilly October night. A soft drizzle slants down out of the black sky. He asks where she'd like to go.

"Oh, I got a place in mind," she replies coquettishly. "You drivin'?"
"Yes."

"Me too. Where 'bouts you parked?"

He points to one of the several rows of vehicles reaching back into the lot. "At the far end," he says. "Last car."

She has to think a moment about the logistics of the matter. "Okay," she says, "we better take both. I'll swing by and you follow me. It's a blue Escort."

He agrees. She hurries to her car, brings it around by his, signals him, and drives out of the lot, pointed west. Darla's living with her boyfriend in a trailer park over on the other side of town. Crummy spot but it'll have to do. You don't get this kind of luck every day of the week. Thinking so, she checks the mirror periodically, make sure he's in sight. Still there.

She steers her Escort down a back road that leads through a thick stand of trees to the park. Pulls up outside a weathered doublewide. Glances in the mirror and sees no headlights behind her. She feels a sudden surge of panic followed by dismay followed by anger. Fuck's goin' on? He lost? Was just back there, last she looked. He's playin' cutesy games, she ain't havin' none.

She waits. The rain picks up. Her anger mounts. Till she sees a figure coming out of the dark, trotting toward her. She recognizes him, experiences an immense relief. Gonna get the old job done after all.

She hops out of the car, beckons to him, and makes a dash for the trailer door. Unlocks it with the key Darla's given her (they've traded keys and confidences; girl never knows when she's gonna need a little, like, hideaway, ha ha). Inside, still a trifle irked, she asks him what happened, where he's been.

"I got turned around."

"So where you parked?"

"Down the street a ways," he answers vaguely.

"Well, least you found it. Guess that's what counts."

She switches on a light, revealing a grimy kitchen to the left, cluttered living room off to the right. "Don't mind the mess," she says airily. "Darla's not much of a housekeeper."

"Darla?"

"Yeah, she's a friend. It's her place. Her and her boyfriend."

"Where are they now?"

"Oh, they gone up north for the weekend," she says, adding coyly, "We got the place to ourselves."

He don't say nothin' to that, just stands there lookin' around like he's takin' inventory or something. So she says, "Maybe you wanna, uh, get outta them wet clothes."

"No," he says, almost snappishly. But then he looks at her and them gorgeous eyes soften. He smiles a sweet tender smile, kinda sad, like, don't seem to go along with the next words, which are, "Not yet."

That *not yet* part, that's what she likes to hear. Dude's got class. Not some animal, gonna wrestle you right to the mat. She likes that too. Welcome switch. "Okay," she grins back at him, "that's cool. We got all night. Whyn't you just step into the living room there and make yourself to home. I'll see what I can find us to drink."

She checks out the cabinets, turns up nothing in the way of hard hooch, silently curses Dar and her squeeze. She opens the fridge and is cheered to discover, in among some molding leftovers and wilting lettuce, a healthy stash of brew. "All's they got is beer," she calls out. "That do?"

"Beer will be fine," he calls back.

So she pops a couple Buds and carries them into the living room where he's sittin' on the edge of an easy chair, which is too bad since she was hopin' he'd take the sofa so's when the time come they could get right at the cuddlin' and squealin' (like the bounce, she gives great squeal). She hands over his beer and plops in the beanbag opposite him, feeling it deflate under her weight and recalling the night she got her carpet munched right here, in this very chair, by a kid worked Produce last summer till he hadda go back to school. What a night that was. What a time.

This one, though, he's lookin' kinda tense. Sayin' not a word. Could be the room. No gettin' around it, place a fuckin' pigsty: stacks of boxes over along one wall, floor to ceiling; toolbox and some strips of wood on the floor; dust on the coffee table so thick you could write your name in it, you wanted. Or the plea "Dust me," which in fact somebody already done, for a joke. She says, "Can't say I didn't warn ya," but he just looks at her funny, like he don't know what she's talkin' about. So she sweeps an arm through the air, taking in the whole room, and adds by way of explanation, "The mess."

He nods thoughtfully. "What's in the cartons?" he asks.

"Them boxes?"

"Yes."

"Oh, Darla's into peddlin' Amway. Thinks she's gonna get rich sellin' soap."

"And the wood?" he asks next. "The tools?"

"Scooter—that's her boyfriend—he's puttin' up paneling in their bedroom. Least that's what he says he's doin'. Been at it last six months."

He cocks his head, like he's remembering something. "Paneling," he says, sounding deeply interested. "Really?"

"Yeah really. Gonna be quite the playpen back there, he ever gets it finished. They even got a mirror on the ceiling. You wanna see it?"

"Maybe later," he says, smiling that same sweet sad smile at her. "All in good time."

Jesus fuck, she's thinking, *this is a strange one.* Say what she just said to any other dude and he'd have you pinned and pumped no time flat, wham bam thank *you,* ma'am. Maybe needs a few brewskies, loosen him up. Except he's not exactly chuggin' the one in his hand there, so she takes a long pull off hers, let him see how it's done, and to make some conversation says, "Okay, you know my name. So what do I call you?"

About that he's got to think a minute, like it's maybe a trick question. "Call me Norman," he says at last.

She looks at him skeptically. "That your real name, or it just come to you?"

"It's my name."

"Okay, Norman. Here's another one for ya. You married?"

"No."

"Yeah, I bet."

"It's the truth."

She gives him a knowing smirk. "However you want it."

"That's how it is," he says, shrugging.

She says, "I am, y'know," elevating her left hand and displaying the ring in evidence.

"I know."

"That bother you?"

"Not if it doesn't you."

"There's some guys like it better that way. Sorta like a challenge."

Again he shrugs. "Immaterial to me."

He takes a small sip of his brew. Gazes at the toolbox on the floor. She looks at him curiously. "Somethin' tweakin' you, Norman?"

"Tweaking?"

"Yeah, y'know, worryin'."

He lifts them gorgeous eyes, stares at her surprised like, puzzled. "Why do you say that?"

"I dunno. You seem kinda down in the dumps."

"It's my natural demeanor."

"Huh?"

"It's nothing."

"Bad day at work?"

"You might say that."

"Whadda you do for a livin'?"

That one gives him some problem too. He rubs a temple, like he's tryin' to remember. She wonders if he's on something, some kinda downer, quacks maybe. Finally he says, "I'm a professor."

Pro'ly another lie—they all of 'em lie. But she don't want to lose the direction of things so she exclaims, "No kiddin'! A professor! So that's how come you talk so good."

"Good?"

"Yeah, real elegant. Refined, like."

"Thank you," he says.

"Where 'bouts you do this professorin'?"

"Hobbes College."

"Hobbes, that's a real class school."

"You think so?" he says, kind of a prickly edge to his voice. "I don't."

"Yeah? Why's that?"

"The president. A terrible woman."

"You got a lady president?"

"Yes."

"She givin' ya grief?"

"Worse than grief," he says, scowling into his lap, where his hands are clasping and unclasping.

Talk about direction, she don't like the way this goin', not one bit, so to turn it she asks, "Whadda you teach out there at the college?"

"English literature."

"No kiddin'," she says brightly. "English, that was my worst subject back in high school."

Here come that smile again, which she takes as a good sign, except it got no words behind it. She's startin' to feel restless, fidgety, so to get the ball rollin' she says, flat out, "Well, you'll be my first professor."

Now if that ain't about as plain as you can put it, she don't know from plain. What does he do? Nothin' is what he does. Sits there studyin' the floor like it's f'chrissake hypnotizin' him. Your basic log bump. Still an awful pretty bump though, young and tender, so she decides to try again, come at it a different angle. Says, "Okay, professor, got another question for ya. Here we are, couple strangers, sittin' down enjoyin' a friendly brew together. Boy'n a girl. Now whadda you s'pose we oughta be doin'? For entertainment, I mean."

"Whatever you like."

Jesus, some talker. And zip in the action department. She's beginning to have serious doubts. Maybe should of just gone on home, see could she get old noodledick get it airborne. Fat chance. Then she spots a deck of cards over on the coffee table. An idea comes to her and that's what she says: "I got an idea. How's about we play a little cards. Have a couple more brewsters. Get acquainted. Get happy."

"Fine," he says.

"Super."

She boosts herself up, goes into the kitchen and returns with two fresh Buds, sets them on the coffee table and slides it over between them, sinks back in the beaner and shuffles up the deck. Her motions are quick, jerky, almost agitated. Not him. He sits with his elbows propped on his knees, chin cradled in his hands, leaning forward, watching her carefully, his eyes alert but calm, and completely detached. Mr. Cool. Makes you a little nervous, all that steady starin'. Other hand, maybe it's another good sign, maybe his engine's gettin' cranked. About time. "So what game y'wanna play?" she asks.

Takes a while for him to answer but when he does he says, "Hearts," blurts it out like it suddenly just come to him, fuckin' inspiration.

"That the one where the hearts count against ya? Got a dump card, queen a spades, I think it is, cost ya all the points?"

"I believe so."

"Why that one?"

"I don't know. I'm not sure. I seem to remember playing it as a child. With my mother."

"Well," she says, drawlin' it out good and slow, so there's no mistakin' the point she's makin' here, "you're not a kid nomore. And I sure as hell ain't your mom."

Minute there he looks like he's in a goddam fog. Like he's not totally convinced either one a them facts is true. And when he does speak, his voice is glum. "That's right," he says. "You're not."

Good thing they got that straight. Motherin' ain't her strong suit. "Anyway, y'gotta have more'n two, play that game."

"Oh."

"An' last I looked, there's just the two of us here. You see anybody else around?"

"No."

"Tellya what. I got a better idea. Poker. Strip kind. Help us do some a that gettin' acquainted I was sayin'. Remember?"

"I remember. But I don't know how to play poker."

"Don't play *poker!* Everybody knows poker."

"I don't."

"I'll teach ya, then. I'll be the professor. Whaddaya say?"

"All right. You teach me."

She explains the rules. "Okay," she says, dealing out the cards, "clothes is the chips. Lose a hand, y'lose one piece a clothes. You get to pick which." With a sly wink she adds, "Game is stud. Five card."

First hand he loses. "Do shoes count?" he asks.

"Yeah, Norman," she says with a sigh. "You can count your shoes, you want."

He removes a shoe.

They play some more. One thing he got right, about poker he don't know diddly. So she directs the flow of the game however she wants, gettin' him first barefoot and then bare to the waist, but throwin' a few hands here and there too, so's to keep things even. Bod she's lookin' at is everything she'd hoped it would be: tight, lean, smooth, hairless, sleek. She's feelin' tingly all over. Squirmy. Got herself down to bra and panties, so next hand she tosses, saying thickly, "You learn real quick, professor." She reaches behind her and unhooks the old boulder holder and puts the ripe melons, their big brown eyes already perkin' up, on show. By now she got a serious wide on, all moist and juicy down at the Y, and when he don't make an instant lunge for hooter heaven she goes, "Okay, how 'bout we try a new game."

"What would that be?"

She rises, steps out of the panties, sits on the floor with her back braced against the sofa, her thighs outspread, knees bent. "Called lickety split," she says. "You do the lickety, I supply the split."

He hesitates. She summons him with a wiggly finger. Dutifully, he comes to his feet, stands over her. Far as she can tell there's nothin' goin' on in crotch country, no steeler in sight. Not exactly your Mr. Groin here, sugar bod or not. She don't know what his problem is, but right about now she don't give a rat's red ass. Little moustache ride do, get her over the mountain. After that she'll get it aloft for him. Plenty ways do that, an' plenty time. Her turn now.

"C'mon, professor. Munchie time. Your tongue still works, don't it?"

She grins at him, urgent grin, viciously cute. Giggles softly. But the giggle turns to astonished gasp when he stoops down and reaches over to the toolbox and removes a glittery ballpeen hammer and, gripping it firmly at the rubberized handle, swings it into the side of her head; and the gasp to muffled howl (for the palm of his free hand covers her widening mouth) as the bones in her cheek splinter; and from howl to chittering screech, the indecipherable vocabulary of pain, when he lifts the covering hand and, simultaneously, brings the hammer down squarely across her face, flattening the nose and collapsing the mouth, from which erupts a bright geyser of blood gaily trimmed with white chips of tooth and bone; and finally, as the hammer falls again and again and the darkness settles behind her eyes, no utterances whatsoever, no sounds at all.

She slumps back against the sofa. Her arms dangle. Plump breasts droop. The battered head, spilling blood, its face no longer recognizable, lolls off comically to one side. He puts down the hammer and grasps her ankles and stretches her out flat on the carpet. Then, retrieving the hammer, positioning himself on his knees next to her body, he pounds it thoroughly, methodically, short rapid blows, rather like a butcher tenderizing meat, neglecting nothing, not toes, not fingers, not limbs, not torso, not throat, shattering bones and transforming the white flesh to a rich purple, dark as wine.

After a while his arm grows heavy. He lays the hammer on the floor and goes into the kitchen and fills the sink with hot soapy water. Washes the blood from his hands and those places on his chest and neck and face where it has spurted. Dries himself with a filthy dishtowel, the only one available, and then soaks the towel, wrings it out and brings it into the living room where he scrubs down everything that his faultless memory informs him he has touched, moving briskly and efficiently but without panic or undue haste. He overlooks nothing, forgets nothing. Each of the playing cards is wiped off individually. Near the bottom of the deck he comes upon the queen of spades, and a thought occurs to him. Perhaps not so much thought as image, lifted capriciously from the chaotic rush of images teeming inside his head. A name attaches itself to the image: Suzanne. He tries to say it aloud but it catches in his throat, emerges a harsh guttural croak.

A firestorm of rage sweeps through him. And as though impelled by an irresistible inner logic, a dreadful necessity, he takes the card over by the body, which lies, as the dead always seem to lie, in a peculiarly lumpish way, eyes full of the unwelcome knowledge of darkness, mouth agape as though in silenced scream; and he finds a ten penny nail in the toolbox, picks up the hammer, searches for a spot on the caved-in skull, from which protrude fragments of bone, settles on what remains of the forehead and nails the queen of spades to it. The queen, her face spiked and blood-smeared, gazes at him sorrowfully.

Sudden as it appeared, the rage passes. He resumes the task of cleaning and when he is satisfied it is finished, he puts on his shirt and jacket, and socks and shoes. He surveys the room. The last thing he sees before dousing the light is a roach creeping out from under the sofa, drawn by the thread of blood leaking from a mangled ear. He recalls a passage Aunt Grace liked to quote, biblical no doubt, a cautionary line: "In the midst of life we are in death."

But it offers no solace, that passage. And driving away through what has become now a shattering rain, his clothes drenched from the half-mile jog to the car hidden in among the trees hemming a stretch of road, thunder booming overhead and forky streaks of lightning splitting the black sky, he feels no sense of release, as on those other occasions in the past when incidents such as this one tonight would occur. No burden lifted, no order restored. Only a certain hollowness in the chest, an emptiness he could not begin to identify or define or name.

17

"Suzanne was her name," Norman was explaining, "something of a velvety, sibilant sound, don't you think? Rather pretty, actually. How she came by it I never did quite understand, perhaps to soften the jarring surname, Croop. Suzanne Croop." He plucked another Marlboro from the thinning deck of reds on the table, lit it, and sighed a plume of smoke at the ceiling, gathering his thoughts. "She was my wife," he continued, his voice pendulating between heavy irony and immense doubt, "Michael's mother, and my crime was—" he hesitated a beat, the word murder stubbornly refusing to issue from his lips—"taking her life. A crime of passion, to be sure, but no less a crime."

Again he paused, slightly longer this time, weighing the effects of a blunt and unvarnished candor. None detectable yet. "Duly adjudged second degree by a jury of my peers," he said, the irony swelling now, "and for which violation of the natural order I paid with eighteen years of my life. A just recompense, some might say."

Across the table Lizabeth stared at him blankly. Saying nothing. Through the bay window behind her he could see white fragments of cloud trooping across a metallic sky. A mild breeze fluttered the yellowing leaves of the maple tree in her yard. The baffled, ticking silence lengthened, and it occurred to him there is no limbo quite so ambiguous and uncertain as that which follows a confessional. And so, partly in summation, partly to fill the silence, he said, "I tell you this so you'll understand my concern over your ex-husband's threat yesterday. For someone with my history, it wouldn't do to be hauled into court. Even on a minor scuffle."

"Where?" she asked.

"I beg your pardon?"

"You were in prison. Where?"

"Stateville. Just down the road."

"Joliet," she said. "I used to drive by it on my way to visit my parents. They lived in Springfield. It always looked so . . . grim. The prison, I mean."

"Well," he said dryly, "it's not exactly your Palmer House."

"And you were there how long, did you say?"

"Eighteen years. It might have been fewer had I learned anything at all of restraint, or even an elementary prudence. Sadly, such was not the case. But then that's another story."

"When did you get out?"

Curious, this line of inquiry, this seemingly urgent need for context. Not at all what he expected. Maybe it was her way of dealing with a revelation of such appalling magnitude, fixing it in time and venue, reducing it to manageable proportions. "I was released three years ago," he said. "This very month." He checked the date marker on his watch. "Almost to the day."

"Which day? Do you remember?"

"Oh, yes. Vividly. October sixteen, 1989. Any particular reason you ask?"

In a voice charged with awe, she said, "October sixteen is my birthday."

"There's a coincidence," he said, truly surprised.

"And I remember exactly where I was that day."

"Where was that?"

"The Bahamas. Nassau. It was Rick's present, probably to ease his conscience. He was bedding a client at the time."

"I see," he said, for something to say.

"I was there, in all that sunshine and warmth. And you were

here." She gazed at him with an attitude of perplexity, brows lifted in wonder. "And those days I drove through Joliet and passed the prison," she went on. "You were behind those terrible gray walls. All those times."

"But dreaming you into existence," Norman said quietly, and a faltering smile crossed her face. A tiny glitter in the corner of one eye revealed the possibility of a tear. And in the sorrowed look presented by that delicate face and the unstained gentleness of that smile he seemed to see again all his own innocence lost or carelessly discarded over the years, and for an instant he felt as if a hole had been opened in his heart.

But then her expression, sifting through a battery of emotions, returned once more to bewilderment, to the stricken wonder, and in that tone of inner dialogue people will sometimes take, wrestling aloud with an enigma too mysterious to unravel or comprehend, she said, "I still can't believe it. You? Killing someone?" She studied him skeptically, as if to say: *It's a joke you're making, right? Own up, now. Tell the truth.* "You? It's impossible to imagine."

Now it comes. After all the meticulous fixing of times and dates and places, and all the ah-ing over coincidental trajectories of two lives, and after the first stunned wave of shock has receded—now comes the pure revulsion. "Believe it," he said flatly. "I did it."

"But why?"

"Why?" He butted out the ash-heavy cigarette, made an impatient motion in the air in front of him. "I don't know why. Maybe she was too blatantly faithless. Or faithless once too often."

"So you were cheated on, too."

"Many times over."

"How did you . . . ? How did it . . . ?"

"How did I kill her?" he finished for her. "I don't remember."

"You don't remember how it happened?"

There was a genuine curiosity in her voice, none of the sly prying malice he had come to expect as a matter of course with the delivery of that question, and in her face a trace of the innocence he had seen, or thought he had seen, before. "No," he said. "My censors have been merciful that way." Yet even as he spoke, another, familiar voice snickered derisively in his ear, and he heard himself adding, "Call it a willed amnesia."

"But there must have been a time, once, when you loved her?"

This question now, this one stalled him, and for a moment he looked at his hands and said nothing. What did he know of love? That perjuring imposter. That clumsy effort to reduce life's insults and griefs to the range of the endurable. *What did he know?* Nothing was what he knew. Less than nothing. And when finally he found the words for these bleak thoughts, that's about what he said: "What can I tell you? I forfeited my right to speak on matters of love. For me even to utter the word is its own blasphemy. All I know is that hate and what you call love share a common border, a shifting frontier. And they watch each other across it. Warily. As well they should."

For a time she was silent again. A great sadness seemed to settle over her. He waited. At last she said, measuring her words carefully, "I can't pretend to understand you, Norman. Or what you say you did. But it doesn't matter. Changes nothing. Whoever you were then was a different man from the one I know." And with those words, that simple declaration and the look that accompanied it, innocent of awe or horror or loathing, all its trust restored, he felt as if he had been awakened from death's vacant slumber.

And having so declared, she rose and gathered up the saucers and cups and plates of their Sunday brunch, by now routinely shared, and carried them into the kitchen. Norman smoked another cigarette. He watched the clouds beyond the window shape themselves into odd configurations, here a strange winged creature—a fish, was it?—gargoyle?—there the blurry outline of mocking face. Unless he imagined them. Lizabeth came back into the room, took her chair, and regarded him in a most calm manner, almost hypnotically calm, before saying, "There's something else I have to ask you."

"What would that be?"

"Where was Michael in all this?"

"He was there, it grieves me to say. Witness to it all."

"How old was he?"

"Nine years old."

"Nine," she repeated, and her head moved back and forth slowly. "How did he . . . react?"

"Numbly, as best I recall."

"And afterward? What became of him?"

"I had an aunt, dead now, lived in Iowa, where I grew up. She took him in. Grudgingly. I had to beg her."

"No one on his mother's side?"

"No. All gone there. And I have no siblings."

"So she raised him, this aunt? Great-aunt?"

"There was no one else. It was that or a foster home. Or worse. Looking back, I'm not so sure it was the right choice."

"Why do you say that?"

The memory of Grace warbling her love of Jesus returned to him, and with a short dry laugh he said, "You'd have to have known this woman. Nothing served by libeling the dead."

"During those years you were. . . ."

"In the joint?"

"Yes."

"If you're asking did we stay in touch, the answer is no."

"Why was that?"

"The aunt pretty effectively poisoned his mind where I was concerned," he said and, shrugging, added, "Maybe rightfully so."

Lizabeth rolled over a palm, a motion of small confusion. "But eventually you must have made contact?"

"Eventually. After he was grown and she had passed on to her reward. We began a stiff correspondence. Initiated by him. I expect he was curious about this monster father."

"And so, after, he asked you to come here?"

"After my release, yes. He was charitable enough, forgiving enough, to offer me a place to live."

"Tell me, Norman. Do you two ever talk about it?"

"Never. It's hardly the sort of thing one cares to reprise."

"But don't you wonder how he feels about it? About you?"

"About 'it,'" he said, a fine edge of defensiveness in his voice, "I'm sure he was badly torn up. Psychically mauled. About me, I'm equally certain there's a great deal of lingering hostility. Buried maybe, but clearly there. You can see it sometimes, in his eyes."

"Yet you've never discussed it? Or gone to a counselor or a therapist?"

"Counselor," Norman snorted. "There are, my dear young lady, some traumas and griefs that refuse to yield to any earnest twelve-step programs."

Again she shook her head slowly, made a wry, meager smile.

"You know, Norman, you talk the way books read. Maybe that's what I like about you."

"You mean it's not my piercingly handsome countenance?" he said, and he threw up his hands dramatically. "Ah! My world topples."

"No," she said solemnly, ignoring the weak quip, "it's your honesty. What you've told me here explains a lot."

"Does it, now. What, for instance?"

"For one thing, why Michael is so, well, ill at ease with women."

"Michael? Ill at ease?"

"You've never noticed?"

"No."

"I don't think he's had much experience with them. Women, I mean."

"That would surprise me. Someone of his appearance. In this age of license."

"Trust me," she said, her gaze turning inward, focused, it seemed, on some private place. "He is."

"About that I wouldn't know," Norman said, a bit uncomfortably.

"I would," she said, and the gaze swayed back to him, fastened on him steadily. "You see, Norman, there was a time—near the end of my marriage, it was, everything in shambles, everything coming apart—when I was very . . . promiscuous. No better than Rick, really. I had other men. Many men."

Norman looked away, acutely uncomfortable now. "Confessions all around," he said.

"The way he was running loose—like you said a while ago, blatantly—it seemed only fair. At the time. I'm not exactly proud of it."

"You've, uh, mentioned this to Michael?"

"No. Not yet, anyway. He's very special to me. Both of you are."

"Wise decision. I don't know my son well, but at the risk of invoking some easy, pop psychology, I'd hazard the guess he'd expect a great deal from a woman. Loyalty, not least of all. There's that much of his father in him, I'm afraid."

"I had that sense myself."

"All the more reason," he said, turning the talk away from these prickly matters, bringing it back to where it first began, "to say nothing of yesterday's little episode. Or that your ex plays a role anymore, even as irritant, in your present life. He might not understand."

"You may be right."

"You've heard nothing more from him?"

"Rick?"

"Yes. Rick."

"Not a word. Like I said, I seriously doubt he'd ever carry through on that threat. Too much the macho egotist."

"But you'll alert me if you hear anything?"

"Of course. I did, though, get a call from Michael."

"Today?"

"Early this morning. From San Antonio. He sounded exhausted."

"He's overworked."

"I know that. But he seemed so weary, so down. It worries me."

"It's the price of his chosen calling."

"He said he's hoping to take a few days off. Between projects."

"Good thought. When will he be back?"

"Depends on when he's finished down there. Possibly Tuesday."

"In time to celebrate your birthday," Norman said, and she looked at him quizzically, as though she'd forgotten. "Remember? October sixteen? This upcoming Friday?"

"My birthday," she said wistfully. "Thirty-five, I'll be. My life's half gone."

What do you say to that? "One half at a time," was the best he could do.

"Do you think less of me? For what I've told you?"

"I'm hardly in a position to think less of anyone. And for what it may be worth, I'm no longer infected with those quaint notions of morality. Arrived at last in the twentieth century."

"What a botch we've made of things, Norman. Both of us."

"Both?"

"Yes," she said, a desolate catch in her voice. "Both."

Before he replied Norman considered the numberless curious scales of regret by which human failures and betrayals and defeats are measured. As many, it appeared, as there were grieving souls to take their measure. He thought of the consoling illusion of some sort of moral macroeconomics at work in the world, presiding over it with pious purpose, apportioning justice evenly, rewarding the good, punishing the wicked. He remembered prison, and also, whimsically, from some remote pocket of memory, the remark he'd read once, somewhere, of the explorer who first stumbled across Yellowstone's fiercely spouting geysers: "Hell must be in this vicinity." Sympathy he could muster for her, this lovely woman, her beauty lit from within and heightened by a transient sorrow over commonplace transgressions and woes. Sympathy, yes; empathy, no. "Well," he said gently, "perhaps it's fair to say I more so than you."

18

At seven o'clock on the evening of October 13, Victor Flam sat at the bar in the lounge of a San Antonio motel, nursing a Lone Star, only his second, but scarfing up a bucket of nachos drenched in a fiery salsa. He was hungry. Little sack tussle with the sleeping pill he'd hired in grew an appetite, but he never liked to go into a face-to-face on a full gut, so the chips would have to do for now. Be time for dinner later.

He'd positioned himself so he had a clear view of the lounge entrance. Place was pretty well lit and most of the small crowd, in for an after-work pop and the freebie snacks, was gone, which was good. Tuesday night, not much action, also good. He didn't want a lot of jungle music and loud yammering going on. Wanted to be able to read every shade of expression and tune in to every rise and dip in the voice. Because, near as he could figure, this was his last shot at a break. You don't catch one here, Victor, whole goddam investigation heading straight down the storm sewer like a dribble piss in a rain shower.

Especially after the past couple weeks in Phoenix, speaking of pissing. His big Gary Cassidy lead, lady-clubber, looked to be the one

for sure gonna crack the nut, turns up a total wash. Girlfriend he bat-
ted around, who Flam talks to first, she's back with him, all is forgiven. Anyway, that A&B charge, that was just a misunderstanding,
by her account, not even her doing. Little lovers' spat got out of
hand, got noisy, neighbors call in the heat. Gary's really truly a
sweet, kind, gentle man, just down on his luck is all. Next in line for
pope, hear her tell it. *Yeah, yeah, yeah.* Flam, he's heard that love-
conquers-all line of scheisse before. Cuts no shit with him. *So
where's Gary at now?* he wants to know, and she says he's out of
town someplace. Where she don't know, interviewing for a job, be
back next weekend.

   So that chews up a few days. And when he finally gets to Gary
what he finds is a dumpy little turd (a long way off Shelley's documented tastes in men, which is the first bad signal) with a perfectly
unmemorable face but with a kind of crafty, elastic quality to it too,
least that's what Flam wants to see in it since he got nothing else to
go on. So he hangs out another week, tracking Gary, but the worst he
can turn over on him is the peckerhead got a couple twats on the
side, no law against that, you don't get caught. And make that second
worst, you're looking at it through Flam's peephole. Because the really bad news is a check of Gary's claimed whereabouts on the day of
the Shelley whacking (done courtesy of Nathan, but in his own Jew
time) stands up.

   Jesus, Flam hated to let that one go, but even he finally got to
admit no corners to be turned with Gary. What you got here is a general fuckup, hornier'n a two-dicked dog, gets by off women, maybe
got a short fuse sometimes but who wouldn't, all that pussy juggling.
Most guys call them happy problems. Which is more than could be
said for his own, way this case was shaping up. Shaping down, be
more accurate.

   "Sir?"

   The bartender, hauling him back from these dismal reflections.
"Yeah?" Flam replies.

   "Last call on happy hour. You care for another beer?"

   One he got still half-full (or half-empty, depending on your angle
of vision, like the old saying said; where he's sitting right about now
the empty be closer on the money), so he shakes his head no. But the
nachos basket, that was empty any way you looked at it, so Flam
adds, "You can bring me some more of the chips, though."

Bartender runs his eyes over him, says, "Well, they come with the happy hour, sir. Have to charge you for them now."

Like he's gonna stiff 'em on some munchies? Everybody busting your balls these days. Whole world going to shit on a diesel-powered handcart. "Yeah, well, I think I can cover it," Flam drawls. "You just tack it onto my tab there." And when the dickweed comes back with a full basket Flam tells him, "Also, I'm expecting a fella, gonna be joining me here. Whatever he's drinking, you put that on there too."

Bartender nods and sidles away, leaving Flam to think, *Least he'd better be showing up,* and before soon, or that bell captain gonna get his palm ungreased, and before suddenly. Double saw bought him the buzz this Michael Woodrow checking out tonight, and it took another double, get the ironclad guarantee Captain Marvel deliver, without fail, the message there's a gentleman in the lounge wants to speak with you, Mr. Woodrow, says it's real urgent. But so far no Mr. Woodrow. Which is another good reason Flam sits where he does, so he can scope not only the entrance but out into the lobby and the front desk as well. Just in case.

Actually, it's a freak of luck (maybe luck, only time tell on that one) he's even here, first place. After he'd given up on good-time Gary and was ready to split Phoenix, he put in one more call to Nathan, had him run a quick follow-up on this Woodrow dude, who it turns out just finished up in Michigan and gonna be down in old San Antone a few days, doing a tuneup on some past job before he gets his next assignment.

That was Saturday. So the next day Flam books a flight into here. Made sense: It's on the way, maybe spare him another stop on the See America First tour, also spare Mother Swales some gelt (about which subject she's getting touchy, close to snarly, last they talked). Day after that (yesterday it was, days start to blur, you're on the road too long), armed with all the Woodrow venues as supplied by Nathan—where he's staying, where he's working, who for—Flam drops by the Jiffy Jack corporate headquarters, see what he can see. Which is not some greasepit garage, like he was expecting, but a brand new office building, whistle clean, piped-in elevator music tranquilizing the air, lots of suits scurrying around.

He asks the receptionist—tall, creamy blonde, great set on her, looks like a pom-pom girl in her skimpy mini there—can he talk with Mr. Zulewski. She asks him back coolly does he have an appointment. No appointment. Helpless shrug. Maybe later today, Flam suggests; and she tells him Mr. Z. is *terribly* busy and, little impatient now, wants to know what this is in regard to. It's a personnel matter, he says; and she kind of sniffs and says, *Oh, employment office is down the hall to your left.* Like she's talking to a pump jockey wants on the payroll.

Well, *I'm not really looking for work,* Flam tells her, smothering his own impatience, and then he explains how he's with AARC (which is the American Association of Registered Consultants, which intelligence he lifted out of that Directory book back at the PBJC library) and how he was hoping to speak with someone could maybe supply him with a little information on a consulting firm they engaged a while back. Possibly Mr. Briggs could help you, she says, but very noncommittal. So what are the chances of seeing Mr. Briggs today? Zip, he learns, after she puts in a quick call. Mr. Briggs tied up all day; however, he could see you for a few minutes tomorrow. Ten a.m.?

Ten be fine, Flam says, and he thanks her and leaves. Goes back to the motel and buttons the bell captain, parts with his first double saw to get what he can on Michael Woodrow. Which is not a whole helluva lot: Mr. Woodrow? Oh yeah, he stayed with us few months last summer, busy man, leaves early, gets back late, keeps out of the bar, eats, when he eats at all, off room service, don't seem to cat around, tips good, good guest. The worm's eye view. And not exactly what you'd call promising.

Because he's not yet actually seen this Woodrow, Flam asks the captain to make him when he comes in that night. Which means Flam's got to hang out in the lobby from 6:00 P.M. on, reading newspapers and stoking himself with Norwegian gasoline, waiting for the grand entrance. About three hours later it comes. Captain signals him with his eyes, and Flam catches a passing glimpse of a slender young man, boss in the looks department by anybody's measure. Expensive threads, expensive attaché case gripped in a hand, determined sober stride on him, man in a hurry, crossing the lobby and vanishing down a corridor. Not so much as a peek in the bar. Mr. Dudley DoRight. Just like he'd feared.

Next morning—that'd be this one—he gets his thirty-minute audience with Dwight C. Briggs, CHIEF OPERATIONS OFFICER and CPA, so the engraved legend on his desk nameplate announces. Flam starts in by telling him about AARC, winging it mostly, getting by on what he remembers out of the Directory, rest of it smoke, which he's good at producing when he got to. Tells him the association is dedicated to maintaining the integrity and the highest professional standards in the consulting industry, mush like that. And as its representative he'd be interested to learn of their experience with the Stoltz organization.

"What, specifically, are you looking for?" Briggs asks guardedly.

"Whatever you'd feel comfortable sharing," Flam says with an easy smile.

Turns out the piss-ugly little numbers thrasher, looks like he'd rather count than fuck, got lots to share. Right up front he makes it plain he got no great affection for consultants generally, the Stoltz people in particular. Comes to them, he's more than eager to dish some dirt.

Except there's none to dish, not on Woodrow anyway. Stroiker now, boozer, gasbag, ass hound ("Why, he even propositioned Gloria, our receptionist," Briggs confides, all a-gasp; which to Flam, recalling those jugs and that sweet can on her, sounds forgivable enough, sounds like envy, though he makes a shocked face for the accountant's benefit), that's a different story, one he'd be delighted to enlarge on. But of no interest whatsoever to Flam, who knows all that already and who gently steers him back to Woodrow and gets, through some pointed questions, the grudging admission that even though his methods are ruthless, Woodrow himself is a tireless worker, good at what he does, and has designed a system that's saving the company a pile of money. And unlike Stroiker, Briggs has to concede, his behavior is altogether professional, his character seemingly above reproach.

Not exactly your boffo news for Victor Flam. With this Michael Woodrow he's down to number five, last name on his list, and from everything he's seen (including the little dance with the old man, up in Illinois) and everything he's hearing, it's not looking good at all. Looking pretty grim, in fact. Five strikes and you're out, Victor.

But not till he sees for himself, up close and personal. Eyeball to eyeball. The Victor Flam wrap and zap test, foolproof and failsafe. What anybody else calls hunch or instinct but what he knows to be experience, twenty-two years' (not including the four in the Corps, an apprenticeship, grammar school) worth of reading the slip-sliding maps of guilty faces and deciphering the messages coded in sounds and stutters and silences. Which years taught him everybody got a nasty secret, everybody a vice, nobody straight. So like they say, it ain't over till he hears Mr. Perfect sing.

So after he's got all he's going to get out of Briggs he comes back to the motel, connects again with the captain, gives him his instructions for tonight, and has him send a mattress up to the room, help pass the long afternoon. Flam figures he's got it coming. All this bootie drought, even Miss Bridget look good along about now (also figuring how he's gonna have to find a spot for it on the expense sheet, under miscellaneous data gathering fees maybe, bury the yard it cost him). She's no Gloria but she'll have to do. After he gets the job done he shoos her out, takes a little snooze, gets up, showers, dresses, and wanders down to the bar.

Where he's been waiting ever since.

He glances at his watch. Quarter past the hour. He's feeling restless. Captain Bell Dick better not fuck up or he'll lean on him hard. He finishes off the last chip in the basket and the bartender whisks it away. Finally has to order another Star, justify his claim on a stool. Give it fifteen minutes more. And that's what it takes, fifteen. At 7:30 his man shows. Michael Woodrow. Number five.

MICHAEL STOOD IN THE ENTRANCE, glancing about the near empty lounge, puzzled and not a little irritated. *What now?* Some last-minute glitch? Last stab at wringing ("free for nothin'," in Jack's eloquent words) one last ounce of advice and direction out of him? The flight to O'Hare, last one tonight, left in under two hours, and the prospect of missing it was not cheering. Was, in fact, deeply disturbing.

It didn't help any that he was exhausted. Almost numb with fatigue, actually; about as weary as he could ever remember feeling. Never mind that he'd given Jack and his bumbling lieutenants three full and uninterrupted days of his absolute best efforts. Hit the Texas ground running, and running nonstop, Sunday to now. Bouncing between the closet of a bird room assigned him (Briggs's doing, no doubt) and the motel, twin axes of his shrunken cosmos; getting by on four hours sleep a night; every waking hour spent feverishly plugging holes, opened only through the grossest incompetence, in the system; restoring order to the scheduling and status reports, badly disarrayed, even as he'd predicted; calming Briggs's bean-counting anxieties; stroking Jack on his small screen performances. . . . Never mind that he'd done all that. There was always more. Out of him, somebody always wanted more.

So he was in something other than the best of humors when, a moment ago, a bellman tapped him on the shoulder at the checkout desk and delivered the cryptic message, "Gentleman in the lounge asking to see you, sir, says it's important." And even less so now, when a burly man, utterly unknown to him, came shambling around the bar, approaching him with hand outthrust, smiling genially, saying, "Mr. Woodrow, glad you could make it. My name's Flam. Victor Flam."

Michael gave the proffered palm a small clutch and, that perfunctory ceremony complete, said, "What can I do for you, Mr. Flam?"

"I was hoping maybe you could spare me a few minutes. Maybe help me out with a little problem I'm working on."

"Are you with the Zulewski organization?"

"Matter of fact, I'm not. Been talking to them though, and your name came up."

"In what context, may I ask."

"Context of this problem of mine. They speak real highly of you out there, by the way. Said if anybody could help, you'd be the man."

"If it's a consulting matter, this problem of yours," Michael said, coating his words with a thin varnish of frost, his rehearsed response to any freebagger (of which there were an abundance, came with the work) trying to score some free advice, "then I suggest you contact the Stoltz offices. I can give you the number, if you like."

Flam put the recently pressed palm in the air, a motion of disclaimer. "Oh no, this one's not a consulting problem. Except indirectly, you might say. If we could sit down here a minute I'll run it by you."

"I'm afraid that won't be possible. I've got a plane to catch."

"Won't take but a minute," Flam said coaxingly. And then, "I think you'll find it real interesting, what I got to tell you."

For an instant Michael wondered if he could be a headhunter, come to tap him for a new and prominent position, more challenge, more opportunity, more reward. Didn't seem likely, this stage in his career. Yet stranger things had been known to happen. Headhunters were notorious for pillaging the management consulting ranks, where only the ablest—and the nimblest—survived. And he had not only survived but advanced, prospered. He looked at his watch. "All right," he said, "but I don't have a great deal of time."

"Like I say, won't take long at all."

They sat at a table next to the door. "I'm having a Lone Star," Flam said. "You?"

"The same would be fine."

Little surprising to Flam, who was expecting to hear diet soda or maybe some kind of fancy Shirley Temple, everything he'd got on him so far. He signalled the bartender with two fingers in the air, and a moment later the beers were delivered. "Good brew, your Lone Star," Flam said affably, swallowing some of his own.

Michael nodded, poured beer in his glass, sipped, made no reply.

"I think they make the best ones down in Mexico, though."

Michael sighed. "And I have to think you may have been misinformed by the Zulewski people," he said.

Flam looked at him puzzledly. "How's that?"

"If this problem of yours has to do with the relative merits of beers, then I'm not your man."

Flam produced a deep clucking chortle and followed it with a smile so engaging that this Woodrow had to smile back in spite of himself. It was stiff and unamused, but a smile all the same, displaying a row of strong white teeth. Perfect teeth, perfect features. Could have been an actor, Flam was thinking, or one of those male models you see parading around in their butt floss underwear. Guy look like that, he's gonna get his share of tail, and more. He said, "No, this problem got nothing to do with beer."

"What, then?"

"Well, y'see, Mr. Woodrow, I'm in the consulting business too, manner of speaking." It was the line he'd used, with slight variation, ever since that first rap with Stroiker. Drop it in, leave it hanging. Good opening.

"Which manner is that?"

"Beg pardon?"

"What's your specialty?"

"Personal research, you might call it."

Or you might not. Another thing Michael had heard about headhunters was their penchant for dancing around the issue, but for which circuitous waltz he had neither time nor patience. So he asked, "What firm are you with, Mr. Flam?"

"Oh, I'm strictly solo. My own firm."

"You're not in executive search, then," Michael said flatly.

Flam laughed again, but only a small chuckle this time. "Well, once in a while this research I do turns up an executive. Not often, you understand, but once in a while."

"Maybe you'd like to get to the point," Michael said, putting some of the distancing chill back in his voice. Clearly, this was no headhunter come to call, come to open up bright new career vistas, broad and limitless. Nothing but a freebagger, just as he'd first suspected. Clumsy one, at that. And here he sat, with an unwanted beer in front of him and no easy exit.

"Point?"

"Your problem."

Flam snapped a finger by an ear and made the kind of face that seems to say, *C'mon, dummy, get with the program.* Which is about what he said. "Oh, yeah, right. The problem. Sorry about that. Taking up your valuable time with all my rambling here."

No response to that, so Flam continued, still in deferential gear, "See, I been working for this lady down in Florida, elderly lady, well-to-do, wants me to see if I can find out, through this research I do, what happened to her daughter."

Still no response.

"Been at it close to six weeks now," Flam said. "No luck so far."

More of the silence from across the table.

So Flam levelled a watchful stare on him, his get-to-grips stare, and fired his first shot across the bow. "Name's Swales. My client, I mean."

Michael returned the stare blankly. Said evenly, "I'm still waiting for that point, Mr. Flam."

"Guess the point is I figured you might be able to help me out. Fill in some of the gaps, this research I'm doing."

"Why would you think that?"

Movie star face, detached and cool, absolutely unreadable. Surprise in the voice, though, which now had a genuine ring to it. Not good. So Flam let loose his second volley. "Well, y'see, this daughter worked at the same place you did a consulting job for. Sanitary Laundry, down in West Palm. Same time, too. About a year back. Remember that one?"

"Yes, of course. But I'm afraid I don't remember anyone named Swales."

"How about Russo? Shelley Russo?"

"I don't recall that name either."

"Yeah, well, I can understand that, whole year gone by," Flam said sympathetically, and he gave it a well-timed beat and pushed on. "Course, she was, like, assistant to the president there, and since I understand you consultants always real tight with the president I thought you might of run into her now and then. Which is why I wanted to talk to you."

Michael sat perfectly still, expression unchanged, no gestures or movements at all. But he asked quietly, "Are you a police officer, Mr. Flam?"

Flam smiled broadly, deliberately, half for Woodrow, half for himself. Sooner or later it always got to that. Except ordinarily there was more fear in the question than he was hearing. Least a little wariness. Neither one there, though. Just that innocent curiosity, same as before, like he was really interested in Flam's occupation. Another of those not-good signs. "No," he said around the locked-on smile, "more a consultant, like I was telling you. Only my clients are private individuals instead of your big companies."

"A private investigator?"

Flam gave a modest shrug. "Some folks like to call it that. Not me. Sounds too much like the movies. Y'know, punching out bad guys, guns blazing, that kind of poot. Myself, I like to think of it as research."

"Researching missing persons?"

"Well, worse even than missing, Shelley's case," Flam said, allowing the smile to settle. He reached inside a pocket and removed a photo, the one of Shelley standing outside the laundry, and laid it on the table. "Whyn't you take a look at her picture here. Maybe jog your memory."

Michael didn't pick up the photograph, but he leaned forward and scrutinized it closely. After a long moment's passing he shook his head and said, almost regretfully, almost apologetic, "Afraid I don't recognize her." Then, still gazing at the picture, he asked, "If she's not missing, what happened to her?"

"What happened is she got herself dead."

Michael lifted his gaze and looked at Flam steadily. "I'm sorry," he said, and when he said it Flam detected an authentic sorrow in his eyes, but the empty kind, remote, kind you feel over death in general but nobody you know in particular, nobody you'd care about.

"It's a shame, all right. Happened the very day you left. You and your team, I mean. Actually, it was that night."

"I wish I could be of some help to you."

Experience had taught Flam that, contrary to conventional wisdom, it wasn't the eyes gave you away but the voice and, sometimes, the set of the mouth. And at not one of the several flash points in their little talk, not the mention of Florida or the laundry, or what it was he did for a living, or Shelley's name, or the sight of her picture or the day of her death—none of them, not a one, excited the slightest twitch or quiver, mouth or voice. And so, reluctantly, he was coming around to accept the gloomy conclusion this was not his man. Which left him nowhere. Square one. If there even was such a square anymore. Fucked if he knew.

But he still had one last cap to pop. Last round in his chamber. "Yeah, me too," he said, and he took out another photo and pushed it across the table. It was the crime scene shot, the one of Shelley's hacked mutilated naked body, or what was left of it. "Especially seeing how it was she got herself wasted."

Michael didn't touch this one either, but looking at it his eyes steepened and his breath quickened and he mumbled, "Jesus."

"Sort of like your before-and-after pictures," Flam said, watching him carefully. "Only this after not showing much in the way of improvement."

"Terrible . . . just terrible."

Flam watched him. Your normal citizen reaction to a shot of a butchered stiff. Nothing out of the ordinary. Except that he kept on staring at it. Except for that curious arched flare in his nostrils and the short, ragged breathing, audible, almost a pant. And except for the message, arrived at just that moment.

For it was just then the bell captain came hurrying through the door, spotted them, and approached the table, saying, "Mr. Woodrow, got a fax here for you, sir, just come in." He handed over an envelope and stood there beaming at him, the toady hover. "Lucky I caught you before you left," he said. Woodrow rewarded him with a couple of bills, and the bellman strutted away, not a glance at Flam.

"Excuse me," Michael said.

"Sure."

Flam turned slightly, to give him the courtesy of space, and he went through the motions of filling his glass with the last of the beer and finishing it off. But he was still alert, still watching. And what he saw was most curious. More than curious. Strange. For the formerly unreadable mask of a face was transformed magically into a display case of emotions: bewilderment, shock, an intense dismay, some remorse in there, something very close to what you could call anguish. And as he read and reread the message his eyes seemed to slide back and forth between it and the photos of Shelley laid out before him, his face paling, as though all the blood were seeping out of it.

Which prompted Flam to break the lengthening silence by asking solicitously, "Bad news?"

"I'm sorry?"

Flam indicated the letter still in his hands. "Your fax there. You looking a little shook."

Michael folded the sheet and put it back in the envelope, and the envelope inside a jacket pocket. "No," he said, eyes glazed over and voice gone flat, toneless as an owl's bleat, "I guess you'd say it's good."

Yeah, right. That's the way you get the good news, Flam'd be real interested, see how you take the other kind. But he said, "Glad to hear it. Good news hard to come by, these days."

"What was her name?"

Momentarily confused, Flam said, "Who's that?"

He pointed at one of the photos on the table, the one of Shelley in stiff mode. "The woman who was . . . killed."

"Swales," Flam said. "Shelley Swales. Married name Russo."

"Shelley," he repeated, and then, as though the words were an incantation, a charm, invoking some mysterious occult force, he said it again. "Shelley."

And in just that instant Flam knew, beyond all doubt, beyond any evidence anyone might produce to prove him wrong, this was surely his man. In a low, careful voice he said, "Wouldn't be something come back to you, Mr. Woodrow? About Shelley? Something you'd like to share?"

Just as instantly was the spell snapped. He hesitated, seemed to compose his wonderstuck features, seemed to get down behind his eyes. "No, nothing," he said. "And I really must be leaving now, Mr. Flam."

"Why sure. I understand. And I appreciate you taking the time to chat with me here."

"No trouble. I'm only sorry I couldn't help."

"Hey, don't you worry. Don't give it a thought."

Michael came to his feet and took a step toward the door. But before he could get to it Flam said, in casual afterthought, "Catching a plane to Chicago, are you?"

He stopped, turned, looked at Flam narrowly, as though he were seeing him for the first time. "That's right," he said coldly.

Flam gave him back a small inverted smile, mouth tucked down at the corners in a suggestion of subdued triumph, not all that far off a jeer. "Well, you have yourself a real nice flight now, y'hear."

19

After the plane was aloft, after the last lights of the city winked away far below, blackened in night, and after he had deflected with frigid monosyllable or withering blankness of expression the peppy conversational stabs of the old woman next to him, Michael got out the fax and read it again, one more time. It was from Russ Marks. Predictably in oafish drummer style, careless of spelling and full of telegraphic dashes, ellipses, and screamers. It read:

Mike,

Just got the word Hobbes project a go . . . full implementation . . . board spanked the iron maiden with a no confidence vote . . . goodbye Dr. R! Who'd a thunk? Go figure. Sensational work Mike—congrats!!!
More good news for you . . . Milwaukee project come through. Guess whose IM? More congrats! Hear your taking

few days off. Enjoy!—you earned it boy! Touch base Saturday with all the skinny.

All best
Russ

In keeping with his tightly compartmentalized life, Michael had, over the past seventy-two hours, squandered not another thought on the seemingly unsalvagable Hobbes College project. Had, in fact, written it off, the harsh strictures of his recommended plan (presented only last Saturday to the regents board—only Saturday, was it? —seemed an eon ago) too draconian for the squeamish educators.

But now he did. And with recall came a discordant clash of memories and images: the board members attending closely, brows pinched, to his impressive show of charts and graphs and numbers. Dr. Hilda sitting off to one side, pursed-lipped, glaring, poised and waiting, taut as a coiled cat about to spring. Dr. H. on her feet in impassioned rebuttal, well-rehearsed, well-delivered, and freighted with well-timed bursts of ridicule ("Crisis? What crisis? I submit to you that a businessperson's grasp of the issues and problems of higher education is likely to be clouded by a, shall we say, bottom-line mentality."). Himself seething under the sneered and wholly gratituous ad hominum assaults; the spineless board, flying in the face of irrefutable evidence, electing to take the Stoltz plan "under advisement" and to render its considered judgment later (for it was, after all, homecoming weekend, and the insistent thump of a marching band could be heard in the distance, a steady pounding in his ears).

The pounding was unrelieved after he gathered up his graphs and charts and beat a hasty retreat, Dr. Hilda's triumphant flinty eyes and parting gloat ("Such a pleasure to have worked with you, Mr. Woodrow. Truly a learning experience.") trailing him through the door. And with him still, internalized, a crescendoed throb inside his head, as he drove back to the hotel and paced the floor of his room furiously, a bottled rage gripping his throat. Wondering what to do, searching his imagination for a way to silence the relentless *thump, thump, thump.* No, more than wondering or searching. Knowing with a terrible certainty what he was about to do.

Melanie, Shelley, somebody called Iris, a Tami Sue in there somewhere, other names, sparked by the memory of that wickedly smirking figure back in the lounge, came to him now, spiraling up out of a whirl of paranoiac darkness. And with them other images, appalling, grisly, swamped in blood, frothy with blood. And now, on a dimly conscious level, his own accusing voice, none other, sounding in his head, the message in his hands a mute and pitiless reminder that the last one, the luckless Melanie, was all for nothing, nothing—only now did he understand for perhaps the first time what it was he had done. Everything he had surely done.

He felt a curious sense of time dissolving around him, as though he had strayed into a dizzying hall of time-warped mirrors whose shimmery reflections—raging man, shrieking woman, stricken child— gave back only demons and from which there was no exit, no flight. He folded the fax and shut his eyes. Behind the shuttered lids he seemed to see two specks of light emerging slowly out of the dark, glittery, piercing, close-set, like the eyes of a jackal. He thought of Victor Flam, and a shiver of fear swept through him. By supreme act of will he banished the thought and the jackal eyes and conjured in their place a vision of Lizabeth Seaver, focused, defined, concentrated, vivid in its particulars. And then another of himself, cradled in her sheltering embrace and safe in her arms.

AND WHILE MICHAEL FASHIONED this dreamy sustaining vision, the flesh and blood Lizabeth sat with his father in a congested O'Hare coffee shop, two steaming Styrofoam cups and a heaping ashtray in front of them. All of the butts were Norman's, for she was trying to quit, or at least cut down. "For Michael," she had explained, somewhat righteously, Norman thinking, *God, not another one.* The brief romance, evidently undimmed by distance, appeared in fact to have flowered into the faultless, enchanted wonder-of-you stage. Certainly her face, glowing with anticipation, and the breathless twitter in her voice gave it away. "I don't know if they believed me at school," she was saying, "when I called tonight and told them I needed time off."

"And what was your excuse of record?" he asked, polite but incurious.

"A death in the family. My grandmother. Oldest fib of all."

"Who can quarrel with death."

"I wish you could have heard the choke I put in my voice," she giggled. "It was absolutely shameless, Norman."

"An award-winning performance?"

"Well, I wouldn't go *that* far. Must have been convincing, though. But it's very chancy, my being there just a couple of months."

"Chance is life's only constant," he said, because such thoughts routinely came to him, and with her he was in the habit of vocalizing them. "If Heraclitus had it right."

"Who?"

"An old Greek. Never mind."

"Still was worth it," she went on, clearly not much taken with the warmed-over wisdom of the ancients, "to have these five days with Michael. You too, of course."

"Of course."

On she chattered. He listened, but only at the edges.

For Norman, deep into a third deck of reds, puffing one right now, it was shaping up a bad nicotine day. Unaccountably restless day. Maybe it was the morning spent in stony gaze at a yellow pad, memory and spirit stalled, both. Or a spiritless afternoon with Montaigne's easy pronouncements on repentance ("I seldom repent, and . . . my conscience is satisfied with itself. . . ."), easy for a Frenchman. Or the surfaced recollection of a morning's chat with a thuggish Sherlock, vigorously repressed in the wan hope it would all go away, all the nagging doubts and suspicions and fears. Or yielding, against all good judgment, to Lizabeth's excited, insistent plea to come along tonight, meet Michael's plane.

More likely was it merely the swarm of people out on the concourse, trooping purposefully from place to place, or the herd of them in here, this feeding station, jostling for position, space. Maelstrom of urgent appetites and agendas and uncertain destinations. Proximity's oppressive lockup, release from which he knew, none better, arrived only through the cultivation of silence, a mystery of the art of how not to need, not to will.

The sound of his name, borne on upward inflection, tugged him back from these wandering ruminations. "Yes?" he said absently.

"You seem awfully distracted. Is something bothering you?"

"No."

"You're sure?"

"Perhaps a mild agoraphobia."

"English, Norman."

"An unreasonable aversion to crowds. Another Hellenism. I seem to be in Greekish mode tonight. Must be the subliminal influence of the gyros posted on the menu on the wall."

Feeble quip, lost on her, or ignored, for she said (and said it in those earnest purling tones grownups will inflict on whiners either end of the age spectrum, sulky brats or querulous bonebags no longer equal to the world's commonplace rigors), "Do you want to leave here? We could go down to the gate. It might be quieter there."

He stubbed out the cigarette and brushed the air impatiently. "Not to fret. It will pass."

"Are you sure it's not something else?" she persisted, same honeyed voice, but with an edge of skepticism in it now. "Be honest, Norman."

"Something else? What, for instance?"

"Rick, for instance. Is it still worrying you, what he might do?"

"Not so long as you continue to hear nothing from him. Which I assume is the case."

"That's right, nothing," she said. But after a hesitation, conviction faltering, eyes sliding away: "Not exactly, anyway."

"Inexactly, how?"

"Well, there was a call last night. Nobody on the other end of the line. Nobody speaking, I mean. Just dead air."

"You think it was he?"

"Could have been. It's happened before."

"Have you considered an unlisted number?"

"I've considered it. But with my job it wouldn't be practical. Besides," she added, brightening some, "I've got a better idea."

"And that is?"

She reached into her purse, removed a small tin cylinder, and held it up in display. Significantly lettered in bold reds and navy blues on a field of white, its logo read *Defender,* and in subtitle, "Your Protection Against Crime."

"Mace?" Norman asked.

"No, the people who sold it to me said mace won't always work against somebody on drugs or alcohol. Which Rick usually is, the alcohol, whenever he's acting crazy. No, this is the real thing. Tear gas."

"May I see it?"

She handed him the cylinder. Near to weightless, it barely filled a palm. He read the instructions, their fine print disclaimer ("Warning: Device not effective against all persons. Do not place undue reliance on this device"), remembered the towering size of her ex, his incendiary temper. Remembered also this delicate wisp of a woman, backed into a wall, cowed and weeping. "And you're willing to put your faith in *this?*" he said.

"Absolutely," she affirmed stoutly. "Next time I'll be ready. Defend myself, next time."

He gave back the formidable weapon, tin cylinder full of the real thing, said, "Yet I'm always at your service, you know."

She laid an affectionate hand over one of his. "I know," she said fondly. "And I do appreciate it, Norman. But I'm sure it won't happen again. Not after what you did the other day. This is just a precaution."

"Just so you know who to call. In the unhappy event your Defender there should fail you."

She nodded, replaced it in her purse. "Let's not talk about it anymore, okay? Let's just enjoy these next days."

"As you wish."

"Speaking of which, can I ask a favor of you?"

"Ask away. Whatever's in my power to grant is yours."

"Will you not mention my birthday to Michael?"

"Not if you'd rather I didn't. But may I ask in return why?"

"Oh," she said dismissively, "I don't want him to feel obligated to get me a gift."

"He'd hardly consider it an obligation. More a pleasure, I should say. If there's one thing Michael is, it's generous."

"Well, there's another reason."

"Care to confide it?"

"The difference in our ages," she said, looking into her lap. "Five years now."

"Five years. What a yawning gap. Unbreachable."

"Don't make fun, Norman. It's significant to me. Bothers me. It's something I've got to work out."

"A scarlet older woman, corrupting innocent youth? Is that it?"

"Will you be serious."

"I'm trying, but I confess it's difficult to share your distress. And the vast difference is actually nearer to four and a half, if that's any small numerical comfort."

"How is that?"

"His birthday is in April," Norman said. "April first, to be exact. All Fools' Day. Conceived in summer, delivered in spring." And saying it, they came back to him now, both days, stark and lucent and rich in detail, like memories preserved in ice, frozen frames in the grim movie playing again and over again in the theater in his head. April 1, 1962. Day of brittle blessing. Perhaps the single blessing of his life. The one thing he did right.

From somewhere outside that darkened theater a voice petitioned him. He wasn't listening. "I'm sorry?" he said.

She gave him an indulgent smile. "You're drifting again, Norman."

"Must be Alzheimer's setting in. Say again."

"I said six months doesn't change anything."

"Narrows the gap."

"All the same, I'd rather you wouldn't mention it."

"Whatever you like."

"I'm grateful for the thought, though."

"And I to you, for summoning it up."

AND WHILE NORMAN AND LIZABETH WAITED at the airport, and Michael's plane winged him steadily nearer to home, Victor Flam was spending a good part of the evening with a phone fused to his ear. Because he knew there would be downtime between calls, he placed them from the bank of phones in the lobby, returning to the bar to review the encounter with Michael Woodrow, run it by in his head, and to weigh and ponder his next moves. Even though he had a pretty good figure on what they were going to be. If he was right about this pretty boy—fuck, no ifs about it, his mind, but you still don't go making any head-up-the-ass moves off a hunch—but if he was, then he was maybe looking at something big. Bigger maybe even than just the Shelley case. Kind of score that gets your name in the papers and your mug all over the TV. Gets you a national rep. That big.

But first you got to be grounded in something a whole lot more standup than a nostril flare and a schizo glaze in the eyes and a zombie pitch to the voice. Got to have more than that. Got to be sure. So his first call had gone direct to Nathan. Where else? And not without misgivings, coming to the Israel well this often. But he needed dish and he needed it now, tonight, to confirm his assessment (hunch he didn't want to call it anymore). And that's what he told him, the urgent part anyhow, to mute the piss and groan sure to follow.

Not that it did. "Tonight!" he squawked after Flam read him the list of questions and laid on the deadline. "You want all that *tonight?*"

"Be a big help."

"Surely even you must understand," he said, squawk turned surly, "such information is not always easy to come by. Requires time. Not to mention expertise."

"Time is what I ain't got," Flam said. The expertise part he left unremarked on.

A long silence.

"Nathan? You gonna help me out here?"

"All right. I'll see what I can do. Call me back in about, oh, say, three hours."

"You got it."

"And Victor," he said, some sly in there now, along with the surly, "we'll need to have that little chat. About this ongoing service I'm providing you."

"Sure thing, Nathan. Any time."

"Tonight."

"You got that one too."

Yeah, right, chat. You don't need no book smarts, put an educated figure on what the little chat gonna be about. The Jew York profit-sharing plan. Pay your friendly yid piper time. Nothing to be done, though. Don't matter, finally, not if he come through with all the happy buzz Flam was hoping to hear, or even part of it.

So for the next three hours Flam held down a stool at the bar, too wired to eat (except for a couple bags of beer nuts), pacing himself on the Stars so's not to fog his head. Scheming, planning, juggling his options, which, if he had it right, reduced to one. For now forget about going home, regrouping; nothing to group there. No, track your man, stalk him, keep in tight, catch him in a whacking, nail him to the wall. After which came all the good stuff: gelt and glory. But only if he had it right.

Fifteen minutes short of the appointed hour, unable any longer to contain himself, Flam walked back into the lobby (nearly deserted now, approaching eleven), picked up a phone and pecked out the number. Took ten—count 'em—dings (Nathan being world class at making you sweat) before an oiled voice came snaking down the line saying, "Let me guess. This wouldn't be Victor Flam?"

"Bingo," said Flam, fraudulent hearty, but thinking, *Wise-fuck kike.*

"Calling in regard to the murder of one Shelley Russo, née Swales, of the moneyed Palm Beach Swales clan, perpetrated on the night of August 23, 1991, and currently unsolved? Am I right about that also, Victor?"

Flam, momentarily dumbstruck, produced nothing at all in the way of reply.

"Victor?"

"Yeah, that one too," he said, because he had to say something, wondering how the fuck he dug it out, impressed and dismayed at the same time.

"Heavy case."

"It's that, all right."

"And doubtless lucrative. For the person—or persons—able to close it."

"That what we're talking about here? That *lucrative?*"

"All in good time, Victor. First let me pass along what I've managed to uncover. As a show of good faith."

"You got something for me?"

"Something for us, Victor. Us. And rather a good bit, I should say."

"So say."

Fuckin' A dog, it's rather a good bit he's got. Yes, there was a woman murdered recently and in most bizarre fashion, as he puts it, in Grand Rapids, Michigan. Last Saturday, in fact, and he goes on to describe what he means by bizarre. Yes, there was another one right here in San Antone, right around Labor Day, similar stamp on the victim. Both women middle-aged, married, reputation for promiscuity. Not unlike Mrs. Russo. And yes, Michael Woodrow, in the employ of Alexander Stoltz and Associates, was in those venues on or about the time of both incidents. As he was, of course, on the occasion of Mrs. Russo's unfortunate demise. Interestingly, in each of these instances he had just completed the consulting project and was about to depart the vicinity. His next assignment, to commence Monday, October nineteen, is in Milwaukee, Badger Manufacturing, Inc., the consulting team to be headquartered at the Grand Milwaukee Hotel.

In the interim he can be found at home in Hinsdale, Illinois, address previously supplied, taking a few much-deserved days off, his first in over two years. Also of some interest, possibly incidental, possibly pertinent, the father, Woodrow senior, was convicted in 1971 of murdering the wife/mother, second degree charge, currently released and residing with the son. "So if this is your suspect," Nathan concluded, "it may be in the blood," adding with small snicker, "No pun intended."

Holy shit, Flam's thinking, everything coming together, all the pieces falling in place. This last one about seals it, his mind. No point mentioning he already had the little face-to-face with the old man, never bothered to look into his sheet, and wondering now where his head was at. Nothing served, revealing that bonehead move. Instead what he says, undisguised admiration in his voice (say what you like about your Jews, they come out on the long end of the brains pole), is, "Y'know, Nathan, you might just be square on the money there," immediately regretting his choice of words.

"Thank you, Victor. I trust all this research of mine has been of some use to you."

Better'n some, Flam was thinking, but anticipating what was due up next he said, cautious, neutral, "Could help."

"In which case we can return now to that other matter."

"What one is that?"

"Come on, Victor."

"So what kinda damage we lookin' at?"

"Oh, a sixty–forty split strikes me as equitable. The sixty yours, of course. For the leg work."

Flam's turn to squawk. "Sixty–forty! Jesus! That's stickin' me up."

"Ask yourself this, Victor. Could you have done it without me?"

"Goddam straight, I could. Just would've taken longer is all."

"If you'd been candid with me at the outset, it would have taken nowhere near as long as it already has. Time is money, Victor, in our profession. And greed, I must say, is not only unseemly but self-defeating."

Ignoring the homilies, Flam said, "Who's huggin' the belt here? That leg work you're sayin', that's me shootin' cube with a body bag. We're talkin' certified whackadoo."

"Point taken. Two-thirds, one-third?"

"S'pose I can live with that. Still a street muggin'."

"With an upfront retainer. In small compensation for my past contributions."

"Case I'm the one loses that dice roll? That it?"

"Perish the thought, Victor."

"How much, this retainer?"

"Oh," Nathan said, humming it out like he had to give it some careful deliberation, like he hadn't long since trimmed it down to the last decimal point, "I should think five long would do."

"Five long! No way! I'm workin' off expenses and a flat per diem myself. Large dollar's strictly contingency."

"I have expenses too, Victor. What would you consider fair?"

"Dime's best I can go."

"Four."

"Two."

"Three, Victor. Nothing less."

Jesus, fuckin' sheenies squeeze piss out of a stone. "Okay," Flam sighed, "three dimes it is."

"Done. I'll look forward to your check."

"Yeah, you do that."

"And you will, of course, keep me abreast of your progress?"

"Do that too."

"Splendid. Because I'll know, Victor. You do understand that I'll know?"

"Like you knew which case this was?"

"Exactly."

"Tell me something, Nathan. How'd you put a make on it?"

"Process of elimination. The screen reveals all, Victor. No secrets from the magic screen."

Except for the sour taste in his mouth about the bones it was going to cost him (still maybe find a way to skim on that yet), Flam was elated. Fuck, make that *charged,* impatient to roll out and bust some moves. About Woodrow, anyway, he was surely right.

So his next call goes to Mama Swales, but that one don't exactly turn up pure aces either. First mistake is he forgets the time, past midnight in Florida, so he's talking at a cranky old twat who's seriously hacked over a break in her ugly sleep. Second one got to do with time too, because when he explains how he's onto a real promising lead, ought to have something solid for her real soon, all she says is, "How soon?"

And when he tells her, "Oh, maybe two, three weeks, month outside" (which is a tight fit but he's trying to put the best face on it, seeing it's been seven weeks gone by already and he got nothing to show but jack shit and a stack of expense vouchers), she starts bitching about those expenses. She calls them "inflated and outrageous," says she's not fresh off the turnip truck and that he's got four more weeks to put a ribbon around it and not a minute longer. Four and counting.

Last mistake is telling her the four do just fine, giving her the old Vaseline rub, letting her know where he'll be staying in Milwaukee and dropping in how he's heading up to Chicago first thing tomorrow morning, tracking that heavy lead.

"There'll be no more flying first class," she snaps. "Back of the plane gets there same time as the front." And then all he hears is a dial tone in his ear. So much for Vaseline. Like he's suppose to be taking the fuckin' Amtrak? Jesus, everybody bending you over lately, everybody giving you grief.

One more call to make, secure a seat (coach, as directed) on a morning flight to O'Hare, and he's through for the night. Least this one goes snag-free, or it does till he's reciting his Visa card number and he senses something behind him, a presence, or the ghost of one. Glances over his shoulder and sure enough there's a dude, sawed-off runt, strolling away. Easy, casual stroll on him. Little too casual. Flam rings off quickly and follows him, hanging back, keeping him in sight. Runt crosses the lobby, turns a corner and ducks into a public john. Flam gives it a beat and then comes through the door and finds him bellied up to the last pisser in the file. Place is otherwise empty.

So Flam walks down the length of gleaming white urinal scoops protruding from the wall and takes the one right next to him. Only he don't unlimber his dick. Instead what he does is say (talking straight at the wall tiles, way you sometimes do when you're leakin' the lizard side by side to a stranger), "Havin' a good night, are you?"

"What's that?"

"Ask if you're havin' a good night."

"Sure," he says, shaking off and tugging at his fly. Knowing something not right here, in a hurry to get gone. "It's a nice hotel."

"Well, that ain't exactly what I meant," Flam drawls, and now he turns and plants himself as solid as a roadblock, looking squarely, though at a steep downslope, into the mobile eyes of a pudding-faced little putz—could be twenty, could be more, with a serious overbite and a swag of black, grease-gunned hair, strands of which he's playing with nervously, and who says innocently, "I don't get it."

"You don't get it?" Flam dances his eyebrows, mock disbelief. This is the part he likes best. Likes to string it out, milk it, make it last. "Lemme see can I help then. Kind of good night I had in mind is surfin'."

"Surfing?"

"Yeah, you know, like shoulder surfin'."

Runt draws himself up to his full height, which got to be a full five-seven, and says bravely, "I don't know what the fuck you're talking about. And if you don't get out of my way I'll . . . I'll . . ."

"Call a cop?" Flam finishes for him. "Y'know what they say. Call a cop, call an ambulance, call for a pizza, see which one shows up first."

Now he's really pulling at the oil-slick hair. Gonna yank himself baldheaded, he's not careful. "Look," he says, voice gone wheedly, all the brave drained out of it, "what do you want off me?"

"Want? Oh, that's easy. All's I want is that Visa number mine you nicked."

"What number? I got no number."

"Well, you better find it or the cleaning crew gonna be suckin' you up with a Dustbuster."

Runt's boxed now, and he knows it. Reaches into a pocket, produces a scrap of paper, and hands it over without a word.

Flam gives it a quick scan, says, "Now ain't that a coincidence. Same number as the one on my card."

Gets back a squishy smile anchored by the two top front buckers, badly stained. "Okay, I done it. I surfed you. Nothin' personal, man. It's a living, is all."

"Hey, I can understand that. Man's got to make a living."

"So you callin' in security, or what?"

"Can't see no need for security, now I got my number back," Flam says charitably. He tucks the paper scrap inside his jacket, tilts his head, like a curious thought just come to him, and he asks, same way, like he really wants to know, "What I'm wonderin', though, is how you surf rats do it, just hearin' it read out loud once. Must take a good memory, huh? Your line a work?"

"Well, yeah. Short term."

"Also wonderin' just how that short-term memory gets scrubbed clean. So's no funny charges turn up, next bill, or the one after that."

"Listen, you don't got to worry none," Runt says hopefully. "I forgot yours already. Like you seen there, I gotta write 'em down or they're gone forever."

"Y'know, that's a real comfort to hear. But I got another thought. On that scrubbin' procedure, I mean."

Flam's the one doing the smiling now. Wicked coil of a smile as he steps in close and catches him in a melon-squashing headlock and drags him over to the scoop, unflushed in his haste to get out of there, and slams his face down into the puddle of piss, bright orange and still bubbling, not enough to drown in but enough for some deep gargling. He holds it there a while, lifts it by a hank of the greased hair, slams it down again, repeats the drill a few times, pausing finally on an upswing to inquire, "Whaddya think? That number gone outta your head yet?"

Head jiggles up and down.

"You're sure now? Cuz we can do it some more. Do it all night, we got to. Always plenty piss."

"I'm sure," he splutters.

Flam releases him, and he sinks to his knees, clutching at his mouth. A trickle of blood seeps through his fingers. "My tooth," he moans. "You broke my tooth."

"Done you a favor, I did."

Flam's over at the sinks now, soaping his hands. Not your most sanitary work, all that hair goo and splashing whizz. Which sparks another thought. "Giveya word of advice," he says, rinsing and toweling off thoroughly. "You oughta watch your diet. Color a that knob drip there, I'd say you been eatin' way too many sweets. Ain't healthy."

And then he's gone, headed back to the bar, little swagger in his exiting stride, smiling to himself, grimly but not without satisfaction, feeling better now, whole lot better than when he was getting a new asshole carved for him over the phone. And though he was not a man given to introspection, he's got a pretty good idea why. His turn, for a switch, do some of that reaming.

•   •   •

AND IT WAS NOT LONG AFTER FLAM had resumed his station at the bar that Michael's plane touched down and taxied to a halt, and after the usual protracted wait ("Please remain seated until the captain has turned off the seatbelt sign") he fell in with the column of passengers shuffling down the aisle. He came up the long sloping tunnel of a ramp and through the gate, where he hesitated, glancing about, an expression near to dazed on his face, as though he were uncertain which, of all the multiple terminals that marked the destinations of his surface life, this one was.

Lizabeth spotted him first. She threaded through the swirl of travellers and greeters and wrapped him in a joyous hug, stuttering in his ear, "Michael, you made it. You're back. I'm so glad you're back." Longer than commonplace welcome would dictate, he held her, clung to her as if to absorb all the electric glow from her slight frame, sponge it right up; and charged so by its wattage the muscles of his jaws trembled and a small stinging sensation pinched at his eyes. Till gradually the crowd thinned around them, and over her shoulder he saw his father backed up to a wall, removed as far as was possible from the jam of bodies. Assembling his face, drawing away, he said, somewhat stiffly, "You brought Norman."

"That's all right, isn't it?"

"Sure."

She looked at him doubtfully. "You mean it?"

"Of course. Let's go collect him."

They walked over to where Norman stood, one hand extended, a rules-transgressing red cupped in the other, giveaway smoke seeping through the fingers. Michael gave the greeting hand a perfunctory clutch. They said each other's names, Norman adding, "Welcome to Bedlam."

"This is nothing. You should try it midday."

"That's an experience I'm content to forfeit."

"Oh, come on, Norman," Lizabeth said teasingly. "It hasn't been that bad."

"I'll be the judge of that."

Rather too curtly, Michael said, "Then I expect we'd better get you out of here."

She looked back and forth between them. Something going on here, not sure what. To lighten things she said, "After just a handshake? You two aren't going to do your Muhammad Ali impression?"

"Not tonight," Michael answered for both of them, and to Norman, "You'd better lose that cigarette. They can fine you now, you know."

"Legislated sanctimony?"

"Just get rid of it, okay?"

Norman shrugged and ground it under a heel, and off they went, through the concourse and into the main terminal and around a series of squared-off corners. Down an escalator and past a long file of slow-spinning carousels thumping out luggage, Michael in the lead, hustling them along, a peculiar urgency in his stride. Lizabeth hurrying to keep up, Norman lagging a step or two behind, panting a bit from the day's nicotine spree, his senses still reeling at this alien world of soaring walls and elevated ceilings, and glass and marble and steel washed in fluorescent glare, and thrumming with voices and voiceover alerts and warnings, dazzled and appalled by its clamor and sharp-angled head 'em up and move 'em out architecture. Architecture of tyranny. Too much. Too many echoes here.

So he was not at all unhappy to find himself next in the shadowy tomb of a high-rise parking lot, Lizabeth out front now, leading them to her Camaro. With some difficulty Michael squeezed his bags into its shallow trunk. They climbed into the car, Norman in the back, Lizabeth at the wheel, Michael, master of direction, pointing the way from the passenger seat, speaking in short, clipped bursts, a curious edge to his voice. "Hard left here. Careful now, watch the traffic flow. Hang right. Your exit's just ahead, quarter mile—"

"You realize," Lizabeth broke in softly, "I've been here before, Michael."

"Sorry. Guess I'm too used to giving orders."

"That's okay," she said and, partly to make a joke of it, partly to include Norman, "but you don't want to confuse me with your father back there."

On cue, Norman deadpanned, "Small risk of that."

"Sorry," Michael repeated, and then he lapsed into silence. No more directions. No more idle chat.

On the short drive down the interstate, Lizabeth did her heroic best to reanimate the talk, keep it alive, asking all those bright, conventional questions one asks of the traveller and getting in reply, and then only after prolonged pauses, answers terse but not caustic or petulant or unkind (The flight? Good, uneventful, and on time. The Texas weather? Agreeable, mild, generally pleasant. His projects? All under control). Answers more depleted, as though he were overtaken suddenly by an immense fatigue, or a great sadness. And strictly a solo effort, For Norman, hunched in the tiny backseat and gazing through the window at a lemony slice of moon like a man transfixed, contributed next to nothing. They seemed to have gotten off into zones remote and intensely private, both of them. It was baffling.

Finally she said, lively as she could pitch it, "Come on, you guys, cheer up. This is celebration time. We're all of us free for the rest of the week. That should be reason enough to cheer."

"There's Columbus Day," Norman said in apparent non sequitur.

"What?"

"Yesterday was Columbus Day. Quincentenary of this hemisphere's discovery by that Great Admiral of the Ocean Sea. Five hundred years of progress."

"You're right. I'd forgotten."

"There you are. A signal occasion. A day."

"So why don't we stop at my place for a drink," Lizabeth offered. "In honor of old Chris. Without him we probably wouldn't even be here."

"Let's do that," Michael said quietly.

"You want to? You're not too tired?"

"No, it sounds good."

"Terrific!"

Norman said nothing. Not until they were pulled up outside her condominium, and then, "Perhaps I'll pass tonight."

"Norman, you can't. It was your inspiration. You have to come in."

"Tomorrow. Or another of those free days."

"Michael," she said, adopting her mock schoolmarmish tone, "talk to your father."

He stood on the porch, volunteered nothing.

She turned to Norman, who was by then backing toward the street. "This is very disappointing, Norman."

"Trust me when I tell you all your disappointments have a far distance to travel before they'll overtake the charming fiction of hope."

From the porch came a heavy sigh. Lizabeth shook her head slowly. "I'm never going to understand you, Norman."

"Don't worry about it. I'll see you both later."

"Yes. Later."

"WHAT'S GOING ON, MICHAEL?"

"What do you mean?"

"Between you and Norman."

"Nothing I'm aware of."

"I have eyes, you know."

He was slumped in a living room chair, gazing at the floor. She sat perched on the edge of an ottoman opposite him. He lifted the gaze, said, "Lovely eyes."

"Talk to me, Michael."

"About?"

"Are you angry that I brought him along?"

"No."

"What, then?"

"Well, there are times I get weary of his pompous riddles. All that ersatz wisdom."

"That's just his way. It's a cover."

"Who should know better than I."

"He cares about you, Michael."

He swept the air with an impatient hand. "I know that too. Why don't we drop it."

"All right. What can I get you?"

He seemed puzzled.

"To drink," she said. "Remember?"

"Oh, I don't know. Maybe nothing."

"Like father, like son."

"I suppose you're right."

She gave him a long, searching look. "If not a drink—what?"

"I'm not sure."

"I am."

Later, she came out of the bathroom and found him sitting on the bed in the dark—stork shouldered, palms at the sides of his head, rocking and swaying. "What is it, Michael? What's wrong?"

"Don't know. Don't know."

"Tell me."

"I didn't do you much good tonight. I apologize. I'm sorry."

She untangled the sheets and eased him back gently, slid in beside him, twining him in her legs and arms. "More good than you know," she said.

And since for her all lovemaking was an expression of longing, a denial of some nameless aching void, she was content to hold him, this strange man-child, and to purr in his ear those sounds transcending all speech.

And for him, head buried in her hair, breathing in its fragrance, enveloped in all the natural perfumes of her, it was as if the candescence of her healing touch carried with it the power to cast out demons, purge them forever, almost as if he were reborn.

AND WHILE THEY LAY TOGETHER, drifting into a clement sleep, Victor Flam sat scowling into his glass, belly churning under the weight of too much beer and too many nuts and chips and not a goddam thing else to eat, nothing solid, like a man needs after a seesaw night like this one been. Ask for a menu and the fuckin' bartender puts on a helpless face and goes, "Sorry, sir, our kitchen closes at eleven." There go the chow plans, fart in a skillet. Everybody dickin' you over. Ball-bustin' world.

Nevertheless and for all of it, all the grief, he was feeling pretty good about himself (except for the burning gut, made you wonder you got an ulcer coming on). Felt like he earned a little party down. For a while he entertained the notion of calling back the mattress, make it a double-feature day, but remembering his pinchass client (speaking of grief) he thought better of it and bought himself a cigar instead, fat turd of a Macanudo, little indulgence, treat. Not as much fun as poom poom, but cheaper.

And as he puffed away, semi-contentedly, his thoughts strayed to money, to sugary visions of all those big buckazoids just around the corner and up the block. And from there to Mr. Michael Pretty Boy Woodrow, and he caught himself mumbling, "Gonna rain on you, boy. Hurricane Victor, blowin' in fast."

Bartender gave him a funny look, said, "You speaking to me, sir?"

"Uh, no. Just thinkin' out loud."

AND WHILE FLAM WAS, quite uncharacteristically for him, giving voice to his thoughts, Norman was doing much the same thing, only on his feet, pacing excitedly, nerves twanging, synapses humming, addressing the stillness of his room, though unlike Flam he was privileged to have a familiar and responsive, if not altogether sympathetic, audience. And he was at that precise moment saying: *I think I have it now. It's the days, you see, the days.*

Days?

Yes. Those watershed days in our life.

Explain yourself.

What I mean is those tiny islands surfaced by the tug of memory out of the currents of time.

How poetic! All that aquatic imagery. None of it, I must confess, very clear to me.

Nor to me. Yet.

So illuminate us.

Try thinking of it this way. If it's true, as somebody once remarked, that all experience represents a fuddled and never-ending process of returning to the source. If that's true, then, don't you see, if I'm able to isolate those islands, reclaim them, maybe I'll understand, finally, what went wrong, what I did.

Who?

I beg your pardon?

Your anonymous remarker. Who was it made that puerile and, it grieves me to say, rather sophomoric observation about source tracing?

No idea. Might have been me.

I thought so. And it's I, by the way.

Fuck you.

You're awfully testy tonight, Norman.

With good reason. I come to you for help and get grammatical niggling.

What kind of advice were you seeking?

Constructive.

Well, perhaps you'd agree you need something a bit more substantial than parlor poetry and water cooler philosophy. To keep your earlier figure afloat, so to say. Ha ha.

Some help.

I'm doing the best I can. Given the murky parameters.

That's your best? More mockery?

A little joke, Norman. Just making a little joke.

Hilarious.

All right. Let me ask you this, then. How many of these "is-lands" did you have in mind?

A few. Not many.

A few. Would the Day be among them?

It's possible. I hope so. We'll see.

Hope? Not good enough. If it's not, then you're merely spin-ning your wheels again. Another exercise in stalling.

I don't think so.

Have it your way.

I intend to. Who needs you, anyway?

You, evidently. Why else are we speaking?

I'm listening. But I've yet to hear anything of value.

Here's a thought. If you must persist with this dubious disin-terment of the past, at least do me the kindness of expunging your idiom of all its astral elegance and limp wit. Speak plainly.

Thanks for all the kind words. I'll try.

Do that. Remember also, Norman, words are deeds. It was Wittgenstein, I believe, remarked that.

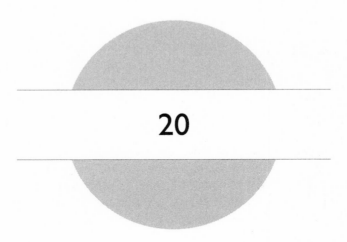

20

P lainly, then:
Grace's parlor. Late on a sun-blasted June afternoon. June 29, 1954, it is. The day after my discharge from the army. I've come here because, well, rather like prison, when they let you out you have to go somewhere. And nowhere else occurs to me.

The parlor (in truth, a tiny, gloomy alcove off the living room) is, I remember, reserved exclusively for entertaining the rare guest in her home. This day I suppose I qualify as guest. Certainly the glass of iced tea in my hand and the plate of sugar cookies on the coffee table between us would seem to confer that status.

Outside, the heat pours down. Thin blades of light pierce the seams of the drapes drawn at the window, slant across the carpet. There is, of course, no air-conditioning, and she bats at her gaunt face with a newspaper folded into makeshift fan. She looks smaller, shriveled, old. Older than what would have been (as I calculate it now) her fifty years offered up to heaven. But then, I'm a callow twenty-two Invulnerable, immortal. What do I know of old? On the all behind her a framed portrait of a cool and ageless, and decidedly un-Semitic-looking, Jesus presides over the room soulfully.

Now and again, at a gap in the stiff conversation (of which there are many), she will offer up a querulous observation on the steamy weather. "Sure is a hot one," she'll say. Or "Air's awful close." Or sometimes simply a "Hot," uttered in telegraphic hiss.

In pursuit of that topic she asks me, "Hot out east, is it?"

"Worse than here," say I. "There's more humidity."

She grunts at this intelligence, seemingly cheered to learn the Lord dispenses His miseries evenly. Cheered enough, anyway, to pop another cookie into her mouth and wash it down with tea, a glisteny sugar bead left behind to ornament a lip. She stabs a bony finger at the plate, directs me to help myself.

"I've had plenty, thanks."

The meteorological talk apparently depleted, she inquires about my trip. It's a thing to ask.

I describe the journey. Caught a military transport flying out of D.C., Omaha bound; arrived dead of night. Taxied to a Greyhound depot; slept on a bench; rode a bus here. I'm still in uniform (to secure the free flight), same one I've worn the past thirty-six hours. Must project a godawful stink. Wasn't too bad, I tell her in summation, a little tiring.

"Where 'bouts was it you were at?"

"Virginia. Fort Eustis."

"No, up north, I mean."

"Labrador, mainly. A couple of times in Greenland." Thule, I could have pinpointed for her but didn't. A literal Ultima Thule.

"Musta been cool up there," she says, the weather analysis not quite exhausted after all.

"It can get cool," I confirm.

"What was it you was doin' up there, again?"

"Working on the DEW line."

"Dew? What's that?"

"Radar stations. DEW, for Distant Early Warning."

"Hope you built 'em good. What with them comm'nists got the a-tom bomb now."

Scattered images of the military and all its waste, sloth, confusion, incompetence, neglect—so unlike the heroic screen sagas of my boyhood—flash through my head. But I say, "They're coming along."

"Y'want my thought on it, we oughta just go over and bomb 'em right now, all them godless reds. China, too. They're no better."

The Grace Woodrow geopolitical theory and strategy. She always fancied herself a well-informed citizen, had probably even read the newspaper employed now to whisk the stagnant air. A woman with an opinion on everything, and expressed in tones that brooked no contradiction. So I say neutrally, "Well, that's a thought."

The fog of international policy sufficiently cleared, she narrows in on the more immediate issue of my future. "Now you're out," she asks, "what you thinkin' to do? Got any plans?"

I have none, and I tell her as much.

This is foreign to her. Disturbing. Everybody has plans. "Goin' back to college?" she persists.

"I don't think so."

"Government pay for it, I hear. Read that someplace."

"They'll help you out some. Not a lot."

"You don't go back to school, gonna have to find work."

"I expect so."

"Hear they're hirin' out to Oliver."

Oliver being a small manufacturing plant on the outskirts of town, its product farm machinery. "Really," I reply, noncommittally and perhaps a trifle smugly. With good reason. What she doesn't know is that tucked inside the money belt cinching my waist are bills totalling very near five thousand dollars, this magnificent sum acquired at great hazard through an illicit traffic in the hard liquor denied, by arbitrary and whimsical edict, the enlisted men working the DEW line (though readily available to officers), the booze supplied by a corrupt lieutenant, myself the middleman, equally corrupt. Five thousand. And here's this crabbed old woman pressing me for decisions, plans. Plans? Assembling hay balers? Languishing in classrooms? Not likely. Not for a devil-may-care gangster like me (like Burt had been, often enough). Not with that kind of plunder.

Grace is frowning. To switch subjects, I remark with a nod at the upright out in the living room, "You still have the piano."

"Been tryin' to sell it, now your mother's gone. No takers though, so far." The frown deepens. "Be a help on those burial costs," she adds meaningfully, "I could get rid of it."

But I'm not listening. Rather, I seem to hear again the tinkly strains of "Ciribiribin," seem to see a gauzy specter bent like a surgeon to the upright, pounding its keys. My mother of the trembly smile and fragile heart. Six months "gone," in Grace's elegant phrase, vanished by death in the gelid grip of winter. Gone by her own hand, wrists opened with a pilfered blade in a nasty stall in a dingy lavatory in a grim state hospital, frail spirit vanishing on twin rivulets of bright blood leaking into a tarnished stool, while just beyond the barred windows, just out of reach, a gusty wind whipped the purifying snow. Unwilling, or unable, to endure another visit to the room down the hall where, thrice weekly, in small mimetic execution, strapped to a table, wired at the temples, bit in the mouth (to forestall the severed tongue, electro-shock therapy being somewhat more primitive in those days), a surge of voltage thrashes the limbs and fries the errant brain cells, and scourges the demons. The voodoo of electricity, inspiring terror, healing nothing.

My spurious birth. Her madness, suicide. Grace's god-lust. My lawless nature. Quite a history we were compiling, the star-crossed Woodrows, stalked, it seemed, like Orestes by the implacable Furies, but for which sins, what crimes, it was never given to me fully to know. And though I couldn't conceive it then, in time they'd all be committed, including finally murder. But now, out of an awakened need to know, I say to Grace, "Did she ever ask about me, those last days?"

"Oh, few times. But she was pretty well out of her head toward the end there."

"What did she say?"

"She worried about you. 'Fraid you was gonna get shot up."

"But surely she must have understood I was in no danger. The war was a continent and an ocean away. Nobody shoots at you in Labrador." (Except once, pursued by MPs in a wild, heart-thumping midnight chase over Goose Bay's corduroy roads, the back of my Jeep stacked with incriminating cases of booze, an incident best left unremarked on.)

"Your mother never had much sense of geography. Much sense at all, y'ask me."

"Why do you say that?"

"Why!" she snaps. "Should think that'd be plain as a pig on a sofa."

Since I'm the one sitting on her lumpy couch, there can be no mistaking the true identity of the figurative pig. "You mean me," I say coldly.

"I mean pickin' up and movin' out to California, first place."

"What was it prompted that?" I ask, my hostility smothered by a natural curiosity.

"Her looks. She was always vain of 'em. Thought they were gonna get her in pictures. Just traipse out there and be a Hollywood movie queen. 'Stead they ruined her life. Lost her morals, lost her honor, lost everything."

"And gained only me," I say quietly to this spiteful, shrunken gnome in floral print housedress, shapeless sack to shroud the withered dugs, unfondled, and the juiceless mound, unpenetrated, unloved.

Who hears me not at all. Voice rising shrilly, make-do fan swatting the air agitatedly, she delivers a choleric litany of slights, offenses, assorted resentments and humiliations. Half a century's worth of nursed grudges, squirming in her chair at the venomed memories, building to a wandering, ranting peroration.

". . . always the pretty one, she was, your mother, always the one somebody got to fuss over. Who cares about Grace? Then when she got no place left on God's green earth to go to, two mouths to feed and not a penny to her name—then, mind you, Grace is good enough for her. Good enough to take the both of you in. Put a roof over your head. Food on your plate. *I* did it. Grace Woodrow.

"Oh, you can bet the men come sniffin' around, first thing she's back. I put a stop to that quick, I can tell you. Says to her, 'Not if you're gonna live in my house. I got a respectable name, this community,' I says. Straightened her out good.

"What do I get for my trouble?" she asks rhetorically, and without dropping a beat supplies the answer. "Teeth. Kick in the teeth," baring them now in injured grimace at this unsurprising revelation. "Use to be I could walk down Main with my head held high. No more. Not since your mother hadda be packed off to the institution and . . . did what she done."

"Also your sister," I remind her.

She looks at me baffledly. "What's that got to do with anything I'm sayin'?"

"Evidently nothing."

"Darn right, nothin'. Got nothin' to do with what I'm tellin' you, now you're old enough to hear how it was. Which was not easy."

"Your many sacrifices, you mean."

"I could tellya thing or two about sacrifice. Just give up the best years of my life is all, for that woman. You too."

The hour grows late. The light softens. On the wall the features of the comely, placid Christ are no longer distinguishable in the deepening shadows of the room. A quirky notion comes to me. I unbuckle my belt, slip it off, remove the bills and stack them neatly on the coffee table. "For you," I say. "For all the suffering we caused you, my mother and I."

"Where'd you get that?" she demands, bug-eyed, mouth ajar. "They don't pay you that kinda money, the service."

"It doesn't matter."

"I don't want your money," she declares, but without much conviction. "However you come by it."

"Give it to God, then."

I'm on my feet now, hoisting my duffel and worn travelling bag, striding manfully toward the door. "Because now we're square, Grace," I say in parting shot and, adopting some of her homely vernacular. "Never have to write or speak or lay eyes on each other again, ever."

And with that I'm gone. Headed, I know not where. Away from here. Not exactly jubilant over the forfeited cash, but not entirely displeased with myself either. It's the sort of lofty gesture of extravagant disdain Burt would make.

But I'm wrong, though. About those forever sundered ties, I'm wrong. Years later I'm on a jailhouse phone, frantically pleading for her charity again, begging for shelter for a scarred son. Like my mother, nowhere left to turn. So in the end it's Grace, God-shielded, who wins.

FOUR YEARS LATER. Another torrid summer day. August, this one. August 24, 1958. A Sunday.

Sunday morning, actually (as my memory, friction-free, reconstructs it now). Early. A perfect silence hangs over the permanent carnival that is the Long Beach Pike. Concessions shuttered. Greasy tarps over the try-your-luck gaming booths. Thrill rides motionless as metal stabiles. Oceanfront promenade deserted, but for the occasional wobbly, retching drunk. A cloud of smog, poison flatus from the urban sprawl to the north, rolls in, pinches the nostrils and nips the eyes.

I'm slouched on a bench at the shore end of the pier. Exactly why I'm here I don't fully understand. A belated pilgrimage? Whimsical search? Perhaps a resolution, of sorts. Impossible to say.

Lived only twenty miles up the road, yet in all the years I've been out here never once undertook the journey. Have, in fact, scrupulously avoided this place (though I've found my way to Newport and Laguna and even down to San Diego often enough, prowling for new scams, new marks).

But the true *axis mundi* of my existence is Santa Monica, that oddly displaced community boxed between monster city and sea, insulated, in those days, as a midwestern hamlet. Santa Monica generally, Vic Tanny's Gym particularly. The original one, down a flight into a cultish, irons slinger's world of slick sweat and hard ripply flesh and a self-rapture near to swooning. And urgent scheming. Anything to avoid work. Nobody works, this fraternity of monomanic scufflers ("Job shafts your training," I'm early on instructed by a neckless gym rat). Myself included.

Over those years I've advanced from innocent idler (skating by on the twenty-six bones a week provided for as many weeks by a grateful government to its heroic Korean Conflict vets), to petty thief. After those weeks expire (my mentor, a Mr. California runnerup, explaining soberly how success in the shoplifting line turns on the assembly of a sunny face and jaunty grin at the precise moment of the boost: "Think about gash," he advises, "what's sunnier'n gash?"), to roller of fags (always in abundant supply, haunting the Muscle Beach weights pen, flashing hundred-dollar bills, smiling wetly). To, finally, hustler of lonely, well-off widows (one of whom, a plump, lusty bluehead, generously pays the rent for six full months before I'm absolutely incapable of performing any longer between those squishy thighs, and who threatens suicide at my abrupt departure but who turns up at the beach a couple of weeks later sporting a new, muscular trophy on her leathery arm).

Now and then, during dry spells or when the local heat leans on our tight little brotherhood of small-time, muscle-armored grifters (or, conceivably, out of some Grace-inspired guilt, some buried sense of shame), I'll take the occasional odd job, the most recent of which is manning a searchlight at supermarket christenings or car lot sale-a-

thons. And maybe it's that peculiar employment, its transparent sym-
bolism—sweeping a stalk of light across a black sky, probing the
night—has brought me here this morning. Or simply a nagging disen-
chantment with the perpetual scramble, the sly hustle. Or, maybe, a
sickness of the soul. Who can tell?

Time ticks by. A mild breeze picks up off the ocean, lifts the
smog. The beach shimmers under a blaze of sun. Out beyond the pier
a vessel slips into the distance, lost in shifting perspectives of sky and
sea. The Pike stirs, unwraps for the day. Knots of tourists, sailors,
squealing kids appear, wander through it. I join them, uncertain
where to begin, or how. Aromas of roasting meat, condiments, sugary puffs of cotton candy thicken the salt air. Rides begin to pitch and
whirl. Brassy music shatters what's left of stillness. Barkers loosen up
their lungs.

I approach one of them, inquire after a Gilbert Ray Mercer (the
name overheard once in some domestic discord, spat out by Grace,
my mother dissolved in tears, has taken root in a memory cell deep in
my head). He registers a blank look, shrugs, says nothing. I move on.
Spot a pair of carnies perched like birds on a rail circling the Ferris
wheel. They look surly. I ask them anyway.

"Never heard of 'im," one says.

"Before my time," says the other after I describe that distant time
horizon. "Y'might try Sammy."

"Sammy?"

"Yeah, Sammy Stokes. Geezer runs a dogs stand down by
the bump cars. Been here since—fuck, I dunno—forever. Knows
everybody."

I head that way. Discover a dingy little box of a concession
whose sign boasts "Real Deals on Square Meals," among which are
listed Red Hots, Kraut Hots, Chili Hots, and something called a
Hammy Sammy. I step up to the rectangular serving window. Behind
it, bent to a grill, his back to me, stands a stooped, wizened spider
monkey humming some unrecognizable tune. I clear my throat elaborately. The humming stops. He turns, presents a tiny, compacted,
age-trenched face, chin collapsed and trailing long cords of sagging
flesh, myopic eyes sunk in withery sockets, nose framed in purplish
burst veins, the only color in skin otherwise the cast of dry walnut.
A nasty, grill-spattered apron girdles his spindly waist, bony hips.
T-shirt bears the chili tracks of one of his own square meals. In a

honking voice, startlingly big for so elfin a figure, he booms, "What
can I do y'for, sport?"

I order a kraut hot.

He tilts his head slightly, revealing a tumorous-looking shell
planted in a nest of wiry ear hair. "Speak up, boy. Sing it out."

I say it again, louder.

"Slaw? Fries?"

"Neither."

"One kraut, comin' up."

An instant later it's up, a tube of charred meat slapped into a bun
and slathered with oily shreds of cabbage. "Getcha anything else?" he
says. "Somethin' to drink?"

"No."

"Be six bits."

I lay out three quarters. He scoops them in, is about to turn away
when I say, "There is one other thing."

"What'd that be?"

"I was told you might know a fellow named Gilbert Mercer."

"You was tol' that, huh. By who?"

"Guy down the line there. Works the Ferris wheel."

He takes a step back, looks me over distantly. "You the law?"

"Law? Hardly."

"Who then?"

"A . . . relative."

"Relative. Sure."

"I'm his son."

"Son?"

"Yes."

Now he leans over the counter, pokes his head through the window, squints me into focus. "Yeah, little likeness there," he allows.
"Don't prove nothin'."

"He had a shooting gallery here. With a trailer behind it, where
he and my mother lived."

"This was when?"

"Early thirties."

"That'd be about right."

To further establish my identity, I fill in those thin scraps of intelligence gleaned as a child. Business is slow, nothing better to do, he

listens. Seems persuaded. Says finally, "Your mother from back east someplace, was she?"

"Iowa."

"I remember her. Little slip of a girl. Pretty. Forget her name."

"Woodrow. Bonnie Woodrow."

He snaps a recollective finger up by the mechanically tuned ear. "There y'go. Bonnie. Tellya, best thing she ever done was flew the coop."

"Why do you say that?"

"Ol' Gil, he was a drifter-grifter. Eye for the ladies an' a taste for the sauce. Always had the big dreams but couldn't hold on to a pee pot. See him kickin' can a beans down the road, y'knew he's movin' on."

He punctuates this wit with a short, barking laugh. "Well," I say, "she's dead now."

"Dead? Shame. Course, so's your old man, better'n likely."

"He's dead too?"

There's a wavery note in my voice, impossible to contain. He's oblivious to it. "Be my guess," he says. "Can't say it for a fact."

"What happened to him?"

"Way I heard it, they caught him bottom dealin', some sawdust joint, Vegas."

"Bottom dealing? I don't understand."

"Y'know, hand-muckin'. Skimmin'."

I stare at him vacantly.

"Cheatin', boy. Where you been?"

"Who?"

"Who what?"

"Who caught him?"

"Wops, ran the place he was dealin' at. They don't take kindly to that. Get you a dirt nap out in the desert."

"When did he go to Vegas?"

"When? Lemme see." He brushes a hand over a perfectly hairless skull, summoning the memory. "After your mother took off. That'd be, what? 1934, 1935, somewhere in there. After that he started hittin' the juice hard. Gallery bellied. It was right over there, y'know."

I follow his rheumy eyes to the place now occupied by a bumper car ride. Seem to see a column of ducks, hear the *plop* of their fall. Feel a curious sense of time slip-sliding around me.

"He come to work for me awhile," he continues. "Didn't last long. Not enough loot in the hots business for ol' Gil. So he gets on with a flat store here on the beach. Learns how to deal a cold deck, skin the rubes. Gets pretty good at it too. Least that's how he tells it. Gets cocky."

"Vegas?" I prompt him.

"I'm comin' to that," he says, a bit snappishly.

Humbled, I wait.

"Okay. One day he stops by, tells me he's met a fella knows a fella can get him a job dealin', one a them casinos over there. Wants my thought on it. This'd be 'bout '42, I remember right. Vegas just openin' up, them days, war and all.

" 'Forget it! Them dagos too sharp for you.' This is me now, talkin' to him. 'Eatya alive,' I tells him. Think he'd listen? Fuck no. Too smart, listen to Sammy."

"When did you see him last?" I ask.

"He come back few times. Stopped by. Last time was, oh, maybe seven, eight years back. All duded up, he was. Got a dishwater blonde hangin' all over 'im. Cockier'n ever. Says he's mintin' money over there."

"How do you know he's dead? For sure, I mean."

"Don't, for sure. Like I said. But y'hear things."

"Who from? About . . . Gil." The word *father* too foreign to frame, too strange to utter.

" 'Nother a your pike flatties. See, bunch of 'em picked up and hauled over to Vegas. Gonna make the big score. Most of 'em, though, come slinkin' back tail between their legs. Outta their league."

"And it was one of them told you what happened to him?"

"Correct."

"When?"

He has to think awhile. Tugs pensively at a rope of flesh dangling from the sheared-off chin. "Be couple years back," he says at last, "maybe more'n that. This fella come by, been over there himself. Used to work a two-way joint here on the beach, so we gets to chewin' over the old days. I asks about Gil an' he tells me what I already tol' you. Says the wops put in that eye in the ceiling, spot Gil runnin' his little game and disappear him. And ain't nobody sayin' where. One day he's dealin', next it's like—Gil Mercer?—who's he?"

"This man, is he still around here?"

"Nope, just passin' through. Ain't seen 'im since."

"You believe he was telling the truth?"

"Got no reason to lie. Anyway, it figures. Gil, he just never could win for losin'. He call heads and the tails come up. I tellya," he tells me, and there's a measure of not dissatisfied spite in the honk of his voice, "it wasn't for bad luck, ol' Gil, he'd-a had no luck at all."

Nothing more to ask, nothing left to say. And so for a moment I contemplate the luckless Gil, his remains unearthed by scavengers of the desert, bones bleaching by day under a furious sun, by night chilling under a vault of cold and distant stars. Ol' Gil, sleeping the long sleep. Visions of cleansing snow appear to me suddenly, much as they must have appeared to my mother, equally luckless, on this very spot a quarter of a century ago.

"You okay, boy?"

"Yes."

He nods at the hot dog, uneaten, forgotten, cooling in my hand. " 's'matter? You don't like your kraut?"

I set it on his counter. "You eat it," I say, and spin on my heels and walk away. I can hear him urging me to drop by again some time, gab some more. But I never do.

The next day, all my earthly possessions stuffed in the duffel and travelling bag, I'm on a bus pointed for Iowa. All I know of home.

JULY 4, 1961. INDEPENDENCE DAY. I'm a guest in the Croop home, a weathered frame two-storey located (in yet another of fate's crude jests) in Waterloo, Iowa. Invited there by the jade-eyed Suzanne, valorously delivered from a bullying suitor only two months back, and now the recipient of her generous favors.

Still, ours is not a tranquil relationship (as they're nowadays pleased to call such primal rutting). Mostly we battle. She doesn't much care for my type, still something of the arrogant swaggerer, a relic of the California years. And with a couple of degrees now, testimony to a certain bunco glibness channelled into the spineless world of academe, and a gift of memory that seals facts, dates, theories, and tortured literary "interpretations" into neat hermetic compartments and disgorges them on order. Doesn't appreciate my swellhead attitude, she says. Insulting her friends, belittling her experiences (she's been out of Iowa twice, both occasions to the Twin Cities), quoting crazy flowery poetry when I'm drunk (which is often lately). Little a that goes a long ways, is what she always says. She's probably right.

For my part of it I'm not all that taken by her. Put off by the Doris Day weltanschauung, life as single-minded quest after Mr. Right. A journey marked by numberless sidetrips—teasing flirtations, endless dissections of mad adolescent crushes, calculating appraisals of the available goods in the room and of the competition. I discover I'm capable of jealousy, or possessiveness, though I'm incapable of understanding where it springs from, or why. Jealous? How can it be? I dislike what I perceive as stubborn ignorance cloaked beneath a breezy candor, good horse sense. She's undeniably a beauty, sleek of figure, velvet of skin, with an abundance of black curls tumbling over a broad, high forehead, wide-set eyes, wide cheekbones with an elegant taper. While she's all that, still there's something about the mouth that annoys me, too tight and too thin for the facial structure, too easily lifted in knowing sneer. Or maybe it's the way her spiked green eyes seem to size me up with incurious detachment, as though she were shopping for a necessary, if unglamorous, appliance, a Mixmaster, say, or a three-cycle washer. No, I'm taken by none of it, but I hang on perversely all the same.

So here I am, on a meet-the-mom visit, a long weekend stolen from my obsessive pursuit of another set of initials to tack to my surname ("Ph.D.'s like a nigger," a jaded grad student at Iowa City tells me, "everybody ought to have one."). Suzanne is an only child, a late in life afterthought, but they're not affluent people, the Croops. The father has been dead for over a decade, sainted in her memory, a public school janitor by vocation. The mother, whose single consuming passion, food, is given away by her mountainous proportions (and who will eat herself into the grave but a few years hence), scrapes by as a grocery cashier.

Mom is unimpressed with her daughter's choice of the moment—so unlike the parade of former boyfriends, *real* jocks and regular young fellas, like to go dancing, have a good time—but she's stiffly polite. Puts me up in a closet-sized second-floor room (Suzanne sleeps down below), studio couch for a bed. Allows it's "nothin' fancy" but invites me, with slack enthusiasm, to "make yourself to home."

To fund her schooling (she aspires to be a librarian, god knows why), Suzanne works summers schlepping drinks in a roadhouse tavern. During her shifts I hold down a stool at the bar, swilling beer, watching her sullenly, her kittenish carriage, practiced hip wiggle, the fuckeye leer on the coarse faces of the louts she services. Wondering what I'm doing here. Powerless to flee. For three full days we feud bitterly. Then have long solemn talks that restore an evening's truce and settle nothing. For her, a teetery disequilibrium seems to fulfill some compelling jaundiced need. I make feeble jokes about the incessant squabbling, but sometimes in the night I'll bolt out of a stupored sleep like an epileptic emerging from a seizure, dazed and stricken with panic. Other times I feel like a suicide who has wilfully elected to step into a pit of quicksand, too late changed his mind, and can't squirm free. A lunatic image sprouts in my head: two fish, hooked and wriggling frantically on jagged lures at either end of a taut common line.

It's the last night of my stay. A Tuesday, I remember. The tavern, predictably, is mobbed. A trio twangs out ear-shattering country tunes. Couples prance or grope, depending on the beat, across a dance floor blurred in smoke. Suzanne, clad in hot pants and tight filmy blouse, flits through the crowd bearing trays of drinks, a perky smile stuck on her face. I'm sitting, beer-fogged, at a corner table. Been there since . . . lost track . . . forgot. A long time. Now it's going on midnight. Through a window I see fireworks igniting a distant sky.

She sashays over, drops into a chair, drops the smile. "Jeez, what a night," she grumbles.

To this I have no reply.

"How you holding up?"

"Still among the living. Last I checked."

"Polished off enough beer."

"It accelerates the hours."

I'm still sulky from the routine morning quarrel, the nub of which escapes me now. She makes a lemony face. "Don't start in, Wood" (her cutesy name for me), she says. "You know I got to work."

Nothing to say to that either. I shrug.

"Anyway, I'll be done, another hour or so." She slumps back in the chair. "Right now feels good just to be off my feet, ten minutes."

"I'm sure it must."

She removes a crumpled wad of bills from a pocket of her blouse, flattens them on the table, runs a quick tally. The smile revives. "Aw-right!" she exclaims. "Close to forty bucks here. Least it's been a good night, tips-wise."

I've seen her coy, breast-brushing moves, heard her high tinkling laugh at some rude quip, some salacious remark. "Good?" I say. "Depends on what you have to do to come by it."

Her mouth tightens. "Just what the hell is that suppose to mean?"

"Whatever you want it to mean, that's what it means."

Her upper lip curls. "Cute. How long it take you to think *that* up?"

"Approximately seven hours."

"You think it's easy, working this room? You try it."

"I doubt the costume would become me."

"Something wrong with what I got on?"

"Not a thing. Be sensational for a girlie show. Tips are even better there, I understand."

She shakes her head slowly, conveyance of supreme disgust. "You're a shithead, Wood. Y'know that? Real shithead. I come over here, keep you company on my break, and you got to pick a fight."

Before I can get off the next round in this escalating duel, a whoop rises from behind her and a pair of beer-toting, certified Iowa corndogs—seed caps, denim shirts, leather vests, scruffy jeans, shit-kicker boots—come weaving out of the throng. " 'ey, Suzy-q, what's up, sugarbuns?"

"Snooker!" she squeals delightedly, mouth stretched back into the jaunty pleasured beam. "Moe!"

They pull up chairs, plunk bottles on the table, settle in. Suzanne supplies introductions all around. Moe and Snooker are identified as "pals from way back, ever since grade school." I'm a friend from college.

They look me over. No hands are offered, none shaken. "*Boy*friend?" Snooker asks, clearly the spokesman for the two. He's got a lean, muleskinner face, furry brows, hawkish eyes.

"Of record," I say.

That established, he directs his attention on Suzanne. "So how's the edge-a-kay-shun business?" he wants to know.

"Coming along," she says. "Slow."

"You still lookin' to be one a them library honchos?"

"Sure. Why not? Beat this place."

Moe nudges me. "Know why she want to do that? Work in a li-berry?"

Unlike his buddy, Moe is plump, round, rosy, saucer-eyed—a corpulent definition of simpleton. I give him a straight-man "Why is that?"

"Cuz one she worked at back in high school there, old McNamara—he was the sissy in charge—he always coppin' a feel off her. Got her all stoked on books. That right, Suzy?"

"Not true at all," she sniffs, mock indignation. "Mr. Mac was a perfect gentleman." Adding with a wink, "Well, most of the time, anyway."

The three of them break into lusty *haw-haw*. Times remembered. I wait till it runs down, say, "There's an inspired career choice."

She glares at me.

Snooker, sensing the sparks, launches into a long, convoluted joke whose bawdy punchline restores her temper. "That's naughty," she giggles. Slaps at him playfully. "Cute, but naughty."

Moe grins vapidly. Evidently heard it before.

"Picked that one up out to the auction barn," Snooker informs us. "Y'hear some good ones out there."

"Veritable gems of wit, I'm sure," say I.

"Huh?"

Suzanne sighs. "Give it a rest, Wood."

Snooker trains his eyes on me. Arches one of the woolly brows. "You got a pro'lum, friend?"

"Matter of fact, I do. Nothing serious. It's the humor. The barnyard bon mots."

"You don't like a little joke?"

"Leave him alone, Snook," Suzanne cuts in. "He's pouting."

Probably I am. Also spoiling for trouble. Hoping Mr. Snook there will rise to the challenge. Instead he turns to her and says, "Whaddya say you'n me shimmy a number? For old times."

"Love to."

They clasp hands, swirl onto the floor. Fred and Ginger. " ' "Now tread we a measure," quoth young Lochinvar,' " I call after them. Snook disdains to acknowledge it with so much as a glance back. Suzanne, however, tosses over her shoulder, "Stuff a sock in it, shithead." They break into a bootie-shaking jiggle.

Moe advances the conciliatory proposition. "They're just pals, is all."

I ignore him.

"You a rassler?" he says conversationally.

"What?"

"Ask if you was on the rasslin' squad, down at the college."

My California-honed physique, the remnants thereof, is on display in snug-fitting T-shirt. Muscles, for Suzanne, are cute (cute being her all-purpose standard of measure), "sexy-wexy" in her cute phrase. "No," I say, "the eighteenth century literature squad."

Moe's not certain what to make of this so he says, by way of apology for his friend, it seems, "Snooker ain't no fighter. He's more a lover."

I shift in my seat, inspect him narrowly. "Hers?"

Cornered, and with imbecile honesty, he allows, "Well, Snook and Suzy, they was, y'know, at it. Once. Long time ago, though."

"How long?"

"Shit, y'got me. Least six months. Year, maybe. Anyways, Snook, he's spliced now. Got a kid."

Moe the diplomat, designated peacekeeper. I turn back to the dance floor. The tempo slows. Some mournful ballad whose whiney lyrics speak to the perfidy of the cheating heart (or should if they didn't, art a pale echo of vulgar life). Snook and Suzy are locked in wraparound embrace. Undulating, pelvic-grinding embrace. I watch, seething. At her. Him. This mean, tawdry place. But mostly at myself.

"You from 'loo?" Moe asks me, earnest at conversation.

"Loo?" (Snook's hands creep down her back.)

"Yeah."

"Waterloo?" (Cup her buttocks, press her in.)

"Yeah. Here. Loo."

"Not any more," I say. Lurch to my feet. Grasp the chair a moment, steadying myself. Then go careening through the crowd, making for an exit. A purposeful man, arrived at a crossing.

But Suzanne, ever the bet hedger, has been keeping an eye on me. She disengages herself from Snook. Beats me to the door. "Where you think you're going?" she demands.

"Away from 'loo."

"For chris'sake, Wood, I'm just dancing."

"That's what they call it now?"

She plants defiant hands on her hips. "You don't own me, y'know."

"None better do I know," say I.

With a temple-flicking salute I'm gone, out into the healing night, trailed by her bawled and redundant epithet: "Shithead!"

Reeling, stagger-drunk, through the night. Chanting "enough enough enough enough . . . ," mantra of survival, deliverance. Victim of an affliction at once loathsome and ludicrous, like the heartbreak of psoriasis, or thistle-sprouting warts, or wet dandruff multiplying at the roots of the hair. But with a miracle cure—tomorrow's early departure—on the horizon. Tomorrow I'm gone for good. Tonight sleep.

Somehow, on foot (for I have no car, no transportation), I find the Croop manse. Tiptoe up the stairs. Collapse on the studio couch. And from down the hall the mother's roupy, adenoidal, fat-lady snores rock me to sleep.

Abbreviated, agitated slumber. Somewhere in its twilight I feel a presence in the room. Peel back crusted lids. See only blackness.

"Who's there?"

"Ssh."

"Suzanne?"

Presence materializes, climbs onto the couch. Coos, "I don't know why you got to be such a shithead."

"I don't know why you can't remember who you came in with."

"Ssh! You'll wake Mom."

I'm still groggy. Head swamped with beer. She snuggles against me. Soon enough we're bucking away to the rhythmic meter of Mom's croaky snores.

And it is out of that angry, joyless coupling Michael Ray Woodrow is conceived. And in time we'll both discover my affliction is ruinous, fatal, final. Not so laughable after all.

IT'S APRIL 1, 1962. ANOTHER SUNDAY. Almost seven months to the day after she comes down to Iowa City and lays on the news. Hearing it, I have a sudden elliptical vision of everything lying in ambush just ahead: squalling infant, spats, scrambling after money, flat obligatory sex, oppressive responsibility, expiring youth. But, bastard child myself, I'm conditioned to do the right thing.

The scrambling begins. I shelve my personal timetable, turn up a thirteenth-hour job teaching freshman rhetoric at the university. Glo-rified grammar teacher, master of the mysteries of the phantom an-tecedent. Forty-four hundred a year. Early that September a sleet-eyed justice of the peace glances knowingly at Suzanne's swelling tummy, pronounces us man and wife.

The birth is not easy on Suzanne, induced as it is. Belly bal-looned, she's ten days past the projected delivery date. Her doctor, a brusquely impatient young man fresh from medical school, deter-mines it's time to get on with it, has her check into the hospital that morning. Gives a nurse some crisp instructions and then vanishes. The nurse opens a vein in Suzanne's arm and a colorless liquid leaks into her blood from a bottle suspended above the bed.

I sit with her. Throughout that long and desolate day I sit. Watch her pass from jittery apprehension through mild discomfort to sharp stitching pain. I feel helpless as she twitches and moans. Words of comfort never came easily to me, and I fumble now for the good sturdy things one is supposed to say. Occasionally I'll leave the room, stretch my legs, gulp coffee, and suck on cigarettes (a habit I've ac-quired recently, convinced it will be shucked off once the graduate school seige is over). But I'm careful to avoid the traditional cine-matic role of expectant father, cluttering the scene with his bumbling joyous presence. It's a caricature I'm not inclined to adopt. The truth of it is I'm vaguely, indefinably glum, none too eager for this new and alien phase of my life to commence. Still, I understand my duty and remain at her bedside, offering up what limp solace I can.

Periodically the nurse pokes her head in the door and asks with a cheery wink, "How's it coming?" By late afternoon the answer is lit-tle more than a groan from the girl tossing on the bed, and from me a sickly smile. It occurs to me to wonder what that coiled fetus, chemi-cally assailed, violently roused from its perfect slumber, would reply, could it speak.

A gray dusk seeps into the room. The nurse pops in again and lays expert hands on the mount of belly. Her face presents the in-ward-turning expression of a seasoned shopper testing the ripeness of a melon. She nods wisely. "Time to call Doctor," she says.

Now I'm instructed to wait in a small room at the end of a hall. I plop onto a vinyl couch, leaf through the pages of a dated *Reader's Digest*. Smoke. Across from me an old man weeps quietly. We exchange glances, say nothing. The dry air carries the hospital perfumes of antiseptics and sour bed sheets. An hour passes, maybe more. Shortly after eight the nurse appears in the doorway, beckons me. "Looks like you're a daddy now," she announces brightly. Gives me the child's gender and vital stats. I work my mouth into a smile.

I'm led up a flight of stairs and down a corridor to a plate glass window. Beyond it, in an orderly file of cribs, squirming bundles shriek soundlessly and tiny rubbery fists beat the air. It's like watching a silent film. The nurse points to the crib that holds my son. With a closer look I can make out a red puckered face with startled, panicked eyes. For a moment I'm reminded curiously of a fluttery bird in a durable cage. But she's watching me, this nurse, waiting for a response, and so I produce the proper fatherly gestures and noises I assume are expected of me.

Next I'm taken to my wife. She looks very small in the bed, very wasted and pale, but she manages a meager smile. It's a night for smiling. There are some dutiful kisses, exuberant words. Then the chipper nurse, who clearly enjoys her minor though well-rehearsed part in these happy-ending domestic dramas, shoos me out. I'm free to go.

At last it's over. I'm sitting at the kitchen table in our three-room basement apartment, a glass of milk and an oatmeal cookie in front of me. Exhausted, thoroughly drained. I feel at that moment rather like an amateur actor winding down from a mediocre performance. Some afterglow of the forced jubilance still lingers. I have a son now and I want things to be right for him. I try to think manfully of my new burdens as merely challenges, opportunities. Solemn vows and extravagant dreams spin through my head. Perhaps, even at age thirty, I can redirect my energies, change my life. Perhaps it's not too late.

But the longer I sit there the more hollow the vows seem. The dreams blur, refuse to stay in focus. What I see instead is the shabby, yard sale furniture, the cookie crumbs on the pink Melmac plate, chalky milk residue clinging to the sides and bottom of the glass. Free glass, comes free with a fill-up at the Supergas station. The gloom that's dogged me all day long settles in again. What do I know of babies or marriage or "providing"? Everything has gone wrong. The future, on this second look, looms bleak as a rutted backroad zigzagging across an arid plain. The past—the mean places I've been and the shallow paltry things I've done, and not done—is hardly

worth memorializing. Up against the stunning clarity of this vision
the past is no comfort at all.

I hear someone, the landlord probably, stirring about upstairs. A
toilet flushes, water swirls through the exposed pipes directly above
my head. I feel like a man waking from a restless sleep to find himself
in a cramped and stuffy room. Windowless, doorless, and with walls
of damp sponge.

NOW IT IS TIME TO SKIP AHEAD to that calamitous day. February 26,
1971. A Friday. Venue is De Kalb, Illinois. Specifically, a main street
tavern, student watering hole, crammed with raucous cretins, throbbing with music. Reminiscent, in a way, of that Waterloo roadhouse a
decade back. Circle ending where it began.

Early evening and already my head is sloshy from the clash of
booze and drugs and assorted stimulants pulsing through my veins.
Caffeine, nicotine, and a dex on waking, to haul me up out of a toxic
sleep; red devil at noon, to glide down off my last fevered classroom
performance of the day (of my life, as it turned out); mid-afternoon
another jolt of crank swallowed on a wash of brandy, to launch the
weekend. Joyless riot of the lately liberated man. Whose face—sallow, stringy, eyes rimmed in pink, hair sleeted with gray—regards me
from the mirror behind the bar.

He fires up another cigarette, that stranger in the mirror, lifts his
glass in toast. Discovers it empty, signals a bartender. A fresh two-pop
is set before him. But he's forgotten what he's toasting. Maybe it's the
six weeks he's been free. Maybe it's Suzanne. Why not? He hoists the
glass in ironic tribute. Here's to Suzanne Croop Woodrow.

It would be easy for me to paint her a villainess, witchy of design, crafty of scheme, scarlet of sin. But not wholly accurate. Not entirely true. Not, at least, in the beginning. For a time, I suppose, she
did her best, tried. To be fair about it, give her her due.

But my kitchen table vision the night of Michael's birth proves
to be prophetic. Rudely plunged from his mother's womb, he
wails ceaselessly through the first six months of his life, as though
the wordless memory of his splenetic conception poisons his
blood. Soiled diapers, steamed baby food, excrement, and vomit
become the fragrances of home. One leaden day of domestic
duty stacked on the next. Vexed, peevish, preoccupied husband,
head perpetually stuck in a book. Spiritless bed sessions, all the

voltage gone out of them. It must have seemed to her as if she'd stumbled out of the sunlight of her youth into a dark and trackless swamp, nothing in sight up ahead but the back of her sullen guide, himself lost. An immense fatigue sets in. Nevertheless she endures. For a time.

. The swamp deepens. Her frustrations mount. Baffled and impatient with my interminable schooling (man's married, got a kid, he settles down, gets himself a decent job), she grows tight-lipped, wire-strung. Tension and exasperation set up housekeeping in her face. Sometimes, in corkscrew non sequiturs introduced into our stormy eruptions over money or the tedium of it all, she'll try to make me grasp the measure of her disappointment and dismay. Who wants to live like a goddam monk? Who needs it? Who gives a rip over dead languages, dead poets, dreary dissertations? Time is fleeting. She's young yet, wants some fun out of life.

Before too many years elapse she'll find it.

Anointed doctor at last, I secure the real job she's been hounding me about. Scrape together the down payment on a house. Fill it with furniture. Pore over pension plans, insurance packages, fringe benefits (among which is that most bizarre and, when you think about it, dreadful of oxymorons, "death benefits"). Except for the barbells secreted in the basement, the last vestiges of my directionless youth are gone. I wear the wardrobe of the Practical Man.

But it's unfamiliar garb for me, a strange fit, comfortable not in the least, like an outfit chosen by a blind man—coat too loose, collar too tight, trousers riding up the crotch, distressing pinched shoes. I'm learning my taint is to learn nothing from experience. Nothing at all.

For nothing is changed. The wrangling persists. Intensifies. Any topic, never mind how innocent, how ludicrous, can trigger a firestorm. You name it. Artichokes, for a single memorable example. Artichokes can be debated on grounds of taste, but for two seasoned marital pugilists taste could never long remain a simple preference. If the innocuous vegetable were the departure point, then matters of taste could readily be extended to a full menu of recriminations and regrets, and what commences as mild discordance of opinion concludes with ugly imprecations hurled along with the glasses and plates.

On such occasions the child looks on, mute witness to the

whirlwinds that seem to sweep, periodic and unannounced, through the cheerless landscape of his young life. By now he has given up weeping. Instead he broods. Once, after an exhausting evening of battling, I climb the stairs and find him crouched in the hall listening, his pale features furrowed into a map of all the griefs peculiar to sorrowing old men. Map of the country of unfathomable woe. In an anguish of guilt I scoop him up and carry him off to bed, murmuring comforting sounds while he lies there wide-eyed in the dark, his thin body rigid as a cadaver, bubbly noises rising to his lips.

It's the guilt that holds me, or so I tell myself. The memory of my own fatherless boyhood. Surely it's guilt, or inertia. Yet there are times I have to wonder if, in our sick alliance, Suzanne and I supply each other some queer, distorted pleasure that annuls any need for harmony, not to speak of that fanciful notion happiness. Like some overarching malignant embrace that binds us closer than any marriage vows ever could, closer than any hostile sweaty coupling. Closer than addictive habit.

The day after Michael is enrolled in school comes the announcement she's taken a job. Education aborted by mothering, she's nonetheless found a place at the college library. Reference desk clerk. An activity, a purpose, reason again to get out of bed in the morning. Fulfillment, of sorts, or the dawn of it.

Often she'll work evenings, and the boy and I eat some savorless gruel I've ineptly concocted. After dinner we play together, vigorous physical games of our own invention. I'm the indomitable wrestler Sweet Daddy Siki, the champion of that time; Michael my relentless challenger. "Find an opening," I snarl fiercely, "find an opening"; and he charges me, childish fists cuffing, shivery with glee. We grapple across the floor. Inevitably, the challenger overpowers this mighty Hector, brings him to shuddering tragic fall.

Often she's late. Comes breezing through the door long after the library is dark. Hair tousled, face lit by secret smile, eyes full of mischief, she offers as airy explanation, "Girls and I stopped by for an after-work drink. Figured you wouldn't mind."

But in the beginning I do mind. Goatish images frolic behind my eyes. Gales of impotent rage storm through my head. We quarrel bitterly. I pitch furious accusations. She taunts me with the reminder, once again, years after the fact, I don't own her.

In time a lassitude sets in, exhaustion of the spirit. I abandon the conflict, leave off accusation, stop petitioning fate for answers to all its sportive mordant riddles. The glacial distance between us widens.

For three more years this diseased union hangs together, bound, it seems, by the force of an animus mysterious and powerful as gravity. And then one day she takes the pulse of her life with me, finds it faint. Insists on a separation. Of the trial variety, no lawyers involved (for this is a cautious woman, nobody's fool). Too weary of the struggle, I agree.

That night I take Michael aside, and in the professorial tones adopted whenever instruction or wisdom is forthcoming, I say, "Your mother and I have decided it would be best if we lived apart for a while. It's nothing serious, you see, nothing to be alarmed about. It's more like, well, an experiment. A little test. I'll be right here in town. We'll see each other practically as much as always."

I hesitate, watch him searchingly. He says not a word. "You have to understand," I continue, eminently reasonable, "it has nothing to do with you. By that I mean we both love you very much. No matter what happens that will never change." He remains silent.

But the next morning, before I pack my clothes and some few belongings, we pass on the stairs and he looks at me puzzledly, as though it's just now occurred to him something unusual is about to happen, something he's forgotten. "You can't leave," he says and gives me a teasing playful punch, challenger assaulting the champion. "You can't leave. I'll beat you up if you leave."

I gaze at my son through tight, pained eyes. Nevertheless, by afternoon I'm surely gone.

So at last I'm free. Near to penniless, sodden with drink, shrunken shell of myself, approaching the benchmark forty. Wreckage of a marriage, hostage son—but free all the same. Yet it's nothing like I'd imagined it to be, this freedom. Sometimes, after the bars close, I'll go tottering through the empty streets of De Kalb. Often these nocturnal wanderings lead me to the street fronting my former home. Always it's dark at this hour, and anguished visions of Michael tossing in his bed appear to me, fill me with such a rush of desperation I'm tempted to storm the door, gather him up, and flee to some safe refuge. But where to run? Iowa? California? Goose Bay? Namaqualand? Wind voices in the branches of trees spangled with blue snow croon, _No place to hide, Norman, nowhere left to go._ The dwindling embers of my cigarette glow like a red eye in the night. Time seems to fold inward. I stand there shivering, grappling with the confounding riddle of my life.

But now, in the steamy warmth of the tavern, a firm hand claps me on the shoulder. Chummy voice trumpets over the din, "How's she goin', prof?"

I shift slightly. Enough to make out a blur of a face. Male. Young. Smirky grin. Dimly familiar. Must be a student. Going fine, I tell him.

"Kickin' back for the weekend, are ya?"

"I suppose you could call it that."

"Enjoyed your lecture this morning."

On Pope, was it? Collins? The melancholy Gray? Long since lost.

"Really learnin' a lot, your class."

"Gratifying," is all I say. Not eager to promote this conversation. Doesn't discourage him. "Y'know that paper you assigned us?"

"Yes."

"Was workin' on it today. Over at the library."

I stiffen. Safe bet what's coming next.

"Saw your wife."

He's watching me carefully. Longing for a reaction. Gets none out of me.

"Yeah, she's real helpful, reference room there, your wife. Stacks too."

Still watching. So finally I say frigidly, "Your thirst for learning is most laudable."

Seems to serve its purpose. Dampens the chat. "Well, gotta be gettin' back to my frat rat buddies," he says. "Good talkin' to ya, prof." He starts away. Pauses. The glued-on smirk enlarges, fills his face. Counterweight to the wicked glint in the eyes. "Oh, yeah, by the way, there's a real funny thing somebody wrote on a crapper in the back. You oughta read it. Get a hoot out of it. Third stall on the right."

And then he's gone, vanished in the crowd. But with malicious seed planted. A "real funny thing" scribbled on a john wall. Pertaining, doubtless, to me. Transparent motive for the dialogue, done on a dare, no doubt.

I sip at my drink. Smoke another cigarette. Give it a decent interval. Give the smirking shitsack—wherever he is, for certain watching—nothing. Or little as possible. Then, moving with solemn inebriate dignity, I walk on back.

What I discover, in among the profusion of scatalogical wit, smutty rhyme, and deviant proposition gracing the wall of that feculent stall, third on the right, is a blunt message in the form of a catalog, compiled by many and various hands. Reads like this:

Suzy Woodrow is:

1. a cocksucker
2. the easiest lay in the county
3. a devout cummunicant (allegedly noted by a Father Timothy Dooley)
4. gives good cumuppance
5. the sandwich spread of champions (followed by two sets of initials in distinct scripts)
6. hostess at cumming out parties (the allegation here of a local catering firm affiliation)
7. gives good cummiseration
8. a two handed handler of whoppers—Burger King, International
9. steamiest shtup in the stacks

Though over the years I have chosen denial, the nature of her sin is known to me. But not the extent. I remove a pen from my pocket, add another notation, number ten, to the catalog: my wife.

As I'm writing I seem to hear a growly voice rising through the room. John is empty, must be mine. I stumble out of the stall. Catch a glimpse of someone in the smeary mirror above the sink. Same stranger from back at the bar. Looks remarkably like me.

Lately I've taken to carrying a bottle of sleeping pills with me wherever I go. It's a comfort, knowing the balm of sleep is only a swallow away. For no good reason I can think of, then or now, some ruinous impulse possibly, possibly some self-immolating need, I fill a cupped hand with icy tap water, gulp a couple of those pills.

Astonishingly, perversely, their effect is tonic. Bracing. Galvanizing. Dark apocalyptic visions swell behind my eyes. All of life's manifold indignities, angular treacheries, baffling defeats telescope into a receptacle narrow enough to contain but a single figure. Just one.

Suzanne. I ache to lunge through the door, the tavern, out into the glacial night. To revel in violence, carnage, blood. Yet I remain there, swaying slightly, rooted to the spot.

The stranger in the glass regards me with an arch, patronizing smile. "You?" he sneers.

"Why not me?"

"The timid professor? Angel of vengeance? I'm sure."

"Not so timid anymore."

"Stout words. But of course that's all they are. Words."

"We'll see."

The appalling visions fade. Another image—calm, familiar, sustaining—emerges in their place: Burt at the tower, scores to settle, nothing left to lose. . . .

That enigmatic stranger in the mirror, that would be me?

The very same.

It's a quaint way you have of ducking the burden of guilt. Bending reality through the prism of an overheated imagination to reflect your fancy of the moment.

And that fancy is?

Why, the devil made me do it, Your Honor. That awful man in the mirror.

You know, there's a truth in there somewhere. Behind all the easy jeering.

Won't wash, Norman. Didn't with the law, won't with me.

Now who's testy?

Certainly not I. It's nothing to me.

Really? I'd never have guessed.

This becomes terribly tiresome. Why don't you just get on with it.

What's the rush? Afraid of something?

Afraid? Me? Aren't you confusing us? Whatever would I be afraid of?

I won't need you anymore.

I'm your man in the mirror, Norman. Remember? You'll always need me.

Don't be too sure.

You say no, I say yes. From tiresome to circular. Your last day is incomplete. Are you going to get on with it or not?

Soon.

Don't tell me I'm going to hear "another time."

Something like that.

What a supercilious milksop you are, Norman. What a coward.

We'll see.

FIVE

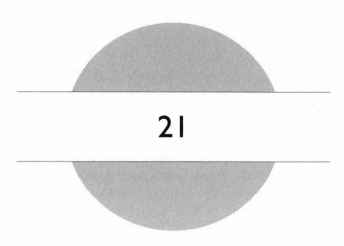

21

"You're sure you won't come in with me?" Lizabeth was coaxing.

"I'd just as soon wait here."

"Might be a while."

"I don't mind."

"I could use another opinion."

"On towels? Afraid I wouldn't be much help."

"On colors, dummy. I just want to see if I can match the shade in my bathroom. Those green ones in there now are an awful clash with the walls."

"Really? I hadn't noticed."

"You're such a ditz, Michael."

"Ditz?"

"Yes. Ditz. Bad as your father."

"Must be genetic. No eye for color."

She gave him an affectionate scolding punch on the arm. "All right," she said. "You wait. I'll try not to be long."

"Take your time. I'm sure I can keep myself occupied."

He could, too. Simply by observing. He was not in the habit of frequenting these places. And this one, Yorktown, a mere twenty-minute drive from home, was utterly unknown to him. And so, while she fluttered through the entrance to a department store, he took a seat on a hard wooden bench at the juncture of two concourses and watched the dazzling swirl of mall crawlers and Saturday morning shoppers. It was fascinating. Look over there. A stout grandmotherly lady in velveteen stretch pants and Jordache sweatshirt, pink sphere of bubble gum inflating at her lips. There a large family of orientals, mother and father trailed by a procession of stepladdered kids, all of them jabbering in high-pitched singsong, marching choir. A lubberly youth, cheeks bulged with popcorn, gigantic thighs sloshing back and forth as he waddled along. Smiling young couple maneuvering a baby stroller through the crowd, the infant, pacifier plugged, a limp bundle of innocent sleep. All that urgent bustle, teeming life, mercantile hum of churning money. All that . . . balance.

He felt very strange. Good, but strange. It was their first venture out in three days. Given her flimsy excuse at work, Lizabeth didn't dare risk being seen anywhere in the immediate vicinity. And anyway, as she put it, the whole point of this fabricated little holiday was for them to spend time together. And that's exactly how it had been. Three enchanted days hunkered down in the tidy security and perfect isolation of her condo, the world at bay. Norman had kept a curious distance, almost as though he were deliberately avoiding them. Once, at Lizabeth's insistence, he came by for dinner, but he seemed to have an uncomfortable sense of his own tinny presence, didn't linger long.

Fine by him. For over the course of those days and under her gentle ministrations, the contagion of her artless joy, some of the unearthed horror at what he'd done, who he'd been, some of it, a share at least, dissolved and scattered like ashes driven by a healing wind. He likened himself to a spelunker lost in the depths of a black and terrifying cave, miraculously come across a narrow passage, tiny portal, and emerging, bruised and shaken, eyes stung by the light, but rescued at last. So maybe it wasn't too late to turn things around. Maybe a shard of deliverance was not out of reach after all. Even for him.

And while he was entertaining these rallying thoughts a short trim girl outfitted in Chicago Bulls jacket, stonewashed jeans fashionably rent at one knee, and scuffed Reeboks came strolling over and plunked herself down on the bench in elaborate show of weariness.

She lit a cigarette, sighed twin jet trails through her nostrils and, on the exhale, said, "Wow, what a mob."

Michael nodded an acknowledgment, polite but distant.

"You'd think it was day after Thanksgiving, all these people."

He tucked back a corner of his mouth in sympathetic smile. He was rusty chitchatting with strangers.

"Hope the smoke don't bother you."

This called for something in the way of reply so he said, "It's no bother."

"Now-days y'gotta ask. All the weenies around."

"This weenie doesn't mind," he said mildly, but he kept his head angled away.

"Take it you don't got the habit."

"No."

"Good for you. Helluva monkey on your back."

"So I understand."

"Gettin' expensive too."

No response required for that. He studied the patterns in the tile at his feet. Let the unwelcome conversation expire.

She took a few more drags on the cigarette, crushed it under a heel. Then, unfazed, it seemed, by the silence, she asked, "You come here often?"

Now he lifted his head, turned, faced her. On closer look he determined this was no girl but rather, under the plaster of makeup, a woman easily his own age, or better. Hair was gamin-cut, bleached; eyes a milky blue; wide white smile displaying the kind of even, prominent teeth that seem to dominate a face, take it over, lend it a certain sluttish appeal. He felt an uneasy stirring deep in his chest. "No," he said, "this is my first time."

"No kiddin'. First time at Yorktown. Where you from?"

"Hinsdale."

"Hey!" she exclaimed, smile levelling on him, enlarging. "We're practically neighbors. I live in Westmont."

"Really."

"Listen, you shoppin' or just killin' time?"

"Killing time. Why?"

"Well, I was thinkin' about goin' over to the food court, grab a bite. You wanta come along?"

Michael hesitated. But only an instant. "I'm waiting for someone," he said.

She looked at him steadily. Sly, conspiratorial look. "That somebody be a wife?"

"Yes."

"Too bad."

He shrugged.

"Maybe another time."

He said nothing.

"You could gimme a call. I'm in the book. Name's—"

He put up a staying hand. "No. Don't say it. I don't want to know your name."

The smile slackened. Eyes narrowed. Then, recovering, upper lip curling, she trilled, "Well la-dee-da. Mr. Clean." Off she huffed, hips swaying, to let him see what he passed up.

He followed her with his eyes. Watched till she was out of sight, indistinguishable in the jostling crowd. The whirlwind in his chest, risen now as high as his throat, gradually subsided. Something approaching calm returned to his face.

Or did until his gaze, drawn as though by some sinister instinct, shifted abruptly to the opposite end of the concourse. Where, for a nanosecond, no more than that, he saw, or thought he saw, maybe it was only a flicker of the imagination, a figure—tall, blocky, only dimly remembered, all but forgotten in the quiet euphoria of these past days. He tried to put a name to it. Elusive. Couldn't bring it up. The man from Texas. Flam. There, that was it. Victor Flam. His breath quickened. Heart thumped. Eyes blinked wildly. He squinted, to steady them, but the menacing figure, real or imagined, was gone.

Now an aggressive band of emotions tussled for control of his face, confusion and panic for the moment dominant, but fear gaining ground, anguish in serious contention, and close behind a terrible, stricken dread. He felt a light touch on his shoulder and recoiled as though from an adder's sting. He spun around, fists balled.

"Michael?" Lizabeth said. "I scared you. I'm sorry."

"Never mind. It's all right. Startled is all."

"You look like you've just seen a, well, a ghost."

He loosened his fists. Reassembled his face. Generated a feeble, wincing smile. "No. No ghosts. Unless you're one."

"Ghost with a sack full of towels," she said, indicating the bag in her hands. "I think maybe, just maybe, I've found what I'm after."

"Good. Then we can get out of here."

"You're not having fun at the mall?" she said teasingly.

"A little bit of mall fun goes a long way."

She gave him a sudden impulsive hug. "You're such a good sport, Michael. I'm glad you came along."

BUT NOT PLEASURE ENOUGH to return for a second time that day. Once was plenty.

Norman, however, fortuitously arrived in the middle of the towels crisis (for she discovered, to her dismay, they were not quite the proper shade after all, wouldn't do, absolutely had to be exchanged), agreed to accompany her. He had stopped by to let Michael know of a letter delivered that very morning, Federal Express. And it was all the out Michael needed: Nobody questions the summons of an AS&A.

So here he sat, silence of his home office, letter and packet of background materials on Badger Manufacturing, Inc., laid out on the desk. Trying to corral his attention, bring it back to a sound utilitarian focus. The anxiety-numbing comfort of work.

But it wasn't all that easy. The letter, that was plain enough: crisp instructions to rent a car, be at the Grand Milwaukee Hotel, south end of town, near the airport, by 3:00 P.M. Sunday, no later. A meet-the-team session, suffer through a Russ Marks pep talk. But the Badger Corporation facts, figures, executive profiles, projections, goals, all of it seemed somehow oppressive, overwhelming. Seemed tedious somehow. His thoughts kept straying. Dreamily, some of them (to Lizabeth, these past days, like a honeymoon must be, he supposed, for normal people, in normal life); others ominously (to the woman at the mall, the shameless proposition declined, but only after a hesitation; worst of all to the persistent image of that shadowy figure who, seen or not seen, like some inarguable truth would not be blinked away).

Finally he gave it up. Put aside the materials, assuring himself he'd get back to them in the morning. Time enough tomorrow. He wandered into the kitchen and fixed a tuna sandwich, poured a glass of milk (lunch forgotten in the speedy Yorktown exit). He ate without appetite, out of habit, but, Grace-indoctrinated, out of habit he finished the sandwich, drained the glass. A memory of her hovering over him, watching, scowling, preaching the gospel of parsimony ("Clean up your plate, boy. Food don't come cheap. Somebody got to pay for it") arrived, unsummoned, across the murk of years. He blotted it, drove it away. Only to find another memory, nagging, related some way, nearer in time, insinuating itself in his head.

He looked at his watch. They'd been gone now—what? Twenty minutes? No longer than that. There was time. He descended the stairs, entered Norman's room, searched through the cluttered piles of books and papers on the desk, discovered what he was after. He took two thick stacks of pages, settled into the chair and began to read.

And as he read these fragmented confessionals of juvenile identification with some has-been actor, macho posturings, protracted adolescence, watershed days in a botched and blighted life, endless ceremonial circling around the only one that mattered—reading them he felt swamped by a dizzying mix of scorn, pity, anger, forbearance, bitterness, and remorse, emptying, when he was finished, into a reservoir of sorrow aching and vast, and with nothing to attach itself to. Perhaps not even a Lizabeth Seaver. It struck him how little he knew this man, his father. But enough now, from this evolving chronicle, to wonder if the virus of madness must inevitably trample the innocence of everything it touched. He didn't know, couldn't be sure.

He squared the pages, replaced them on the desk. Sat there awhile, head cradled in his hands. His mouth felt dry. A curious stinging sensation nipped at his eyes. They roved about the room, out the window at an orange dome of sun settling on the horizon, came back to rest on a calender bearing, opposite the date, an ambiguous alert, at once inspiriting and alarming: Time to reorder.

"WHY SO GLUM, MICHAEL?"

"Who's glum?"

"You are. Glum, or melancholy, or preoccupied. Whatever. You've been quiet all evening. Is something wrong?"

"Everything's fine. About as near to perfect as it gets. In my experience, anyway."

"You mean it?"

"I mean it," he said, and there was in his voice a certain strained sincerity. Why shouldn't he mean it? Eased back on her couch. Basking in the contented afterglow of an elegant dinner at a secluded, intimate spot. Lizabeth snuggled against him, her head nestled in the hollow of his shoulder. Glasses of Chambord in hand. Flickering candlelight. Tranquil music sedating the air. Soft rain pattering the roof. Perfect in the way of some saccharine cinematic conception of romantic bliss. The world as it never was. Reason enough for glum.

"It's been such a lovely few days," she said, almost wistfully.

"I know. Too bad they're coming to an end."

"Maybe there'll be others."

"It's possible."

"I hope so."

"So do I."

She lifted her head, searched his eyes. "If you mean that too, if you're serious—"

"I'm serious," he broke in, thinking, more serious than you could ever understand, ever be allowed to know.

She laid a stilling finger on his lips. "Wait. Let me finish. If this thing, with us, is going the direction I think it's going, then there's something we need to talk about."

"What would that be?"

"I want you to know that I know about . . . about Norman. And your mother."

He said evenly, "I see."

"He told me everything."

"Everything?"

"Well, what happened. What he did."

He leaned forward and set his glass on the coffee table. Stared at it for a long moment. Said finally, "I'm not sure I want to get into any of this."

"I think we should, Michael."

"Why? If he's already told you, what's the point?"

"So there'll be no empty places between us."

"What is it you want me to say? He killed her. Went to prison for it. I went off to live with a shrewish aunt. End of sorry tale."

"Somehow I don't think that's quite all of it."

His eyes, loaded with suspicion, shifted from the glass to her. "I don't understand what you mean," he said carefully.

"I care about you, Michael. I want to know how you feel about all these terrible things that happened to you. It's important to me."

"Which things, exactly?"

"About Norman, for one."

"He's my father. I feel what I'm expected to feel."

"You're not bitter toward him?"

"He did what must have seemed right for him. Can't be undone.
I try not to think about it."

"Your aunt. What about her?"

"Toward her I suppose I'm a little less kindly disposed."

"Why is that?"

If it was bitterness she was probing for, there was more than
enough in that God-poisoned well. More than he cared to plumb. He
said, "It was not the happiest arrangement. For either of us. Let's
leave it at that, all right?"

"All right. Tell me about your mother, then."

"Nothing to tell. I barely remember her. It was a long time ago."

"You were nine, Michael. Norman told me. Surely you have
some memories of her."

"Afraid not."

"None at all?"

A pair of images, female, dispatched from opposite poles of
time, appeared to him suddenly, warred in his head, merged gradually into the features of a single lewdly grinning woman.

"Michael?"

"Cards," he mumbled.

"What?"

"She taught me card games."

"Your mother?"

"Yes. We played together. The two of us. She liked games."

"That's what you remember? Card playing?"

"She was a spirited woman. Pretty, I think. Generous. As lavish
in the giving as in the taking away."

"But you loved her?"

He swept the air with a vexed hand. "What do I know
about love?"

She smiled privately, said nothing.

"You find that amusing? Strange?"

"You know what's strange, Michael?"

"What's that?"

"Your father said something very much like that. When I asked him the same question."

"You asked him that?"

"Yes I did."

"Why is it you have to keep pecking at this? Why not let it rest?"

"Because I believe you need to sort things out, Michael. I'm five years older than you. I don't want you mistaking me for her."

He looked at her with the saddest of eyes. "You know," he said, "I'd rather you didn't put it that way."

"I've hurt you. I'm sorry. It's just that I want you to be sure. About us."

To that he had no idea what to say. And because just then the phone rattled he was spared a reply. She sighed, crossed the room, picked up the receiver, and spoke an irked greeting. Then she was silent awhile, appeared to be listening. From where he sat he could see her foot tapping an agitated beat on the floor. After a prolonged pause he heard her say "No . . . no," and again, sharply, "No!"

Down went the receiver. She came back and dropped onto the couch, shaking her head slowly, display of annoyance. "It was one of those, you know, phone solicitors," she volunteered in explanation. "Wanted me to contribute to the fireman's fund, or something like that. I wasn't paying attention."

"Odd time to be calling."

"Oh, they'll call any time. You name it. Nights, weekends, dinner hour's big, too. Always the worst times."

As though in willed confirmation, the phone rang again. A violent twitch shook her. She looked stunned. "I can't *believe* this," she said.

"You want me to get it?"

"No," she said quickly. "I'll handle it."

It was handled in a voice short, flat, stony, almost callous. A voice such as he had never before heard out of her, never imagined her capable of. "Yes? No. No, and I want you to stop calling here. Is that clear? Do you understand me?" Evidently the other party understood. All the same, the receiver, he noticed, was left off the hook.

"They're so obnoxious," she said, sitting beside him again, her shoulders tight, face grim. "So persistent."

"They're salesmen. That's how you define persistent."

"Still is maddening."

"You need an answering machine. Screen your calls."

"I'll think about it."

"I could have Norman get you one tomorrow."

"We'll see," she said vaguely and, waving the topic away, "look, Michael, would you mind terribly if I had a cigarette?"

"Of course not. You don't have to reform for me."

"I want to, though. I'm trying."

She fumbled through her purse. Produced a cigarette. Lit it with a trembly hand and smoked it down to a tiny stub. For a time nothing was said, the earlier conversation seemingly lost or forgotten. He watched her curiously, not at all unhappy to leave off poking into the past, sorting emotions too tangled to identify or interpret or confront. But baffled too, wondering what was going on. Reaction all out of proportion to trivial event. Curious side of her, new to him, foreign and troubling. And so to put something into the widening silence he said, "I guess it's my turn to ask about glum."

"I'm sorry," she said, voice softened some, steadier. "I don't mean to sulk. But things like that, intrusions like that, well, they bother me."

"A couple of nuisance calls?"

"Yes. They're upsetting. Such terrific timing."

He pointed at her glass, emptied along with the urgent pulls on the cigarette. "Maybe you'd like another."

"I think I've had enough to drink tonight."

"And enough talk?"

"That too," she said, and took his hand and led him back to the bedroom.

22

True to her word, the castle dragon calls him at his room in the Grand Milwaukee Hotel (nothing grand about either of 'em, sackhouse or town, you want his take on it) and before he can even grind the sleep out of his eyes says, "Your four weeks are up, Mr. Flam, what do you have?" And when she hears what it is (which is a handful of Jell-O, never mind how you slap on the whipped cream) proceeds to bend him over, takes about five pounds of his ass, and fires him on the spot. All the dancing, dodging, weaving, wheedling, squirming earns him is your basic squat. She's snapped wise to that gas, heard it all before. No shuckin' her. He's off the payroll as of that moment, midnight, November 10, four weeks on the fuckin' button. Old reliable Mother Swales. Freeze dry must of had a timer going down there in sunny Palm Beach.

Up here though, scuz town, Flam's wide awake now and feeling like he just got the old fudge tunnel snaked with a rusty flagpole. World-class ream job, do a D.I. proud. Course the hard truth, you want to own up to it, is she's probably right. Probably chasing his tail. Four weeks gone by and he hasn't budged the Woodrow needle, not one tick. It's like trying to catch a pimple-face kid chokin' the chicken. Never know when the floggin' itch gonna come on.

You could bag the four-day stakeout, that Chicago burb. That close to home base, nothin' going down there. And after their little San Antone chin'n grin his man's maybe figured something's up, gone to ground. Only thing comes close to any action is when he finally pops out of his hole, split in tow. Flam tracks them to a mall and, later, out to dinner and then straight back to her crib again. Big night on the town. Some action.

Next morning she drives him to a car rental spot and after a lot of gooey kissy-face farewells (twat plainly got to be the girl back home, not a heavy candidate for a whacking), he's on the road to Milwaukee, Flam in his own Hertzmobile a couple of car lengths behind. At the hotel he asks for and, with a little juice, gets a room at the end of the same wing Mr. Woodrow's in, far end. His thought is to keep in close but to keep down too, so's not to spook him. What he's looking for is to nail him in the act or, more likely, right after the act. Shame, but you want an omelette you got to break the eggs. Another one of those hard truths.

First thing he does is grease a bellman, lock in a hot line to our Mr. W's comings and goings. Which are exactly none the rest of that day, though Flam learns a bunch of suits show up at the room, stay late. So next morning Flam's up bright and early, hangs out in a corner of the lobby and follows him and his squad of suits to a big plant located in a bugspeck called Oak Creek, few miles south. But he can't charm his way past the security gate here. Best he can do is get one of the toy cops aside and lay on some cush to keep him posted, the Woodrow arrival and departure times. Which leaves Flam with nothing to do but come back to the hotel and sprawl on the bed and watch the TV and wait.

And that's what he's been doing, four weeks now. Four zippo weeks. The Woodrow drill's same as it was in Texas: out to the plant all day, squirrelled in his room at night, eats off of room service, avoids the bar like it's an AIDS ward. Goddam monk.

Consistent though, got to give him that. And if his M.O. is to wait till the end of a job, do his psycho number and blaze outta town, then that's the problem right there, and Flam knows it. Could come to a whole lot of thumb up the ass time, all of it giveaway, now the Florida float money dried up. And he's never been big on charity.

Tells himself let it go, Victor, ain't your problem anymore, world's full of one oars, people getting smoked every day, every place, crime's a growth industry, plenty of work.

Except it's all dogflop, all that good common sense, because what he really wants to do is burn this pretty boy, spike him right to the timbers, and he knows that too. If he could just get a fix on that wrap date. Even ball park be a help. Least help him plot his next move. Or make up his mind. Trouble is there's only one way to find out and it's for sure no gimme, his p.r. out in Jew York City being not all that sensational lately.

So he stalls awhile. Thinks it over. Checks the clock. Half past twelve, hour later out east. That's okay, Jews never sleep, too busy scheming how to skin the goys. What the fuck. Might as well gnaw the old dum-dum, Victor. What's to lose?

He puts through the call, lets it ring, finally gets a sluggish greeting and says back, pitching it real chummy, "Hey, Nathan, how's your hammer swingin'?"

"Hammer?"

"How you doin'?"

"This could only be Victor Flam," he says, voice alert now, all the drowsy finger-snapped out of it, lot of winter in there, though.

"Bingo," says Flam.

"What time is it?"

"Oh, 'bout midnight out here in cornpone country."

" 'Here' being Milwaukee, no doubt."

"Right again, Nathan."

"And how are you finding that fine city?"

"Not so hot. Sun just don't wanta shine, Milwaukee."

"Is that a metaphor?"

"A what?"

"Never mind."

The way Flam figures, thing to do is lube the gears a little, slide into it easy. So he says, "Fact is, birds fly upside down out here cuz there's nothin' worth shittin' on."

You think it gets a laugh? Not even a snicker. There goes easy. "Amusing, Victor. But I suspect you didn't call at this hour, and after this long silence, to discuss the relative demerits of heartland communities."

"Well," Flam allows, "couple other items too."

"Such as?"

"You remember the Swales case?"

Nathan snorts at that. Says, "Indeed I do."

"Been meanin' to bring you up to speed on it but the time just got away, all the jackin' around I been doin'. You know how she goes."

"No, I've no idea 'how she goes.' Tell me."

"Shapin' up good. I'm on top of this dinger, got him wired in tight. Just a matter of time till I yank his chain."

"Very encouraging. You must feel cheered."

"Oh, yeah. Except for this little snag come up."

"Snag," he says flatly, no question to it, like it's what he's waiting to hear.

"Yeah, see, right now he's playin' at solid citizen. Doin' the righteous walk, straight and narrow. And we know his pattern is to hold off on the icing till the job's over with."

Flam leaves it hanging there. Smart Jewboy oughta be able to fill in the blanks for himself. But all he says is, "We, Victor?"

"That's right. You'n me, partners all the way. Like we agreed, last time we talked."

"Which was, by my calender, exactly four weeks ago. This very night."

Flam knows what's coming next but he tries to skate around it anyway. Never hurts to try. Nothing else, buy a scrap of time. "Been that long, has it?" he says innocently.

"That long. And I've yet to see the agreed-upon retainer."

"We talkin' about that three large?"

"Please, Victor. Don't insult my intelligence."

"Okay, here's what happened. The old lady, Mrs. Swales, she bounced me. Wasn't bringin' the felon to justice quick enough for her, guess."

Flam figures Nathan don't need to know the boot came less'n an hour back. Nothing served, telling him that. Besides, rest of it's straight up, and the truth oughta be worth something.

Worth dick. In a voice coated with frost, direct out of cold storage, Nathan says, "Whatever arrangement you have—or had—with Mrs. Swales is quite independent of our own. No longer any of my concern. But the retainer is. And I don't appreciate being stiffed."

"Nobody stiffin' you, Nathan. It's just a little glitch is all. Anyway, them dimes gonna look like birdseed once we tie this one up."

"Which one? You've been fired."

"So we work on spec. Think about it. We bring him in and they'll put us on your *60 Minutes* there. Pro'ly make a movie out of it." Maybe make the cover of *Time*, kike of the year, Flam wanted to add but didn't.

"Working for glory is hardly my style, Victor. Yours either."

"Who's talkin' glory? Business gonna come pourin' in. Big-time offers, downtown. Fartin' through silk, partner."

"You're fantasizing, Victor. It's not like you."

Flam sucks in his breath. Hesitates. He's not sure how to put this, or if he even wants to. But the bait's running low, down to the last worm in the can, so he gives it his best cast: "Look, Nathan, we both know he's our man. No argument there, right? So we got to nail him. It's like a, y'know, duty."

"What's this? An appeal to ethics? Moral obligation? How very quaint, Victor, coming from you."

"That mean you're out?"

"To borrow your expression—bingo."

"Okay, that's how you want it. Okay. But you could maybe do me one more service. Small one. Won't cost you but a minute of your screen there."

"So at last we arrive at the point of this call. Took long enough. Let me guess. This small service wouldn't be the determination of a completion date for the Badger project?"

"You're way ahead of me, Nathan. Like always. Whaddya say?"

"No."

"No? You're sayin' no?"

"You heard correctly."

"But I gotta have a target date," Flam says, trying without success to smother the pleading in his voice. "Even a range help. Otherwise I'm out on a limb here."

"It's your tree of choice, Victor. You're sitting in it."

On a sudden desperate impulse Flam says, "Do this one thing for me and you can forget the two-thirds, one-third split. I'm willing to go halves."

"Half of nothing. You've been pink-slipped, and I'm still looking for my three thou."

"Suppose I was to get it to you?"

"Oh, I'm counting on it. Debt's a debt, you know. But as for the rest of it, I wash my hands."

"Come this close and you're gimpin' on me?"

"Let me give you a word of advice, Victor. Obsession—and that's clearly your problem—can be insidious, dangerous. Malignant, even. Like any disease, it can take over your life. And success in our line of work demands a certain clinical detachment."

Flam's had a bellyful. Begging's not his style either. He growls, "Yeah, well, detach your sheenie needledick," and bangs down the phone. Fuckin' yid. Who needs him. Fuck his advice.

Curiously, it strikes Flam that in all their years of doing business he's never once met Nathan, never actually seen him. Nasal whine coming over the line, across the miles, that's all he really knows of him, and for an instant he wonders if there was in fact a real face behind that whine. Wonders if he hasn't just dreamed him up, all them years, imagined him into being.

That's bughouse, thinking like that. Doing way too much of it lately: pondering, reflecting, weighing, considering, analyzing, disecting, fretting, brooding . . . talking to yourself, f'chrissake, blowing bubbles out your ass. Ain't healthy. Man needs action, movement, decision.

So what's it gonna be, Victor, that heavy decision? Fucked if he knew. Smart thing be kill the light, clear the head, log some Z's, pack the bags in the morning, and catch the first plane south. That'd be the smart thing.

What he does is get up and walk his gut around the room. Glimpse of it in the bureau mirror there, bulging his skivs, reveals just how flabby he's become, these past weeks. Face peering out at him displays the pained grimace of a guy holding back a thunder fart. Comes of all that thinking.

So he yanks open a drawer and gets out his gear and brings his shoes over by the bed and polishes them up to a spit shine, real jarhead gloss, kind where you step in close to a fluff you're gonna catch a peek of snatch reflected off 'em. And then he gets out his cleaning kit and his ordinance (9 mm. Ruger P89 semiaut with the Black Talon slugs, erupt on impact, claw the meat), and he gives that a good oiling too.

Already he's feeling better. Feeling like a regular strak troop set to go waste some Cong, even though he'd never been to Nam, never had hostile fire come his way, did his whole hitch at Portsmouth re-educating the fuckups, and even though he's sitting here in his underwear, Milwaukee hotel, middle of the night, talking to himself. Still feeling good. So maybe a couple bridges gone up in flames, and maybe it ain't been exactly your banners and bugles night for Victor Flam. So what? Don't count him out yet. Not yet. Life's full of downs and downs, but his turn for an up got to be coming. He's overdue.

23

Eight days later that up Flam's looking for arrives at last. Along about half-past seven, just about the time the eagle scout's ordinarily tucked away in his room for the night, bellman calls and tells him Mr. W.'s on his way out, better hurry.

Flam knows how to hurry when he got to. Grabs his piece (dealing with a dinger, y'never know, always best to be strapped), pulls on a jacket, bolts down the hall and through the lobby and out into the lot in time to spot him swinging onto Layton Avenue. Flam follows him west couple miles, then north, then down some back streets, slowing to a crawl and watching his head go bobbing back and forth, like he's searching for a particular address. Appears finally to find it when he turns in at a little restaurant on a corner, some dago name to it. Flam parks in the row behind him, lets him get past the door, gives it some wait time, shivering there in the chill air, before he goes on in. Wouldn't do, get made now, freak him. Not if it's mischief he got on his mind. Better to shiver.

Outside, place don't look like much. Inside's another story. One of them cozy intimate joints, all soft lights and hushed music and whispery talk. Gas log glowing in a fireplace, some moon-eyed fish

floating in a tank. Flam picks a seat at the bar where he's got a slanting view of the dining room. Fair crowd for a Wednesday night.
Takes him a few sweeps before his gaze lights on Woodrow sitting at
a table off in a corner, his back turned. Sure enough, he's got a broad
with him, and sure enough she's a perfect match for the mold. Older,
late forties easy, little on the chunko side, pair of heavy headlights
swelling her blouse, mane of bottle-black hair, wide slash of red
mouth, good bones, might of been dish in her day, couple of re-
upholsterings back. Lookin' promising, Victor. Except it don't quite
fit the pattern, seeing there's been not signal one the job's anywhere
near finished, and last he got off the bellman the Stoltz crew rooms
booked ahead indefinitely. Still lookin' good. Maybe his man got the
itch early. Schiz, how you gonna know? Breach like this one in his
lockstep drill, tonight could be the night. Never dog on the old gift
horse, is Flam's motto.

They order drinks. Talk, twat doing most of it, that red mouth
going mile-a-second, lots of smiley face and twittery gestures. Probably fuckstrated, counting on her young stud there to lay some steeler
pipe, clean the cobwebs out of Little Miss Fuzzy. Probably soaking
her silkies right now. She had any idea what's around the bend she'd
blaze for the nearest exit. Flam's thinking maybe, though, with some
luck, she won't have to end up crowbait. Depends on the circumstance, and on his timing. She still gonna take a ton of hurts before
this night's over. Too bad, but what're you gonna do? That eggs-
omelette thing again.

More drinks. More of the schmooze. Must be close to an hour
this drags on. Flam don't mind. He's patient, he can wait. Something
got to break soon.

But when it does, it's like nothing he's expecting. She's yapping
away, and all of a sudden Woodrow just shoves back his chair,
lurches to his feet, wheels around, and comes weaving through the
tables. Flam ducks his head, follows him with his eyes. Sees him get
his coat from the check booth, stop at a phone by the door, tap out a
number, and start right in talking, free hand chopping the air furiously. Back at the table the lady's sitting there with her jaw dropped
to her chest, wide-open mouth looking like the bull's-eye on a target.
Fuck's goin' on? No way to tell, and no time either, because once he
puts down that phone he's gone.

Flam slaps some bills on the bar and takes off after him. Tracks him onto the 894 freeway east, then south on 94 at the Chicago exchange. Flam's first thought is he's headed back to the hotel, somehow must of got skittish with the winter chicken back there, but when he zips on by the exit that don't wash. Same thing at Rawson Avenue, which would've taken him over to the Badger plant, which was Flam's only other thought, though fuck knows what he'd be doing there, this late hour. Don't leave much. Chicago is what it leaves, and that looks to be where he's pointed.

Turns out that ain't right either. One of the Kenosha exits he peels off and pulls up outside a grunge motel. Flam keeps in tight, parks near the entrance, and watches him march inside, get registered, and vanish down a hall, stepping smartly, in a hurry. Only thing Flam can figure is he's maybe hired in a hooker. Still stoked maybe, motor still in overdrive, still looking for some of his sicko action so he decides to take it out of town. Could be, even if it don't square with the M.O. Whackadoos got their own logic. Least that's how Flam hopes it's coming down.

Wrong again. Can't be more'n twenty minutes later a Camaro swings into the lot and a fluff climbs out and goddam if it ain't the girl from back home, same cunt, the very same. Fuck's goin' on here anyway? What is it with this guy? Date night? She goes in and raps with the clerk, who gives her a smirk and points her to the hall and then she's outta there too. Leaving Flam shaking his head, thoroughly baffled. Don't make sense, none of it.

He sits there a while, trying to put some kind of figure on it. Comes up zip. Two of 'em plainly bedded down for the night, he might as well pack it in, get out of the cold. That's what he oughta do. Except that ding-dong logic keeps coming back to him. Suppose it was to take a serious twist tonight? Okay, not likely maybe, but just suppose. It did, and you ain't in the immediate vicinity, you're back in the hotel snoozing, then score of a lifetime's flushed right down the Chinese whizzer, Victor. Too much time and too much money invested, let that happen. Even if it's gotta mean a night camped out in a vehicle in the fuckin' Wisconsin deep freeze.

So with his mind made up he goes inside and oils the clerk for the room number (dumb fuck registered under his own name, which is not your best sign; other hand, it requires only a saw to get the buzz, sleep cheap like this, which is something of a bargain and he's been trying to economize lately). Then he brings the car around to the end of the wing where that room's located, but before he parks he spots some golden arches, couple streets over. And since his gut's sending out distress signals and since there's nothing but time, he drives that way, indulges himself with an order of two Big Macs, large fries, and a jumbo coffee. Night like this, man's got a little indulgence coming. He'd've known how it was gonna shake down, would've brought along a jug, keep him winterized.

Back at the motel, he inhales the chow, chucks the bag out the window, and watches the wind sail it across the asphalt. No lights on in the room, far as he can tell with the drapes pulled shut. Probably knocking boots in there right now. Whatever's going on got to be better'n out here, sitting with the collar of his summer-weight jacket turned up (kicking himself in the ass for not getting a heavier one) and teeth rattling quick time. Nobody said it was gonna be easy, Victor.

He settles in. Sky is black, clear, dense with stars. Out on the highway cars go shooting by, a steady, hypnotic whoosh. Periodically, he starts the engine, kicks on the heater. Helps a little, not much, and not for very long. Just makes him drowsy. Visions of a brilliant Florida sun spin through his head, followed by steamy images of his busty manicurist down there, and even of the acrobatic Ms. Vatchek in all kinds of pretzel postures.

Caffeine's wearing off. He reaches inside a jacket pocket, removes a small plastic bottle, shakes out two pills, and swallows them with the last of the chilled dregs of the coffee. He's no routine popper, but sometimes you need a little crank, keep you pumped. Times like now.

Once the speed takes hold he's feeling tight again. So wired he could hear an ant pissin' on cotton at a hundred yards. Except there's no ants. And no cotton. And no action from out of that dark room. He sits there listening to the accelerated thump of his heartbeat, watching his breath appear and dissolve in a fine mist and then appear again. Like watching your life leak away by the numbers. And that's how he sits, the long night through.

SHE WAS A MELD OF BRITTLE CHARM and studied grace and sexy neuroses, this Dolores ("call me Dee Dee") Bruce; and for Michael she was, from the beginning, a vaguely disturbing presence, like some dull subclinical affliction, a canker on the lip, say, or a kink in a joint. Too trivial to medicate, too persistent to ignore.

They had met on the first day of the project, first wary once-over for consulting and executive teams. The Badger CEO, one Frank Root, supplied introductions all around, Ms. Bruce identified as VP in charge of something called Human Relations. Root was himself a paunchy, fiftyish man with a repertoire of narcissistic expressions and mannerisms that appeared to be mirror-rehearsed. To convey a deep deliberation he shuttered his eyes and stroked an earlobe. To suggest decisive commitment he squared fatty shoulders and rippled his prow of a jawbone. Obviously enamored of the baritone peal of his voice, he was given to pronouncements on the health of the economy generally, the vigor of Badger, Inc., particularly. The latter of which was not good. With the sudden and entirely unforseen demise of the cold war, order rates for their principal product, marine propulsion gear drives, had fallen off an alarming forty percent in the past eighteen months. No more warships, no more call for gear drives, and no fat government contracts on the horizon. Business, in short (or in long, if the interminable gas of his "opening remarks" was any measure), had slumped dangerously, and the future of the company was in serious jeopardy. "But that's what we're all here to turn around," he declared stoutly, in merciful conclusion.

He invited each of his executives to spell out his/her (one female and one solemn black the pair of conspicuous tokens at an otherwise all-male, all-white conference table) management philosophy. Ms. Bruce's, when it came her turn, was novel indeed. She believed it vital to foster an atmosphere of warmth and trust between management and labor. To that end she had initiated a number of dramatic changes: the removal of all time clocks, elimination of individual production incentives, implementation of an equitable salary structure, standardization of benefits packages, expansion of employee participation in the decision-making process. And the catalog of fashionable innovations rolled on.

Undeniably, she was good on her feet. A once-handsome, full-bodied, plump-breasted woman, she presented an altogether seasoned get-to-business air in her tweedy power suit (except for that swag of dark hair, stylishly coiffed but tumbling to her shoulders, concession, it seemed, to a ghost of girlishness). Had her facts and stats and sources at tongue-tip. Spoke in a husky assured voice and, like any veteran speaker, established frequent and sustained eye contact with a selected member of her audience. Who just happened to be Michael Woodrow.

He showed her his thoughtful listening face, inwardly smiling at her brisk recitation of a "philosophy" held in supreme contempt at AS&A, whose own doctrine was securely grounded in the motivational force of fear. Listening, but thinking of the substantial overhaul ahead. And thinking also the earnest Ms. Bruce would be among the first to go, once the Badger house was restored to order. But in meeting that practiced gaze he detected, or thought he detected, a familiar shimmer behind the ceremonial reserve in her eyes; and he felt a queasy stirring in the pit of his stomach that had nothing to do with conflicting management theories and techniques, the troubling sense of having been down this road before, more times than a few.

And so for the past four weeks he had done his best to avoid her. It wasn't easy. Impossible, in fact. Wherever he turned, there she was. Executive staff meetings (of which there were many, Root being the sort of leader who liked to, in his words, "keep a finger on the pulse of the plant"), she was there. Retreat to the factory floor and she followed, shouting considered opinions and unsolicited advice over the nightmare din of grinding metal, whirring machines. She found reasons to pop into the bird room, unannounced and uninvited. It was on one of those visits she urged him to call her Dee Dee, adding with coy sidelong glance, "All my friends do, you know, and I hope we'll be friends."

His hopes were something altogether different, and to shore them up he buried himself in the project, numbing savage mutinous appetites with work and nightly calls to Lizabeth. But of course eventually, inevitably, Ms. Bruce suggested they get together for an after-work drink, run by some ideas she had on productivity enhancement strategies. And with the adrenal rush of a man courting disaster, he agreed.

"Terrific," she said. She knew of a quiet little place, convenient to his hotel. She gave him the address, directions. "Eightish?"

Eightish would be fine.

So it was he found himself, that Wednesday evening, in a darkened corner of a small and elegant dining room, attending to the animated chatter of this woman with the preposterously cute name. As the brandy flowed, she steered the conversation expertly, almost imperceptibly, from matters of business to personal revelations. Without asking, he learned she had been with Badger some seven years now ("Loved every minute of it," she gushed. "Frank's such a sweetheart to work for, and *so* intelligent"); was M.B.A. degreed; the divorced mother of a grown son. "His name's Bradley," she said. "You remind me of him in some ways."

One of those gratuitous observations for which there is no adequate reply.

"You married?"

Negative toss of the head.

"Ever been?"

"No."

"Take my advice. Don't."

"Yours was not a happy one?"

"I'd say, not! My ex was such a shit. He simply couldn't bear it when I finished my degree and went to work after Bradley left for college. Much too threatening. He was a very insecure man."

With good reason, Michael was thinking, but he asked, "What was his profession?"

And, remarkably, she answered, "Teacher. High school math. A wannabe egghead, but without the capacity. Math suited him. He lived by the numbers."

"Of course," he said mildly, "so do we."

"Believe me, there's a difference."

Perhaps, but he had no interest in exploring it. Echoes enough here already. He said nothing.

Alert to the subtlest shifts in mood, she turned the talk another direction, inquiring brightly, "Tell me, how do you like Milwaukee so far?"

"No way to judge. All I've seen of it is the plant and the hotel."

She wagged an admonishing finger at him. "You work too hard. You know what they say about all work and no play."

"And what do you do for play?"

The crimson-stained mouth opened in an impish, dimply smile. "For diversion?" she said. "Or play?"

"Either. Both."

"Well, for diversion," she began, and proceeded with an agenda of voguish activities that carried the tinny ring of a singles ad: DWF, attractive, young forties, professional, loves golf, skiing, Bucks and Brewers, symphonies, good books, travel to exotic lands. Absent only was the ritual moonlight strolls on the beach. A pathetic stab at making herself "interesting." He listened, overtaken alternately by chills and a peculiar burning sensation, like a fuse ignited and burning fast. And when the salutary docket was complete, she fluttered her lashes, brushed a hand through her thick locks and said, "Those are my diversions. Play, now, that's something else again."

"How, exactly?"

"Can't you guess?"

"No."

"Try."

"I'd rather you'd tell me."

"No," she said, voice dipped to a teasing purr, "you tell me what it is *you* like. For play, that is."

He lowered his eyes. Seemed to see in the theater of his mind a panicked figure fleeing down a blackened subterranean tunnel, walls of granite, floor of wet sand, a pack of howling beasts in pursuit and gaining ground, narrowing the gap. Heard himself murmuring, "Cards."

She tilted her head, lifted a brow, coquettish smile gone slightly askew. The puzzled look of someone eager to share in a joke but uncertain of its punchline. "Cards? Hardly what I was expecting to hear."

"Do you play?"

"Well, yes, bridge sometimes, with the girls. And when Brad was young we used to play gin."

Legs pumping, breath coming in great hawking gasps, the figure emerged at the distant end of the tunnel, escaped into a blaze of light, vanished in the redeeming light. He wanted to cheer. Instead, he hauled himself up out of the chair, said, "I have to leave now."

"Leave? Why? It's early."

"No, it's time. I'm sorry."

"But—what is it? what's wrong? I thought—" Voice stuttery now, eyes full of confusion.

"You were mistaken."

He made it through the room, but unsteadily, swaying a little, wavering. Made it to the door but, unlike the man in the tunnel, the lucky one, he wasn't delivered yet, and he knew it. Not yet. He could stop right now, adjust his face, walk back to the table, concoct a pacifying tale, resuscitate the suggestive dialogue, lead it wherever he liked, bring this ugly encounter to its foreordained conclusion. All that was in his power to do. Or he could pick up the phone on the wall, last slender, loosening link with the substance of a sanctuary formerly unknown to him, alien to his experience. But not anymore.

    He called Lizabeth. And within an hour he was restored, reclaimed. Delivered. Maybe even absolved.

"ONLY AN EMPIRE IN SERIOUS DECLINE," Norman was pronouncing, "would supplement the weather report with something called a 'pain index.' "

    Lizabeth's smile was tolerant, amused. "I'm not so sure about that. Certainly can't be all bad. At least not for those people with, you know, arthritis, asthma, things like that."

    "An alert to the misery ahead? Only hurts when it rains, and it's about to rain? Is that what you mean?"

    "Better to know what's ahead."

    "Forewarned is foredoomed."

    "Ssh! I want to hear this."

    They were sitting in what she called her "person" room (a small basement space converted into snug retreat, carpeted and fully paneled now, walls and ceiling), she on a sofa, he in a cushy chair, tuned to the local news: a couple of routine murders on the south side, jittery-looking retailers confidently predicting a brisk upturn in holiday sales, an armed robbery in La Grange, charitable group shown piously doing good for the less fortunate, sanguine prognosis on an injured Bear lineman, forecast of showers and temperatures unseasonably chilly, clammy. All of it periodically interrupted by commercial messages extolling the blessings of deodorants and beers, or public service announcements, earnest celebrities issuing calls to arms in wars on assorted evils—drugs, illiteracy, AIDS—while background pianos plinked buoyant chords of harmony and hope.

    And Norman had an opinion on all of it, a running commentary delivered in arch and ironic style, mannered enactment of his role as designated skeptic. Lizabeth, for her part, assumed the tut-tutting character of concerned citizen, righteously appalled by his perverse asides. It was a ritual they had fallen into lately, an entertainment, he the extemporizing performer, she the willing foil. A kind of good-humored fencing over polarized world views: hyperbolic cynicism over against determined cheeriness. In neither case a perfect fit, but suitable for the lively little playlet.

What she wanted to hear was one of those signing-off dispatches designed to spark a wry chuckle. The anchorman smirked into the camera and announced: "Now here's a piece of news for any of you who've run out of things to worry about. Seems some British astronomers have discovered this giant asteroid pointed in the general direction of Earth, and they're telling us it's due to enter our atmosphere in the year—" eye-rolling pause for comic effect—"2026. So you'd better not put off that vacation to Rio too much longer." Another pause, this one to allow the face to liquify in a just kidding smile. "Of course, they're also saying it could miss us by a couple million miles, so you might want to wait on those tickets. What can I tellya? G'night, folks."

"Now *that's* positively eerie," Lizabeth said.

"Rather an intriguing notion, when you think about it. An enormous chunk of rock come streaking out of the blackness of space to cancel our assumptions with a cataclysmic sneer."

"What a comforting thought."

"Humbling, actually. All our petty human scrambling, lofty aspirations and fretting dreams squashed in a fingersnap by a Zeusian bolt from a cloudless sky. Maybe the Greeks were right."

"You don't really believe that."

"Oh, but I do. Your asteroid is simply a metaphor for all the random capricious elements of experience."

"I haven't the slightest idea what you're talking about."

"Give you an illustration. I knew an inmate in Stateville, a meek and gentle soul, embezzler, who had the wicked luck to choke to death on a grape seed the day before he was to be paroled."

"Grape seed? You can't choke on a grape seed."

"Might have been a peach pit. Don't be so literal minded."

She looked at him dubiously. "And the day before he was paroled? Sounds suspect to me."

"All right, maybe it was a week. Or a year. Time tends to blur in there."

"Now it's a year?"

"If the story grows a bit in the telling, in all the significant aspects it's essentially true."

"Come on, admit it. You made the whole thing up."

Fact was, as he summoned it now, the hapless embezzler had been so relentlessly buggered he took his own life by swallowing battery acid in the prison garage. Exactly when, in relation to the abortive parole (if indeed parole was even a factor), he couldn't recall. No matter. The tale had the trappings of truth, and it reinforced his point. "Believe what you will," he said, shrugging. "Anyway, as the imbecile on the tube there suggests, I wouldn't worry too much. In the long run we're all wormfood."

"You're a real treat to be around, Norman, you know that? Real joy."

"That's what all you ladies say."

She shook her head in mock disgust. Norman merely grinned. Anymore it felt easy, natural, to allude to those dark days, the whitewashed surface of them anyway, the rascally characters, bizarre episodes, twisted humor, the sorts of things free-worlders could handle. And in the waggish spirit of debate he was about to amplify his ill-formed theory with another joint anecdote, of which there was an abundant supply, when the phone sounded.

They exchanged quick glances. Calls to this house still carried the potential for alarm. "It's probably Michael," she said, and she glided across the room and lifted the receiver and spoke a cautious greeting. Instantly, a relieved joyous glow came into her face and, needlessly, for Norman's benefit, she shaped the silent word "Michael." He nodded, turned away, fixed his gaze on the television. But in the confines of this tiny room it was impossible not to overhear her end of the conversation:

"No, it's fine. Your dad's here. We were just watching the news."

"Whatever you ask."

"Now?" Voice faltered a little. "Tonight?"

"Is there something wrong, Michael?"

"Of course I will. Have to leave early in the morning, though. I just can't miss another day of school."

"No, no, it's all right."

"I'm sure."

"How far?"

"An hour?"

"Four? Yes, I'll remember."

"But I *do* want to, Michael. I'll see you soon."

She put down the phone and stood there a moment, brows pinched, eyes on the floor.

Norman cleared his throat. No response. So he said quietly, "You know, it's difficult not to eavesdrop in here."

"What?"

"I've been listening."

"Oh."

"Trouble?"

"He wants me to meet him."

"I gathered."

"In Kenosha. Tonight."

"Rather short notice. For Michael. Spontaneity was never one of his virtues. Or faults."

"He sounded awfully . . . agitated."

"No crisis other than romantic, I trust."

She flushed slightly. "I don't think so. Probably not. He remembered to remind me there's four tolls. Said I'd make better time if I had exact change."

"Well, no one ever accused him of inattention to detail," Norman said, trying to make light of it but distressed in spite of himself, all the unsettling thoughts of his son censors-subdued over these past tranquil weeks, all but erased.

"Still is mysterious. Middle of the week like this, and his work up there as demanding as he says it is."

"But you're going."

A small, private smile crossed her face. "Yes."

"Drive with caution. Remember the predicted showers. And the pain index."

"You don't approve, do you."

In a voice detached, self-shielding, he said, "Quite the contrary. I think you should go. And if it should be anything else, some other sort of . . . problem, perhaps you'll give me a call."

"Of course."

"If you think I can help."

"Help right now if you had some toll change to spare."

He stood and searched his pockets, produced two quarters and a dime, and came over and handed them to her. "Best I can do," he said.

"I'm sorry to run out on you this way."

"Don't be. I understand."

"You can stay and watch television if you like. Just lock up when you leave."

"No, I should be getting along now too."

She looked at him appraisingly. "Norman?"

"Yes?"

"Thanks."

"For what? The coins?"

"For being who you are."

Which was who? he wondered, watching her hurry up the stairs, wondering also if in the end, after all the stealthy inspection of the past, with all its blunders and betrayals and rusted hopes and collapsed dreams, and after all the anxious speculation on the future's murky perilous frontiers—if, after all of it, the only thing that finally mattered was the simple longing in the heart for another guileless, blameless human presence in the room.

WHICH WAS NOT ALL THAT FAR OFF what Lizabeth wondered, two hours later, lying next to this man in the perfect buttery limpness that follows on passion run dry. Wondering about the urgent and still unexplained summons that brought her here, no hesitations, no questions, and about these two strangers, father and son, like two halves of the same man, come into her life at a critical juncture to shape its course irreversibly and, she hoped, forever.

"Michael?" she whispered.

"Yes."

"You awake?"

"Yes."

"You want to know something?"

"What's that?"

"I'm glad you asked me to come."

"You're not sorry?"

"It was a beautiful idea."

After a small silence he said, "Would *you* like to know something?"

"Tell me."

"Remember when you asked me about love?"

"Yes I do."

"I never really understood how to speak about it before."

"But now you do?"

"I think now I do."

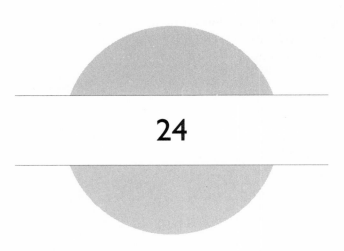

24

By about 5:00 A.M. Flam's coming uncranked. The numb in his legs and ass creeping north, lids drooping, head sinking toward his chest, mind a pleasant void. What saves him from crashing right there is the urgent call of the trusty old hose in serious need of a draining. He cracks open the door and steps outside, every joint creaking, and gives the asphalt a splashdown. The bitter air stings his face and nips at poor exposed Mr. One-Eye down below. Braces him a little, but it's not going to be enough to do the job and he knows it. So he holsters his shlong and climbs back inside the vehicle, and even though he don't like to lean too heavy on the wizard pills he pops a couple anyway, figuring two more can't hurt, swallows them with a juiceless gulp, mouth feeling worse than dry, feeling like it's coated with soot.

He switches on the ignition and the heater and waits for the jolt to kick in. Takes a while but when it does it comes on a hotwire rush, nerves prickling, thoughts tumbling, filling the vacancy in his head. Most of them disjointed, some downright weird, none exactly cheering. Looking at the gradually lightening sky, color of a wicked bruise and not a trace of a sun anywhere in it, he's thinking how someday they'll write in the history books that people actually lived up here, strange place called Wisconsin, way they write about Eskimos livin' up in the Arctic now-days. And watching objects emerge moment by moment out of the dark, he speculates dreamily on the mysteries of shape, form, substance, singularity, identity. Take that Dumpster over there, other cars in the lot, one he's sittin' in, himself—in the border-less blackness of the night how you gonna know, for sure, where one ends and the other begins. Which is probably what it's like when you're dead and there's nothin' but night, and when you been dead a million years your stretch just gettin' underway. And seeing the wing of the motel framed in that gray cast of dawn, he gets to wondering if maybe he's been wrong all along, if maybe this ain't his man in there after all. Or even if it is if maybe Nathan's right. Charity don't make no bank. It's not like you're working for Goodwill Industries, Victor, or got yourself commissioned captain in the Salvation Army. And that's about what this deadend gig worth to him anymore, fuckin' Sal-vation Army doughnut, unsugared at that.

This last dismal thought is reinforced, a few minutes later, by the sight of the happy couple coming through the door, hanging all over each other, got the boinked-out beam on their faces. And why not? Night of harmless bone-jumping, no law against getting your nuts cracked, last he heard. Fuck, Flam, he'd be beaming too, it was him. Instead of scowling like he is, wondering all the more what he's do-ing here, eight hours shivering through the cold and the dark, scorch-ing the brain to keep awake on the longshot odds of scoring the big banana. Shoulda known better. Shoulda seen it for a sucker bet right out of the gate. Can't even trust your hunches no more, f'chrissake.

After a long huggy-bear goodbye they head for their respective cars, roll out of the lot and onto the street leading to the interstate, Flam well behind, keeping a cautious distance. Fluff takes the ramp pointing south, Woodrow north. No surprises there.

As for Flam, he's arrived at a crossing of his own. Run out of pa-tience, fresh out of moves (not to speak of dwindling resources, all the cush pissed away tracking a maybe, maybe not one oar), starting to feel like a candidate for the cackle box himself. And thinking that way, it comes back to him what Nathan turned up on the old man, daddy Woodrow, smoked his missus. He wonders if it might do some good, go have another chat with him, see if he can see is there any-thing to that Jewboy theory says bughouse infects the blood. Other hand, could be his own logic's bent. Might spook junior too, after fa-

ther and son sit down for a heart-to-heart, which for sure they'd
be doing once Victor Flam come to call. Course after last night it's
looking like junior ain't too tightly strung no more either, so a seed-
planting visit with daddy maybe just the ticket, nudge he needs,
boost him over into loopyland. Could go either way.

Crunch time, Victor, shit or vacate the pot. He pulls over onto
the shoulder, ponders a moment. Consider where you are, where
you stand. What you got right now is a shrinking wallet, mounting
bills, headful of lame hopes, buy you a handful of dog flop. So what's
to lose? Nothin' else, get your head straight on this whole kinked
business. Put you on the bus or off it, one or the other.

He gives the dreary landscape a tough glance, swings back onto
the road, turns at the ramp and drives south.

AT ABOUT THE TIME VICTOR FLAM was urinating on a motel parking lot,
some forty miles north, Norman was contemplating the drift of papers on his desk, gazing at the pages of cryptic notes, murky jottings,
whimsical and irrelevant reflections (in the solitary life there was a
tendency to collect and hoard extraneous details), anemic words
strung together in senseless scribblings. Page on page of false starts
and bold new beginnings that invariably dribbled away in rambling,
scarcely coherent digressions, their pertinacity (never mind meaning) long since lost. The sterile product of five weeks' grappling with
the Delphic riddle of that terrible night.

All his inventive and recollective energies seemed exhausted,
stalled in the arid mind wastes of this final expedition into the abyss
of the past. What he felt like was a magician no longer able to whisk
the rabbit from his sleeve. And what he was discovering was the
harsh and unforgiving truth that merely to label an object or an act or
a memory was in no way to penetrate it.

Nevertheless, he remained stubbornly rooted to his desk. Now
and then he would swivel about and address the walls of the room in
long, troubled monologues. But mostly he sat in silence, chaining
reds and listening to the voice running like a tape in his head, albeit a
defective tape, its sound distorted, accelerated, jeering quack of a
spunky critter in an animated cartoon: *Th-th-th-that's all, folks.*

But it was unmistakably his own voice this time, none other, furious voice of the man he had been that lurid lunatic night two
decades gone. If he could just slow it down, restore it to normal pitch

and tempo, perhaps then he could break the code, isolate the fragments, secure the salient ones, and discard the rest. Perhaps produce the bunny and exit to thunderous applause after all. Why not? It was his tale to tell.

Was it fear that paralyzed him? If so, of what? Overlooking something? Peering too deeply into your own mangled, scurvy heart? Or an even more primal fear of arriving finally at journey's end and facing up to all those bedeviling doubts and confusions over Michael that still assailed him whenever he allowed them in? Impossible to know.

Beyond the window the darkness lifted slowly and without auroral fanfare, exposing a leaden November sky. The promised rain fell in soft soundless drizzle. Somewhere around seven the familiar Camaro pulled into the Seaver drive. He watched her step from the car and sprint to the door, hands shielding her head against the rain. Thirty minutes later she emerged, outfit changed, umbrella in one hand, satchel of books in the other, smiling serenely to herself and moving purposefully but with an unhurried, almost careless, grace. And watching her, Norman felt a sudden jarring dissonance between this delicate young woman, who seemed to glide through the world in a state of perpetual dazzled innocence, and himself, freighted with the gloomy substance of experience and shackled by the compulsion of his own grim and secret vocation.

But not nearly the dissonance he would feel when, thirty minutes after that, the two-toned chime of the doorbell would rudely snap him from these bleak reveries.

NO SOONER DOES HE CROSS the Illinois line than the sky got to open up and needles of rain start pelting the windshield. Jesus fuck, you'd think travelling south, even if it's only for a few miles, the goddam weather cooperate a little. Way it's suppose to work. Deep-six that good idea, Victor.

No question about it, he's amped. Jolt got him by the nuts now. Fingers drumming the wheel, head going at breakneck speed, one thought toppling into the next. Slow down, boy. Nothin' but time. Don't want to get there too early, haul the old bugger out of the sack, get a door in the face for your trouble. Anyway, you could use some of that time, settle the tummy, which is still doing flips under the weight of last night's burgers and fries banquet. Back door detonating some foul thunder off that feast. Worse'n swamp gas. Good thing you don't smoke. Light a match in here and the vehicle go up in flames, you with it.

Traffic picks up. He slides over into the middle lane, sets the cruise at fifty, lets the hacked-off drivers roar up behind and zoom around him, either side. Fuck 'em. After a while he don't even notice. Too busy attending to the hypnotic rhythm of the wiper blades slapping across the glass. Listen close and you can recognize some tunes in there. Familiar ones, oldies. There's "Lady of Spain." Here comes "Bye Bye Blackbird." He warbles along. Helps get the mind right.

Ogden Avenue exit, dead ahead. He pulls onto it, stops at the first station and bolts for the crapper. Nick a time, too. It's a powerful load he's got to lay, godawful stink to it. Next guy in here a goner for sure. Pro'ly have to evacuate the area. That's okay. Chance to assemble all those vagrant rushing thoughts, set 'em in order. Some of your better thinking gets done on the throne.

Thoroughly emptied and an easy ten pounds lighter, he hitches up his pants, steps out of the stall and rinses his hands. Glances in the mirror over the sink, recoils, startled at what the reflection gives him back. Hair matted, gluey; blue stubble of beard; eyes a couple orange piss holes in the snow; cheeks flushed color of a slab of raw meat. Not good, Victor. Looking like a fugitive from the wig factory yourself. All the more reason to bust a smart move, turn the corner on this shitsack case, one direction or the other, don't matter which no more. Get yourself straight again.

So he scrubs his face, towels off, runs a comb through his hair. Helps a little, not much. Best he can do.

Ten minutes later he's standing on the porch of the Woodrow condo. He squares his shoulders, sucks in the gut, and lays a finger on the bell.

"SO. WE MEET AGAIN, MR. FLAM."

"Lookin' that way."

"And what brings you by this time?"

"Thought maybe we could have another little talk, you'n me."

"On what matter?"

"You got no idea?"

"Why don't you tell me."

"Well, same matter as before, more or less."

"I expect that means you'd like to come in."

"Be nice, get outta this rain."

Norman looked him up and down. Almost unrecognizable. Almost, though not quite, like a different man. Like he just came off a three-day jag, laundry direct out of the tumble dryer, whiff of sour rankness to him, face a shadowed bloat, cracked impression of a smile stuck on it, peculiar varnished sheen in the eyes, but with all their flinty meanness still intact. That much was the same. "I don't think so," Norman said. "Not this time."

"You're a hard man, Mr. Woodrow."

"And not a very patient one. If you've got something to say, better get to the point."

"Point," Flam repeated, enunciating as though it were a word unfamiliar to him. "Yeah, well, guess that point, you wanna get right down to it, is I got reason to believe your son's been whackin' some ladies, his spare time after work." He paused, let it settle in. Mr. Chill there says nothin', never once lifts the frosty glare. So Flam asks, real cordial-like, "You know what that means, that whackin'?"

"Oh, I understand the term."

"Figured you might. Man with your wide life experience."

"And how did you arrive at this absurd notion?" Norman said evenly.

"Couple ways. Y'see, seems like every city your boy's doin' a consulting job, some poor lady turns up dead. That one down in Florida I tol' ya about, last time we talked, San Antone, one over in Michigan—you name it, he's there."

"Along with several hundred thousand other people, those places you've cited."

"Well, that's a fact too. But lemme finish here. See, pattern's always the same. Always a lady pushin' into her forties, that range, married, cheatin' on the hub. Always gets herself iced on or about the day your boy's foldin' his tent and bookin' town. Real brutal snuffs they was, too. Messy. I ever show you a picture, one a the victims?"

"No, I missed that part."

"Think I got one here," Flam said. He fished the photo of the butchered Shelley out of his wallet, held it up in display. Watched him study it. Gotta give the old boy credit, he don't flinch. Don't wince or stiffen. Don't so much as blink. "She's the Florida lady, got me started on this case, first place," Flam explained. "One that worked the same plant your boy was at."

"Life is full of coincidences, Mr. Flam. Have you established any link between Michael and these incidents?"

"Not exactly. Just it happens he's always in the vicinity."

"But no solid link?"

"Nothin' stand up in a court of law. Least not yet."

"Then how is it you've got the audacity to show up at this door and advance this preposterous, offensive, and, I might add, potentially litigable accusation?"

Flam swiped a hand across his brow, mopping phantom sweat. "Whew!" he whistled. "All them words go right over my head."

"Let me simplify it for you. I'm asking why, if you have no hard evidence, you suspect Michael."

"Call it a hunch."

"That's what brings you here? A hunch?"

"Something like that. Remember how I said I got a couple reasons?"

"I remember."

"Well, other one is, course a my research I come across the fact you had a little trouble your own, while back."

Flam leaves it hanging out there. Watches him steadily. Now he stiffens. Locked-on stare don't waver none but it glazes over some, turns inward, like a nerve been tweaked. All he says is, "That's right. I did."

"Done some time, I understand."

"Eighteen years."

Flam shook his head sorrowfully. "Lot a years. Musta been tough, educated man like you. All them coloreds in there, joint monkeys."

"Not so bad. It's how you carry yourself."

"Listen, I know about that. Done some time myself. Only on the other side of the lockup."

Norman tucked his lips back slightly, a smile guarded and molecularly thin. A hack. Should have guessed. Same oxen power of stupidity, same rodent cunning. "And where was that?" he asked.

"In service. Portsmouth Correctional Facility."

"I would've tagged you for the Big Eight. Or Schofield."

"I was Corps. Anyway, heard them places went pussy."

"But not Portsmouth?"

"Nothin' pussy about Portsmouth. Real gladiator college."

"Do any batting practice in there?"

"Yeah, we hadda do some a that, inmate got unruly."

"Heavy slugger, were you?"

"I swung a few bats, my time."

"Bet you did."

Flam can see the hard bitter glint comin' into them zombie eyes. Don't escape him. An image of that spook they zapped, thousand years ago, Portsmouth, flashes behind his own. Have a caution, Victor. Walkin' the high wire here, in your combat boots. "Well, them was the bad old days," he said, dismissing them with a brush of a hand. "Both of us."

"Worse for some than others. Depends on your end of the bat."

"Ain't that always the way. Nothin' fair, this sorry old world. Anyway, gettin' back to what we was discussin', time you done, that was for poppin' your wife, was it?"

"Why is it I think you already know."

"Hey," Flam said, voice lowered to a molasses purr, "I'm makin' no judgment calls, y'understand. There's some women drive you right outta your skull. Known a few like that myself. Like they say, be a bounty on 'em, they wasn't sittin' on top that world-class persuader."

"Appreciate the thought. Very comforting. But I'm still waiting for your point."

"You don't see it?"

"Help me out."

"Kinda touchy. Sure you wanta get into it?"

"Try me."

"Okay. Long as you're sure. See, I got this associate, been consultin' with him on this case. Real intelligent fella. Jewish."

Significant pause. As though the elusive point were suddenly deciphered, laid bare. "So?" Norman prompted.

"Well, it's his thought, mine too, there's maybe a connection, your boy, what happened to you."

"A genetic link? Stain in the blood? Like father, like son? Is that what you're suggesting?"

"Guess you could put it that way," Flam said mournfully. "Now I know it ain't easy, thinkin' bad about your own flesh and blood—"

"What I'm thinking," Norman cut in on him, "is you're selling wolf tickets here, Mr. Flam. You know about wolf tickets?"

"Believe I heard the expression."

"Figured you might. Veteran like yourself. Corrections officer. DiMaggio with a bat."

"Could be you're right. 'Bout them tickets, I mean. Wouldn't plunge to it, though."

"I would. And this conversation's over, Mr. Flam. I've got nothing more to say to you."

Flam put up conciliatory palms, backed away. "Hey, that's okay, I understand." But before the door swung shut on him he laid a thoughtful finger on the bridge of his nose, added, "Y'know, we're all of us consultants, one way or another, you think about it. All got our little areas of expertise, little secrets to share. And I wanna thank you for sharin' yours with me this morning. Owe you one."

"Maybe I'll collect one day."

Flam's face crinkled around a huge nasty grin. "Maybe you will at that."

WOLF TICKETS, FLAM'S THINKING, steered north on the interstate and tooling right along, chuckling to himself. Your hardcases same the world over. Spook, spic, slope, white, old, young, educated, pig ignorant. Peel away a thin layer of polish and you got the same scarred oak underneath. Equal opportunity badass.

And this one about as badass as he's leaned on, good long time. Turn your back on that old joint dog, be a shank in it for sure. Flam's got street eyes too, knows what he sees. Also what he hears. Like father, like son? You said it, badass, not me. Stain in the blood? Your words, wisefuck, not mine.

Other side of the Wisconsin line the rain lets up. Flam's jazzed head starts to quiet down some. A message, clear, emphatic, resonant in the hush of the car, arrived like a signal beamed across a vast expanse of space and time but delivered by a sturdy familiar voice, instructing him to *follow your instincts, Victor*, hang in there a while longer. Ain't over yet. We'll see who it is peddlin' the wolf tickets here. See.

LIKE FLAM, NORMAN WAS, that same moment, attending to an interior voice counseling him to remain calm, still, to draw in long slow breaths, the way you learned to do in the darkness of the hole, let the whistle of the breathing and the steady rise and fall of the chest persuade you of your existence. It wasn't easy. Even down here, returned to his desk, the air was thin. A man like Flam takes all of it with him when he leaves.

He tried to get his mind around this utterly alien ideation, but it was too staggering to comprehend, rather on the order of last night's asteroid hurtling through the heavens, targeting no one but you. Michael a merciless killer? Unthinkable. Grotesque. A concept so profoundly black it leached all the colors from either end of the moral rainbow. Impossible to entertain, groundless as coincidence, and certainly false as its loutish grinning courier.

Except if you've learned anything at all, Norman, it's that certainty, like mercy, is one of those propositions for which there is no corresponding reality. At the bottom of the heart anything is thinkable, anything possible. And lurking around every treacherous fork in the road is the ineradicable specter of the past, waiting to confirm your grimmest forebodings.

And so to escape those auguries it was that past he retreated into now, confronted at last, lifting a pen and spilling words across an empty page with a burst of renewed energy, and an urgency fierce and final.

25

The thing about graffiti is that, like myth, it taps the darkest well of our collective spirit, mocks our petty achievement, cackles at our pride, dismisses all our loftiest institutions and symbols and aspirations and received wisdoms with a sniggering line, and it cautions that our noblest enterprises must come ultimately to nothing more than, to invoke the vernacular of the art itself, diddly squat. In his introduction to *The Uses of the Past,* that seminal study of history's abundant ironies, Herbert Muller describes the satirical drawings of bishops etched on the columns and balustrades of the Cathedral of Hagia Sophia in Istanbul. On some of the more ornate panels he discovered the crudely chiselled initials of artisans, made apparently to claim payment for their work. (Though who can ever know for certain? Surely your own initials are preserved in the concrete slab of a sidewalk somewhere, your personalized plea to history: *Remember me! I lived! I was here!*) At any rate, Muller concludes that the builders of that magnificent monument to Christendom, that is to say the men who actually did the dog work, were perhaps motivated by something other than pietude and holy zeal.

But it's those scribblings gracing the walls of men's rooms (some of them succinct little pearls of wit and whimsy and convoluted irony) that, I think, best celebrate the sardonic spirit of the underground man lurking in each of us, and topple all our pathetic posturings with a jeer. Who, for example, can forget his first introduction to the subtle paradox of that familiar couplet:

> A man's ambition must be mighty small
> To write his name on a shithouse wall

Or its mordant, if for our time "sexist," counterpoint:

> But a woman's ambition must be smaller still
> To sell her ass for a dollar bill

What about the taunting indictment:

> Some folks come here to sit and think,
> But *you* come here to shit and stink.
> Others come to sit and wonder,
> But *you* come here to fart, like thunder (italics mine)

Or the pitiless judgment of:

> People who write on shithouse walls
> Roll their shit in little balls.
> But those who read these lines of wit
> Must eat those little balls of shit

And which male adolescent, puffed with pride over his magically sprouted organ, has not glanced up from a urinal to read the deflating query/admonition:

> What are you looking up here for?
> The joke's in your hand

Now, I would not want to overstate my case. To be sure, much of it is coarse, uninspired, banal—the lackluster issue of dull, disgruntled minds. Nevertheless, I would maintain that the finer models of this folk art perform no less a service than, say, those hellfire Sunday sermons whose function it is to remind us of our sickness of soul and mortality's cankered rot. I would go further: Behind all this anonymous twitting foolery and waggish good fun is the somber message of catastrophe's certainty, disaster's foreordination. Or, put another way: The joke, my friend, is finally, inescapably, on you.

I would, of course, like to believe such keen insights occupied at least a share of my thoughts that calamitous winter night so long ago, but the sorry truth of it is nothing of the sort occurred to me. After reading the scurrilous catalog of Suzanne's sins, so bent was I on confrontation my fogged head would accommodate nothing more subtle than the wordless constricted vision of a frenzied rush to reckoning. And so, propelled on a tidal wave of fury, I strode manfully from the tavern john, shouldered my way grimly through the crowd, pushed through the door and out into streets clotted with snow, pointed purposefully in the direction of what had once been home.

And soon discovered myself coatless, that garment left draped over a barstool, forgotten in the theatric exit. I hesitated, ankle-deep in exhaust-blackened curbside snow. And for a splinter of an instant, shivering there in the gauzy silver light cast by a moon flat as a coin embossed on the frigid night sky, I toyed with the soundly practical notion of turning back, recovering the coat. And many times since have I speculated, as old men are wont to do, on the numberless scenarios that might have unfolded, the phantom, happy-ending lives that might have been lived, had I done just that.

Here's an alternate script:

I return to the tavern. Its steamy warmth and ersatz intimacy calm me. Another drink dulls my passions. And the pills, gulped so recklessly, gradually numb my senses. I stumble, coat-shielded, back to my mean digs, fall into a sodden sleep. The next day, or the one after that, I encounter a lovely, sensitive, compassionate woman, a Lizabeth Seaver for that time (don't ask how: my script, my plotting devices). The affinity between us is spontaneous and immediate. We become friends, confidants, lovers. Her gentle touch heals me. We marry. Produce children of our own—bright, comely, well adjusted. Michael, recognizing his mother for the slattern she is, elects to live with us. In that ambience of perfect harmony he blossoms, flourishes. My career does the same. I publish the definitive critical biography of Mad Nat Lee, a work hailed for its impeccable scholarship, trenchant style, and vast learning. Professorships come my way, honors, distinguished chairs, fat stipends, accolades of peers, the rich contentment of a productive life, quietly and sensibly lived. . . .

Music swelling, the scene dissolves, trailing a rosy afterglow.

Like most visions of peace and balance and order, this one, needless to say, is pure fancy, a script unrehearsed, never performed. Coat? Fuck the coat. Who needs it? Not Norman Woodrow, aka the valorous Burt, who shrugs away discomfort, feels no pain. He slogs on, a monster of vengeful appetite, fortressed in righteous wrath.

But the clashing stupificants in the blood—dex, booze, sleepers—slow this monster. He staggers and reels in a muggy, narcotized daze. His head feels swollen as an outsize tuber, one of those botanic aberrations proudly displayed at country fairs, tomatoes big as pumpkins, melons mammoth as barrels. He stops to lean against a tree (an evergreen, in this reconstruction, its bark coarse to the gloveless touch, its needles spiky), steady himself, stay on his feet. An icy wind pierces the thin fabric of his shirt. He sustains himself with chanted maledictions. For there's a commitment here, something demanding to be done. Exactly what, he's not quite sure. Wrongs to right. Lessons to teach.

Deliberately do I slip into third person here, not to distance myself through the feeble fabrication of some brutish golem composed, in my case, of malignant incantation and chemical bravado, but rather in the spirit of fidelity to fact (to know all, as some charitable soul once allowed, is to forgive all). No, this was no doppelganger. Let it be understood, I was I, none other. Conscious of every thought, answerable to every deed to follow. For consciously did I press on. Arrived eventually at the house. Stormed through the door, fully expecting to discovery some rutting, two-backed beast.

And found only a woman and child sitting cross-legged on the living room floor, a deck of playing cards spread out between them. What I had burst in on was an innocent game of cards.

My shoes were wet. Clothes flecked with snow. The moist heat of the room dizzied me. For a moment I forgot why I was here. To take my place on the floor, was it? Join in the fun? Resume my rightful role in this ruptured household? Later, doting father, to tuck the covers around a sleepy son, and then, forgiving, dutiful husband, to lie down beside a sullen wife, murmuring soft words of appeasement, renewal, repair? Dumbstruck, I gaped at them both, stupored by confusions, paralyzed by doubts.

Till a glimpse of those wicked green eyes, fastening me with that look of revulsion ordinarily reserved for odious slimy bugs, rekindled my purpose. For there was a flicker of fear in them, too, and if shame were foreign to her, it was time she made acquaintance with something of fear. Past time.

Not that her stance, on her feet now, hands planted defiantly on hips, or her strident voice, "Hell are *you* doing here?" she demanded—gave any of it away. Not this harpy.

"To call you to account for the amplitude and enormity of your sins," said I, ever the pedantic schoolmaster.

"Look at you. You're drunk. Disgusting. I got nothing to say to you."

"Ah, but I have a great deal to pass along to you, my love. And I should expect by now you're no stranger to disgust."

"I'm not having any scenes with you. Won't stand for it. You got no right to be here."

"No scene, Suzanne. Merely a lesson in the wages of sin."

She wagged a thumb at the child, still on the floor, cards still gripped in a trembly hand. "Not in front of him," she snapped at me.

"And why not? It's time he learned of his sainted mother's transgressions. Could be instructive."

"Mikey"—that being her cute name for him—"go to bed."

He watched us curiously, a puzzled fascination scrawled on his pale, stricken face. An expectation. He didn't move.

"Tonight's topic, then, is betrayal, treachery, deceit," I declaimed in orotund, if slightly slurred, peal. "In a word, sin. As recorded on the wall of a pestilent men's crapper."

"Hell're you talking about?"

"The graven testament to your faithlessness."

"Jesus, you *are* crazy. They oughta lock you up."

"Remember that archaic notion, Suzanne? Sin? Probably not. You wouldn't recognize it if it snuck right up and buggered you."

"Maybe not. But one thing I do know is you better get out of this house, you sick son of a bitch, before I call the cops."

She glared at me, fierce and unblinking, and with a loathing bone deep, the riddled marrow, perhaps, of all cancered unions. But I was unfazed. Unintimidated. Wasn't I Burt, after all? Larger than life. Bulletproofed by rectitude (and a variety of analgesics). Indestructible. Who could touch me? Police? Laughable. "Call them," I growled toughly.

"Okay, that's how you want it. Try out your big professor words on them. See what they got to say."

Here I must pause briefly and alert you to the fact that my best recollections of everything that followed are little more than a scattering of vagrant image linked only by that teetery, vertiginous sensation peculiar to all fractured experience outside one's power to control. Don't mistake me. This is not, I say again, to condone my subsequent actions or to absolve me of culpability (for that would test the charity of an angelic host, let alone the earthly judgment of a jury of one's peers), but simply to attempt to reconstruct my disordered state of mind. For you see, acts, events, faces, voices, assorted sights and sounds—all tumbled together in a firestorm of rage, seemed to flash by at time-warp velocity.

There is Suzanne, marching toward the kitchen, site of the phone. There am I, unaccountably (in light of my fearless rejoinder to the threat) tracking her. And there is Michael, silently watching us both.

I stumble over a coffee table, topple face first onto the floor. The graceless fall thumps the wind from my lungs. My breath comes in panting gasps. And lying there, I'm obliged to conclude this is no movie, and I no cinematic hero. Rather, something of a buffoon. Something of a fool. The acrid scent of ashes from a heaped, upended tray stings my flaring nostrils. Over the years, Suzanne has become a prodigious smoker, and it occurs to me to wonder how many packs (cartons?) she's consumed in langorous stolen moments of post-coital bliss, naked beside some sated lecher under soiled and sweaty sheets. And it's just that image that impels me to my feet.

I'm in the kitchen now. Suzanne is yelping frantically into the phone (". . . yes, yes, that's the number . . . and hurry, will you . . . he's acting crazy . . ."). I jerk it from her hands, rip it from the wall and, employing the dangling cord as sling, sail it across the room. She backs away, maneuvers behind a table still littered (for Suzanne keeps no immaculate house, never did) with the residue of the evening's meal: cups, saucers, silver, food-spattered plates, the remains of a roast chilling in a pan. I stalk her. She ducks left, I right. She to the right, I left. No words pass between us. Deadly mime of the child's game of tag.

I soon weary of the game. With a single furious swipe of an arm I clear the table, lunge over it, and bring us jarringly to the floor in a tangle of flailing limbs. Suzanne trys to wriggle out from under me, but even in my groggy and wilted condition I'm much too strong for her. Much too charged. I straddle her waist, pin her thrashing arms. Alongside my knee, in among scraps of food and slivers of shattered glass, is one of those pieces of kitchen cutlery commonly and, as I see it now, aptly called a "butcher" knife. I seize it. Lay its blade across her throat. Her face is chalky, eyes steep with terror. In a burbly voice she pleads for mercy: "For god's sake, Wood! Don't hurt me! Please!"

But mercy is for me, just then, a commodity in woefully short supply. Vengeful voices howl in my head. Oddly, though, the memory of a bit of dusty lore, long forgotten, returns to me now: crusaders claiming for Christ, through the harsh redemption of slaughter, the lost souls of infidels. And in the instant before I bear down on the blade I declare: "Thusly do I claim thee."

A fountain of arterial blood erupts. Sprays my face and neck and hands in rhythmic pulsing spurts. I seem to hear a long siren wail, piercing and unnaturally shrill. A shriek, is it? Not exactly. More a whooping squeal. Ever so slowly, it dwindles to sluggish groan, to raspy gurgle, then to no sound at all. She shudders once, convulsively. Abruptly slackens. Her mouth is ajar, chin slick with warm emergent blood. Rootlets of shock burnish those ice green eyes. But all of the fear is gone out of them now, all the desperate yearning; and a perfect serenity settles over her features, still delicate, still lovely, as though she merely slumbered, her placid sleep absent of any but the most enchanted of dreams.

I remove the knife from her torn flesh. Fling it away. Disengage myself from her. Slump back on the floor. The spiraling screak of a siren rises in the distance. Real one this time. Coming for me.

I sense a presence in the doorway. Michael, gazing at me quizically. "Is Mom dead?" he asks.

"Yes."

"Did you kill her?"

"Yes."

"Why?"

"I don't know," I reply, and speak the truth.

"Are you going to kill yourself now?"

"No."

"You promise?"

"I promise."

"Because if you do, then I'll have to too."

"You won't have to, Michael. You can't. I need you. Want you to go over to the neighbors now. Tell them there's been . . . an accident. Wait there for me."

"You'll come get me?"

"Yes."

"When?"

"When I can."

"You won't leave again?"

My eyes are flooded with tears. "No," I lie. "Go now. Hurry."

Obediently, he turns and trots out the back door.

I try to stand. Want to be on my feet when they arrive. My knees feel rubbery. I brace myself against a wall. There's a toaster on the counter and I catch a glimpse of a weirdly elongated reflection of my own face peering at me from a rippled strip of chrome. Almost comical, that face, thin as an arrow, splotched with blood, otherwise white as bone dust and punctuated by two damp savage specks of eyes. I'm wonderstruck by the curious configuration of events that's led me to this moment, this grimy kitchen, this irreversible act. Metaphysical questions occur to me: butterflies with bizarre dreams of manhood; the silent echo of trees falling in remote forests; the occult riddle of sin, its mysterious collaborative essence.

But these are to be the last of my weighty deliberations for this day. The siren is suddenly stilled. I hear footsteps in the outer hall. Time running out. Pragmatic matters to attend to. Hastily, I fumble through a pocket for my bottled deliverance, shake its contents into a cupped palm, stoop down and stuff the pills inside a sock. Nick of time. For when I look up, two uniformed officers are standing in the doorway, inspecting the scene gravely. No weapons are drawn, none needed. One of the officers says, "You did this?"

"I did."

"Gonna have to ask you to step over here, sir."

I rise, approach them with bloody wrists extended in docile acceptance of the cuffs. Solemn, courteous, they pat me down, advise me of my rights. After some routine questions, routine business, they lead me to their car.

At the local jail I'm stripped of belt, shoelaces, cigarettes, lighter, wallet, change. Someone, the booking officer, I believe, reminds me of yet another privilege. A single phone call. Just like the movies. But who to call? What to say? Anyway, I'm having difficulty staying on my feet. "Maybe later," I mumble.

He looks at me narrowly. "Good idea," he says.

Wobbling like a burlesque comic in broad imitation of a drunk, I'm escorted to a cell. The barred door, first of many, clangs shut behind me. Lord, Thou hast delivered me up into the hands of mine enemies. But my sock runneth over.

In the corner of the cell there's a rust-blasted sink. I retrieve the stash of pills and, heedless of the pledge to my son, wash them down with a mouthful of brackish water. I stretch out on the bunk, head dangling over one end. Thin blades of yellow light from a bulb in the corridor cast long shadows, blackening pockets of the stone floor. My vision blurs. And the last I remember is the sour stench of the dank woolen blanket covering the bunk and gripped tightly in my blood-streaked hands.

Some thirty-six hours later I floated up from the bottom of a dreamless sleep, peeled back crusted lids and discovered myself strapped to a bed in the ward of a state hospital reserved (as I would soon enough learn) for the criminally insane. In the adjacent bed a plump, rosy-cheeked youth with an IV vine sprouting from an arm chanted in nursery rhyme singsong: "Plague is coming, plague is coming." Other inmates shuffled up and down the aisle, trailing flatus.

Periodically, a surly attendant stopped by to lay two fingers on my wrist and frown into his watch. After a while he unfastened the straps and helped me sit, shaking, my bare legs hanging over the side of the bed. He brought me a bowl of soup and a plastic spoon. Famished, I ate noisily, slurping. "Better go easy," he advised. "Your gut took a serious pumpin'."

Soon I was pacing the aisle myself, naked buttocks exposed in the floppy hospital gown. Part of the procession. I undertook some knee-bends but my joints were stiff, my balance precarious. Ten push-ups on the floor set my triceps quivering. The young man with the needle in his arm watched these salutary exercises curiously. "Why do that," he asked, "when plague is coming?"

YOU'LL REMEMBER THIS SOMEWHAT FRAGMENTED narrative began with a meditation on graffiti. Not, I trust, without a certain relevance, however oblique. For the walls of the ward's squalid communal john were, you see, adorned with a veritable riot of messages, most of them purely scatological, but a few profoundly disturbing. Among the former was a bit of doggerel verse composed, no doubt, by some demented riddler. It read like this:

> *If a pig drinks buttermilk before he starts;*
> *Can run a mile before he farts;*
> *The farther he runs, the farther he gets;*
> *How long will it be before he shits?*

And, more ominously, among the latter a line of gloomy prophecy penned by a lunatic of truly Sophoclean vision:

> *If Fate promised you to pass by here,*
> *You will.*

Each, in its own way, seemed addressed to me.

Now I ask you: Where do these seemingly alien voices come from? What is their source? I would advance a theory:

They spring from a schizophrenic darkness latent within us, all of us, and we write the messages to ourselves. They arise out of our disequilibrium in a world sundered in two, spinning off on wildly divergent courses, the one elevated, purposeful, constant, noble and fine; the other swamped in mockery, subject to no order, bearing witness to the arrogance of our pride and the folly of our dreams. No accident the best of them are found in those temples consecrated to human stink and ordure. Here the grinning ape in dressup clothes squats to make his mess and is himself made mindful of the noxious perfumes of all his own soiled illusions. And here his devil of self-contradiction concocts a wicked wit to thumb his nose at them all, the No in Thunder of a shithouse jest. Saint, scoundrel, prig, renegade, and roaring clown fused in one, he reminds himself of the death-bound road we all travel, walking wormfood, armored in defiant mirth against griefs of every measure and proportion and kind.

Fascinating theory, Norman. Speaking of lunacy, as I believe you were in there somewhere.

You.

Surprised? Surely you didn't think you were shut of me yet? Your dependable scapegoat in the mirror? Or the toaster, in this self-serving, not to say vulgar, chronicle.

I gather you're unimpressed with my theory.

Well, I do have to doubt it would stand up to close scrutiny.

And why is that? Because it's exclusively my own? Because you had no hand in it whatsoever?

No. Because it's preposterous beyond all credibility. Ludicrous. Flimsy and transparent apologia for your crimes.

Aren't you being a bit hyperbolic? A bit overwrought?

If I were—which I'm not—I daresay it would be perfectly justifiable. Shameful, it is, imputing your own dementia to an entire populace, staining their innocence with the tarred brush of your psychotic ravings.

Very touching, this sudden concern for others. But as you say, it's my dementia. I don't recall soliciting your opinion.

The more fool, you. I might have been of some help. At very least might have steered you clear of these tortured circumlocutions.

Perhaps. But you see I didn't need you after all.

So you didn't. And look at the result.

I'm not dissatisfied.

Awfully smug, Norman.

With good reason, I think.

Which enigmatic reason is?

You and I are quits now. Finished. I'm free of you at last.

Free, are you? I wonder. Freedom, like adventure, is in the journey, Norman. Not the destination.

Now who's enigmatic?

Not clear? Very well, let me put it another way. In frater-

nal, parting gesture, you understand, since I'm being dismissed so cavalierly.

I'm listening. Get on with it.

A timid reminder, then. Life has all manner and any number of quirky surprises up its sleeve. As who should know better than a lavatory philosopher like yourself.

Part

SIX

26

The morning of Thursday, November twenty-six, came up murky and sullen and gray, as if in ornery denial of the festive day ahead. Dense, sluggish clouds packed the sky. Patches of ground fog coiled in off the lake, nudged along by a raw breeze. A wintry tang seasoned the air.

Inside the Grand Milwaukee Hotel, Michael sat alone at a coffee shop table. He was dressed casually and for him uncharacteristically in suede sport coat, tieless twill shirt, chinos, sneakers. An overnight bag lay on the floor at his feet. Apart from himself and a uniformed couple, airline pilot and stewardess, the place was otherwise empty at this early hour. The sight of the woman generated a fleeting memory of Max Stroiker and his Atlanta "squeeze." Poor Max. He wondered what the one-time mentor would make of this impulsive decision, as uncharacteristic as the wardrobe and as remote to his disciplined nature as the dark side of the moon. Probably wouldn't approve. Or, given his own reckless disregard for the iron Stoltz code (which recognized no holidays for the duration of a project), maybe Max would.

He was marking time, Michael was. Stalling, actually. Wrestling

with doubts, second thoughts. He was not in the habit of taking unau-
thorized and wholly indefensible time off. Word of his apostasy
would certainly spread like a brush fire. Leak to the Bunker. Blemish
his flawless record. Still not too late to return to the room, change
into conventional suit, cancel the message left for his deputy in command (at best a contrived and flimsy excuse for his absence), gather
up his materials, and proceed as always. Another routine business
day. On the other hand, the Badger project was beginning to shape
up nicely, as testified by his latest progress report. The modish Ms.
Dee Dee (who no longer acknowledged his existence or, if she did,
cut him with a haughty glare) had been effectively neutralized. And
with her soft, ruinous policies discredited and reversed, productivity,
fear-inspired, was on the rise again. So his performance, to date,
could be faulted by no one. So maybe there was nothing at risk after
all. Or next to nothing.

A chipper waitress intruded on these conflicting thoughts, offered to fill his empty cup. "No more, thank you," he said.

She knew him. By now he was an early morning fixture in here,
familiar insomniac sedulously poring over notes and charts while nib-
bling at an unvarying breakfast of juice, muffin, coffee. "All set for
turkey day, are ya?" she asked conversationally.

"More or less."

"You fellas gotta work today?"

He glanced at his watch. Six-thirty. Any minute now the other
team members would come trooping in. Join him. Look askance at
his outfit, puzzled. Want to know what was up. He arrived at his
choice. "They do," he said. "Not I."

"Hey, lucky you."

Lucky, indeed. Or foolhardy. One or the other. Time would tell.

He signed the check, gripped the bag, walked through the lobby
and out the door. He crossed the parking lot, unlocked the car, slung
his bag onto the back seat, slipped behind the wheel and pulled
away. Out of habit he drove south on Howell. Passed College Avenue. In the distance, emerging from the haze like accusing fingers
pointed at the sky, the line of Badger smoke stacks spewed gritty
black vapors, sooting the air. Plant was plainly running full steam.
Everything in order, on schedule, under control. As he drove on by
the gate he felt a small twinge of guilt, but he took comfort in the
knowledge that employee holiday pay had been reduced, at his rec-

ommendation, from double-time to time-and-a-half. By that single stroke (presented to the union as nonnegotiable, take it or we shut down for the day; pure bluff, of course, but a successful one) had he saved the company large dollars and set a significant precedent. In the finest Stoltz tradition, he was doing his job. Doing it well. Tomorrow, the weeks ahead, there would be other cost-cutting measures to uncover and implement. For the remainder of this one stolen day he could erase all of it from his head.

He turned west on Ryan Road, picked up the interstate a mile over, and swung south again, headed for home. At a Kenosha exit he caught a passing glimpse of the motel, site of last week's troubled rendezvous. Only last week, was it? Seemed a thousand years ago. Another man's life.

For he was not the same man anymore. Of that, he was certain. An image of Lizabeth, catalyst for this magical transformation, floated behind his eyes. He thought about her. Her satiny voice, crossing the miles night after night, steadying him. Magnetic tug of her smile, drawing him, this very moment, down the highway. Soothing balm of her touch. Almost mystical, it was, like a God-licensed healer's laying on of hands. He could picture her astonished delight, discovering him at her door later this morning. Pictured the warm familial contentment of the upcoming day (for Norman was in there too, on the periphery). Moved ahead in time to picture their life together, wedded, parents perhaps, himself settled in a comfortable executive position somewhere nearby, no longer on the road, on the run.

Head full of dreams, he drove on.

The lingering scraps of fog scattered, dissipated. Off to his left, ribbons of orange light appeared on the horizon. The brown fields shimmered under a silvery crust of frost. A car passed him on the right, edged over into his lane. A young couple, not unlike the Lizabeth and Michael of his time-sprung vision, occupied the front seat. He accelerated enough to keep in close behind. Close enough to watch them. They seemed to be chatting animatedly, mouths in motion, heads bobbing, hands rending the air. The implied intimacy of their gestures and movements gladdened him.

Unless he was mistaken. Unless it was argument they were engaged in. Some bitter squabble. Fiery verbal duel. Impossible to tell, the way a caw of pain might be mistaken for passion's peculiar groan.

He eased up on the pedal. Watched their car speed away, minia-

turize in the widening distance. He weighed the polar possibilities of
the snippet of life he'd just witnessed. Arrived at no conclusion. A
powerless sense of isolation overtook him suddenly, sealed there in
his own vehicle, an enduring loneliness, vast and incurable.

NORMAN WAS FEELING SOMETHING of a similar desolation, that same
hour, as he left the condo and set out walking, hands stuffed in the
pockets of his winter jacket, shoulders bunched against the wind.
Not so much loneliness, if he had to put a name on it, as loss, the
wistful sense that comes of emotions thoroughly tapped. Habit's
gravity continued to wring him from sleep, rouse him early, and draw
him to the desk, but he was exhausted of words, barren of memory,
and he knew it. Nothing really left to say. A useless appendage, a
relic, whose only function anymore was to gaze vacantly out the window, occupy space.

Been a week now, he'd felt this way. But this morning, on mutinous impulse, he skirted the desk and took a walk instead. Went over
to Madison and up Fifty-fifth Street, turned west and tramped through
Clarendon Hills, Westmont, on into Downers Grove. The sharp air
nipped at his face and punished his smoke-charred lungs. Sky was full
of purple-bellied clouds, heavy with the threat of snow. Streets were
empty this holiday morning, but for the occasional passing car, one
of which arrived at an intersection the same moment he did, came to
a squealing stop. Pedestrian and driver waited obediently, if less than
patiently, for the light to turn. A thunderous boom erupted from the
car's radio. Norman glanced over and saw a punkish adolescent regarding him through the window and across the yawning genera-
tional gulf with a patronizing smirk, as if to say, *It's our music,
freeze-dry, you wouldn't understand.* He gave back a sneer, and the
punk, pulling away, flipped him an impudent bird.

Oddly, the muffled whomp trailing from the receding vehicle
sparked an incongruous recollection of a different sort of music.
More precisely, of a theory he'd come across somewhere, advancing
the proposition of a soundless sympathetic music capable of trans-
mitting the characteristics of one person to another, abstract as readily as bacterial, evil, in this theory, as communicable as, say, the flu.
Flu? Why flu, exactly? Some repressed association. He traced the
vowel echo: flu, flom, flim, flem . . . flam. Flam. Victor Flam. The image of that wickedly grinning hack (street clothes notwithstanding,

he was purebred hack, and once a hack, always a hack); the ugly accusation bluntly delivered; the hostile music resonating between them, poisoning the air—all of it came rushing in on him, unwelcome, unsummoned, and with it all the dreads held at arm's length this past week.

He confronted them now. Could it truly be he'd dispatched, through the shrill symphony of a moment's madness, some dissonant chord amplified in his son to caterwauling wail echoing down the years? Was it possible he'd transmitted, through the toxic seed of an angry coupling, some monstrous genetic legacy? No. Couldn't be. Defied logic. Unless, of course, his own logic was blurred and bent by whatever he knew or understood of the slippery notion of love.

A noisy flock of southbound birds winged across the sky in tight symmetrical formation. He was reminded of those ancient seers who claimed to see the future in patterns of birdflight. He saw nothing. He passed a church whose outdoor bulletin board declared "Religion Can Be Holy and Hilarious," insipid theme for an upcoming sermon. He turned away scowling. On the Downers Grove main street he spotted a bank marquee announcing, in sniggery pun, "A smile increases your face value." He was unamused. A sign in the window of a grimy eatery assured him, "Your [sic] a stranger here only once." He walked on by.

The world was full of messages, some more portentous than others. But none of them spoke so eloquently to the inevitable derailment of dreams than those angular, jeering communiqués addressing us from the walls of men's rooms. He wondered idly if they were the exclusive property of males. Did women scribble them too? Perhaps later today, over the holiday feast to be shared by the two of them, he'd ask Lizabeth. Coming from him, it was a question she'd not be uncomfortable with.

And soon (he made a sturdy vow to himself), next time Michael was home, whenever that might be, he'd find a way to approach him on that other matter. Casually, roundabout. Set the dreads to rest. That's what they'd do, have a chat about it soon.

LIKE THE WOODROWS, father and son, Lizabeth was experiencing an acute distress just then, though of an altogether different variety and from a source much more easily identifiable. Source was sprawled on her couch, face buried in a cushion, one arm limply brushing the floor. Source snored rudely, dry sputtery honks.

When he appeared at the door last night she'd been too startled to block his entry. Too slow. Also too fuddled, yanked up out of sleep, to remember where she'd left her reliable Defender (purse, was it? Dresser? nightstand?). Turned out she didn't need it. Clutching a bottle, he ducked around her, tottered into the living room, and sank onto the couch. She stood over by the table, keeping a wary distance. Very coldly, she said, "It's late, Rick. Past midnight. What do you want?"

"Come say g'bye."

"You're going somewhere?"

"Goin' Omaha."

"Omaha?"

"Omaha. Got a job there. Couldn't take it anymore, bein' same town as you."

"When?"

"Huh?"

"When are you leaving?"

"Couple weeks. Get my affairs in order."

"I imagine that will take some doing."

"Whaddya mean?"

"Your affairs."

"Be nice, Liz."

"I'm trying. It's not easy. And it's Lizabeth, by the way."

"Have a drink with me, Lizabeth."

"No. Say your good-byes and leave."

"It's Scotch. You used to like Scotch."

"Not anymore."

"One. For old times."

She looked at that sad crumply face, liquid-eyed, pleading, all the princely arrogance gone out of it. Face of the man who had once been an essential, defining part of her life. "One," she said, "and then you're out of here."

That was her mistake, right there. For of course the one led—for him, not her—to another, another, till finally he tilted the bottle to his lips, bubbled down the last of the Scotch, and slumped over, mumbling something about the anguish of lost love. Worse than useless, all her best efforts to budge him off the couch, get him to his feet. Easier to revive a corpse.

And reflecting on it now, this morning, far too late, she had to wonder what could have been in her head, where her wits had gone. Out the narrow window of pity, she supposed, or some lingering ghost of sentiment, or maybe just a blessed relief over the prospect of all that geography between them. Unless he was lying about Omaha, which he was perfectly capable of doing. Another cunning ploy. Anything to repossess a discarded toy.

But her problems were more immediate than the honesty, or lack of it, of Richard Charles Nagel, attorney-at-*lie*. One of them, at least, was under temporary control. Last night, after she'd given up trying to wake him and gone to bed (chair wedged against the door, recovered cylinder of tear gas at the ready on the nightstand), it came to her like a phantom augury in the twilight of sleep, an image of Rick's Corvette, for certain parked in her drive. She bolted out of bed, tiptoed into the living room, searched his pockets, and came up with the keys. She went into the garage, backed her Camaro out, and replaced it with the Corvette. Dead bottom on the list of things she wanted or needed was for Norman, notoriously early riser, to spot it and come storming over, replay that violent scene. So that was one disaster forestalled. For the moment, anyway.

Which didn't do much to quiet her present anxieties. All of which telescoped into that single source, snorting and wheezing on the couch there. Somehow she had to get him up and out of here. From harsh experience, she knew it wasn't going to be easy. Never was before, wouldn't be now. Stiff, groggy, aching, he'd surface from a boozy sleep spoiling for trouble. With Rick, that's how it always worked.

Had to be a way. She could try conciliatory, caring, kindly even, if that's what it took. She could try that. Or maybe firm would be better, assertive. Threats, if necessary. She couldn't decide, didn't know. Maybe coffee would help. Bring him around, make him semi-reasonable. She'd try coffee.

FLAM'S SLEEP HAD BEEN SPASTIC, tossing, and visited by weird dreams, but once he was awake and on his feet he was jacked, no doubt about it, locked, cocked, and ready to rock heads and stomp ass. Must of been middle of the night, call come through, jangle of the phone weaving itself into the crazyquilt fabric of one of those dreams. Felt like middle, anyway. Voice on the other end a muffled, urgent whistle: "Mr. Flam? Horace here. Got some buzz for ya."

Fuck was Horace?

As if in spontaneous reply to the unuttered question, voice goes, "Horace Kurtz. Bellman."

"Oh. Yeah. Horace. Time's it, Horace?"

" 'Bout half past six."

"Six o'fuckin'clock in the A.M. This better be good buzz, Horace."

"Think it is. He's up. Been sittin' in the coffee shop since it opened an' he's—"

"That's your buzz? He's always in there this time a morning."

"Lemme finish. Got a bag with him today. No suit on, like normal. Don't look to me like a man on his way to work."

"Bag? Like a travelin' bag?"

"Correct. Travelin'. Overnighter."

"Sure it ain't a briefcase?"

"Bags my business, Mr. Flam."

"And no suit?"

"Nope."

Don't compute. Word he got off his Badger security mole was today just another workday, Stoltz people scheduled to turn in at the plant, same as ever. "He's there now?" Flam asked.

"Yeah, but you better hurry."

"I'll do that, Horace."

He did, too. Bounded out of the sack and flew into the head and emptied his hose and splashed his face with cold water (no time for your basic shave, shit, shower, and etc.) and pulled on some laundry, not neglecting to remember his piece (could be nothin', could be the break he's lookin' for—either way, he's strapped and steady), and blazed on outta there. In the lobby, Horace, catching the spirit of the chase, shot a tells-it-all glance at the door and, lips barely parted, barely moving, said, "He just left."

"Good man, Horace. I'll take care of you when I get back."

Whenever that might be. Lookin' late. Maybe even tomorrow. Whole fuckin' weekend maybe, all Flam knew. One thing for sure, he ain't goin' to work. Horace dead on the dollar, that one. Tools right on by the plant, spins over to the interstate, points south. Just like last week. Maybe got the old itch again, gonna meet the twat at the

Kenosha motel, scarf some Thanksgiving pussy today, 'stead of bird. Jesus, Flam hoped not. Wasn't sure he was up to another all-nighter, that parking lot. Make that all day too, this time out.

But he got lucky, least the way he measured luck anymore. Got spared the squat'n squint drill. His boy zipped past the Kenosha exit, chewin' up miles, man in a sweat to get wherever it is he's goin' to. Which got to be home. Where else, this direction? Home for the holiday. Some luck.

Except they got into Illinois and he starts drivin' real strange, real erratic, slowin' down, pickin' up speed, droppin' back again. Fuck's goin' on? Something rattlin' the squirrel cage. Way a man drives tell a whole lot about him. Tellin' Flam it's a strung-out schiz behind that wheel. And what's he doin' here on the highway, first place? Ain't like it's in the Michael Woodrow profile, duckin' out on work.

Something not right here. Something gotta be comin' down. Maybe the little chat with the old man last week finally mintin' some gold coin. Maybe schiz senior finally got his nuts stiff enough to put in a code red call: Hurry on home, boy, we got some serious rappin' to do, serious trouble. Got him tweaked. Why else he doin' that stutter step?

Flam cut him some road leash. Kept him in sight but put a mile or so and a line of vehicles between them. Wouldn't do, spook him now. Not if there's anything to that drivin' theory. Hoped to fuck there was. 'Bout time for a break, Victor. Past time.

He tracked him up the Ogden Avenue ramp, through the quiet Hinsdale streets, on into the condo complex, still keepin' a caution gap, givin' good space. Watched him creep by the girlfriend's place, scopin' it, and then pull up outside his own and lug the bag inside. There was a small visitors' parking area off the street between the Woodrow crib and the twat's. Flam nosed his car into one of the spots, killed the motor, and hunched down in the seat, eye level with the dash.

He waited. Tiny puffs of snow, airy as smoke, fragile as glass, appeared on the windshield, melted instantly, vanished. Called to mind all his own cashed hopes, these three long months gone by. No good thinkin' that way. This time he's onto something. Something heavy. He can feel it. Right down in the old jingleberries, can he feel it. Feels good. Like you're on a moneyroll, Victor. For a welcome switch.

• • •

THE SEDATIVE POWER of the engine lulled him. Road-tranced, he lost track of time, distance, velocity. Some cars swept around him, others he passed. Familiar landmarks flashed by, gauzy as hallucinations. Only the periodic toll booth stops restored a measure of sensory perception. Without them he might very well have missed his exit altogether. As it was, he veered off at the absolute last moment, the driver behind him laying on a furious horn blast.

He slid the window down a notch. The chill air, flecked with snow, braced him, cleared his head. The streets of home, treeframed, domed in silence, all but empty of traffic at this hour, comforted him, seemed to lift a share of that streak of loneliness he'd felt back there on the road. Small share, but something was more than nothing. More still, when he passed Lizabeth's. He slowed, considered stopping, thought better of it. Too early.

Bag in hand, he came through the door, purposely banging it behind him in announcement of his presence, fully expecting to find Norman at the foot of the stairs, momentarily bewildered by his unexpected appearance. No Norman. He called his name. Perfect stillness. Curious. Mornings Norman was always here. Vague misgivings stirred on a distant horizon in his head, rose in dark funnel clouds of assorted catastrophe scenarios: brutal crimes, seizures, collapses, selfslaughter. Any of which was possible.

He dropped the bag and hurried down the stairs. Bedroom was empty. He searched the house. No sign of Norman. But none of any of those fancied disasters either. Windows were sealed, doors bolted, Nissan in the garage. Nothing out of place, no cause for alarm. Probably out for a walk, honing an appetite for Lizabeth's holiday dinner.

His fears ebbed. He unpacked the bag, went through the stack of accumulated mail. Some bills, some solicitations, nothing of interest. He wandered through the house restlessly. Eventually those wanderings led him back down the stairs and into Norman's room. Stealthy as a cat burglar, he crept over to the desk, parted the sea of loose paper, and came across a slender sheaf of pages clipped together, typed, numbered. He slid them out carefully, cautious not to disturb some imagined order. He settled into the chair and began to read.

And as he turned those pages the buried past seemed to unreel in slow motion behind his eyes, and the amnesiac shadow of that swamped, savaged night lifted; and as he read on, he experienced a

peculiar sensation of time's undulations, rocking back and forth in
time, man to child to child masquerading as man; and when he was
finished, a powerful sense of release surged through him, of purga-
tion, repair, like a disease willed into miraculous remission, no longer
fatal. Sense of a kind of private triumph, resistant to definition, too
secret to yield up a name.

Lizabeth would understand. He'd tell Lizabeth.

STILL CLAD IN THE OVERSIZE T-SHIRT habitually worn for sleep, Lizabeth waited in the kitchen for the coffee—full pot of it, extra-
strong—to brew. She puffed feverishly on a cigarette ransacked from
a dusty pack in the back of a drawer. The clock on the stove read
quarter past eight. Time was ticking. A small turkey, centerpiece of
her elaborately engineered meal, thawed in the sink. Irrelevantly, she
remembered Norman's wry description of a typical Stateville Thanksgiving, feasting on turkey pot pie, Banquet brand, in commemoration
of the holiday. This year will be different, she'd promised him. This
year they'd have a traditional dinner, all the trimmings, even if it had
to be scaled down to accommodate just the two of them.

Maybe they would yet. She ground out the cigarette in an ashtray
on the counter (the lead crystal one, Norman's thoughtful gift), filled
a cup, and carried it into the living room. Set it on the end table next
to the drained Scotch bottle. Stood there for a long moment, summoning her nerve. Or stalling. Why, she wasn't sure. After all, curled
in the palm of a hand was her trusty Defender. Nothing to fear. She
raked the other hand through the tangle of her hair, drew in a sustaining breath, kneeled down on the floor by the couch, and touched
his dangling arm lightly, gingerly. No reaction. She leaned in close,
murmured in his ear, "Rick, wake up, it's morning, you have to
leave." Got a smothered groan for her efforts. She jabbed at the
arm, not so gentle now. He grunted, belched, rolled over on his side.
Didn't stir. She reached for the cup and held it under his nostrils.
Maybe the steamy aroma would rouse him.

And that was her posture—on her knees, T-shirt riding up her
bare thighs, hair disheveled, cup extended as though in adoring service of a slack-limbed sot—when a key turned in a lock and she
glanced over her shoulder and discovered Michael standing in the
doorway, assimilating the scene, uttering not a word but measuring
her with a sorrowed stony gaze, the blood pooling darkly in his face.

•   •   •

NORMAN'S FIRST THOUGHT, seeing the unfamiliar vehicle parked in their drive, was of some careless guest of some negligent neighbor. It had happened before, visitors ignorant of or indifferent to the rules, infringing on private space. That was the trouble with all communal living, either side of the walls: defending your space. He'd have to have a word with the people next door or the ones across the street, whoever it was entertained the intrusive visitor. Even though he had no intention of taking the Nissan out today, it was still a matter of principle. Relaxed holiday good fellowship notwithstanding. A matter of standup.

But not now. Later. Now he was weary from the extended hike, bone-cold and ready for a smoke. Little bit of pure ozone went a long way. But once inside, he sensed something altered, nothing visible, some slight tonal variance in the silence of the rooms. Occupy a place in solitude long enough and you pick up every oscillation in the air. He went to the door of Michael's bedroom, peered in, saw the bag, and immediately made the connection with the car in the drive. A surprise appearance. Very unlike him. Nowhere in evidence, must have just popped in and gone directly to Lizabeth's, heedless of the early hour. She, of course, would be joyed. Ardor embraced opportunity, passion scorned clocks. His own feelings, however, were mixed: glad Michael had somehow arranged to be here, but reminded once again of that disquieting issue yet to be trotted out, inspected, demystified, properly interred. Maybe later, if the occasion arose, he'd get him aside, circle in on it. Or maybe not, not today, disrupt the festive spirit.

He'd have to think about it. He descended the stairs, gravitated naturally to his desk. And even as before, entering the house, he was conscious now of something amiss, something out of order. He fished through the confusion of paper, found the last installment of his chronicle, held it in his hands. Bars of wan morning light filtered through the window, danced across the pages. Instantly, out of a knowledge sturdier than reason, innocent of proofs, he knew they'd been gripped by other hands, scanned by other eyes. Michael? Who elevated privacy above all other values, kept jealous guard over his own? Seemed impossible to conceive. Yet who else? And if so, what new colorings would it bring to the emotional electricity forever crackling between them? If indeed it were true and not merely another baseless figment of an imagination infected with doubt, diseased by suspicion. Or, if it were, to wonder if he had not in some way, by some unspoken signal, invited the covert prying through his darkest secrets. To wonder if confession hadn't been the destination all along.

There would be no time to ponder it that morning. For when he put down the pages and glanced out the window, what he saw was a most remarkable sight: a blocky figure tearing across the frost-burned grass, yanking a gun from a hip holster as he ran, making straight for the flung-open door of Lizabeth's condominium. And even from the back, Norman could recognize that figure as no one other than Victor Flam.

"MICHAEL!" she said, voice full of genuine astonishment. And then, setting down the cup, standing, turning to face him, she said it again, rising inflection this second time.

He said nothing. He came through the narrow entry and crossed the living room and seized the empty bottle and shattered it on the edge of the table. His stride and his motions were not so much hurried or agitated or even irate as methodic, deliberate. Lizabeth took a halting step backward, stammering, "Michael, please. You don't understand. Listen—"

He wasn't listening. Nor did he look at her as he came around the couch and stooped over the lumpen figure, who was stirring slightly, nettled it seemed by all the commotion and clatter, eyes blinking, peeling back just in time to see something odd, the jagged end of a bottle swooshing toward him, and to feel it puncture his throat, cleaving the flesh in a grinding motion, choking off what would certainly have been a screech of unbearable agony, though from somewhere else in the room an audible scream, shrill, vibrato, reached his rapidly closing ears. His hands clawed at air. He gargled up a thick froth of blood. For a moment he shuddered and twitched, steady as an engine, eyes wide open now, and spinning. Abruptly, the twitching stopped and his arms fell and he sagged back, still squirting blood, but the dying done.

"Why?" Lizabeth wailed. "You killed him. *Why?*"

Michael gazed at her puzzledly. "You don't know why?"

"He's my ex-husband."

"Was," Michael corrected her. "He's gone now."

"He was drunk. Passed out. Harmless. There was nothing between us."

"Well, now there's nothing."

"What are we going to do? We have to call someone. Norman . . . the police . . . someone."

"Why would we do that?" he said quietly. He lifted the bottle, examined it as though it were some peculiar surgical instrument, foreign to him, yet stained from recent use. Then he lowered it, thrust it out ahead of him like an extension of a greeting hand, and advanced on her.

Confusion, disbelief bleached her face. She backed away. "Michael," she said, her voice catching now, clotted with fear. "It's me, Lizabeth. You wouldn't hurt me."

"It shouldn't hurt much."

"You love me."

A wild smile creased his lips. He kept coming.

She put up a quivery arresting hand. Gripped in the other was the tin cylinder, pointed at his eyes. "This is tear gas, Michael. Don't make me use it. Please don't."

AS IT HAPPENED, she didn't have to, for Flam came charging through the open door, piece levelled, bawling, "Freeze it right there, dickeye!"

Michael spun around. A startled, almost sheepish expression came into his face.

"Now lose that poor man's shank you're packin' there and get your hands up top your head."

Michael lowered his eyes. Gazed at the floor. Didn't speak. Didn't move.

"Do it! Now! Or you're boneyard dead!"

He did it. Released the bottle. Clasped his hands on his head.

"Turn around and drop on them knees."

He did as he was told.

"That's good," Flam said. "You learn real good. What I want you do now is back over here, nice'n easy. Think y'can do that?"

He could do that, too, but only awkwardly. A slow, choppy progress across the floor, like a defective windup toy winding down, or like an awkward child engaged in some playful childish game.

Flam took in the whole scene with a quick sweep. Stiff on the sofa, twat shivering in a corner, lookin' about to faint, or zuke. Stone dead stiff, witness, perp on his knees—all the goods. Flam knew this was gonna be his day, knew it. He was feeling pumped now, stoked. So when Michael got in range he said, "You're a real assassin, boy, know that? Assassin likes the taste a blood, so you better get down there and lap some up." He planted a loafer squarely between Michael's shoulder blades and shoved, sprawling him face-first into a stream of blood oozing off the couch and threading across the floor.

Twat let out a pained yelp, like it was her the one takin' the hurts, said, "You don't have to do that to him."

"Lady, you just lucky you got a healthy set a lungs on you. Otherwise be a pair a stiffs to draw to in here."

"Who are you?"

"Man who just kept your mail from comin' federal worm express. Now I got a little chore for you. Want you to get on the horn and dial your basic nine-one-one. Tell 'em send somebody over here, collect this piece a dog shit."

She hesitated. Only an instant, but in that sheared beat Flam saw something in her eyes, and he whirled about, too late to dodge the lunging figure and the looping arm that slammed something into the side of his skull just above the ear, something solid, hard, weightier than a fist. And though he did his best to hold on to the Ruger, he could feel it slipping from his hand in the long, spiraling, brain-swizzled plunge to the floor.

NORMAN FLUNG AWAY THE ASHTRAY, plucked from the counter in the furious spearing tackle, and scrambled over on all fours and recovered the gun and lurched to his feet, gasping and swaying. He surveyed the room. Sifted and processed everything he saw: his son coiled in fetal posture on the floor, hugging his knees, rocking and whimpering; ex on the couch in a puddle of blood, no more briefs to prepare, fresh out of cases to argue; Flam a crumpled groaning heap, also effectively out of things, for a while anyway, not long; Lizabeth backed against a wall, eyes glassy, smeary, breath drawn in short gulping sobs. And then there was himself, still standing, more or less, weapon in his hand. A thick nausea bubbled up in his hammering chest. He swallowed, gagged it back down. A notion, formless yet, more resolve than idea, gathered in his head. He approached Lizabeth, reached for her hand, and steered her gently toward the door, saying, "Come along now. It'll be all right."

"He killed him, Norman. Michael killed him. Why'd he do that?"

"I don't know," he said, that one a lie too, the way the flimsy assurance everything would be all right was the purest of fictions; the way he'd understood all week long, at some submerged level, the absolute certainty of his son's guilt, as ordained and inescapable as his own.

"I tried to stop him. Explain it. He went crazy. Nothing I could do."

"There is now."

"What? What can I do now?"

"Listen to me, Lizabeth. Listen. It's important that you trust me."

Some mournful keening spirit in his voice, at once collected and grave, seemed to steady her. "I do," she said. "I trust you."

"I want you to go over to our place. Sit down. Smoke a cigarette. Take your time. And when you're finished I want you to call the police. Tell them to come out here. Don't tell them what's happened. Say there's been a . . . domestic disturbance. Can you do that for me?"

"I'll do it, Norman. If that's what you want."

"There's one thing more. Not to do. To know."

He paused, unclear himself what it was he intended to say. Could he speak of connections? Distances shrunk, spanned? The motley seasons in his life, this brief one perhaps the finest of all? In the movies, fitting summary words sprang nimbly from the lips of a Burt. Not so, he. What he required was time. Time to shape them, revise, edit, pinch, and prod them for grace, implication, meaning. No time. She stood framed in the doorway, watching him out of those still-vacant eyes, sapphire blue. He looked over her shoulder and, for something to say, said, "I think I just saw two alike."

"What?"

"Two snowflakes."

"What do you mean?"

"Nothing. Just making a little joke. Go now. Hurry."

He turned quickly, stepped around the fallen Flam, and went back into the living room, her retreating footsteps sounding in his ears, carried along on a whisper of the wind; and along with them a familiar voice rising from the far side of a long silence, murmuring,

What did I say, Norman? About those quirky surprises, what did I say?

HE CROUCHED BESIDE HIS SON. If the words had been elusive before, in the doorway, they were fugitive here, skittering off in every direction. He touched his shoulder.

Michael unlocked his knees, rolled over on his back and dug at his eyes. Like a child emerging out of a hard sleep. "Dad?" he said, peculiar cheeping tone. "That you?"

"Yes."

"Is she dead?"

"She?"

"Mom."

"Yes. Dead."

"Will you stay?"

"I'm not going to leave you, Michael. This time I'll stay."

But circumstance was to make a liar of him again. Over in the entry Flam was boosting himself up on his elbows, looking around dazedly. To Michael, Norman said, "Wait here a minute. Don't move. Something I've got to attend to. I'm not leaving. I promise." He rose, hefted the gun, and came across the room, stopping a few paces short of Flam. And to him he said, "Better stay down."

Flam massaged a purpling bruise blossomed from beneath the roots of his hair and flowering over a temple. "That's a mean wallop you pack, Mr. Woodrow," he drawled.

"It's the ashtray," Norman said, certifying it with a glance at the floor. "Wasn't me."

"Still a thumper."

"Smarts a little, does it?"

"Little. Guess that must be the one I owed you. Remember me sayin' that?"

"Vividly."

"Guess that makes us square now, right?"

"Tabula rasa."

"Huh?"

"Yes. Square."

Flam hauled himself upright. Leaned into the wall for support. Shook his head vigorously, the way a drenched hound shakes water from its fur. He smiled crookedly, said, "So maybe you wanna hand over that artillery, mine."

"I don't think so."

"C'mon, Mr. Woodrow. You're a badass, but you ain't no shooter."

He took a wobbly step toward him. Norman motioned him back. "Don't be too sure."

"That's a Ruger you're holdin' there," Flam said, patient, tutorial, still smiling. "P89. Got them Black Talon slugs, put a wicked hole in a man. You wouldn't wanta do that."

Norman backed away. This wasn't part of his ill-formed notion or idea or scheme, whatever it was. If indeed there was any scheme. "Not unless I have to," he said.

"Face it, old man. You ain't got the nuts for it. Gimme the piece."

Flam extended an open palm, took another step. His smile had warped into tight, downslung sneer, skeptical and tough, but with a hint of a crack in it too, dollop of fear. And in that thin crease of fear Norman recognized the craven doubts of all the spite-smirched bullies he'd encountered, one guise or another, all his life. The pettifogging hoax of Authority. Cheered him to see it. Quite mildly he said, "I never cared much for hacks, Mr. Flam. You're the only hack in the house, so this is for all of them."

He trained the gun on Flam's left knee, and an explosion shook the walls, and Flam let out an astonished bellowy whoop and toppled, the whoop swelling to piping howl, then trailing off in stuttery moan. Norman watched him. Gave it a moment. To be sure. Flam elevated a jaw beaded with saliva and glared at him, banjo-eyed, teeth bared. "You shot me," he said, voice an uneven mix of ragged whinny and snarl. "Cocksuck, you *shot* me!"

"Count your blessings. You're lucky to have a pulse."

NORMAN RETURNED TO THE LIVING ROOM. Michael, obedient to his directive, lay there, stretched across the reddening carpet, gazing blankly at the ceiling. Norman positioned himself behind his head, squatted down, and stroked his hair.

"Dad?"

"Yes."

"You came back."

"I said I would."

"Where are you? I can't see you."

"I'm right here, Michael."

"What was that noise?"

"Nothing. Thunder."

"Is it raining?"

"Not yet."

"What's going to happen?"

"Nothing will happen."

"I killed him, didn't I."

"It doesn't matter."

"I loved her. She deceived me."

"Try not to think about it."

"What will they do to me?"

Do? He didn't dare allow himself to think what they'd do to someone like this in a place like Stateville. A dreadful image came streaking across the years: A joint queen, Boris by given name, Heather by tag, discovered free-chipping by his jocker cellie, and hobbled forever with a severed Achilles tendon. A cluster of other like images, embalmed and buried, swarmed out of the tomb of memory. He said, "I wish I'd been a better father for you, Michael. Better man."

"Maybe you still can, Dad."

"How?"

"Come back for good. You and Mom try harder."

"Begin again?"

"Yes. Again. Can you do that?"

"Maybe I can," Norman said, and he lifted the gun and pointed it downward and squeezed the trigger and reclaimed his son forever from all his demons; and for Michael, who was about to express his joy, there was for a shred of an instant a gigantic starburst, and then a sudden darkness fell over him like a lid rudely slammed shut, and the nothing he had searched for and anticipated all his life, the no-thing, was upon him at last; and for Norman, staring at the mingling of bloods seeping into the nap of the carpet, hemorrhaging his own current of grief, there was the curious whimsical thought that God, if Plato was right, always revealed His mysteries through the perfect symmetry of a celestial geometry, and that if blood could sing, its song today would be, "I am the son of the father, closing the circle, proclaiming a truce."

He inverted the gun and slid the barrel partway into his mouth. Its taste was hot, brassy. From somewhere outside his ears, a jeery voice squawked, "You'd better yank that trigger, suckwad, or they gonna put you on permanent ice, they don't fry you first"; from within them another voice whispered, *The freedom, you'll remember, is in the journey, Norman, not the destination.* He considered that moist, spongy glob of tissue and fibers and charged neurons at the end of the barrel, source of all the words yet to be strung together in the improbable, uninventable history of his days.

Through the bay window he caught a glimpse of a black and white fleeting by, crimson cyclops eye twirling. After a moment he heard footfalls on the porch. A shadow fell across the open door. He removed the barrel from his mouth, laid down the gun, and called out, "I surrender." And then he settled back on the floor and waited for them to fall on him, and they did.

· A NOTE ON THE TYPE ·

The typeface used in this book is one of many versions of Garamond, a modern homage to—rather than, strictly speaking, a revival of—the celebrated fonts of Claude Garamond (c.1480-1561), the first founder to produce type on a large scale. Garamond's type was inspired by Francesco Griffo's De Ætna type (cut in the 1490s for Venetian printer Aldus Manutius and revived in the 1920s as Bembo), but its letter forms were cleaner and the fit between pieces of type improved. It therefore gave text a more harmonious overall appearance than its predecessors had, becoming the basis of all romans created on the Continent for the next two hundred years; it was itself still in use through the eighteenth century. Besides the many "Garamonds" in use today, other typefaces derived from his fonts are Granjon and Sabon (despite their being named after other printers).